A DARK REFLECTION

ALSO BY MICHAEL A. BLACK

A DARK REFLECTION

MICHAEL A. BLACK

ROUGH
EDGES
PRESS

A Dark Reflection
Paperback Edition
Copyright © 2025 by Michael A. Black

Rough Edges Press
An Imprint of Wolfpack Publishing
1707 E. Diana Street
Tampa, FL 33610

www.roughedgespress.com

This book is a work of fiction. References to historical events, real people, or real places are used fictitiously. Any similarity to real persons, living or dead, is purely coincidental and not intended by the author.

Paperback ISBN 978-1-68549-390-5
Ebook ISBN 978-1-68549-389-9
LCCN 2025941844

For my buddy, Dave Case

A DARK REFLECTION

PROLOGUE

OCTOBER 17TH, 1987

The last vestiges of fading, late afternoon sunlight filtered through the streaked window panes, dappling the old, wooden stairway with an occasional, bright speckle. The windows of the narrow landing were painted shut and the pervasive smell of stale urine was so strong it made Detective Roger Colby cough. His partner, Fred Dix, grinned.

"Stinks, don't it?" he whispered.

Colby nodded, the sweat breaking out on his forehead. The place made him want to disinfect his whole body starting with the soles of his shoes. But they were close now. Real close.

He was dog-tired, which wasn't good. Tired men make mistakes, but he marveled at Dix's stamina and resolve. Colby was having trouble keeping up, despite his partner having ten years on him. They'd been working the case of the abducted Swanstrom twins nonstop for the past twenty-four hours and had finally tracked the suspect, Morgan Laird, down to the room in this sleazy SRO flop house. Their adversary was not only Laird, but the ticking clock as well.

For the sake of the twins, Colby prayed they weren't too late. The desk clerk had told them there weren't any little girls in the room, but he was sure Laird was.

A sudden squeak of the floorboards jarred Colby as they cleared the landing. Dix frowned and pulled out his snub-nosed .38, pointing down the hall.

Room 33.

Colby nodded and took a position on the opposite side of the door, his gun out too. It was a four-inch stainless steel .357 Magnum. "We're at the top," he whispered into his radio. It crackled a reply and Colby grimaced. He'd left the volume on too high. Had Laird heard it?

Dix must have thought the same thing. He pounded on the door and announced, "Police! Open up." Then they both stepped back.

Just as Colby was about to give the bottom half of the door a good kick, a muffled voice came from inside the room. "Hold on, I'm coming."

Colby and Dix exchanged glances.

Seconds later, a myriad of tiny splinters fluttered in a haze of smoke and dust in front of them as a round hole ripped through the cheap wood right below the number with an accompanying roar.

"Shotgun!" yelled Dix.

Colby fired a round through the door and kicked it. The door shuddered but held. He cocked his leg to kick again, just as he faintly heard a rhythmic metallic clacking despite the ringing in his ears from the gunshot.

They exchanged glances and Dix said, "Fire escape."

Colby yelled into his radio for the backup officers in the alley below to intercept him.

More shots—pistols, followed by the heavy blasts of the shotgun.

Colby hurled his shoulder against the door and it crumbled inward. The momentum carried him through the portal. He fell heavily on top of the shattered door. Dix raced over him to the window and peered out. The shotgun's roar sounded from below, then Colby saw his partner firing downward.

"Dammit," Dix said, grunting. He ducked back, hit the cylinder release of his revolver, and started to reload.

On his feet now, Colby sprinted across the room to the window. Down below, Laird was running toward one of the open squad cars. Colby aimed and fired. Laird kept going, showing no sign of being hit.

Where the hell were the two containment officers?

A second later, he knew as he climbed through the window, his shoes clanging on the metal framework of the fire escape. Fifty feet below, two uniformed coppers lay in the alley, darkening puddles spreading out beneath them, a sawed-off shotgun lying between them. Colby skipped down the steps three at a time, using the handrail for balance. The marked squad car peeled off toward the street. He could hear Dix's ragged breath above him. Two more uniforms came running down the alley.

Colby reached the bottom. He ran to his closest fallen comrade. Faint pulse, shallow breathing.

"Jesus, what the hell happened?" one of the new coppers asked.

"Call for an ambulance," Colby said.

Dix was next to him now. "Laird stole their squad."

Colby ran to their unmarked and got behind the wheel. His lungs were burning from exertion. Dix jumped into the passenger side as Colby slammed the car into gear and took off, leaving a trail of burned rubber. The oscillating red-and-blue lights of the stolen squad car bounced down the far end of the alley before disappearing from sight.

Dix jammed the red bubble-light onto the dashboard and plugged it into the cigarette lighter.

"He ain't going far in that squad," Dix said. "Too recognizable." He yelled the pursuit information into his radio, holding the red light down on the dash. "He stole one of the copper's guns. Looked like a semi-auto."

Turning onto Vermont Street, they spotted the squad car barreling through the intersection fifty yards ahead, scattering the pedestrians coming from the commuter trains. Colby hit the siren and kept going.

Laird raced toward Western Avenue against the red light and seconds later smashed into a blue Volkswagen, sending the smaller car careening into a vehicle in the next lane. The squad car bounced straight, its front fender a crumpled mass, and kept going. He was a hundred yards ahead of them now, the friction of the metal against the tire emitting a stream of black smoke, the emergency lights on top whirling as he lurched through the tangle of vehicles, bashing some and forcing others onto the sidewalks in desperate avoidance.

Colby followed seconds later, slowing to traverse the maze of smashed cars. They felt the abrupt crunch as one of the cars struck their rear fender.

"Keep going," Dix shouted. "Don't stop."

Colby kept watching the plume of smoke on the road ahead of him. The burning rubber stung his nostrils. They were gaining. Slowly, but they were gaining...maybe sixty yards back now.

"His tire won't last much longer." Colby pressed the accelerator to the floor. He saw Laird swing around a stopped minivan before going under a viaduct.

Thirty more yards to go.

Colby swerved to avoid the stalled van. As the fleeing car entered the darkened section of the tunnel, a red flash winked at him from the shadows. Milliseconds later, a bullet smacked against the top of their windshield, the impact causing a web of fanning cracks.

Dix grunted and said, "Hold her steady." He rolled the passenger side window down and stuck his gun out, resting his hand on the side-view mirror as they entered the tunnel.

Another red flash from Laird's car. Colby instinctively swerved. This time there was no impact. They bottomed out on a low point in the roadway. Dix fired three rounds, the flashes lighting up the corner of Colby's peripheral vision. It was impossible to tell where the rounds went, or even if they were close, but he felt better that they were shooting back.

The smoke from Laird's tire hung heavy and thick in the air. He was less than a hundred feet in front of them.

"Pull up alongside," Dix said. "I'll blast him."

"We need him alive. The twins."

An oncoming vehicle bore down on them, horn blaring. Colby jerked the wheel, and felt the gut-wrenching scrape as the two cars sideswiped each other. Straightening the wheels, he glanced in the rearview mirror.

"Screw 'em," Dix said.

Ahead, the road split into a T-intersection, with a trucking storage facility on the right side. To the left, the street dipped under another small viaduct with huge cement pillars.

"Come on," Dix said. "Get up next to that—"

Before he could finish Laird's squad begin to skid, turning sideways, then straightening out, before swinging all the way around and crashing through the cyclone fence to the right, in front of the trucking facility.

On top of the adjacent viaduct, a slow-moving freight train clattered by.

Colby hit the brakes and controlled his skid, following Laird's path as best he could, but avoiding the collision with the fence. He and Dix were out of their car as soon as it stopped.

They paused by the ruptured fence. Laird had gone completely through and crashed into the side of the flimsy, sheet-metal building about forty feet ahead. A trail of noxious smoke floated upward from the smoldering tire.

Colby felt for his radio and suddenly realized it was in the car.

"Dix," he called. "Radio this in."

In the moment it took for his partner to turn his head to reply, a shot rang out and Dix grunted and fell to one knee.

Colby ran to him.

"You hit?"

Dix grunted again, holding his side. Blood poured through his fingers.

"I'm all right. Get that asshole."

Colby ran toward the gaping hole in the building made by the squad car. The interior was dark. To go in without backup was suicide. He instinctively reached for his radio again and felt the empty space on his belt.

Shit, is anything gonna go right today?

At least the building looked deserted.

Another flash brightened the darkness and a bullet whizzed by his head. Crouching, he leveled his gun toward the spot where he'd seen the burst of yellow and fired off three rounds. There was no way he was going to let that bastard escape. To lose him was to lose the last chance they had of ever finding the Swanstrom twins in time. Those two little girls were depending on him.

If they were still alive.

He ducked through the torn metal, gun outstretched, reaching into his pocket for his mini-mag flashlight, and looking for movement in the inky blackness, waiting for another flash, another round.

Instead he heard a scrambling sound and saw a large, overhead door trundling upward. A loading dock. He shone the light in that direction, and Laird jumped under the rising door against the backdrop of a rapidly darkening sky.

Colby ran toward him but something caught his foot and he went down, his gun discharging onto the floor in front of him, the little flashlight going instantly dark. Cursing as he pushed himself to his feet, he pocketed the mini-mag and moved with a cautious haste toward the big door, which was now fully open. Colby paused at the edge to avoid making himself an easy target.

Laird was already across the street, scrambling up a gravel incline toward the railroad trestle, a blue-steel semi-auto in his right hand.

I got him now. He aimed at Laird's lower back.

The hammer fell as he squeezed the trigger.

Nothing happened.

Out of ammo.

Colby flipped the cylinder open with his right thumb as he reached into his pocket with his left hand for his speed-loader. He quickly ejected the spent cartridges and fitted the new bullets into place, twisting the release dial. The bullets fell into the holes and he snapped the cylinder shut.

Laird had already crested the top of the incline, a barely visible dark silhouette against the velvet sky. Colby climbed through the opening and made the four-foot drop to the ground from the back loading dock. He ran full-out across the street and began to scale the gravel hill.

If Laird were up there waiting, Colby knew he'd be an easy target. But if he hesitated, he'd lose him for sure.

The squealing and grinding of the rumbling train obscured Colby's own ragged breathing. Gasping, clawing, stumbling up the incline, he skinned his knuckles and knees on the sharp gravel, his street shoes slipping with each step. As he neared the top, he debated whether to go right over or pause. He elected to prone out on the rough surface, sliding down slightly, allowing only enough space to peer over the edge.

He was surprised to notice how dark it suddenly was. It had been nearing dusk when they'd gone up those stairs in the hotel, but now it seemed almost totally black. Beyond the crest of the hill he saw four sets of parallel railroad tracks, with the train rumbling north on the farthest set. In the ambient light Colby saw Laird running alongside the slow-moving freight about a hundred and fifty feet away. His arm snaked out and he caught a rung of the ladder on the side of a boxcar. He pulled himself up and onto the small, grated platform at the front of the car. The train continued its ponderous trek as Laird moved out of sight.

Colby was up and running parallel to the train, jumping over the other tracks as he tried to get next to the space where Laird had disappeared. The cool night air burned his lungs.

A shadow moved on the ground on the other side of the moving train.

Laird had gone between the two boxcars and jumped down on the other side.

The train began to pick up speed.

Colby dropped to his knees and tried to get a fix on Laird's running legs but it was like looking through a stroboscope with the rapidly moving wheels and hanging wires providing no more than episodic glimpses. No clear shot.

Another set of the large wheels squealed past him. He had no choice. His only chance to catch Laird was to go under the moving train. Colby hesitated for a few seconds, taking pause at the squeal of the massive, rotating wheels. One wrong move, one miscalculation...

Gritting his teeth, Colby lurched forward and rolled under the middle of the passing boxcar, flattening out on the heavy ties and gravel bed. The floor of heavy wood, metal rungs, and dangling wires rumbled above him as he rotated onto his back. A few inches above his face sparks spewed all over and a pungent stench filled his lungs. He stretched out to let the boxcar pass over him, knowing he was a sitting duck if Laird saw him. Colby waited as the next set of massive wheels clacked toward him. Some box-like gear mechanisms with drooping wires looked low enough to snag him. Colby reached up with his free hand, hoping to grab something and be carried along for a few yards, like they did in the movies, to avoid being snared by the wires. But his fingers brushed against a long steel rod and slipped off, covered with a grimy smear.

He decided it was now or never, realizing that to hesitate was to risk getting dragged to death or cut in half by the unforgiving wheels. He rolled again, feeling his shoulder bump against the second track, then pushed up and over the smooth rail, landing on a gravel surface. Seconds later he suppressed a shudder as the lethal wheels squealed by him only inches away.

Stretching out his gun in front of him, he scanned the area.

No sign of Laird. The noise of the train nearly obscured the sound of something else. Something familiar. A rhythmic clacking again, just like back at the hotel.

Steps. Metal steps.

Colby got to his feet and ran toward the sound. A banister came into view, followed by a set of stairs going down the other side of the incline. He saw a figure running on the street below briefly illuminated by the overhead glow of the street lights. Colby raised his gun and fired instinctively. The figure jerked but kept going toward the superstructure of massive pipes and cement pumping towers fifty yards away. The odor was unmistakable: an oil refinery.

Colby descended the steps as fast as he could. He took out the mini-mag and shook it. The light came back on and he shone it over the ground in front of him. Spots of blood on the cement sidewalk marked the way. A blood trail. Colby felt a surge of adrenaline. For the first time in the chase he felt he had the upper hand, but Laird had disappeared.

At least he had a bullet in him. A wounded man couldn't go far.

An eight-foot high cyclone fence surrounded the refinery's perimeter, the top bracketed by three strands of barbed wire. No way Laird could climb over it.

As Colby drew closer, he saw the break in the fence. The bent, pulled-back section near the support post would easily allow someone to slip through. The crimson trail led right to the opening, smears of blood marking the round post.

Colby squeezed through, peering around at the massive conglomeration of pipes and ladders, sheet-metal buildings, large cement towers, and chimneys belching out plumes of acrid smoke. The smell of oil and sulfur were heavy in the air, along with a cacophony of loud, clanging sounds. Colby moved up to a trailer and squatted behind its yellow flange.

Christ, he could be anywhere, Colby thought while trying to assess his next move.

The area before him was an unending maze of twisting pipes, and narrow corridors, but the lighting was good. Getting to his feet, he jogged to the closest cement tower. An implanted ladder led upward, toward several platforms.

He reached out and was about to start climbing, hoping to get high enough to see Laird from above, when he spotted the blood trail again; red spots dotted the way on a long, concrete driveway toward a section of lighted buildings. A new fear gripped Colby. If this place were on three shifts, then there'd be workers here. That meant he couldn't shoot at the first thing that looked like a man, but Laird would have no such compunction.

He cursed his forgotten radio.

He knew he needed to find a phone and get some help as he followed the blood trail toward the next cement tower.

A distant wail of sirens weaved through the ubiquitous hissing and clanging of the refinery. Then, in between the intermittent noises, he heard something else. A man's voice screaming, followed by a shot.

Colby ran toward the sound. The network of twisting pipes parted to form a widening aisle illuminated by a series of overhead mercury vapor lights. About thirty yards away, the aisle opened into a larger, paved area of lighted shacks next to a long driveway. In the middle of it, a man in a hard-hat lay on the ground. Laird was several feet beyond the supine figure, pointing a pistol at a man in a truck and yelling.

Their words were indecipherable under the canopy of

noise, and Colby didn't waste time yelling any commands. Instead, he raised his pistol, struggling to control his breathing. Bracing against the side of the building, he cocked back the hammer and sighted in on Laird's back. It was a risky shot, but he knew he had to take it.

A second later Colby squeezed the trigger and saw Laird jerk forward, take two small, stuttering steps, and fall face-first onto the ground.

CHAPTER 1

TWENTY-EIGHT YEARS LATER

Colby couldn't get comfortable in the cushioned chair. The sweat was trickling down from his armpits, and the studio's bright lights just about blinded him. He glanced quickly toward the phony curtains covering the mock window that supposedly looked out on downtown Chicago. Behind it, he knew, was just more empty space in the TV station's expansive sound stage.

"And did you later find out where your shots hit him?" Pierce Nolan, the newscaster for "Chicago Today," asked. The guy's handsome face was the perfect picture of concern, but Colby knew the expression was no more real than the ersatz office façade.

"My first shot, the one that gave me the blood trail to follow, hit him in the left calf." Colby waited before adding, "The second one hit his spine."

Nolan's brow furrowed. "And that's the one that paralyzed him?"

Colby nodded.

"Were you at all concerned about shooting Laird in the back?"

Colby stared at him before answering. The stupidity of the question both angered and amused him. "No, I wasn't."

"I can understand that," Nolan said, nodding in agreement. "After all, you were trying to take out a vicious killer, weren't you?"

"I was trying to stop him," Colby said. "And to keep him from killing the civilian in the truck." This interview was turning into one hell of a mess.

"But you were too late to save the Swanstrom twins."

Colby took a deep breath and nodded his head. "Laird subsequently told us where he'd hidden them, but by that time, it was way too late."

"And ironically, that was the case that took the death penalty off the table, correct?"

Colby nodded.

"And is that the reason you've dedicated your book to them? The twins?"

Colby nodded again. He felt like a puppet, but his throat was too tight to answer.

"Well," Nolan said. "That's quite a story." He paused and smiled.

The guy was a lightweight. Colby found himself wishing they'd assigned the Black girl, Carmel, interview him instead of this jerk. She was sharper, not that either of them was interested in anything but their likability quotients and ratings.

Holding up the book, the newscaster looked directly into the camera and said, "There you have it folks, the real story from a real-life hero, Chicago Police Detective Roger Colby." He paused, lowered the book, and resumed what he must have thought was a pensive expression on his face. "Now I have to ask a serious question."

Colby waited, his cop instincts taking over. He was essentially a counterpuncher, waiting for the other guy to speak first.

The newsman's mouth jerked into a smile. "You've described to us how difficult it was for you to bring Morgan Laird to justice twenty-eight years ago."

Colby shifted in his chair.

"And now," Nolan continued, "he's been released on parole, back into society."

Colby noticed him abruptly shift his gaze away from him and toward the blinding lights. Toward the camera. This guy was a real ham.

He held up two fingers, ticking off his points. "One, how does that make you feel, and two, do you think that Morgan Laird is still a threat to society? After all, he is confined to a wheelchair."

Colby cleared his throat, trying to figure out what to say. The questions hadn't been among the ones submitted in the pre-interview script.

I'm here trying to push my book, he thought, and Mr. Blow-dried throws me a curve ball.

"A man like Laird is always a threat," Colby managed to say before a voice from off stage interrupted him.

"He damn sure is. That's why I taught Detective Colby everything he knows. So he could keep fighting the good fight after I hung up my gloves."

The voice was unmistakable. Colby's head shot around as a grin spread over his face.

"Dix," he said, rising.

Nolan sat there like a grinning fool, but Colby couldn't have cared less. He walked over and embraced his long-retired partner as the co-anchor, Carmel Washington, walked him across the floor.

"All I can say is," Dix gave Colby a light punch on the arm. "You'd better have spelled my name right in that damn book."

It'd been almost ten years since they'd seen each other. Dix was heavier, with silver-hair swept back from his forehead in the styled perfection that only a really good hairpiece could provide. He looked like a beardless Santa, smiling, with a twinkle in his eye.

"Because if you didn't," Dix said, "you'll be hearing from my attorney."

"Detective Colby," Carmel said, "Mr. Dix contacted us right after we had your interview set up. He insisted he wanted to surprise you. I hope that's okay."

Colby smiled. "It's great."

"He knows I was always the brains of the outfit," Dix said, sitting in one of the additional chairs. "Like I told you, I'm the guy that taught him everything he knows."

"Plus, he took a bullet capturing Morgan Laird," Colby said.

"And what you were saying about Laird still being a threat," Dix continued, "my partner's absolutely right. The only time he'll stop being a threat is when he quits breathing."

"But perhaps," Carmel said, "others would argue that the man has served his time. And, the man is in a wheel-chair now."

"That's justice." Dix patted Colby on the shoulder. "But only because my partner was such a good shot."

Colby remained silent, his mind racing back over those split-seconds: aiming, estimating the trajectory, trying to control his trigger pull, his breathing.

"He shoulda been in another chair," Dix added. "The one they used to call Old Sparky."

"I think they'd switched to lethal injection by then," Colby managed to say.

"Either one of them would've been fine with me." Dix snorted. "Better than what we got now."

"We'll have to save the debate about the abolition of the death penalty for another show, gentlemen," Carmel said, turning to smile into the camera. "Attorney Lance Fontaine has been quoted as saying that Mr. Laird lived up to the arrangement that was made, and he's now paid the debt that society ascribed to him."

Dix snorted again. "At the time, we all thought the son of a bitch would be behind bars forever." He shook his head. "They assured us he'd never be released."

Great, Colby thought. This was spiraling out of control. He tried in vain to glance over to check if the copy of his book was still standing upright.

"We're out of time," Carmel said, her smile seeming a bit strained now, but still dazzling, nonetheless. "Once again, we've been talking to police detective-turned-author, Roger Colby, about his new book, *Blood Trails*, which describes the tracking down and capture of now-paroled serial killer, Morgan Laird."

Dix reached down, grabbed the book, held it toward the camera, and grinned. "And I'm Fred Dix, the real hero of the story."

Carmel smiled, this time more genuinely, as the cameraman counted them down and then out. She stood and smoothed out her skirt. Colby saw Dix checking out her legs.

"Thanks again for the interview," Colby said, extending his hand toward Nolan and then Carmel.

"Yeah," she said. "Too bad they let that man out of prison. But at least he doesn't seem to be capable of causing any major hurt."

"Never underestimate a criminal, my dear," Dix said, stepping between Carmel and Colby. "In fact, he could be lurking in your parking garage. You should let an experienced law enforcement professional like myself walk you to your car."

She smiled. "We have our own security, sir."

"Sir? Please, call me Dix. How about I escort you for lunch, then?" He raised his eyebrows a couple times. "We could get a drink or two and I could tell some real good stories."

"What would your grandkids say?" Carmel asked, smiling as she walked away.

Colby placed an arm around Dix's shoulders and steered him off the sound stage. "Come on, partner, I'll buy you a cup of coffee and we can catch up."

Dix went along, looking over his shoulder to ogle Carmel in her tight skirt. He turned back to Colby. "Maybe I should tell her there's snow on the roof, but there's fire in the furnace. I think she's got the hots for me,"

"Yeah, right," Colby said. "Only she doesn't know it yet. What'd you do, stick up a Viagra van?"

Before Dix could answer two figures stepped into the aisle next to the heavy, floor-length curtains. The man and woman were both conservatively dressed—him in a dark blue suit and her in a blue pantsuit.

Suits, Colby thought. That can only mean one thing.

"Detective Colby," the man said, holding up a wallet-sized, black leather case with a gold FBI shield affixed to it. "I'm Special Agent in Charge Pearson, and this is Special Agent O'Keefe. We're with the bureau." He paused, obviously for the maximum effect, then added, "We need to talk with you."

"About what?"

Pearson's face was impassive. "We can discuss that at our office."

Knox edged the BMW up to the sign that warned all firearms must be declared before entering Canada. He reflected that bringing his Walther across the border would have made the upcoming task much easier, but he couldn't afford to take the chance it might be discovered at this checkpoint.

Besides, the knife made things more up-close-and-personal. It was a bit more problematic in the grand scheme of things, but his specialty was solving problems after all.

The lane opened up in front of him and he gathered his long, blond hair into a ponytail and secured it with a band as he pulled up to the booth. He wanted to make sure his face matched the picture on the passport. He'd get a crew-cut afterward. The mustache and goatee would have to go as well when he got back to Chicago.

The pretty, dark-haired Canuck smiled at him and said, "Welcome to Canada." She looked about twenty-five. Nice teeth. Nice neck, too. "May I see your passport or identification, sir?"

He handed her the passport listing his name as Vernon Krems.

She looked at it and typed something into her keyboard. Knox knew the name would come back clear with a valid driver's license.

"Your destination, Mr. Krems?"

"Toronto," he said.

"And what's the purpose of your visit?" She looked at him. Obviously, she had run a check on the license plate, which would have come back to New Genesis.

Knox thought for a moment before answering.

"Sir, the purpose of your visit?" the girl persisted. "Business or pleasure?"

If she only knew.

He flashed a benign smile. "Business," he said,

shifting and suddenly feeling the solid pressure of the knife's metallic hardness against his left side as he shifted in the seat. "But some pleasure too, I hope."

The girl glanced back at the screen and typed something else, then handed him back the phony passport.

"Enjoy your stay," she said, her mouth forming a cute smile.

"I'm sure I will," Knox said.

———

Colby glanced at his watch as he shifted in the uncomfortable chair. They'd kept him waiting in this outer office for twenty-five minutes, after saying they'd be "right back."

Right back my ass. The secretary looked up from her computer keyboard and smiled nervously as if she could read his thoughts.

Colby stretched, felt the relief of a few pops in his back, and stood up.

The hell with this. He took out one of his cards and approached the nervous looking girl at the computer monitor.

"I'm going to shove off," he said, holding out the card. "Tell Agent Pearson to give me a call."

Just as he was speaking, a shadow came up on the other side of the glass door that separated the office area from this waiting room. Pearson stepped out and motioned for Colby to enter.

The guy was holding a copy of *Blood Trails*.

Maybe he wants my autograph, Colby thought.

"I thought you forgot about me," he said, pocketing the card in his jacket.

"Hardly," Pearson said. "A call from Quantico." He tucked the book under a file he was carrying.

Quantico, Colby thought. As if that explained everything. Pearson led him down a hallway with offices on each side. Most of the doors were open, but the offices looked empty. A far cry from his own station-house where everybody was busy.

Of course, for the most part, the feds had the luxury of picking and choosing which cases they wanted to investigate.

And I wonder what they want with me.

"In here," Pearson said, pausing and opening a door at the end of the corridor. As soon as Colby entered, he knew it was one of their interview rooms. No outside-view windows, no pictures on the walls, no desk, no phone. Just a nondescript table and a couple of chairs. Colby glanced at his reflection in the mirrored section on the left wall. One-way glass.

The next thing, they'll be handing me a rights-waiver form.

The female agent from the studio stood in a corner by the glass window.

"Sit down," Pearson said, indicating the "hot seat" chair.

Colby frowned and looked at Agent O'Keefe.

She was kind of pretty. In an official, federal sort of way. Pearson, on the other hand, looked like Timmy from *Lassie*, all grown up.

Colby remained standing. "You want to clue me in about this?"

Pearson ignored him, fiddling with something inside the manila file folder.

"Excuse me." Colby was making no effort to hide the irritation in his voice now. "I asked you a question."

"If you don't mind, Officer Colby," Pearson said, "we'll ask the questions."

"Fine. Then ask them, because I got a lot of work to do. So far, this has been a big waste of my time."

Pearson's eyes shot toward O'Keefe, who raised her eyebrows.

They do more nonverbals than Penn and Teller, Colby thought. And they were almost as irritating.

"In your interview this morning you mentioned you thought the handling of the Laird case was a miscarriage of justice," O'Keefe said.

Colby nodded and then waited for a follow-up. When none came, he added, "Yeah, it was. The State's Attorney's Office took the death sentence off the table if he'd show us where the other bodies were buried. They guaranteed that he'd die in prison, but now he's out. I'd call that an abortion, not a miscarriage, but I didn't want to use those words on TV."

O'Keefe sat there for several seconds, as if assessing this, then said, "He was only paroled three months ago. You wrote the book pretty fast."

"Yeah, well, I'd been working on it for a while. Fountaine's been trying to get him released for years."

Pearson removed an eight-by-eleven color photograph from the folder and handed it across the table.

"Does this photo look familiar?" he asked.

Colby looked at it. A crime scene photo. The body of a nude woman lay on a bed, her face canted off to the right, her tongue protruding grotesquely, most likely due to the tightened ligature around her neck. The woman's arms had been bound to the bed frame, her legs left splayed open. It was gruesome, but nothing he hadn't seen before, although somehow the picture struck a chord of familiarity within him, although he couldn't immediately place it.

Pearson's eyes narrowed. "Just what can you discern from that picture?"

Colby stared at the FBI man. What was going on?

He thought about just walking out, but then he'd

never find out what their game was. He took a deep breath and reassessed the photo.

"Appears to be a homicide, possibly a strangulation murder. The decedent looks like a female, white. Probably late twenties to early thirties. From the position of her legs, I'd say sexual assault was probable."

"What else?"

Colby scanned the area surrounding the body. It was obviously a bedroom. Women's clothing was strewn over a nearby chair, and a big, round-faced alarm clock was next to the bed.

"It looks like a bedroom. Possibly the victim's. The alarm clock says this photo was taken at three o'clock, although AM or PM, I'm not sure."

Pearson's mouth gave a little twist at both ends. Something akin to a smirk. Like the mention of the clock was significant.

"What would you say if I told you that the clock this photo was inoperative?" Pearson said. "That it had been set at that time?"

What the hell is he driving at? Colby managed a noncommittal shrug. "I'd take your word for it."

The FBI man's face twitched.

"You'd do well to be serious," he said.

"Great. Then give me something to be serious about."

Pearson removed the copy of *Blood Trails* from under the folder and pushed it across the table.

"Now that's a subject near and dear to my heart," Colby said. "You want me to sign that for you?"

"Page one-eleven," Pearson said, nodding at the book.

Colby heaved a sign, picked up the book, and turned to that page.

It showed a black-and-white photograph of one of the crime scenes. Jenise Williams, naked and bound to her bed, with black boxes strategically inserted to block her face, breasts, and pubic area. Colby had insisted that the black lines be inserted to preserve the last modicum of dignity for the decedent's surviving family, even after they had agreed to allow the photos to be included to show the heinous nature of Laird's deeds. But the similarity in the positions of this body and the one in the new, color photograph Pearson had given him were unmistakable. Not only that, but the alarm clock on her nightstand was a dead ringer for the one in the new photo. The hands were also set at three o'clock.

"Look at this portion of the new photo," Pearson said, holding the tip of his pen like a pointer to the bed stand.

All Colby could see was a black plastic device next to the alarm clock.

"Know what it is?" Pearson asked. He waited a beat, then answered his own question. "It's a *radio* alarm clock."

Colby could see the plastic shape more clearly now.

"What does that tell you?" Pearson asked. His voice rose a half octave. O'Keefe seemed to be watching intently. Maybe there were more feds behind the one-way glass watching, too.

Colby shook his head and shrugged.

When Pearson began to scowl, Colby said, "Look, are we gonna play games, or what? Tell me what you're getting at. Are you implying that this is a copycat crime?"

Pearson leaned back in his chair, looked toward O'Keefe.

"The CSIs who processed the scene found something interesting, Detective," O'Keefe said.

Ah, Colby thought. Maybe this is a federalized version of good-cop-bad-cop.

"The techs found a good deal of fingerprints," she continued. "Mostly the decedent's, on everything except that second alarm clock."

"It was wiped clean," Pearson said.

Colby was considering the implications, but Pearson filled in the blanks.

"As I said, it wasn't running, either." Pearson tapped the open page.

"It's our conjecture that the offender purposely brought the clock to the scene and set the hands at three to mimic the crime scene photo in your book."

Colby blew out a slow breath. This was really shaping up to be one of those "aww, shit" days.

———

It was time for Matthew to become Morgan Laird once again. He slowly selected the next manila envelope and bent back the clasps that secured the flap. The sheaf of reports and eight-by-eleven crime scene photos spilled out. This one was another woman. Almost all of them were. Except when the men were incidentals, like the couple in the car or the farmers. Unless you counted the fag.

Matthew smiled.

The farmers. That had been his first one. Certainly not Laird's first. No, he'd claimed that his mother had that dubious honor. Too bad Matthew had never known his own birth mother. But the host of surrogates had served him well enough.

Onward and upward.

Still, the thoughts of that first time... What had the old lady said when she'd walked in the kitchen when he'd been washing his hands?

"Where's my husband at?" Her voice had an irritating countrified lilt to it.

The old cow. She'd howled loudly as she died, but there was no one around to hear her.

After copiously researching the account of Morgan Laird's first documented homicides in the state of Illinois, Matthew had searched laboriously for a suitable farmhouse. One just like the house described in Colby's book. No photos of that crime scene for that one, so Matthew had to delve into the special crime scene files to make sure he got it right. Luckily, the book did contain a photograph of the infamous clove hitch knot, and that, he decided, would be enough of a clue for this one.

His *clue*... His *gift*, was more like it.

He'd parked his car a mile or so down the road, removed the license plates, and screwed the stolen temporary plates onto the bumper. A note in the window saying, "Out of gas. Be back," was all the subterfuge he needed. Then he set off on the little trek across the field toward the farm house. He remembered how friendly the old man had been when he walked up.

"Howdie do, young fella," the farmer had said, pausing to wipe some sweat from his face. "What can I do for you?"

His voice had that southern Illinois twang. Like a redneck's. Matthew had mimicked Morgan's own southern Missouri accent when he'd answered.

"Sir, I've been on the road a spell. I sure would appreciate a glass of water. I'd be glad to help out with some of your chores, too, if you could see your way clear to give me a good meal in exchange." He hiked the sparsely filled backpack up on his shoulder, trying to make it look like it contained all his worldly possessions.

The ersatz Southern charm, heavy on the mint julep, had worked. The farmer told him to hop on the tractor and headed for the house. It was just like he'd pictured it. A big, two-story place painted white, with a swing on the porch. The same type that Morgan must have seen back when he'd wandered up that road coming from his second prison incarceration.

"Ma, we got us a guest for supper," the farmer had said. "We're gonna be doing some of that baling in the barn."

The woman smiled, and Matthew thought she looked like a happy barnyard beast. Big-boned and heavyset, with lackluster brownish hair turning gray, and a washed-out print dress covering her fat belly. Bovine. All she needed was a bell around her neck. He made sure he showed her his most polite smile, just like Morgan must have done.

The old man made it easy for him, turning his back after he'd handed Matthew the pitchfork and told him to move some hay. The old guy's expression was one of total surprise when Matthew said, "Hey? Like this?" and the farmer turned around, probably half-expecting some dumb question, designed for reassurance. Instead, he got the prongs of the pitchfork jammed into his gut. He lay curled on the dirty floor, holding his belly and moaning as Matthew took his time flipping the end of the rope over the cross support beam before slipping the noose around the farmer's neck. The old coot was heavier than he looked, and it took Matthew three tries before he mastered the leverage and pulled enough of the rope over to the perpendicular shaft and secured the modified clove hitch. Just like the one described in the book.

It was a good thing he'd brought his own rope. Who knew how long he would have had to search around in that pigsty for one of the right length and texture. No, bringing it was perfect. A masterstroke. The first of his many masterstrokes.

"Where's my husband at?" the woman asked as Matthew was washing his hands in the kitchen sink.

Getting her into the bedroom was more problematic

than he'd anticipated. But luckily, he'd brought his own knife, too. He left her lying on the bedroom floor, mimicking the crime scene photos from the special file, hopeful that at some point the cops would connect all the dots. Hopeful, too, that the clove hitch would provide the associative clue they needed to begin assembling the big picture.

That first one had been hard to set up, but each time it got easier, and a lot more fascinating. By the time he'd gotten to the boy and girl in the car he had really begun to enjoy the game.

Matthew smiled and looked at the next crime scene photograph. Another nondescript house.

This was almost too easy, but after all, it was in his DNA.

CHAPTER 2

Dix waved the waitress off when she came by to offer them more coffee. He leaned forward. "So why the feds involved in this anyway?"

"One of the victims was abducted and transported across state lines."

Dix raised his eyebrows. "That all?"

Colby blew out a slow breath. "It looks like someone is mimicking Laird's crimes. Setting the new scenes to match the ones I had in the book."

Dix raised his eyebrows and then licked his lips.

"How many so far?" he asked.

Colby held up three fingers.

"Which ones?" Dix asked.

"Jenise Williams for sure. Even went so far as to bring one of those old style wind-up alarm-clocks. Then there was a murder downstate." Colby sighed again, looking down at the table. "Remember that farm couple? The Browns. The FBI thinks a new one might be another copycat crime. Had the same kind of knot that Laird tied, same positioning of the victims. And a young couple abducted in a car in Cal City and killed in Indiana, just like Judy Thompson and Henry Snow. The crime scene photos are so similar, they're scary."

"Those are ones he got immunity for, right?"

Colby nodded, disgusted by the series of miscarriages of the judicial system that had corrupted this case, which was the driving force behind him writing the book. Once it was announced that Laird was being released from prison, something the state's attorney had guaranteed would never happen, Colby felt compelled to write an exposé of the injustice.

"Hey," Dix said, patting Colby on the arm. "You can't go blaming yourself for the actions of some crazy psychopath."

"Yeah, I know, but..." Colby grabbed his cup and took a sip. The coffee was cold and bitter, just like his mood. "This whole thing makes me sick."

Dix patted his right side. "I got a little silver flask in my pocket that could warm things up for you."

Colby shook his head. "I'm on duty, remember?"

"So take the rest of the day off. We got things to discuss here."

"We do?"

"Sure," Dix said. He leaned across the table again, getting close and lowering his voice to a whisper. "You think Laird could be involved somehow?"

Colby shrugged. "No idea."

"Can't you call in a couple markers...get yourself assigned to these new cases?"

"I'm knee-deep in unsolved homicides now. I'm not looking for any more." He sighed. "Besides, so far they ain't in our jurisdiction. The suspect crossing state lines has brought the *federales* in. They don't need me."

Dix snorted as he sat back. "Don't you see the potential? You gotta get on this task force. It's dynamite stuff. I can see another book in the making." He held his hands up, as if framing an imaginary title. "*Copycat*. That's what we can call it. Imagine, you and me on the talk show circuit. We'll be getting laid every night."

Colby smirked. "What's gotten into you? First you're flirting with that pretty news gal this morning, and now you're sounding like a frat boy anticipating his first beer party."

"I'm just realizing my full potential, that's all," Dix said. The leering grin appeared again under the well-trimmed mustache. "Getting divorced will do that to you. Leaves you all debonair and da-boner."

"I'm divorced, too," Colby said.

"Are you?" Dix raised his eyebrows and frowned. "We shoulda stayed in touch more."

Colby said nothing. It had been years since Dix had reached out to him.

"But anyway," Dix said. "Think about it. I can run down any leads you need help with."

"I don't know…"

"Just think about it, okay?" Dix dug into his jacket pocket, removed the silver flask, and unscrewed the cap. "Here, a little toast. To our success."

Colby held his hand over his cup. Dix shrugged and poured the amber liquid into his coffee. He lifted his mug and tapped it against Colby's.

"Here's to justice being served," he said. "One more time."

––––––––

Knox glanced at his watch. 5:09. The conference didn't begin for almost two hours, and Norton's speech wasn't scheduled until eight. Knox removed the black nylon bag from the trunk, placed it on the front passenger seat, and removed his laptop and makeup bag.

He opened his laptop and looked up the file labeled Employee Information Files. After a few deft clicks, he found the section where Norton's personal information was listed, including his credit history. He copied the credit card numbers, closed the file, and selected another program. After entering Norton's card number password, Knox clicked on recent purchases. A list filled the screen giving dates, locations, and amounts.

Knox quickly found the one he was looking for: a reservation at the Royal York Hotel, Toronto, Canada.

That meant Norton would have to travel from his hotel to the convention center.

Knox shut down the laptop, slipped it back into its case, and pulled on his thin, black leather gloves, the kind he used for driving and special jobs. Next, he took out the second laptop he'd purchased for this assignment—the same model as Norton's—and stuck it into the brown leather valise Knox had taken from Norton's office at New Genesis. It would suffice if he had to make the exchange in a crowded place. The old magician's dodge: keep the audience focused on something else, while you accomplish your switch.

It would be better to intercept him before he got to the conference. Less of a challenge, of course, but also less chance of getting caught.

He unzipped his makeup bag and took out his hairnet and wig. After tucking his ponytail up under the net, he adjusted the gray wig on his head and looked at his reflection in the mirror. Close, but it needed something more. He took out a pair of round, wire-rimmed glasses, put them on, and studied his reflection again.

Nondescript, average, unremarkable looking. Perfect. All that he had to do now was add the gray to his mustache and beard.

Matthew stretched the girl's body out on top of the bed. She'd struggled a bit, but he was a lot stronger. The pleading expression on her face almost caused a twinge of regret. Regret that he couldn't spend more time screwing her. He wondered if it would keep on getting easier. If he'd reach the point, like Morgan had described, where he wouldn't feel any remorse. The chase this time had proved to be an elementary exercise after finding the suitable target. He'd followed her from the commuter train, watching her walk to her fancy car. She was one of those do-nothing automatons who worked downtown at some office building each day, probably toiling away at some meaningless job in front of a computer, doing non-essential busy work designed to keep the mundane economy moving. No more than an insect, an animal in a maze, a guinea pig.

Matthew had shadowed her as she went into the grocery store and picked up a few small food items. Obviously buying for one. That sealed it. He wondered as he watched her in the aisles, if Morgan had used a similar hunting technique. No, he had been more spontaneous. More hit-and-miss, selecting his targets as the opportunities presented themselves, which explained why he was eventually caught.

Too much serendipity. Matthew smiled. His own game required more planning, thinking several moves ahead, like a game of chess. He was smarter than Morgan, even though they were cut from the same cloth. He was better, and he'd prove it.

He'd timed it perfectly, coming up the walk just ahead of her. She jostled a bag of groceries as she fished for her keys, smiling and murmuring a "Thanks" as he held the door for her. She hadn't even given him a second look with his clean-cut appearance. Like he was a non-entity to her, the stupid bitch. Too self-absorbed to realize his real importance, and that angered him. He wondered if Morgan had felt a similar rage rising within him before it spurred him to action.

But that was the difference between them: emotion versus intellect, spontaneity versus planning, hot versus cold. Impulse versus revenge. And, as they said, revenge was a dish best served cold.

He paused to admire his handiwork before removing the crime scene photo from his pocket to study it again, although its subtleties had been etched in his mind. Her leg was wrong. Too much bend at the knee. And her face wasn't turned at a sharp enough angle. After correcting these minor things, he paused and took out the pack of cigarettes.

Pall Malls, just like Morgan had smoked.

He peeled off the latex gloves and stuck them in his pocket. It was time for measured exactness, the next clue. After sticking one of the cigarettes in his mouth, he flicked the lighter and held the flame to the end. He drew in a mouthful of smoke, just to get it going, and blew it out, as if it were venom from a snakebite.

A filthy habit. One that he was glad he never started. The smoke stung his eyes.

Disgusting.

But necessary.

He watched patiently as the cigarette burned, the smoke curling off the end.

If they'd had DNA analysis back then, they might have identified Morgan sooner. He wondered how long it would take to trace it to him in this case.

The cigarette in the crime scene photo had been smoked down more than halfway. Almost to the end. But the smell was making him sick. He held the burning butt away from him and tapped the lengthening ash onto the floor.

One more drag to make sure they have enough juice, he thought, and brought the tip to his lips once more. His stomach wrenched at the pungency, but he persisted.

After all, he had to get this right. Exactly right.

———

It took Knox the better part of twenty minutes to locate Norton's car in the Royal York's parking garage. A beige Lexus, the red, white, and blue Illinois Land of Lincoln plates standing out like a banner in a sea of white and blue Ontarios. The GPS tracking device took a scant thirty seconds to snap in place under the right rear fender where no one would notice it. Knox got back into his BMW, pulled about a hundred feet away, and stopped. Despite the coolness of the October weather, the wig was making him sweat. He wiped his face with some paper napkins and threw them on the floor. He couldn't afford to leave any trace evidence, even a drop of sweat, though the probability that they'd find it and make the connection was remote. Very remote. But still, why take the chance? It was all about minimizing risks.

His laptop was open on the seat next to him, and he clicked on the icon marked Trace.

It took a few seconds for the program to load, and a few more for the signal to bounce off the orbiting satellite. The map of Toronto etched itself across the screen and the hourglass symbol came on. The small automobile materialized, off Front Street, in the stationary position indicating that the vehicle was parked and non-mobile.

Knox shifted into drive and pulled out of the underground facility, circling the streets until he found a suitable parking spot. He could check inside the car later, after he had Norton's keys. For now, he was content to wait.

He glanced at his watch. Six fifteen p.m. That meant it was five-fifteen in Chicago. Time to check in with Jetters. He picked up his cell phone and punched in the numbers.

———

Colby slammed the copy of the file down on his kitchen table.

Damn, it shouldn't have worked out like this.

Taking a deep breath, he tried to sort it out again. He tried to remember exactly whom he'd given the file copies to when he'd done the book. Yeah, he'd been careless, but hell, the case was over twenty-eight years old.

His editor had seen them. His agent. The proofreaders.

Shit, it was impossible, but, from what the feds had told him, this copycat dude had known things that went far beyond the photos and info detailed in the book. No, someone had access to the actual police files.

Colby sat forward, elbows on knees, and contemplated.

Pearson's skepticism, the sarcastic lilt in his tone, floated in Colby's memory. It still stung.

"You aren't trying to tell us you wrote this yourself, are you?" the FBI man had said. "I mean, you had a ghostwriter, right?"

That had come at the tail-end of the interview, when Colby was debating whether or not to walk out, or give this asshole fed a knuckle sandwich.

"No," he said. "I didn't."

"Detective Colby." It was Agent O'Keefe's turn. She managed to get something akin to a compassionate expression on her face. "We're not the enemy here. We're on the same side."

"Could've fooled me," Colby said as he headed for the door. "I'll look over my files and get back to you. In the meantime, why don't you go check out Lance Fontaine?"

Fontaine. It had to be him. As Laird's attorney, he would have total access to the police reports. Those hotshot feds needed to check the lawyer's discovery motions instead of hassling an honest cop, who just happened to write a good book.

He toyed with the idea of going to Fontaine himself.

No, that would only give the prick more ammunition. He'd just claim client confidentiality and clam up. It would be a wasted trip.

Unless...

Colby mulled over the possibility of breaking into the defense attorney's office and then shook his head. With his luck he'd get caught on candid camera and be awarded a one-way ticket to the joint.

———

The small auto-shaped icon began to move just as Knox was finishing his conversation with Dr. Jetters.

"He's moving," Knox said. "I have to go."

"Stop him," Jetters said over the cell phone. "He must not speak at that conference."

"Leave it to me," Knox said, glancing over his shoulder as he pulled out. Luckily, the evening traffic was very light here for such a large city. Nothing like New York or Chicago. Knox braked and checked the screen.

The Lexus pulled out of the parking area, and seconds later the auto-icon moved onto the ribbon-like section labeled Front Street going east. The icon turned left on

Bay and left again on Wellington. When he saw it turning right on John Street, going back toward Front, which was one-way, Knox knew Norton was heading for the convention center and tailed at a respectable distance. The tracking device was superfluous now, except as insurance. But minimizing the odds against mistakes was what separated the professionals from the amateurs. Thinking of professionalism, he made a mental note to retrieve his GPS locator once the personal interaction had been completed.

Norton's Lexus signaled and turned right, going into the parking area for the convention center. Knox followed, collecting his entrance ticket and watching the Lexus's taillights as it braked and went left. He gunned his own car, cutting down the closest entrance ramp and finding a vacant spot next to the sign that pointed toward the convention center entrance. Beneath the ground the city was quiet and deserted. Hardly any cars. Hardly any noise.

He readjusted the wig and fake glasses as he got out of his car. His gloved fingers rested on the knife in his pocket, his thumb ready on the hollow eyelet that allowed for the one-handed opening of the blade. The stairway to the next level down, the one where he assumed Norton would be on, was only about fifteen feet away. With a few brisk steps he was there.

Looking around, Knox saw a few people hustling toward the stairs. A car shot past him. He paused in the aisle and studied the parking area, and then he saw the Lexus. Knox casually removed the knife from his pocket as he began walking. Norton closed the door and hit the remote, causing a slight beep of the horn. Knox flipped open the blade and held it against the inner aspect of his wrist. It felt cool and hard.

Norton was fussing with his laptop case, glancing at

his watch, totally unaware of his surroundings, probably mentally rehearsing his speech. He looked a little nervous, but he didn't need to be. It would all be over shortly.

"Professor Norton," Knox said, the pleasant smile still gracing his lips.

Norton's head shot up, his face a quizzical knot. He pressed the laptop to his chest, like a schoolgirl carrying her books.

"Who are—" The realization apparently dawned on him, despite the disguise. "Knox? Is that you?"

Still smiling, Knox shortened the distance. They were perhaps seven feet apart now. He rotated his head, looking for witnesses.

No one around.

"I hope you're not here to try and dissuade me," Norton began. "I know he's angry with me, but it's time. The world has to know. They have to be told."

"Certainly," Knox said. "But over there…" He pointed off to an imaginary point over Norton's right shoulder. The man's head turned slightly.

Three feet now.

Two.

Knox readjusted the knife, curled his fingers around the handle, and brought it up in a quick motion striking just under the sternum.

Norton's gasp was barely audible, and Knox worked the blade around inside the other man's abdomen.

Knox grabbed Norton's arm with his left hand, carefully gripping the laptop to secure it, and walked the man back toward the Lexus. No one was around, no one to see them. Knox could feel the warm blood seeping between the glove and his wrist. Norton stumbled along, like a drunken marionette, his legs dragging a little more with each step. When they were between the cars, Knox let

Norton sink to his knees. His face was already draining of all color, his tongue curling upward at the side of his mouth.

After another quick look around, Knox dropped Norton on his side, wiped off the blade, and snapped it shut. He checked to see how much of the other man's blood had gotten on his jacket. It was dark and the blood didn't show much. Stooping down, he grabbed the laptop and set it on the rough cement, away from the draining crimson puddle. The floor was canted in such a way that the stream was running toward the center of the aisle.

Designed that way for drainage purposes. Convenient. He worked his fingers into Norton's back pocket and removed his billfold.

Flipping it open, he found the Royal York room keys.

After slipping the wallet inside his own coat and going through the rest of the dead man's pockets, Knox hit the remote and opened the Lexus. The blood was running toward the center in more copious fashion now.

Must have hit a major vessel, Knox thought. *Have to buy myself enough time to check his hotel room, too.*

Knowing it would be better to move to a safer location before tossing it, he grabbed the laptop, slipped inside Norton's Lexus, and started it. As he pulled out of the space, he rolled up and over the body of the now late John H. Norton.

CHAPTER 3

Leslie Labyorteaux pulled her brown hair back in a ponytail, despite knowing it would make her appear younger. The alternative was worse; accidentally brushing it back and getting blood on it. And she'd been told there was a lot of blood.

At thirty-three, she'd finally worked her way up to detective, after having labored in patrol for five years and property crimes investigations for four-and-a-half. Getting this far had been costly: her marriage, her social life, her family relationships... This was her first homicide, her first whodunit. A dead body in the parking garage at the convention center. What more could a girl ask for?

She flashed her badge at the officers standing guard at the entrance and they motioned her car through after giving her one of those looks. The kind that carried the assumption that she was sleeping with somebody higher up to get a plumb assignment like investigator. She'd paid her dues and would tell anybody that.

But not tonight.

Tonight, she had something better to do: a date with a dead man.

Another officer motioned her to stop, and she brought her detective's shield up again. He nodded.

"They radioed me you were coming," he said. "Inspector Graven's already up there. You might want to pull in here and walk down. It's only one flight."

She thanked him and steered her Honda into the open space. As she got out, she reached in her purse for a pair of latex gloves before going down to the next level where a gaggle of men worked behind a ribbon of yellow crime scene tape.

Inspector Graven looked up from a small circle of men in trench coats, his face in its perpetual scowl. He nodded to Labyorteaux.

"Glad you could make it, luv," he said. "Hope we didn't break your boyfriend's heart."

"Actually, I was just going for a run, sir."

"A run? This time of night?"

"On the treadmill," she added.

Graven frowned again. "What bigger waste of time is there than running and not getting anywhere?" He took a deep breath and tapped another man on the shoulder. "Benson, give her what you've got so far."

Benson, a red-haired, overweight guy, flipped open his pad and began reading quickly.

"At nineteen-ten hours, this date, a patron of the establishment was walking back to his car." He read off the patron's name and the information about the vehicle. "As he proceeded down this aisle, he stepped in what he thought was an oil or antifreeze leak." Benson paused again and pointed to a set of male footprints several yards away. A photographer was standing by the prints snapping pictures. The flash made a bright wink in the cavernous parking garage. "It was at this point he saw the body by that car, and realized that it was not oil or antifreeze, but blood."

"Cut the superfluous crap," Graven said, his voice a low growl. "Give her the damn highlights and hurry the hell up."

Benson's face reddened to almost the same shade as his hair. "The victim was stabbed in the gut. Looks like your typical mugging gone bad to me."

"And keep your opinions to yourself," Graven said.

Labyorteaux saw more techs snapping photos. The flash winked again, its sudden illumination bouncing off the inner recesses behind them. A man lay twisted in the shadows, next to the rear bumper of a parked car, his tongue twisting out of his mouth, locked between frozen jaws.

"Has the victim been ID'd yet?" Labyorteaux asked.

"No, his wallet's missing," Graven said. "So get to it, *Detective*."

The way he said "detective" let her know that failure, as they say, was not an option.

———

The next morning Colby felt hungover and dehydrated. He'd spent last night mulling over the case files with his old buddy, Johnny Walker Red, while too many repressed images of the dead Swanstrom twins kept lingering in his mind. One drink turned into two, and two to four...He was drinking doubles, or, as he put it after downing several, only multiplying by two. The stupid thought had occurred to him in the midst of a drunken stupor that did little to quell the gnawing feeling of guilt in his gut. The Swanstrom twins' pale faces floated in front of him again.

He'd failed them. He hadn't gotten to them in time.

After stopping at the water cooler, he was downing his second cup—multiplying by two again—when Bosworth, the detective Colby liked least in the division, slapped him on the back hard enough to cause him to spill the water on his necktie.

Colby swore at him.

"Hey, hotshot, looks like you got a wet spot on your tie." Bosworth's face split into a large grin. "Oh, the LT wants to see ya."

Colby thought about how sweet it would be to punch the asshole's face in. "What about?"

"Shit if I know." Bosworth laughed as he walked away. "Maybe he wants you to sign a copy of your book."

Colby went down the hallway and spotted Lieutenant Kropper behind his desk, talking on the phone, the little man's waspy frame looking totally agitated. Colby walked to the open door and knocked.

"You wanted to see me, lieu?"

Kropper's steely gaze met his. He put a hand over the mouthpiece of the phone and said, "Come in and close the door."

A closed-door session, thought Colby. This can't be good.

He debated whether it was better to sit in the "hot seat" chair in front of the desk or remain standing. He elected for the latter, remembering one of the "power tips" from his agent: "Standing forces them to look up at you. It's a position of dominance."

A second later Kropper mumbled a "Yes, sir. Ten-four. Will do," and hung up the phone. He snapped his fingers and pointed, indicating the "hot seat."

So much for the position of dominance, Colby thought.

As he settled into the chair he could see the lieutenant's face was more flushed than usual.

"How's the book tour going?" Kropper asked.

"All right, I guess."

Kropper nodded, the dash of red still dappling his cheeks. "I got a call from the FBI this morning." He paused, letting the words sink in. "Special Agent Pearson. Know him?"

Colby knew that Kropper had been on the job long enough not to ask a question without already knowing the answer. He decided to play it straight and close to his vest.

"Yeah, I talked to him yesterday."

"What about?"

Colby shrugged. "They were looking at a couple of homicides that might be copycats of an old case I worked."

Kropper smiled. The man had little teeth that slanted inward, like a small rodent's. "Rog, you're being modest again." He folded his hands behind his head after smoothing his thinning black hair. "Don't you mean *the* case?"

Kropper sprang forward so quickly it shocked Colby. "Didn't I tell you when you wrote that damn thing, that the department had better not come off looking bad?"

"Lieu," Colby began.

Kropper raised his index finger, pointing it like a revolver. "Let me finish." He took a deep breath, and said, "Maybe it's time you decided if you want to be a cop or Ernest fucking Hemingway." Kropper kept his finger extended, his eyes locked in what he must have thought looked like a fierce stare.

Colby compressed his lips. He wasn't in the mood for this. He met the lieutenant's gaze with one of his own.

After all the years of interviewing suspects, he wasn't about to let anyone, even his boss, stare him down.

Kropper's gaze wilted, then he dropped his hand. "How does your caseload look?"

Colby shrugged. "The usual."

"The feds are requesting you," Kropper said. "They're setting up a multi-agency task force. They want you there as some kind of consultant."

"A consultant?" Colby said, a tiny bit irritated. Although he was curious about this copycat thing, there were a lot of old ghosts he didn't want to revisit. "What kind of bullshit is that?"

"Don't worry. I ain't gonna give you up without a fight." He showed Colby the small teeth again. "Especially at the end of the month with Comp Stat looming." Kropper's face twitched slightly, then he blew out a slow breath. "Take today to sort through your cases. You can start with the feds tomorrow. You got any slam-dunks that can be administratively cleared, give them to Bosworth. Anything else, farm out to Dicarlo and Wilson. I want to have something to show the brass."

Colby nodded, his mouth drawing tight. As much as he hated the thought of handing Bosworth a bunch of easy closures, Colby cared enough about a few of the open ones to see they got good homes. And despite the bad memories, part of him did want to check into this copycat thing.

Who knows, he thought, shifting his weight to stand up, maybe Laird himself might be somehow connected to the crimes.

After all, the son of a bitch was out of prison.

———

Matthew ran his fingers over the edge of the blade, testing the sharpness. This one was going to be a bit trickier. Not a lot of time to assure exactness. He folded the knife shut and slipped it back into his pocket, allowing the metallic clip to hang on the outside of his pants. Taking the gold stud, he switched the magnet from his left earlobe to his right, and snapped it in place.

Did the fags still do that? No matter. Even if he was a bit passé, he knew he had to fit into the scenery. Fade into the background. The rental car would help, too. It was a black Lexus. Plenty of trunk space. He remembered to spread the heavy tarp down first. Any clues he left had to be part of the master design, not left out of carelessness. And this one required an obvious clue, in the name of expediency.

He turned onto Belmont and proceeded up toward the glowing neon lights and it wasn't even dark yet.

What an ostentatious affectation.

Matthew smiled at his choice of words. Good choice for a college student. He hoped that none of his professors had dropped the dime on him to the old man. But why would they? What did they care if he attended class or not, as long as the New Genesis Foundation paid his tuition? Except for that bastard, Dr. Sellers. He was the busybody type who would gladly stick his nose in where it didn't belong.

I'll deal with him later, Matthew thought, remembering his focus. Morgan's seventh Illinois victim had been a young male prostitute that Laird had said came on to him. He'd left the fucking faggot gutted in an alley.

A red Dodge Viper turned in front of him with a belligerent honk. Matthew slammed on his brakes and gave the driver the finger. A bunch of twenty-something girls, out for a night of drinking and carousing, shuffled across the street. For a moment he thought about following them, and making them into number eleven-plus, counting the ones in Indiana, but that would be deviating from the plan.

Concentrate on the task at hand, he thought. No deviations, no matter how pleasant the thoughts.

For a moment he envied Morgan's freedom to act on impulse, rather than follow a carefully scripted plan. Chasing the rapture. No, that wasn't right. With Morgan it had been more Darwinian. A version of natural selection, the predator's natural dominance, rather than merely rapacious serendipity.

The rapture came in a different bottle for Matthew. It was tied to the ultimate goal. Executing his master plan. The perfect plan. Exposing the truth...redemption... escape.

The sign up ahead spelled out: Rainbow Bistro. This was the place. Two queers walked hand-in-hand down the block. He cruised by slowly, then went around the block again. They all looked like couples.

Fags of a feather, he thought. Then he saw him. The young man, waif-like, with longish hair, obviously dyed black, a rainbow ribbon pinned to his jacket lapel.

Matthew slowed the Lexus and looked the waif straight in the eye as he rolled down the passenger window with a deft push of the button.

"Hi," he said, trying to keep that certain, vibrant, effervescent quality in his voice. "You going my way?"

———

Knox drove up to the large metal gates and ran his passcard through the electronic scanning slot. The oval eye of the camera stared blankly at him and he saw a convex distortion of his face as he waited.

Finally, the gate on the left swung open and Knox

drove forward. The entrance opened to a beautiful, manmade lake as the narrow ribbon of roadway split in two, each going off in the opposite direction to run parallel with the shore. Beyond it, the vastness of the square brick buildings was silhouetted against the setting sun.

Knox went past the line of trees toward the main building, the edge of sunset filtering through the leaves to dapple the asphalt. He took out his cell phone as the road twisted toward the first set of buildings and called.

The phone rang several times before Jetters answered.

"I'm at the lab," he said. "Meet me at section C."

That was all. Knox knew it was one of the old man's quirks. Not wanting to talk on cell phones. Always convinced that Big Brother was listening, even here, in his own little fiefdom.

What does he have to worry about? Knox wondered. The son of a bitch owns both sides of the aisle in DC, as well as the damn White House.

Knox swung the BMW over toward the second set of square, brick buildings set in front of still yet another artificial lake. This one had several swans skimming over the surface. A white security car cruised by in the opposite direction. The uniformed guard waved to Knox, who ignored him.

It was getting late, he'd been on the road since early morning, and now all he wanted to do was relax in a hot tub with a drink, not be reporting to some self-aggrandizing asshole. He found the special parking space marked Head of Security and parked there. He shifted into Park and plucked the new pair of driving gloves from the seat next to him, slowly working his big hands into the form-fitting confines.

He didn't want his fingerprints to be on merchandise

when it was delivered. Thoroughness. That's what made a pro.

Knox watched his reflection in the opaque windows as he walked up the cement section toward the front entrance: a tall, athletic man carrying a briefcase, and marveled as to how fit he looked. Like a movie star. Did that make him a narcissist? He wondered for a moment how others saw him. A lawyer, perhaps? A judge was more like it. Or, better yet, an executioner.

Taking out his card, he swiped it in the box next to the door. Inside the synthetic decorum of solid rock walls, fifteen-foot waterfall, and the tropical garden looked as trite and phony as ever. This place was all illusion, all smoke and mirrors. Nothing, Knox reflected, was as it seemed, nothing was truly real.

The rush of the flowing water echoed in the large, empty room. Knox walked past the winding staircase of steel, black slats and Plexiglas that wound over the fountain stopped at the elevator. He pressed the button and waited. In the mirrored wall in front of him, Knox saw the reflection of the solitary figure standing at the top of the staircase, hands clasped behind his back, the errant white hairs curling away from the large skull. He almost looked like an artist's version of Einstein gone mad, except for the aquiline nose.

The elevator doors slid open. Knox stepped in and pressed the button for the second floor. When the doors opened, Jetters was standing a few feet away.

"Good evening," Knox said, feigning politeness.

"How was Toronto?" Jetters asked.

Knox shrugged. "It wasn't Vegas." He knew his wit wasn't appreciated.

The old man's lower lip tucked over his upper, vibrating with rage. His eyes stared so coldly at Knox that he felt a sudden urge to take his hands out of his pockets. Knox had seen him slap people during his legendary temper tantrums.

But the old coot sure can't afford to take a swing at me, no matter how mad he gets, Knox thought. And if he tries, I'll break his fucking arm.

"When I ask you for a report," Jetters said, "I don't expect flippancy. That's not what I'm paying you for." He rose up on his toes, but made no further physical movement.

Knox allowed himself to relax a bit.

The old bastard did have a point. The money was good. Plus, being a professional meant delivering the goods in the crunch. Knox walked over to the adjacent handrail, set his briefcase on it, adjusted the knobs to the proper combination, and lifted the lid. Reaching inside, he removed the laptop and held it toward Jetters.

The old man's eyes lit up.

"This is his?" The veined hands grabbed the laptop and he held it to his chest, like a child receiving a much anticipated Christmas gift.

Knox nodded.

"And John?"

"Tactically neutralized," Knox said. He removed something else from the briefcase and held that out also. "Here's the hard drive from his main PC, as well as two flash drives I recovered from his home."

Jetters' eyes narrowed. "Any problems there?"

Knox shook his head. "Only a minor one. I took care of it before I left before I left for Toronto. His partner walked in on me."

"Peter?" Jetters blinked rapidly several times. "What happened?"

"I made it look like an accident," Knox said. "A fall from a high place. A fractured neck."

The old man's sigh was audible. "I never wanted that. I liked him, but I guess it couldn't be helped."

Knox thought of a felicitous reply, but kept it to himself.

Jetters looked up and licked his lips. "We have another problem."

Knox waited, tugging off the thin leather gloves, one finger at a time. "What's that?"

"Matthew," Jetters said, "is missing."

CHAPTER 4

Leslie Labyorteaux looked again at the photos of the dead man. It was going on thirty-six hours since the body had been discovered, and she had yet to get the victim identified. The textbooks said that the first twenty-four to forty-eight hours were the most crucial in terms of solvability. She felt the case slipping away.

Refocusing herself, she studied the file again. There were no fewer than twelve convention events scheduled at the center the night in question. So far, she'd been unsuccessful in determining if the victim had been connected to any of them. Graven had expressed his opinion that it was a random mugging gone bad. A review of the "thug file" of known offenders who frequented the downtown area had so far proved less than elucidating, as well. She decided to concentrate on what she did have.

The autopsy that morning had been especially telling.

"He had a heart transplant," the attending doctor had told her.

That, in itself, was not totally unremarkable. But the body bore other surgical scars, too.

The doctor's fingers, glossy white in the latex gloves, probed the decedent's right side. "Looks like other organs as well. Most likely a liver, maybe more."

She remembered the doctor's thoughtful expression as he stood back after sifting through the man's open chest cavity.

"His organs are in remarkable shape for a man his age. I estimate him to be in his late seventies, but these organs look much younger." He laughed. "If I didn't know better, I'd say they almost look brand new."

"Maybe he went in for a complete overhaul," she said facetiously, trying to keep her mind off the putrid odor and horrendous sight of a human being sliced up the middle like a field-dressed deer.

She remembered the doctor's perplexed expression as he continued to shake his head.

"Never seen anything quite like it," he said, as he stared down into the gaping hole. "The anti-rejection drugs were doing an extraordinary job."

Medical operations like that would be recorded, she thought. At least that's something to go on.

Still, it had taken longer than she anticipated to get the victim identified. His pockets had been completely devoid of anything remotely personal, except for a roll of breath mints, a comb, and a handkerchief. No wallet, no hotel keys, no car keys. No record of the dead man's fingerprints through Toronto PD, the RCMP, or any other Canadian database. She'd submitted them to Buffalo PD, Erie County, NYPD, and also to the New York State Police.

Good luck hoping for them to put a rush on it, she thought. If only things moved as fast in real life as they did on those American TV shows.

She also submitted a request to the AFIS system of the Federal Bureau of Investigation, hoping for a sympathetic ear, figuring maybe the feds, as the Americans say, would see her as something more than a pesky Canuck.

Hopefully, something else would break soon, giving her a more substantial lead. It had to, if she wanted to solve her first homicide.

———

After locating the silver Corvette in the parking lot of Matthew's apartment building on the city's southwest side, Knox tried to place a tracking device on the undercarriage. The burglar alarm had been engaged, and the car began an incessant honking and blinking. Turning, as if totally disinterested in the noise, Knox picked up his black leather briefcase and went back around to the front of the building. Inside the small foyer, he glanced in the mailbox for apartment 2B.

M. Jetters.

It was surprising that the old man had allowed the kid this much freedom. Moving off the New Genesis compound, having an apartment, a sharp car. He'd been raised exclusively on the compound, being home schooled and never allowed to venture into the outside world unescorted. And it showed. To say he was a weird little fucker was an understatement. Now it looked like Jetters had given him free rein, but he was the only normal one in a group of retards. Almost as if Matthew was actually Jetters's surrogate son.

Almost.

Strict conditions were in place, like closely monitoring the kid's cell phone, computer usage, and credit card activity. It kept Knox and his security team busy. Obviously, their surveillance had not been sufficient.

Knox took out his lock picking kit. He concentrated

on the mailbox first, slipping the gaping, jagged lock in easy fashion.

It was full. Obviously, no one had emptied it in at least two or three days. No wonder the old man was concerned.

He sorted through the mail, pocketing any bills he could find, and sticking the ads in his other coat pocket. After a quick glance around, he stuck the thin blade of the pistol-pick into the security door's lock and applied a gentle, simultaneous pressure with the L-shaped wrench. After a few flicks of the trigger, all the tumblers lined up and he felt the lock twist open. He carefully closed the door behind him and went upstairs. At apartment 2B, he again used the pistol-pick. It took even less time than the first door.

The apartment was dark inside and smelled musty. Stacks of papers, books, and magazines littered the coffee table and chairs in the living room. The bedroom was just as bad, the bed a twisted mix of sheets, blanket, and pillows.

It was evident that no one had slept here for at least a few days. The red light on the answering machine blinked in the solitary darkness.

After switching on the lights, Knox listened to each message. There were three, all unremarkable. School related. One from his graduate adviser informing him that she still hadn't received the proposal for his thesis project. The second from the research librarian advising him that the books he ordered were in, and the final one from the adviser again, more petulant in tone than the last, once again reminding him that his proposal was due this week.

I guess it pays to have a rich old man footing the bills, thought Knox.

He settled in to the task at hand, switching the

computer on. The message box, requesting a password, sprang into view.

Knox frowned, feeling the growing sense of urgency to get this damn thing done. He removed his tablet from his coat pocket, connected it to the computer, and selected the override program. Twenty seconds later, Matthew's computer opened to the screen saver, a selfie of the Matthew holding a gun to his head. The weapon looked to be a BB pistol, but the effect was clear: this kid had more than just a couple of screws loose.

Knox went through the computer quickly, hacking into Matthew's emails and checking for social media listings. There were none, but Knox hadn't expected any. Jetters had been clear that was forbidden, harnessing Matthew with another abnormal restriction. What normal kid today wasn't on Facebook? But then again, Matthew was anything but normal.

Knox continued to review the files until he found the ones allowing him access to the recent credit card information. The card was listed under *New Genesis, Inc.*

He checked the list of recent charges. Three were of interest. Two at a gas station on the north side, and one from three days ago at the Bel-Aire Motel, on the south side. The gas purchases were substantial amounts. Knox didn't think the Corvette would be that kind of a guzzler. Did he have a second car?

The third charge piqued Knox's interest more. Why rent a motel room when he had his own apartment?

Knox figured the obvious answer was that he wanted to do something that he didn't want his neighbors to know about. Drugs? Parties? Hookers? Maybe all three?

It was unimportant. He didn't care what vices the little punk was into. Knox just wanted to find him quickly. Still, the discovery of this unexpected wrinkle had piqued Knox's interest. The game was afoot, and he was beginning to enjoy it. He moved the mouse to see what else he could find.

———

The break in the homicide case came four hours after Leslie's initial request to the FBI.

She looked at the email:

Attention: Detective Labyorteaux, Toronto Police Dept.

The fingerprints you submitted have shown to be a positive match with the following FBI number: GS 44399010003. Norton, John H. DOB: 03-19-1933.

It took her a few phone calls to find out what the information meant and where it led.

"GS is the designation for Government Service," the helpful man at the Bureau of Identification said.

"Do you show any home address?" she asked, and heard a soft chuckle.

"I couldn't find that without narrowing it down more," the man said. "Know what state he lived in?"

"No idea. Isn't there a central listing of all US residents?"

"Not really. There are way too many people for that."

The initial ebullience she'd felt was fading rapidly. "This is the first break I've had in this case. Do you show a last known address?"

Another chuckle. "This entry is over thirty years old. I'd have to do a manual lookup. They don't even keep these files on the computer anymore."

"How soon could you do it?"

The chuckle turned to an irritated laugh.

"You'll have to submit a request through NCIC," he said. "You can tie into that up there, can't you?"

Labyorteaux told him she could and thanked him.

Red tape. The Americans reveled in it.

She tapped her pencil on the tablet where she'd written the name and date of birth. At least she had something to go on now.

An American in Toronto. That, in itself, limited the possibilities, unless he'd moved here. Plus, with his medical conditions, he'd have to be listed on the health care computer system. It was worth a shot to send an inquiry to the border stations, too, to see if they had any record of his recent crossing. And she could now cross-check his name with the lists of conference attendees.

After running the name on her own computer system, and drawing a blank as far as Canadian residents, she sighed and put her head in her hands. When she looked up, she saw Inspector Graven standing in the doorway of her cubicle. Sitting up straight, she managed a weak smile.

"Good afternoon, sir."

He frowned.

"How's the investigation going on that stabbing murder at the parking garage?"

"I've finally found out who he is." She tapped the tablet page. "He was an American. I'm waiting to hear back from the border stations."

Graven worked his hand over his chin.

Was he checking to see if he remembered to shave this morning? Or was it a sign of annoyance?

"Check the conference attendees' lists and the down-town hotels too," Graven said. "If he's not a permanent resident, he's got to have turned up missing from one of them. Probably came in as a report of an unpaid bill."

"Already on it, sir," she said.

He seemed unimpressed. "And go through that list of plates I had the uniforms copy down. It was every car up and down two levels from where we found the body. I think there were a couple American ones in there."

"I planned on doing that, too," she said.

Graven smiled ever so slightly and, in his usual gruff tone, said, "Okay, luv. Keep me posted."

———

"We were expecting you yesterday," Special Agent Pearson said, his lips forming into a small pout.

Colby grinned. "What can I say? My boss is an asshole." For once, he'd told the truth in making an excuse, and felt good about it.

Pearson expelled a loud breath through flaring nostrils and held the door to the inner offices open. "Come in."

Colby followed Pearson to the same interview room that he'd been in before. It gnawed at him that they were still treating him like a suspect, or something.

And they talk about "inter-agency cooperation."

Pearson held out his hand indicating the chair and sat opposite him, staring at him from across the table. The FBI man then opened the manila folder he'd been carrying.

"There's been a new development," he said.

"Another homicide?" Colby asked.

Pearson nodded and held up two fingers.

"Once again, we have reason to believe that the killer, or killers, purposely recreated the scenes of Morgan Laird's series of murders. Four in Indiana, six here in Illinois."

Colby felt a tightening in his gut. "You think it's the work of more than one guy?"

"We assume nothing. Our VICAP program indicates that it is, most probably, the work of one individual, but he may be working in concert with another." Pearson paused and raised his eyebrows. "Serial killers are typically loners, but this is no ordinary perpetrator."

Typical fed, Colby thought. Spread the bullshit on so thick, that no matter how it eventually plays out, you're covered.

"However," Pearson continued, "as I said, there's been a new development." He let the sentence hang.

Colby waited, his irritation growing. "You gonna tell me about it, or you want me to guess?"

The FBI agent's mouth tightened into a thin line. He withdrew an 8x11 color photograph and slid it across the table.

Colby looked down at the photo. It was the cover of *Blood Trails*.

"Recognize that?" Pearson asked.

Colby nodded.

Pearson reached into the folder again and removed a photocopy of the title page. Above the bold print name was a practically undecipherable signature.

"Is that your signature?" Pearson asked, setting the photocopy on the tabletop and resting an index finger on the penned scrawl.

Colby studied it. Where the hell was this leading?

"Looks like it," he said. "I signed a lot of them."

Pearson's eyes narrowed.

"This book," he tapped the photo of *Blood Trails*, "was found at the latest crime scene."

Colby raised his eyebrows. It was a message. A message to him.

Pearson continued. "The vic was a young homosexual, strangled and dumped in an alley in Boystown. The section about Benjamin Pike bookmarked with the new victim's big toe."

"You dust the book for prints?" Colby's voice sounded coarse, hollow.

"Of course," Pearson said. "In a case of this magnitude, we put a rush on all of the forensics."

Colby felt the tightness in his gut ratcheting up another notch. Why couldn't this son of a bitch just spit things out?

"Find any?" Colby was ready to jump out of his chair and grab the file right out of the asshole's hands.

"We did." Pearson pointed to the top of the title page. "Several, including an exceptionally defined latent right here. His triumphant little smirk was cut short by Colby's reply.

"It was mine, right?"

Pearson's lips compressed, then he nodded. "Yours and a host of unidentifiables. Not on file. Some smudged partials."

"But none, you believe, belong to the suspect." It was more of a statement than a question. Colby had to start showing these assholes that he was as quick on the uptake as they were. Fortune favors the bold, he thought.

"Don't you think it's time I got assigned to this task force as something more than a consultant?"

The FBI man frowned. "Detective, while your input here might have some value, it's our consensus it might be a mistake to involve you more fully at this time."

"Why the hell not? The prick's obviously taunting me."

"Therein lies the problem," Pearson said.

"What problem?"

Pearson sat back in the cheap plastic chair and clasped his hands behind his head.

"For you, I'm afraid," he said slowly, "this is far too personal."

Colby's brow furrowed. "Then why am I here?"

"You're here so that we can gain insight into the unsub," Pearson said. "Not as an investigator."

It had taken Leslie most of the day, but finally things were starting to fall into place. Cross-checking the plates recorded in the parking garage had yielded six American ones. Three from New York, one from Michigan, one from Minnesota, and one from Illinois. It was the last one that rang true. It had been found parked two levels down from the spot where the body had been found. The license plates were registered to the New Genesis Corporation in Oakbrook Estates, Illinois, Leslie found a driver's license record for John H. Norton living in that area also. After a quick phone call to the Oakbrook Estates Police Department asking them to do a death notification and to contact her, she searched for the town, finding it near Chicago. Next she crosschecked the events at the convention center the night of the murder and found another tie-in: a geneticist convention. One of the scheduled speakers had been Norton, but he'd never showed.

"Mr. John H. Norton?" Leslie asked Dr. Carroll, one of the Canadian scientists who had been a keynote speaker at the conference. "Did you know him?"

The scientist's hesitant reply made the hairs on the back of her neck stand up. She was on to something.

"Yes," Carroll said. "I knew him."

"What can you tell me about him?"

She heard a deep sigh on the other end of the line. "Dr. Carroll?"

"Well, I, um, don't wish to speak ill of the dead."

"Please, Doctor," Leslie said. "This is very important."

She heard him sigh before answering. "I always found him to be a rather odd bird."

"In what way, sir?"

Once again, the scientist's answer was slow in coming and riddled with uncomfortable pauses.

"He was a very capable, oftentimes brilliant man. But, if I had to put my finger on it, I'd say he had something of a...personality problem."

"Can you be more specific?"

She heard another heavy sigh. "My associate, Dr. Leavitt, was nominated for a Nobel Prize for his work in stem cell research," Carroll said. "Norton spoke in a very disparaging manner about it. And when those scientists in Britain cloned that sheep, and when that woman paid to have her dead cat cloned, he hit the roof. He was so angry at the attention and acclaim they received. My guess is, he had research projects in those areas himself and resented them for beating him to the punch."

"Beating him to the punch?"

"Yes, well, a Nobel Prize, even though my colleague didn't receive it, is a strong motivator."

"I see," Leslie said, making a mental note to check into Norton's work more closely. "Do you know where Mr. Norton was based?"

"In the States. Somewhere near Chicago, I believe."

"Was he associated with a company called New Genesis?"

"I do believe that it was something like that," Carroll said.

After making sure Norton's car was towed and processed by the evidence technicians, she began checking the downtown hotels and, sure enough, there had been a John H. Norton registered at the Royal York. He'd never checked out, leaving his luggage, a sparsely packed suitcase, in his room.

"What did you do with his things?" Leslie asked the hotel manager.

"I guess we still have them in storage."

"Good. I'll send someone by to pick them up," she said, a smile working its way across her face. Finally, she was getting somewhere.

Inspector Graven was impressed, too, but not quite enough.

"So it's taken us this long just to find out who he is and where he's from?" His expression was grave, sour. Like someone had poured curdled milk into his coffee. "We need to get moving on this one, luv."

"I'm going to the lab now to speak with the techs," she said. "They're going over the items from his hotel room."

But that turned out to be another disappointment. Not only were Norton's things unremarkable in content, the hotel housekeepers had packed all his belongings in his suitcase, depriving her of any clues the layout of his clothes would have provided. Not that they would have yielded much anyway, in all probability. From all appearances, this still appeared to be a random crime. A robbery. The victim's wallet was missing, and the thorough search of all the trash cans in the area had been done the first night. They either missed it, or the killer disposed of it in another fashion.

Maybe he kept the wallet as a souvenir, which would be nice if they caught him with it. But that was looking like a pretty big "if" right now.

Norton's car proved to be another matter.

The head of the forensic team was a short, skinny man with a fringe of grayish hair around his ears and tiny, gold-framed glasses. Leslie knew him as Tab, which was how all the detectives referred to him. His last name was something long, Polish, and unpronounceable.

"Nothing remarkable," he said.

Something in his expression caught her eye.

"What?" she asked. "You noticed something, didn't you?"

Tab took off his glasses and rubbed the bridge of his nose.

"Like I said, nothing remarkable. Plenty of prints all over the interior of the car, the windows, the doors. But..."

"But what?"

"There's absolutely nothing on certain areas. Like the button on the shift lever. Usually, you put your thumb on it to press down to shift it from Park." His lips drew together. "No prints at all. None on the steering wheel or the trunk area. It'd been wiped clean."

Leslie's heart jumped. That meant the killer had gone through Norton's car, taking the time to move it to a place different from the body. Why? What was he looking for? Another piece of the puzzle, but one without a definite answer.

"Did the body look like it'd been dropped?" she asked.

Tab shook his head. "Hardly. With the mashed right foot and leg, postmortem, I'd say the perpetrator killed the man, then drove off in his car."

"Then why not just keep going? Ditch the car someplace else, not two levels below the crime scene?"

Tab raised his eyebrows.

"It would make sense," he said. "But then again, I'm not a killer."

Leslie appreciated at his laconic humor, but her mind was racing. Maybe, just maybe the killer didn't want to drive Norton's car away because he had a car of his own. But he still went to the trouble of moving it and wiping it down. Too bad there weren't more surveillance cameras in the area. The recordings they'd confiscated had yielded nothing significant so far.

Regardless, this was shaping up to be a bit more than your run-of-the-mill mugging turned bad. She was going to have to learn more about the late John H. Norton, which is what she told her boss when she got back.

"Makes sense." Graven rubbed his fingers over his jaw again. His expression looked as dour as ever. "We'll have to backtrack him. In the meantime, there's been a development."

"Oh?"

The right side of his mouth drew up in a weary-looking smile.

"As it turns out, this Norton fellow was a pretty important guy. The Americans are a bit upset by his demise and are putting the pressure on for us to solve it fast."

Leslie felt her stomach tie into a knot. Was he going to take her off the case?

"Lieu, I'm doing the best I can. I just found out who he was, and it's not like we have a lot to go on."

Graven's mouth twitched slightly in what he must have thought passed for a smile. He walked to the window in his office and stood, looking out at the bleak darkness. The glow from the artificial lights of the parking lot made the scene look particularly glum.

"I know, luv, but nonetheless, we have to try to appease our neighbors to the south."

"Meaning?"

He turned. "Meaning, we're going to have to step it up a bit. Put on the old dog and pony show to demon-strate how much we're doing. I still think this was a robbery gone bad, so I'm assigning two other detectives to check things out."

It felt like he'd given the knot another twist.

"Well, I can certainly use a little help," she said, her

voice cracking faintly. "Am I still the primary investigator?"

Graven sighed. "I prefer not to think of things in those terms."

It felt like a sucker punch. He was trying to let her down easy. It was a matter of faith, and his in her was obviously lacking.

"I see." She fought to hold back the sudden hotness in her eyes. Was her first homicide slipping away?

Graven seemed to sense her despair and smiled, his voice conciliatory and soothing at the same time. "Attempts to notify family in the US have proved negative," he said. "Apparently, the victim's domestic partner is also deceased. A fall of some sort."

This struck Leslie as a bit odd. "That's interesting."

"Interesting, but a bit too far out of our bailiwick." Graven considered this for a moment and then clapped his hands together. "Anyway, like you said, we need to find out more about the victim. Pack your bags, and take your toothbrush. You're going south to backtrack through the gent's personal affairs."

"South? You mean to the United States?"

He nodded. "To Chicago, specifically. I happen to know someone there in law enforcement. Worked with him a few times. I'll give him a call, and he can help you along."

"All right, sir," she said. At least she was still connected to the investigation. "What will you being doing up here?"

Graven assumed a thoughtful expression, as if weighing the scope of his answer.

"Oh, we'll putter along," he said, "and round up the usual suspects."

CHAPTER 5

The boozy air hit Dix like a breeze from heaven, and he suddenly longed for a smoke, even though he'd given up cigarettes fifteen years ago. Booze, on the other hand, was still his frequent companion. More frequently of late, he reflected as his eyes narrowed to scan the dimly lit interior. He spotted Colby at a booth near the back. Dix waved to the bartender on the way there and paused to pat the waitress on the arm and order another round of whatever she'd brought to his buddy's table.

"On second thought," he said, watching Colby drain his glass, "better make his a double. I'll have scotch on the rocks."

She nodded and angled off toward the bar.

Dix flashed a broad grin when he got to the booth and slid in across from Colby.

"Man, you look like shit," Dix said.

Colby shrugged. Maybe he'd been drinking doubles already.

"Thanks for coming, brother." Colby's eyes looked like twin roadmaps. The glass in front of him was still half full.

The waitress came with their drinks, setting down a whiskey soda in front of Colby along with a napkin and Dix's scotch.

"Hey, what's this?" Colby asked. "I was still working on this one."

"A gift from an angel," the waitress said as she winked at Dix and then walked away.

"Hey," Dix said, pushing the second drink toward him. "You should see if she wants to go home with you tonight."

"Yeah, right," he said. "Just what I need. More complications in my life."

"So," Dix asked after sampling a small bit of his drink, "what's so important that I had to drag myself down here to this scene of the crime?"

"Déjà vu," Colby said. "You know what that means?"

"Yeah, it means you're drunker than you look if you think you can speak French."

Colby sipped some of the amber liquid from his glass. "You're right, partner. I am getting drunk."

"Tell me something I don't know," Dix let his expression get serious. "What's eating ya?"

Colby downed more of the whiskey before answering. "I told you about those copycat murders?"

"Yeah." Dix narrowed his eyes and waited.

"There's been a couple more," Colby said. "Remember Sally Borders? Benjamin Pike?"

"Borders? The college coed?" Dix said. "And Pike... He was that male prostitute they found in the alley over on Belmont and Halsted."

Colby nodded. His expression looked beaten. He tapped a thick manila envelope on the table in front of him. "This is the file on the new ones. Carbon copies of the old Laird murders."

"Damn."

"And you wanna know the worst fucking thing about it?" Colby took another sip of his drink. "This new asshole is leaving copies of *my* book around at crime scenes. *My* book, that I signed."

"No shit?" Dix considered the possibilities. "Sounds like he's taunting you."

"And the damn feds," Colby said, twirling his glass. "They're starting that task force I told you about, right?"

Dix nodded again, his smile eager and earnest looking.

"They don't want me in," Colby said. "Except as a consultant."

"A consultant? That's bullshit. Nobody knows the Laird case better than you." Dix had to refrain from adding, *except for me*.

"It's too 'personal,' they said. Too fucking, in-your-face personal." Colby slammed his fist down on the table causing his near-empty glass to topple over. "They just invited me by to quiz me about the original case, and collect their little facts so they can do their VICAP bullshit."

Dix snorted and took a long pull of his drink, feeling the good burn all the way down. "Ain't that the thing they used back on that East Coast sniper case? Where they predicted the shooter was an evil white guy in his forties who was mad at the government, and it turned out to be two Black guys hell-bent on extorting money by creating a wave of terror?"

Colby nodded. "Dammit, Dix, this is the kind of case I should be working. People are dying out there and this fucker's taunting me." He paused and started to take a drink, then stopped. "Leaving my book there…What's that, if not a message? An invitation?"

"The feds won't budge, huh?" He glanced down at the file on the table between them.

Colby shook his head, then started to get up. "I got to take a leak."

Dix nodded as he signaled the waitress again. "What are they afraid of? That you might crack the new case and hog all the credit?"

Colby shrugged, shook his head, and walked toward the men's room.

Dix waited until his ex-partner was inside the john. Then he opened the flap of the envelope and dumped the papers into his waiting hand. It was a thick collection of reports, crime scene photos, and notes. A case file. He looked closer. A few of the photos looked startlingly familiar.

The copycat file.

Out of the corner of his eye, he saw the waitress and motioned to her.

"Hey, sweetie," he said. "I need a big favor." He winked and held out a twenty.

"Anything for you, big guy," she said, pocketing the bill.

"You still got that big, old copying machine in the office?"

She nodded. "Yeah, but Fred gets pissed if we use it."

"Grab me a stack of them fliers over on the bar," Dix said, glancing quickly toward the men's room. "And hurry up."

The waitress raised her eyebrows, went over to the bar, and handed him the shelf of papers. Dix jammed them into the folder and stuck it back into the envelope. He then hid the file under his jacket and stood up.

"Meet me in the back hallway," he whispered to her. "You're gonna let me in the office."

"I can't do that," she said. "I'll get in trouble."

"No you won't," Dix said. "It's police business." He saw Colby exiting the men's room and patted her on the ass. "Besides, I got Andrew Jackson's twin brother waiting for you once I'm done."

The waitress compressed her lips and nodded.

Colby regarded both of them as he got to the table.

"I just ordered us another round," Dix said. "After which, I'm driving your drunken ass home."

"I can drive myself," Colby said. "I'm not drunk."

"Fine, you can drive me, then." Dix laughed and grabbed his stomach. "Hold down the fort, will you? I think that Metamucil stuff that the doc prescribed is about to cause me to go give birth to an FBI agent."

Colby grinned.

As Dix was walking toward the back, he glanced over to make sure Colby was facing the other way. He was, like any good copper, not sitting with his back to the door. Dix moved to the office hallway instead of the john, and watched as the waitress glanced around nervously and unlocked the office door. He went inside and saw the nice, big, fancy copying machine against the far wall. Taking the file from under his arm, he systematically removed the staples, placed the sheaf of papers into the top tray, and pressed the *START* button.

As the machine began its copying cycle, Dix took out his cell phone and glasses, then sorted through the business cards in his jacket pocket. He found the one he wanted and dialed the number, straining to see in the subdued light.

The phone rang several times and an automated operator answered, offering a variety of choices to proceed.

Dix scrolled through the list of options until the automated voice instructed him to say the name of the party he wished to speak with.

"Carmel Washington," Dix said into the cell phone.

After about ten more seconds, a sexy female voice said, "This is Carmel Washington of Chicago Today. I'm sorry, I'm not available at this time, but leave your name, number and a brief message and I'll get back to you."

Dix waited for the beep, then repeated his name and cell number. "And listen, babe," he said. "Make sure you call me back ASAP. This is about the story of a lifetime, and I'm giving you first crack at it."

He disconnected and watched as the final pages of the case file passed through the copier.

———

Knox looked at the luminous dial of his watch. Three twenty-six a.m. Ordinarily, he would have been exhausted, considering that he'd driven back from Canada the day before, and had been going on very little sleep for the past several days. But the thrill of the hunt invigorated him. He felt close to victory now, if you could call chasing down a wayward punk a challenge. Still, it helped to keep the skills honed, and he was getting paid handsomely for it. He went back to the green-tinted view that the night scope afforded him.

The parking lot of the Bel-Aire Motel was only partially full. Most of the traffic, Knox had noted, was of the quick-encounter variety. A seedy place, but from what he'd seen on Matthew's hard drive, the choice of domiciles wasn't a surprise. The only surprise had been in how long it had taken to run the kid to ground. Perhaps he wouldn't even show. He could have even changed motels to suit whatever was his perverted agenda.

But Knox was betting otherwise.

So when the dark, windowless van pulled up and parked in front of room 230, Knox wasn't surprised to see who it was. From the plate, it was obvious the vehicle was a rental.

Shielding his eyes from the intrusive and blinding

glare from the brake lights, Knox watched as Matthew got out and looked around, trying and failing badly to affect an air of nonchalance before going to the rear doors. He rummaged around in the van's interior for a few moments, removed a plastic bag, and, after another quick look around, slammed it shut.

Christ, didn't that punk know anything? All he was doing was calling attention to himself. And why did he rent the van in the first place?

Knox used the night scope again to watch Matthew move toward the stairs and up to his motel room. He carefully slipped the lens cap on the night scope and placed it back in its case, wondering what was in that bag.

He would look into it after he'd secured his quarry.

———

Matthew set the bag of goodies down at his feet and stuck the key card into the lock. The light on the door changed from red to green and he twisted the knob.

What to do, what to do?

He flipped on the lights.

This whole process was so exhilarating, racing along, leaving clues for the cops, knowing all the while that there was no way they would even get close to him, no way they would figure it out...Until he was ready for them to.

He set the bag on the bed. One more night in this dump. Maybe two, and he'd go back to his apartment, get caught up on classes until the weekend, and then have some more fun.

Fun and games, fun and games.

Just then he heard a scraping sound coming from the door and he froze.

The police? Could they have followed him here somehow? Had he slipped up? Given them too much, too soon?

He didn't know whether to feel relieved or worried when the tall, athletically built man with the blond ponytail opened the door and stepped inside, quietly closing it behind him.

"What are you doing here?"

Knox strolled toward the bed and reached for the bag, but Matthew recovered in time to snatch it away.

"That's mine. You have no right."

Knox moved back, standing in front of the door, preventing any exit.

"I asked you a question." Matthew felt his voice crack. He hoped it didn't make him sound like a girl. Or a fag.

"Your father wants to see you." Knox spoke with a quiet deliberation. Like he was tired, or bored, or both.

But Matthew didn't care. He wasn't about to let all his careful planning go down the drain.

"He's *not* my father."

Knox shrugged. "He wants to see you anyway."

"Tell him to go to hell." Matthew noticed the contempt he felt raising the inflection of the last word. Again, he hoped it didn't sound effeminate. To add more force to his words, he reached in his pants pocket and took out his folding knife, using his thumb to open the blade. "Now get out of here. Unless you want some of this." He brandished the open knife.

Knox rolled his eyes. "Put your toy away and come on. I've had a long day."

"What if I refuse?" As soon as Matthew had finished saying the words, be realized how ridiculous it sounded, with him holding the knife. He should be dictating from a position of strength. Issuing ultimatums.

Knox smiled and reached in his pocket. "Nothing

would please me more." He withdrew some kind of gun and held it down by his side.

"Don't even pretend that you're going to shoot me," Matthew said, trying for bravado, but cognizant his knees were feeling a little weak. "*Father* would never allow that."

"Wouldn't he?"

Knox raised his hand with the gun quickly and pointed it. The barrel looked squared off, funny.

An instant later two bees stung his left side and a gut-twisting paralysis gripped him and knocked him to the floor.

He thought his joints would snap, it hurt so much. The knife had fallen from his limp fingers. He couldn't move. The pain...drool oozed down his chin and he knew he'd piss himself if it kept on much longer.

Knox stepped over and picked up the knife.

The pain ceased, and Matthew felt like he'd been kicked in the stomach. He saw two gold-colored wires looping upward to connect with the gun. Before he could brush the connecting barbs off his body, Matthew felt the mind-numbing pain grip him again.

After several seconds it vanished once more.

"Ready to go back now?" Knox asked him.

Matthew tried to swallow, but found it hard to make everything work right. Finally, he managed to get the words out.

"You bastard," he said.

———

The next morning Colby woke up to a jarring alarm clock and the delicious smell of frying eggs and strong coffee. It took him a minute to remember last night, and when he did, his head immediately began to pound.

Oh, Christ, he thought. Seven o'clock. It hurt to move. He laid his head back down on the pillow and tried to let the pounding in his temples subside. It had faded slightly when he felt a hand roughly shaking him, which brought the pain back, full force.

"Here," an authoritative voice said. "Take these."

Colby opened one eye and saw Dix standing over him with a glass of orange juice and an aspirin bottle. It was a moment before Colby could get the words out. "What are you doing here?"

Dix laughed and held out the glass, the orange liquid looking less than appetizing. "I sacked out on your couch, remember? I figured you'd probably need some-body to wet-nurse you through breakfast. Now here, take some of these." He held up the aspirins.

Colby felt like taking the whole bottle, but Dix only shook out three. They went down like sandpaper over his parched throat.

"Go take a shower," Dix said, waving his hand in front of his nose. "How do you like your eggs?"

Colby sat up slowly, feeling that unsettling twinge in his stomach. He eased his feet to the floor. "If I wanted a wet-nurse, I'd have stayed married."

"You know no broad would put up with you." Dix turned and left, calling out over his shoulder, "How you want your eggs?"

Colby thought for a moment and then yelled, "Scram-bled." It hurt his ears.

"Tough shit," Dix yelled back. "I only know how to do over-easy."

"Marvelous," Colby said, as the patches of cold floor sent shock waves up through the soles of his feet.

"And hurry up," Dix yelled. "We gotta go pick up your unmarked at the bar, and I have to meet somebody very special this morning."

By the time Colby made it to the office, it was close to ten thirty. It was going to be a black coffee-and-aspirins kind of day. Bosworth, his fat face looking more smug than usual, came up and yelled in Colby's ear as he was pouring himself a cup of the hot coffee from the pot.

"Late one last night?"

Colby grimaced as the hot liquid ran over his fingers.

Colby set his cup down and grabbed a paper napkin to wipe his hand off. "Bosworth, you should've been a detective."

The big man smirked in a self-satisfied way. "I'm what they call a detective's detective, palie."

"Yeah, everybody says you're a real *dick*, all right." Colby turned away and headed back to his desk, taking a much-needed sip of the dark brew.

"Ha ha. Very funny," Bosworth's said. "The LT's been waiting on ya, smart ass. Wants to see ya as soon as you stagger in."

Colby reached the relative safety of his desk and looked at Ray Brewer, another detective sitting in a desk opposite.

Brewer nodded. "Kropper is looking for you. And he has a hair up his ass."

Great, Colby thought as he nodded a "thanks" to Brewer and took another sip, scalding his tongue. He set the cup down and reached in his pocket for his supply of breath mints, thankful that at least he'd had the presence of mind to bring that vital piece of equipment.

As he raised his hand to knock on the lieutenant's closed door, he heard a gruff voice filter out from behind the frosted glass. It wasn't Kropper's, and it didn't sound happy, either.

The door opened inward with an abruptness that

made Colby glad he'd left the coffee back on his desk. He saw a big, reddened face and a white shirt with two gold stars on the collar under a blue blouse. The round crown, with the golden scrambled-eggs on the brim, sat on Kropper's desk, and the LT sat behind it looking like he'd been caught stepping on his dick.

"You wanted to see me, lieu?" Colby managed to get out before he read the name tag on the other man's uniform blouse: *MANNION*. Colby nodded at the standing man.

What was the deputy superintendent of operational services doing here?

Mannion's stare was baleful. "Get in here and close the damn door."

Colby did and Mannion pointed to the hot seat chair. When he sat down, Colby was eye-to-eye with an obviously distraught Lieutenant Kropper.

"As I was telling Ken here," Mannion said, throwing a glance at Kropper. "I got a call this morning from some broad at *Chicago Today News Magazine*." He paused and let the words sink in. "Any idea what they asked me about?"

Colby tried to look as dumbfounded as he felt.

"No, sir."

Mannion's eyes narrowed.

Oh, Christ, he's trying to read me, Colby thought. He sat up straighter and tried his best to look sincere and without guile.

Mannion shifted his gaze back to Kropper. "They asked me to confirm a rumor that we've been purposely excluded from a task force investigating the Laird Copy Cat Murders." He said the last words with a slow relish, pausing to smile and nod knowingly.

Colby felt like he'd gotten clocked by a punch from left field. "I wouldn't think they'd give a shit."

"Neither would I," Mannion said. "Do you know what I had to tell 'em?"

Colby glanced at Kropper, who swallowed hard.

"Well, I *didn't* tell 'em that I never heard of the Laird Copy Cat Case, even though I hadn't."

"Good thinking, boss," Kropper started to say, but Mannion cut him off with a look.

Kropper's face blushed. "Sorry."

Mannion placed his fists on his hips, leaning over Kropper's desk slightly. "So I do a little checking and come to find out that you been in contact with the feds on this already. This special agent in charge...I forget his damn name—"

"Pearson," Colby said.

Mannion's head whirled. "You know him?"

"I talked to him the other day."

"You knew about this?" Mannion asked, looking back at Kropper.

The LT gave a quick nod.

Mannion's neck looked as red as lobster tail. "And you didn't see fit to tell me?"

"Boss," Colby said as gently as he could. "It's not really his fault. The feds didn't give us much info at all. They're being really anal on this one."

"Show me one of those goddamn sphincter-puckering assholes that ain't anal," Mannion said, "and I'll show you one that don't have his head stuck up his fucking ass." He sighed. "How many of these damn homicides are ours?"

Kropper shrugged. "One, maybe two."

Colby suppressed a skeptical look. With the dumped body in Boystown, it had to be more like four. But he didn't want to say anything that would further embarrass Kropper. Shit, after all, rolled downhill.

"Detective, how heavy's your current caseload?" Mannion asked.

Colby shrugged. He had to tread gingerly here.

"It's not bad, sir. Luckily, Lt. Kropper and I already discussed the possibility of me maybe going to the task force eventually, so I've been divvying up my slam-dunks."

"Good thinking," Mannion said, looking back to Kropper.

After a few seconds of silence, Mannion clapped his hands together and pointed at Colby. "Okay, unload the rest of what's on your plate, I'll make the call to the feds. Colby's going to the task force, no if's, and's, or buts."

"Ten-four, boss," Kropper said.

"And track down the other cases. See who's working them. Let's show some coordination on this thing." Mannion took a deep breath. "We can keep running our own investigations on our end, but this task force can devote a lot more attention to them than we can."

"We'll get right on it, boss," Kropper said. He reminded Colby of a kid who'd gotten caught sleeping in church and then ordered by the priest to get up and pass the collection baskets.

Mannion picked his round crown off Kropper's desk and started to put it on, but stopped. He looked down at Colby. "Just make sure, when all is said and done, that we come off looking good for our part in this. I got a hunch this whole goddamn thing's gonna stink to high heaven when it blows wide open."

CHAPTER 6

Matthew was furious. He walked ahead of Knox, down the long, tiled corridor to the elevator that would finally get him off the fifth floor. The Blem floor, as he called it. The noise of their constant and inane grunting and screaming had kept him up all night, until he'd screamed and pleaded for security to let him out of his locked room with the padded walls and stainless steel toilet. It was like being trapped in a zoo.

God, he hated this place. And he hated the Others. Blems, he called them, and that's what they were. Blemishes! Every one of them was an inferior, incomplete, *subhuman*—even though Matthew knew that each one of them was an ersatz version of himself, of Morgan. From the moment he'd first learned about his own genetic history, and of the Blems, their very existence had been a blemish on his life, his future. And now he was back with the creatures.

He shot an obvious look of contempt at Knox, but the prick paid no attention. He'd brought Matthew back last night, his hands, feet, and legs tied with some kind of plastic restraints. And he refused to loosen them during the long drive. By the time they'd arrived at New Genesis, Matthew could barely move his limbs. He flexed his fingers now as Knox inserted his special key into the wall slot and the elevator doors clicked open.

"Get in," he said.

Matthew pursed his lips. At least he'd be getting off this fucking floor of retards. If only he could get his hands on an elevator key. Knox looked like he could read Matthew's mind, because he smiled as the doors slid shut. Knox reinserted the special key, twisted it, and pressed the button for the second floor.

Going down to see *father*, thought Matthew. Oh, I can hardly wait.

But something else worried at him: the rented van. Had Knox left it sitting in the motel parking lot? What if it got towed? Matthew hadn't had the chance to make sure the interior was washed out and vacuumed real well. What if some of the dead faggot's blood was there? Matthew had put the plastic down when he'd transported the body, but afterward, could something have leaked from the bag?

The elevator jerked to a slow stop, and the doors opened. Matthew stood there, unmoving until he felt Knox's powerful fingers dig into his shoulder.

"Come on," Knox said. "You know the way."

"Just don't touch me," Matthew said, faking a bit of bravado. In this environment the prick would be more restrained, but Matthew didn't want to see how far he could push it. He had too much to worry about: the plastic bag with the dead faggot's bloody clothes, the rented van, his overnight stay here...they all upset his overall timetable. He remembered something else, too. The knife.

Matthew was conscious of Knox close behind him as they moved down the hallway, past the opaque glass walls of the lab, to the office with Dr. H.A. Jetters's name on it. Knox rapped gently on the solid oak door and a muffled voice told them to enter.

Matthew tried his best to out-stare the old man as he caught his gaze from behind his desk. The desk, like everything else in the old coot's life, was perfectly organized. Not even a paperclip out of place. His eyes were unblinking. Like a reptile's. His array of degrees, honorary and otherwise, hung in several rows behind him. It was the only a concession to vanity. Or personality. Everything else in the office, from the tightly stacked bookcases, to the immaculate black board, was utilitarian. The old man must have been a Spartan in a past life.

"Well, what have you got to say for yourself?" Jetters's voice sounded authoritative, imperial. The perfect tone for a man who gave out orders and ultimatums all day long.

Matthew returned the stare as best he could until, finally, he looked down. Shit, he knew he'd have to grovel to get out of this one. He had to get back on track with his plan, otherwise it might unravel. But it would look too suspicious if he gave in too quickly. Instead of answering, he looked at the pair of darkly tinted windows beyond the old man's head.

"Dammit, I asked you a question." Jetters's voice had gone up to the next level—the one before he'd lash out with a slap. "Answer me. I am your father."

Rather than deliver the same comeback he'd snarled at Knox, Matthew pursed his lips.

"What are you going to do, *Father*?" he asked. "Have your hired goon Taser me again?"

He was pleased. The retort immediately cast him as the victim, while sidestepping the entire issue about his recent activities.

"Don't use that tone with me," Jetters said. His gaze then focused on Knox. "You did that to him?"

"I had little choice," Knox said. "He pulled a knife on me."

"A knife?" Jetters's voice lowered an octave with the second word.

At least I had the foresight to clean it off, Matthew thought. The clothes in the bag, though... He wondered again if Knox knew about them. He must. But did he bring them, or leave them there? So many wrinkles that could upset the damn applecart.

"He hurt me for no reason," Matthew said, affecting as much outrage as he could muster. "I didn't give him any cause, either. He's just a sadist. If you really cared anything about me, you'd fire this fascist right now." His voice had taken on a whiny lilt, which he regretted, but found uncontrollable.

Jetters turned back to him. "Why have you been cutting classes?"

If the old fart only knew what I've been cutting, Matthew thought. He pursed his lips. "They bore me."

"Aren't you interested in studying medicine anymore?" Jetters asked, his voice sounding almost quasi-paternal now. "I've been rewarding you with more freedom lately. Is this how you repay me?"

Christ, Matthew thought. If he only knew.

"Well?" the old man said.

Matthew's mind raced, trying to think his way out of this. He'd had all night, but every excuse, every plan that he'd come up with evaporated as he stood there before that withering stare, eventually lowering his gaze to the floor.

Jetters turned to Knox again. "Do you have anything to add to your report?"

Matthew caught a glimpse of Knox's eyes. They were

flat, unemotional. Like he was staring at a deer he contemplated shooting, even though he didn't need the meat.

"Just what did he tell you, Father?" Matthew blurted out, trying again to seize the initiative. "What lies is he spreading about me?"

Jetters' brow furrowed a bit, and he took off his glasses and massaged the bridge of his nose. "Do you have any idea how paranoid you're sounding? Not to mention the strange behavior."

"What are you talking about?"

"Have you been involved in something illegal?"

Christ, the whole thing's coming apart. He tried another bluff. "What's the matter, Father? Afraid the bad genes are beginning to surface? *Illegal.*" He rolled his eyes and put what he hoped was the right amount of contempt on the last word.

Jetters sighed and replaced the frail, gold-rimmed spectacles on his face. "I know about the motel, and the rented van. I want an explanation."

"All right," Matthew said, "I was out trying to score with some chicks. Didn't want them to know my real name. Where I lived. Satisfied?"

Jetters continued to stare at him. Slowly he reached down and opened a drawer, removing the brown plastic bag with the bloody clothes.

"And this?"

Matthew swallowed hard, then licked his lips. The old bastard had suckered him. In desperation, he grabbed at one of the flimsy lies he had formulated last night.

"I was with a friend of mine," he said quickly. "Another guy. We got jumped by a bunch of skinheads, and he got stabbed."

Jetters's face showed no emotion. "Who is this friend?"

"Just some guy I started hanging out with at school."

"His name?"

"Rodney." He looked down. "I don't know his last name."

The old man stared at him. "And where did this happen?"

"In the city somewhere. Lake View, or someplace. I don't know exactly."

Jetters waited a few seconds before speaking again. "And did you notify the police?"

"He might have, I don't know." Matthew glanced to his left. "I drove him to the emergency room."

"Which hospital?"

"I told you, I don't know." Matthew frowned and then grabbed the name of a nerdy guy in one of his classes. "Okay, I remembered his name. It's Rodney Potts."

The old bastard's piercing stare was making Matthew sweat.

"Were you trying to buy drugs?" Jetters asked.

"No," Matthew said, shaking his head. At least that much was true.

Jetters looked at him a few moments more, then turned to Knox. "Check on the veracity of his story. Let me know what really happened."

Knox nodded.

"Look," Matthew said. "I have to turn in that rental van, and close out the motel room." Matthew said.

"Mr. Knox will see to that also," Jetters instructed. "You have this knife?"

Knox gave a slight nod.

"Bring it to me."

"I'd prefer to handle things myself," Matthew said. "That is, if it's all right for me to leave. After all, I do have classes to attend."

"You can request extensions," Jetters said. "In the meantime, until you're ready to be more forthcoming, you'll stay with us for a thorough examination. Take him back upstairs."

Matthew felt Knox's hand grip his arm.

"Upstairs?" Matthew said. "With them? No way!" His mouth twisted as he felt Knox's fingers dig deep into his biceps.

———

Leslie Labyorteaux watched the taxi's meter click. She'd never seen so many tall buildings clustered so close together. Several of them looked as tall as the Tower. Nor had she ever seen traffic like this. It made Toronto's rush hour look like a soapbox derby. Cars stacked one behind the other in lines so long that you couldn't even see where they began or ended. And this damn cab was traveling at glacial speed. People walking were moving at a faster rate. It was a cold, gray day to match. Everything about Chicago looked blustery and unfriendly, from the rickety elevated trains that moved along with a harsh clatter, to the turbulent lake, which looked more like a small ocean. Waves of the dirty green water slapped the shore with a repetitive fury, and changed to a rich blue farther out, conveying a cold deepness.

The taxi moved up about three feet and jerked to a halt as someone cut in front of it. The driver blew his horn.

Why the hell would anyone want to drive in this?

The meter clicked again. It was already up over fifty dollars from her trip from O'Hare.

"Get a receipt for all your expenses, luv," Graven had said. "Just make sure they match up with whatever charges you make on the departmental credit card."

"Is it going to be all right? My taking it?"

Graven's face puckered into what she took as a semi-reassuring expression. "Of course it is. You're on official business."

She knew the boss just wanted to get rid of her so they could begin doing things their way—rousting every local thug in the province of Ontario. *Probably figured to have the case solved by the time I get halfway finished with this wild goose chase.*

The meter clicked again.

They'll hit the roof when they see my expense report for this little foray. But that actually brought a smile to her lips. After all, Graven had directed her to go on this excursion, and he'd have to approve it as long as she had legitimate receipts. Nothing frivolous, of course. And since she'd converted all her Canadian dollars to American dollars, she'd wait till she got back and pocket the difference on the black market exchange rate. It wouldn't be much, but it would soften being shifted to the bench on her first homicide.

The taxi edged forward.

"Excuse me," she asked. "Are we getting close?"

The driver, an Indian or Pakistani type, just shook his head. He'd been busy chatting on his cell phone the whole trip.

Thinking of the turbulence of Lake Michigan again, and how different it was from Lake Ontario, she longed for the breakfast view of the placid water at sunrise in her apartment back home.

Homesick? Already?

She was being silly. This was, after all, an important part of the investigation. Backtracking the victim. In order to find out who'd killed him, they had to gather as much information as possible about him. So perhaps this wasn't so much the wild goose chase she thought it was.

Maybe, just maybe, she would glean some crucial bit of info that would help crack the case. Or an insight as to who would want the victim dead.

A lane opened up to the right and the cab driver swung into it, accelerating very quickly and passing a bunch of cars on the right. He twisted the wheel and turned left, went down a short block, honked at a delivery truck blocking the street for a solid minute. The meter continued to click all the while. Finally he pulled up in front of a pair of black, metallic buildings. They were all girders and dirty windows, and were set back from the street by wide, pebbled sidewalks. Signs and arrows along the glass wall advised that the closest set of entrance doors were closed, and pointed to a set of circular revolving doors, behind which stood a uniformed guard.

"Here you are, miss," the driver said, shifting into Park and getting out to open her door. He scampered to the trunk for her suitcase as she stepped out.

Looking up at the tall exterior, which at this angle extended out of her line of sight, she thought the building looked hard and unforgiving.

––––––––

Dix closed the open file and took off his glasses. The late afternoon light was just beginning to filter into his through his kitchen windows. He'd used that table because it was the biggest, and it was now awash with papers, files, and stacks of old reports. He'd pulled out all his old Laird stuff to compare with this new, copycat file. Whoever was doing these new killings knew the Laird case, that was for sure.

Dix got up, looked at the clock, and poured himself two fingers of Jack Daniels in a coffee cup just to help him think. He rummaged through the papers on the table for a clean sheet and a pen, swearing as these items eluded him. Finally, he went to his den and grabbed a new tablet and a pencil from the desk by his computer.

Time to do it the old-fashioned way, he thought.

Sitting down he organized the old Laird file, then reshuffled the copycat file, and set them side-by-side. Some other papers fluttered to the floor but he left them.

Focus, he told himself, then took another sip of the whiskey. As the burn crept down his esophagus, he opened both file folders and jotted down the sequence of events.

The first time he and Colby had come to suspect Morgan Laird was in the Swanstrom Case. The two young girls, twins, disappeared while walking near a construction site. A neighbor had reported seeing a man in the area, driving a beat-up old van with out-of-state plates, talking with the twins. They'd traced the plates to a third party in Valparaiso, Indiana, who admitted selling the van, with the plates on it, to a guy named Morgan Laird for eight hundred bucks. A computer check on Laird showed he'd served time in Texas, Oklahoma, and Missouri for a host of crimes, including rape and murder. He'd been in and out of prison virtually all of his adult life and looked good in connection with the case.

Dix and Colby were confident that they had their man but finding him was another matter entirely. The Swanstrom twins had been missing for almost forty-eight hours, and with each tick of the clock they were slipping further away. With a bit of luck, they found that Laird had picked up a few days' work as a laborer at a construction site and had given the address of a seedy, transient hotel in Blue Island. When they'd gone there to pick him up, intending on sweating him about the Swanstrom girls, all hell broke loose.

Dix swallowed some more of his drink and watched as the light seemed to fade through the window. If only he hadn't been the one who'd caught that bullet, if it had been him who'd chased Laird down, it'd be his name on the book cover instead of Colby's. Oh sure, he would have given the kid his due, but the fame, the notoriety, it should have been his. He was the one who found the construction site connection. Dix sighed and patted his substantial beer gut. Even if he hadn't caught the bullet twenty-eight years ago, there was no way he could have run Laird down like Colby had. Of course the kid was a decade younger, and in great shape. Hell, he still looked like he was. How did the guy look so good after all these years?

Shit, I was so outta shape back then, Dix thought, I probably had about as much chance of catching the bastard as I do scoring with that Carmel broad now.

She'd been nice to him when they'd met to discuss the story. He remembered her eyes widening when he showed her a few select pages from the copycat file. They were pretty eyes, but he didn't kid himself. It was only a business deal for her, a hot story. Dix knew that all he was to her was a source.

On the other hand, if he could somehow solve this new case, it would mean big things. Maybe a second book—*his* book, this time—detailing how he'd cracked this new case, rather than that bunch of FBI task force clowns. Maybe it could be turned into a TV movie. That would get people to sit up and take notice.

He swallowed the rest of the amber liquid, relished the residual burn, and set the glass down.

Aww, hell, he thought. I still gotta catch this new asshole first.

Colby was still mildly irritated by Pearson's latest directive, "Report to the third floor of the federal building at three-thirty sharp for the afternoon briefing."

Three-thirty sharp. The fed didn't even use the twenty-four-hour time designation. He was more civilian than law enforcement. Plus, the asshole had sounded so condescending on the phone: "I have no problem with you joining the task force as long as you can be professional. You'll have to keep your personal feelings out of this investigation. But I want an assurance from you that you'll not go to the news media again behind my back."

Colby felt like telling him to go to hell, but he didn't. For one thing, his head hurt too much.

"It wasn't me," he said.

"Right." Pearson added insult to injury by finishing with, "We'll do our best to bring you up to speed when you get here. Then it'll be up to you to keep up."

Bring me up to speed, Colby thought. I've forgotten more about homicide investigation than that guy ever learned.

He wondered who had dropped the dime to *Chicago Today.* Regardless, things had turned out the way he wanted. He was now actively involved in this new case. Or should he say cases? Regardless, there was a monster loose using Colby's book as a template for murder. Pearson was right. It was personal. But it was also something Colby had to do. He had to run this new killer to ground; he had to stop him. And this time, the guy was going to die in prison, like Laird should have.

He pulled into the underground parking at the federal building off Dearborn and showed the security guard his badge. After a brief conversation, the guy raised the gate and waved him through. Colby parked in the first open spot he found, and took out the bottle of aspirin.

How many had he taken since breakfast? He'd lost

count. Shrugging, he popped two more into his hand and washed them down with the remnants of his cold coffee, grimacing at the taste. He looked at his watch: fifteen-forty.

He remembered Pearson's admonishment: "Be here at three-thirty sharp." But, hell, traffic had been heavy. Plus, he didn't need to explain himself to that stuffed-shirt fed.

He took his zippered case with the notepad and papers inside. The copycat case file was thick, but it would fit inside easily.

I'm ready, he thought, as he went to the trunk and sorted through his briefcase, finding his notebook, a handful of case reports, but no copycat case file.

What the hell had he done with it?

His mind raced. When was the last time he'd had it? Pearson had given it to him yesterday. He'd started to peruse it once he'd gotten back to the office and remembered taking it with him when he met Dix at the bar.

Dix, he thought. Maybe he knows where it's at.

As he walked across the expanse of cement toward the elevators, he checked his cell phone for Dix's number. It wasn't in his contact listings. Frustrated, he re-clipped the phone to his belt and pressed the button for the elevator. He'd look for the file later, certain now that he must have left it at home.

Damn, his head hurt.

————

Knox pulled up to the space nearest the motel office and got out of his car. A quick glance reconfirmed what he'd already noticed. The rented van was nowhere to be seen. He sized up the seedy establishment in the fading daylight as he opened the office door. A buzzer sounded and he saw an overweight, bald man, behind a thick

Plexiglas window, glance up with a look of irritation, toss down the skin magazine he was reading, and push himself out of a cushy chair.

This chump probably wouldn't have a very good relationship with the cops, judging from the look of this dive, Knox thought, fingering the phony badge and ID in his jacket pocket. Better go with another angle.

"Can I help ya?" the bald guy asked.

"I hope so," Knox said, taking out his wallet and letting the man see his New Genesis identification. "I'm with corporate security. I'd like to ask about someone renting a room here with one of our credit cards."

Baldy's nostrils flared.

"Look, I ain't gonna give out no personal information to nobody. Not without some kinda warrant saying I have to."

What an idiot, thought Knox. If the Plexiglas hadn't been there, he would have been tempted to collar the son of a bitch and smack him around. But that wouldn't accomplish the task at hand.

"A warrant?" He took out a fifty. "How's this one?"

Baldy's face perked up when he saw the money.

"Whatcha need?" He held his palm near the slot at the bottom of the thick glass.

"The person who rented room fourteen," Knox said, lowering the bill, but not releasing it just yet. "Can you describe him?"

"Average looking kid, a bit on the thin side. Dark hair, kinda long. Maybe twenty, twenty-five. He done something?"

"Perhaps," Knox said. "You know his name?"

Baldy's face soured again, but the venal gleam in his eyes as he cast a surreptitious glance at the fifty told Knox he had the asshole hooked.

"When was this?" the Baldy asked, pulling out a box of file cards.

Knox gave him the dates he'd gotten off Matthew's credit card record. The guy flipped through the cards and came up with an index card with several pieces of paper attached to it. One of them was a crude copy of Matthew's driver's license.

"May I see that?" Knox asked. He pushed the fifty through the slot toward the bald guy, who grabbed the bill. After a quick check to see if it was real, the bald guy pushed the index card through the slot toward Knox.

"I ain't seen him today," Baldy said.

In addition to the copy of the driver's license, the card had an imprint of the credit card and a license number scrawled along with "dark green van."

"Where is this vehicle now?" Knox asked.

"The cops towed it," Baldy said. "Got broke into last night. Somebody tried to steal it. Busted the window. See all that glass out there by the room? Now I gotta go clean that up."

"Why'd they tow it?"

Baldy shrugged. "Couldn't find the kid. Wasn't in the room. The cops said it came back as a rental, so they towed it for safekeeping."

"Who towed it? What agency?"

Baldy shrugged again. "Ask the fucking cops."

Knox could almost see the light going on behind the dull eyes. Wheels were turning beneath that slick-skinned skull. Better end this quickly before he starts asking too many questions. No sense giving him more than he needs.

"So what's the story on this?" Baldy asked. "That card stolen or something?"

Knox didn't answer. He put the motel registry in his jacket pocket.

Baldy's eyes narrowed. "Hey, I needed that credit card info."

Knox removed some hundreds from his wallet. "I'll take care of the bill now. How much is it?"

"Thirty-nine-fifty a night. For five nights, including today. Plus tax."

Knox placed three hundreds into the slot on the counter.

"You know," Baldy said, "I'm supposed to keep that registration card by law."

Knox put another hundred on the counter near the Plexiglas slot.

Baldy raised one eyebrow and asked if Knox if he was going to need a receipt.

Knox shook his head and shoved the money through the slot.

Baldy palmed the bills. "A pleasure doing business with ya, Mister."

Knox nodded.

CHAPTER 7

In the elevator, Colby glanced at his watch again, fifteen-fifty. Close enough for government work.

He smiled at his own bit of feeble wit as his temples continued to throb. Why had he drunk so much?

If he hadn't wanted to be part of this damn thing so bad, he would have just stayed on the elevator and ridden it down to the basement again and gone home.

Fishing out the bottle of aspirins, he debated dry-swallowing two more. Maybe there'd be a water cooler in the feds' office. Hell, there had to be. Just get in and out, as fast as possible. I'll tell him the traffic was murder, he thought. Tell him I'm not feeling good. He just hoped he wasn't going to have to explain the absence of the copycat file to Pearson.

The doors opened and he moved down the now familiar hallway to the secretary's station. She had apparently been expecting him because she grabbed a visitor's badge and held it out as soon as she looked up.

Colby worked on flashing what he hoped was a grateful looking smile.

"Go right in, sir," she said, indicating the frosty glass door behind her.

Colby nodded—another mistake, another ache, but he covered well, strolling past her.

As he got into the hallway, he saw Pearson standing by an open office door. Despite his dark-blue suit and power tie, he looked almost casual, with his arm stretched out and positioned against the corridor wall in a relaxed lean. He was jaw-jacking with some female in a dark jacket and matching skirt. Colby noticed that she had nice legs. A dark blue suitcase, with a retractable handle, sat on the floor next to them.

Pearson looked up and frowned, straightening and making a point to be very obvious as he looked at his watch.

This immediately rubbed Colby the wrong way, despite all his mental preparations, and he forced a big grin and a nonchalant wave.

"Good afternoon," he said. His head throbbed and his gut wrenched at the same time. He managed to freeze the smile and hold it.

"It's three fifty-three, Detective," Pearson said, still holding his watch arm horizontal for emphasis.

Colby glanced at his watch and nodded, saying, "Mine must be a little slow. I've got fifteen-fifty-one."

He noticed the woman turn toward him, brown hair pulled back into a French braid, dark-brown eyes, with a hazel cast, and a face that could only be described as angelic. In other words, a babe.

"Regardless," Pearson said, dropping his arm to his side, "we've concluded the briefing for today."

That rubbed Colby the wrong way, too. Even if he was a little bit late, he'd sort of busted his ass to get there. Couldn't the federal prick at least give him a thumbnail sketch?

"I'm sorry to hear that," Colby said, regaining some of his composure. He still needed to be part of this, and didn't want to have to explain how he pissed-off the special agent in charge on the first day. Kropper would shit if he heard that, and so would Mannion.

"I'll bet you are," Pearson said. "But there is something I need to talk to you about." He turned to the woman. "Detective Labyorteaux, would you mind waiting in my office for a few minutes? Or better yet, there's a break room down the hall and to your right." He pointed behind them. "I'll join you there in as soon as I've finished briefing Detective Colby here."

Detective? Was she some kind of copper?

He noticed the suitcase and figured she must be from out of town.

Wouldn't mind working a case with her, he thought as he watched her get up and walk down the hall pulling her little, blue suitcase-on-wheels behind her. Pearson cleared his throat and stepped briskly into his office.

Colby followed, checking out the decor. Several dark wooden bookcases crammed with law volumes were opposite a big desk. It was made of the same wood as the cases. Nice veneer. Everything on the desk was arranged in neat stacks and perfectly aligned. An obvious reflection of the man behind it: totally anal.

Colby remembered hearing once that an organized desk was the sign of a small mind. God, his head ached.

Pearson sat in his padded leather swivel chair and indicated the hard wooden one in front for Colby. Behind the desk, the wall was covered with framed letters and certificates: the National FBI Academy, an FBI Certification as a VICAP Specialist, Special Operations Commendations, and one stating that Marion Steven Pearson had successfully completed two investigations in hostile territories.

Marion? Christ, no wonder the guy was so anal-retentive. Colby questioned the veracity of the commendations, too, as he eased his tired ass onto the hard chair.

He figured preemption was the best technique with someone like Pearson.

"Look," he said, "I'm sorry about being late. I got tied up on an interview, and then the boss called and—"

Pearson cut him off. "I didn't bring you in here to discuss that. The briefing was truncated for another reason."

His tone was terse. Something was up. Had there been another copycat murder?

"There's been a new development," Pearson said. He leaned forward, placed his elbows on the desk, and tented his fingers.

Colby's headache was throbbing, full force.

"Are you gonna tell me?"

Pearson's lips pursed and he dropped his hands.

"In due time," he said. "First, I want to make something clear." He paused, obviously seeking the maximum effect of withholding the knowledge. Colby noticed the man's Adam's apple bob quickly. He'd swallowed hard. This dude was nervous.

"I received a call from my section leader today, telling me that you were coming on board the task force," Pearson said. "I expressed some reservations, but, nonetheless, it was presented as a *fait accompli*."

Whatever the hell that means, thought Colby.

Pearson canted his head ever so slightly, as if trying to adopt an expression of superiority. "It seems that my boss received a call from a Deputy Superintendent, who assured him what an asset you'd be to the investigation."

Colby smiled at that. It still hurt, but the aspirins were starting to take effect.

"And," Pearson said, "I did agree that you would add a degree of depth to the task force. However…"

Here it comes, thought Colby.

"Deputy Superintendent Man-ni-on." Pearson took special care in enunciating each syllable. "I assume you know him?"

Colby nodded. "He's a real copper's cop."

"Whatever," Pearson said. "He convinced me—against my better judgment, I might add—to include you in this task force. But let me emphasize that the bureau has the lead in this one. Your Deputy Superintendent is totally behind me on that." He paused to stare at Colby. "In other words, I am in charge."

"Certainly," Colby said, nodding.

This seemed to take Pearson by surprise. He'd obviously been expecting to lock horns. Colby's passive approach had thrown the fed off his game. It was sort of like counterpunching.

"All that said," the FBI man continued, "I want to reiterate that I will not stand for any undisciplined heroics, unauthorized stunts of any kind, or someone not following my orders. Understood?"

Colby thought about asking if disciplined heroics and authorized stunts were permissible, but he merely nodded. His head hurt too badly to think about any more repartee. He just wanted to get the hell out of there, find a familiar hole, and crawl inside. He'd worry about finding the damn missing file and getting up to snuff tomorrow.

"Is that it?" Colby gripped the arms of the chair and started to get up.

"No, it isn't."

Colby let himself sink back down.

"I believe I mentioned the new development," Pearson said. "The one that caused the briefing to be canceled."

"You did."

"It has to do with someone leaking information about the investigation to the press," Pearson said, his lips twisting into a frown. "I want to make it clear that no information—absolutely *no* information—is to be released to any press personnel without prior approval from me."

"No problem," Colby said, but Pearson's stare indicated there was more.

"And that includes Ms. Carmel Washington," Pearson said with a measure of disdain. "The host of *Chicago Today*. You know her, don't you?" He added this last question very quickly.

Colby shrugged. "I wouldn't say I *know* her. She interviewed me about my book a few days ago, is all."

Pearson's eyebrows rose. "Oh? Are you sure that's 'all?'"

Colby straightened up. "Meaning what, exactly?"

"Meaning, that someone's been feeding her inside information."

"What kind of information?" That had to be what Mannion had talked about.

Pearson's lips compressed into a little pout. "Information about some of the murders, and the formation of this task force." He paused. "As I said, we've got a leak. Someone with an ulterior motive."

"And you think it was me?"

The FBI man arched his right eyebrow. "I'll bet it would sell a lot of your books, wouldn't it?"

Colby resisted the urge to get up, tell Pearson to go fuck himself, and storm out of the office. Instead, he used another counterpunch.

"Hey, you're right. I hadn't thought about that," he said, rubbing his chin and grinning. "But, I didn't do it."

The two men sat in silence, facing each other over the Spartan desk. Colby was used to staring people down, the benefit of a thousand interviews. He wasn't about to lose this one.

Finally, Pearson blinked and looked away. "I'm not saying you did." His voice was tentative, hesitant. "My point is that we all have to be on the same sheet of music regarding the press. We have to be extremely careful about what we release, and when."

"That's standard procedure in any homicide investigation." Colby held the stare a moment more, then added, "I hate dealing with the press, anyway."

Pearson nodded and pushed his chair back, standing up. "All right, with that settled, we'll reconvene tomorrow morning at nine."

Colby had to stop himself from asking, "Sharp?" He stood, too.

Pearson paused and cleared his throat. "Say…" He let the word hang out there for second before adding, "I need a favor."

Colby shot him an inquisitive look.

"That young woman I was talking to in the hall," Pearson said. "She's from Toronto Police Services. You know, Canada?"

"Yeah, I've heard of it."

"An associate of mine, from the Great White North, contacted me," Pearson said, breaking into an uncharacteristic smile. "Her superior attended my serial killers course at Quantico." Pearson raised an eyebrow. "Have you attended the National Academy?"

Colby shook his head. "Just the University of Hard Knocks. What's the favor?"

"She's down here doing a background follow-up on one of their homicides," Pearson said. "Inspector Graven, that's the fellow I know, asked if we could kind of look out for her. Take her under our wings, so to speak." He paused and flashed the smile again.

Colby was thinking he liked the guy better with a sour expression. He scratched his jaw. "And?"

"And, I told him we would steer her in the right direction."

"That something you want me to do?"

Pearson nodded. "I would appreciate it."

"Okay," Colby said. "As long as it doesn't keep me from getting up to speed on this copycat thing."

"If you wouldn't mind," Pearson said. "I'd appreciate it if you could drop her at her hotel. I'll be tied up here with some paperwork for a while."

Driving an out-of-towner to her hotel wasn't such a plumb assignment on his first day with the task force. He hoped this wasn't a sign that Pearson wasn't going to try to sick him with all the do-nothing assignments. But his stomach was starting to growl and he wanted to grab something to eat real quick, not to mention finding where he'd left that damn file.

"Sure, no problem."

"Thank you," Pearson said, standing. "I'll see you in the morning."

————

It was time to do a more thorough check of Matthew's hard drive, Knox thought as he adjusted his thin leather gloves before attaching his tablet to Matthew's computer. He'd spent the morning in the kid's apartment, going through his stuff as well as checking all the emergency rooms, clinics, and police stations for information on the alleged stabbing of Rodney Potts. His sources, along with his computer search, had turned up nothing. Nothing at the Medical Examiner's Office, either. There was a student listed by that name attending St. Xavier, and after hacking into student information files, Knox found out Potts lived in Pacelli Hall. With another two keystrokes, Knox had his phone number and called him.

"How are you feeling?" he asked.

The voice on the other end sounded stupid and dull, as well as confused. "Okay, I guess. Why? Who is this?"

"This is Mr. Butler with the student health services. I heard you'd gotten injured the other night. Just checking to see if you needed further treatment."

"Huh?" The voice sounded genuinely perplexed.

"You weren't involved in a fight on the North Side?"

"Huh? I ain't even been to the North Side in weeks. I mean, I live up in Winnetka, but alls I been doing is staying here in the dorm, boning up for my midterms."

An English major, no doubt, Knox thought, allowing the sarcasm to go unheard. "Are you a friend of Matthew Jetters? He was supposed to be involved, too."

"Who? Matthew, oh, okay. I know him. We got a class together. Sometimes he says hi to me, but we never really..." He let the sentence trail off, then added, "Is he in some kind of trouble, or something?"

Or something, Knox thought. But he didn't want this idiot to start any rumors, either. "He listed you as a reference for a part-time job here. I thought he said you were ill. But, no matter. Study hard." He hung up.

So much for loose ends. With a few more keystrokes, he was rerunning the check for Matthew's passwords and then began opening his emails. Mostly, they were useless spam and a few college related messages. No sign of any friends, male or female. He started checking the most recent sites visited. Several were law enforcement sites:

the FBI, Chicago Police Department, and South Bend, Indiana Police Department.

But the kid was pre-med. Why the interest in crime?

He checked further and found recent checks on the *Chicago Tribune* and *Chicago Sun-Times* sites, as well as several other papers both here and downstate. *The Indiana Times* showed up too. Most of the articles referenced were crime related. Murders. He minimized the internet field and clicked on documents. A lot of articles had been copied about a particular case. A serial killer named Morgan Laird. Knox began printing them.

Maybe material for a paper?

Knox didn't think so. That special feeling started to tingle in his gut. He got it whenever he was investigating a particular problem and had a sudden flash of inspiration that he knew would pan out. He went back to the internet and did a Google search on *Laird, Morgan*, with *serial killer* in parentheses. The references began to pop up. It wasn't until Knox saw one particular reference that he stopped and scrutinized it.

Blood Trails, a memoir by Roger Colby. A tough Chicago detective tells the story of how he caught a brutal serial killer, only to have the system fail…

Knox clicked on the link and went immediately to Amazon, which displayed an image of the book's red and black cover along with a short description and price. Knox didn't click further. He got up from the desk and walked over to a closet that he'd searched earlier. He opened the door and pushed some clothes aside, checking two stacks of books piled on the floor in by the rear wall. The ones on top were textbooks, but underneath them were several copies of the same book with the red and black cover.

Knox stooped and counted them. Seven copies of *Blood Trails*, all signed by the author. One of them had a somewhat battered look and several pieces of paper stuck in it. He opened the cover. Notes in black pen covered the margins. The last section bookmarked was titled "The Murder of Benjamin Pike." It had something scrawled in pencil in the upper part of the page. *Belmont and Halsted, the Rainbow Derby.*

That was a gay joint. Was the kid exploring that side of the coin?

Knox considered this, then perused the chapter. It had a picture of the victim. Clean-cut looking punk with doe-like eyes. Knox skimmed the text and found out that Benjamin Pike had been a male prostitute who'd been murdered and left in an alley years ago. Like twenty-eight years ago.

The tingling sensation crept over him again, and Knox read further. Morgan Laird had stabbed Pike in the gut, then strangled him. It was listed as another of the confessed murders for which he'd been granted immunity.

Sounds he had a good lawyer, thought Knox. This Laird must have been quite a busy guy. Flipping through the book, Knox looked at the several pages of pictures. A few were crime scene photos. One of a naked woman tied to a bed with blocked-out lines covering her breasts and pubic area.

Jenise Williams was tortured and brutally murdered by Laird. It is a crime to which he admitted after he was granted immunity.

Knox turned the page and saw an old, black-and-white picture of a young Morgan Laird, taken at age twenty-one, when he was a member of the Merchant Marine.

Knox studied the face in the picture. Morgan Laird looked like a piss ant trying hard to play a tough guy. His hair was slicked back, and his lips were twisted in a truculent sneer. Obviously, the guy was a real charmer. Still, there was a strange familiarity about him. Knox looked at it again, and then something clicked.

Knox smiled and closed the book.

Funny how things fall into place when you least expect it.

———

Matthew scrutinized the attendants at each feeding time, silently counting the seconds to himself. One thousand, nine-hundred and eighty seconds, or thirty-three minutes, until they got to his room, the last room. It was an approximation, but close enough for his purposes. He stood and moved to the door, removing the paper from his mouth and wadding it in his hand so he could be ready. He heard the keys jangling, and then the sound of the lock on the door to his cell twisting open.

He knew something else from listening, too. They didn't use the deadbolt portion until it was time for the nighttime lock-down. Too much hassle using the key twice for each door.

It swung open and the two white-suited attendants blocked his view of the day room. They looked shocked he was standing so close, so he shifted his weight to his rear foot.

I could kick them both from here if I wanted to, he thought, but smiled as benignly as he could.

"What's for dinner this time?" he asked.

"The usual," the smaller of the two men said. "Meat

loaf, mashed potatoes, and corn. With a chocolate bar for dessert."

"But..." the other one said, his face breaking into what he must have thought was an ingratiating grin.

Matthew wondered what his chances of getting away would be if he stabbed one of them now. Instead, he merely feigned compliance and shrugged. "I know. My meds first, right?"

The smiling attendant nodded.

Matthew held out his open palm. "Can I at least have some juice this time to wash them down?"

"Only water," the small one said, holding out a waxy paper cup.

Matthew reached out, moving closer, so that he could almost lean against the doorjamb. The larger of the two attendants moved forward to discourage any escape from the room. The smaller one placed the two blue pills in Matthew's palm. Tranquilizers. Probably ten milligrams of Lorazepam.

"Oops," he said, letting the pills spill out of his hand as he brought it toward his mouth.

Both men's eyes followed the bouncing pills for the split second it took for Matthew's right hand to press the small wad of wet paper into the latch-hole. It was a deft movement, and neither attendant seemed to notice.

"Sorry." Matthew flashed a sheepish smile. "Butterfingers."

It's a good thing these dopes were chosen for their easy dispositions, he thought, accepting another set of meds. This time made a show of carefully placing them into his mouth. The small guy handed him the paper cup, and he brought that to his lips and drank.

"Ahh," he said, wiping off his mouth with the back of his hand. "Can I have some juice now with my food, please?"

The small guy popped open a can of apple juice and poured it into the paper cup. He then handed him a Styrofoam box with the food inside. The big guy held out a plastic spoon.

"We'll be back in ten minutes," he said. "Place the—"

"I know, I know," Matthew interrupted. "Place the cup, the spoon and any uneaten items in the box for pickup, and you will check for the spoon. Right?"

The big guy nodded, looking unperturbed.

"Say, I think I've got lice." Matthew pointed to his long mane of dark hair.

"We'll tell grooming in the morning," the smaller one said. "He can give you some special shampoo."

"Okay," Matthew said, holding the box of food. "Maybe I'll just get it cut short like the rest of the boys in here."

"That's up to you," the big attendant said, motioning for Matthew to step back.

"At least give me an extra candy bar, okay?" Matthew said, trying to make his voice sound plaintive.

The two men glanced at each other.

"Come on," Matthew said, sensing that he had them. "You guys know me. I shouldn't even be in here, right?"

The smaller guy reached into another of the Styrofoam packs, removed a candy bar, and held it toward Matthew.

"Thanks," he said.

As soon as the door closed, he leaned against it, stuck his fingers in his mouth, and removed the blue pills, which he had tucked between his cheek and gums. He went to his bed and sat, carefully lifting the plastic-coated mattress. Four more of the blue pills lay on the solid metal bed slate. Matthew picked up one of the candy bars and carefully worked the end wrapper loose, separating the folds of paper. He then used the spoon to cut open the bottom of the candy bar and stuck the blue pills into the rich caramel and chocolate. After refolding the wrapper, he checked it and could barely notice that it had been opened. Smiling, he set it in plain sight on the bed next to the other candy bar.

If you want to catch a Blem, he thought, you have to sprinkle a little sugar around.

———

Colby was actually beginning to feel better as he walked back to where he'd parked the car. The basement felt cool and brisk, with a bit of a breeze, like he'd splashed icy water on his face. Detective Leslie Labyorteaux walked behind him, tugging her little suitcase. He'd offered to take it for her, but she'd declined.

"You got your gun in it?" he asked.

"Gun?" She shot him a look askance. "I didn't bring one."

"No?"

"We don't even carry our guns off duty. We check them in and out of the armory for work."

"Wow," Colby said, grinning. "Well, hopefully, you won't need it down here, but I'll see if I can find you one if you do."

She said nothing.

"Here's my car." He stuck the key in the lock and raised the trunk lid.

She nodded, stopping and collapsing the extendable handle.

She started to lift it, but he said, "Let me." and bent down to reach for it only to have the top of her forehead collide with his right temple.

Damn, that hurt, he thought, recoiling upward. She jumped back, too, and the suitcase fell over.

"Oh, my god," she said, "I'm so sorry."

For a moment he was certain the old headache would come skating back, but it didn't. He even managed a weak smile.

"My fault," he said, pointing to the suitcase. "You go ahead. I won't try to stop you."

It was her turn to smile, and she did, and he caught a flash of amusement in her brown eyes.

Maybe she's just glad she didn't knock me out, he thought.

After the suitcase was safely tucked inside, Colby slammed the lid, making sure to check that his fingers were out of harm's way first.

"Where you staying?"

"The Marriott Hotel." She began to dig in her purse. "I have the address here."

"No need. I know where it's at."

He exited onto Clark Street and headed south. It was close to four-thirty and traffic was reaching its apex in the Loop with everybody in the midst of going home. After fighting his way over to Van Buren, Colby went west a few blocks then cut back north again. He stole a glance at her as they crawled in the stop-start of rush hour. She seemed enamored with the all the activity.

"Is it always this busy here?" she asked.

"Nah. Sometimes it's worse."

She laughed.

That was a good sign. "Is it a lot like Toronto?"

"Population-wise, it's about the same size, but your streets seem to be more crowded." She turned her head to follow the sweep of the river as he turned onto Wacker Drive.

"Pretty icky looking, isn't it?" he said. "You should come back for St. Paddy's Day. They dye it green."

"It already looks green."

"I mean, really green. Bright Kelly green." He came to a stoplight, waiting to turn onto Dearborn. "You know, we've got an Ontario Street two blocks north of here."

"Really? I'll have to get a picture of that before I leave." Her smile was nice.

Colby took Grand Avenue east to Rush and pulled up in front of the hotel. There were two cars parked in front of them. Colby assessed the state of his lingering hangover and decided, what the hell. Why not?

"Say, after you get settled in your room, I wouldn't mind showing you Ontario Street," he said. "They got a couple of good restaurants around there."

"Oh, thank you, but I should probably go over the case some more. Plus, I'll have to check in with HQ," she said. "I've got my superior breathing down my neck on this one."

She must have an asshole for a boss too, he thought. Maybe we got more in common that I figured.

The phone jarred Dix awake. Sitting up and blinking, he glanced at the wall clock. Five-fifteen. Had he really fallen asleep this early? Christ, he only remembered laying his head down for a second.

I ain't quite the man I used to be, that's for sure, he thought as he got up and headed for the phone. Hell, he remembered the time he used to work on a case around the clock on coffee and adrenaline, racking up the overtime. But he always got results.

The phone rang again and Dix grabbed the caller ID box to see who it was before answering.

A cell phone. He answered.

"Dix, it's me," Colby said.

"Hey, buddy. What's up?"

"You remember what I did with that copycat file last night?"

Dix smirked to himself. Yeah, he remembered, all right. "File? What'd it look like?"

"It was in a manila folder about an inch thick. Had an FBI stamp on the front."

"Oh, that. I think I put it on your desk. You dropped it when we got into your house."

"You sure?"

"Sure, I'm sure." Dix licked his lips. "Why? Don't tell me you got assigned to that task force?"

Colby's reply was hesitant. "Yeah, I did."

"That's great. Just what we hoped for."

Another hesitant reply. "Yeah."

Dix suddenly began to wonder if Colby might have it figured: the benevolent ex-partner buying doubles, staying over to fix him a good breakfast. "That's great news. You deserve it." He paused to let the compliment sink in, then added, "I hope you'll keep me in the loop, at least."

"Sure."

"And if you want to run anything by this old, retired war-horse, I'm here."

"Thanks," Colby said. "I'll call you later."

Dix chuckled softly as he hung up, figuring Colby would probably still be holding his head from all that booze. It looked as though giving Carmel a few select pages from the file and urging her to make an FOIA request with the bureau had caused the right amount of heat in all the right places. Just like he figured. Probably got Colby in a little trouble with his boss, but hell, you had to break some eggs if you wanted to make an omelet. And Colby was good at thinking on his feet.

After all, Dix reflected, he was taught by the master.

But his ebullience was short-lived. He'd been poring

over this new file for hours, and still didn't have the slightest idea where or how to begin. Maybe he had lost more than just a step or two. Maybe he just didn't have it anymore. Whoever had been committing these new crimes had certainly studied Laird's old ones. That much was obvious, but Dix suddenly realized he didn't have the resources he'd once had. He wasn't a copper anymore. He was just another fucking civilian. Where could he go from here?

A vague idea floated in front of him: if he could find out who had access to the original file, it might lead somewhere. But how could he do that? He'd probably have to leave that one for Colby to figure out, and pry it out of him later.

Dix looked at the chart he'd been working on when he'd fallen asleep. It compared Laird's actual murders to the ones done by this new killer.

He and Colby hadn't known about all of Laird's handiwork when they'd chased him from that seedy hotel. That all came later, when he began singing, as part of his plea bargain. *Show us where you stashed the Swanstrom twins, in exchange for us taking the death penalty off the table.*

What had that damn state's attorney been thinking? The twins were already dead by the time the offer was made. If it had been the real old days, Dix would have gotten the answer out of Laird real quick, even in a hospital room.

Dix sighed. But this sure ain't the old days anymore.

And then it had gotten worse: that fancy mouthpiece, Fontaine, had secured the sweetest deal for Laird *He'll tell you about his other crimes, the locations of other victims, in exchange for immunity. So you can put the family's minds at ease. Give them closure.*

Immunity...they gave him the deal, and Laird started talking up a storm. By the time they realized what kind of monster they were dealing with, it was too late. The state's attorney had already signed off on it.

Yeah, a whole shitload of unsolved homicides got closed, but Dix suspected the families got little satisfaction. Closure was one thing, retribution was another. Plus, at the time, they guaranteed that Laird would spend the rest of his life in a prison cage.

Boy, did they get taken.

CHAPTER 8

As the elevator in the federal building made its ascent up to the fifth floor, Colby glanced at his watch to verify that it was eight-fifty-one. He was early and feeling relatively comfortable with the copycat file in his leather valise, tucked securely under his arm. He'd found it last night on his desk, right where Dix said it was. But something bothered him. While looking through it, he realized that some of the reports had been re-stapled, leaving an extra set of twin holes in the upper left corner. He couldn't remember if it had been like that before, or not. Could it be a sign of some kind of incremental disorder, like a warning light flashing on his dashboard, and then fading out? It could also mean that, unbeknownst to him, Dix might have somehow copied the file. That could explain who leaked the info to Carmel Washington.

But it didn't matter. Colby felt good. The workout he'd taken after finding the file had done the trick, purging all the residual alcohol from his body. Hitting the bags always proved beneficial for him. He'd boxed Golden Gloves in high school, and won his division. The small, gold boxing glove medal sat buried in his dresser drawer somewhere, but he'd never forgotten it. And this time he was able to imagine SAIC Pearson's face in front of each punch.

The elevator doors opened and he strolled forward, smiling and ready to go a couple more metaphorical rounds with the uptight fed. When the secretary smiled and allowed him to pass without even a question, he took it as another good sign.

Maybe, she read my book, he thought.

As he went through the door, he was pleasantly surprised to see Leslie there, talking to Pearson. Like déjà vu. He moved down the hall toward them and nodded.

"Where's the briefing at?" he asked, pointing at his watch. "I heard it was at nine sharp."

If Pearson was irritated, he didn't let on. Instead, he cocked his head toward Leslie.

"Detective Colby, you remember Detective Laby-orteaux, of—"

"Toronto PD," Colby finished for him. Then, turning to her, said, "I hope you enjoyed your first night in Chi-town."

Now it was her turn to smile and nod.

"Actually," Pearson said, leaning forward a bit. "The proper title is Toronto Public Services." He cast a knowing eye at Leslie, then turned back to Colby. "The briefing's in the conference room at the end of the hall. We have coffee in there, too."

Colby considered another smart ass comment, like asking if it was real coffee from Dunkin' Donuts, but figured he'd better not. After all, he was right where he wanted to be: about to get an update on the progress in the investigation.

Pearson started down the hallway and Leslie followed, glancing back over her shoulder at Colby.

He caught up to her with two elongated strides.

"So, you back for directions?" he asked.

She nodded and shot him a lips-only smile.

A Canadian Mona Lisa. Although he certainly didn't mind her being there, it struck him as a bit strange. An anal prick like Pearson wouldn't normally allow someone not connected to the investigation to sit in on one of his briefings.

Pearson paused at the door and held out his hand, ushering Colby and her into the room, which was already filled with people. The blinds on the far side had been closed, shutting out the morning sunshine. Agent O'Keefe was standing off to the side, and Colby counted half a dozen more suits. But that didn't surprise him half as much as seeing the big, grinning face staring at him from the other side of the long, wooden table—Bosworth, with a half-eaten chocolate-frosted donut on a small paper plate in front of him. He smiled, showing traces of yellow dough along his gum line.

"Hiya, Colby," Bosworth said, popping the rest of the donut into his mouth and not bothering to worry about the little bits that shot out as he continued talking. "The LT thought you might need a backup on this task force thing, so here I am."

Colby was about to say it wasn't an "ass force," but Pearson jumped in saying how grateful they were to have two experienced CPD detectives working with them on this investigation. His double-talk rang in Colby's ears as he sat down.

Pearson moved to the front of the room. A laptop rested on the table next to him. He tapped his pen on a lectern and, as if on cue, O'Keefe stepped over and turned down the lights.

"Shall we begin?" Pearson said as he picked up a remote. An overhead projector came to life, illuminating the image of Morgan Laird's old mug shot.

"I'm sure that most of us know who he is," Pearson began. "But for the sake of overall clarity, I'm going to review everything."

He was obviously somebody who liked to hear himself talk.

"Twenty-eight years ago," Pearson continued, "this man, Morgan Laird, committed numerous murders in this region, the extent of which was not known until his subsequent apprehension."

It's called *an arrest*, asshole, Colby thought. Otherwise known as, *good police work*. What's next?

A second later, he found out.

"Although he was a suspect in the kidnapping of the Swanstrom Girls, Laird was initially charged with aggravated battery to a police officer, and attempted murder when he was taken into custody," Pearson said, flipping the remote to go to the next image: a black-and-white picture, obviously scanned from the newspaper, showing Laird in a wheelchair, being pushed along a sidewalk by a trio of uniformed officers, one of whom was carrying a shotgun. Pearson turned slightly, and the edge of the projected light partially illuminated his face. "Needless to say, Laird, a derelict, was indigent and had to be appointed counsel."

He flipped to the next image. Lance Fontaine, resplendent in a three-piece suit, his long hair brushed back, stood looking dapper by a bookcase full of law books, holding a pair of glasses.

Enter asshole number two, Colby thought.

The picture was at least twenty-plus years old. Pearson had done his research, but how was this history lesson relevant to what was going on with the new homicides?

"In this case," Pearson said, "Mr. Lance Fontaine, fresh out of law school and seeking to make a name for himself, stepped forward to represent Laird pro bono. His motivation was unknown, but as an outspoken critic of what he called 'brutal police tactics,' perhaps he felt a compulsion."

Colby felt his irritation ready to boil over. He knew that the shyster had represented Laird for one reason, and one reason only: an opportunity to get in front of the news cameras on a heater case. Colby felt like saying something, but he knew that Bosworth would immediately relay anything untoward back to Kropper faster than Morse code.

"So," Pearson continued, flipping to the next image, "Fontaine, despite what we, as law enforcement officers might think of him, did his job, and did it well."

Colby braced himself. He knew what was coming next.

Another image shot onto the screen: a newspaper headline reading, *CHILD-ABDUCTOR SUSPECT PLEA BARGAIN*.

"As you probably already know," Pearson said, "Laird was a suspect in the case of missing twin sisters, age ten. Since there was hope the girls might still be recovered alive, the state's attorneys immediately entered into negotiations with Laird and his attorney."

He clicked to the next image. This one said, *TWINS FOUND DEAD*.

"In exchange for taking the death penalty off the table, Laird agreed to tell where the girls' bodies were."

A subsequent image showed a crime scene photo of Elsa Swanstrom being removed from a fifty-gallon metal oil drum.

Colby averted his eyes, although the image had been indelibly burned into his nightmares for almost three decades. Could he have done anything differently back then?

Another image materialized, showing a close-up facial from the autopsy. The child's eyes were closed, and she looked angelic lying on the cold, metallic surface.

"Even though the girls were both deceased when they were recovered," Pearson said, "negotiations didn't stop there." He paused, his face still partially lit up from the light from the projector. "One of the problems of making a deal with the devil, so to speak, is that you never know what you're going to get. And we really can't blame the police and prosecutors for this."

Colby heard someone barely control a derisive sounding snort. It had to be Bosworth, the prick.

"In exchange for immunity on his previous crimes," Pearson said, "our friend, Mr. Laird, began singing like a canary."

Pearson flipped the remote again and another headline materialized: *LAIRD CONFESSES TO MORE KILLINGS.*

"Laird's attorney said his client wanted to help the families of missing loved ones find closure." Pearson paused and flipped through several more crime scene photos of unearthed graves in desolate fields. "Regardless of our skepticism about Laird's sudden altruism, he did lead authorities to the graves of three more missing victims."

The next image showed another headline, *MORE BODIES FOUND*, along with a grainy newspaper photo of Laird in a wheelchair in a grassy field, surrounded by police.

"It wasn't until then that the enormous scope of the man's monstrosity became apparent." Pearson clicked to another image of a headline: *SERIAL KILLER'S PLEA BARGAIN STANDS.* "At the time, the prosecutors thought that Laird would be spending the rest of his life behind bars."

Colby noticed Agent O'Keefe moving toward the lights. She turned on half of them. Pearson left the last image projected against the screen. "However, we now know, that Laird was eligible for 'good time credit' for time served while being a model prisoner. That meant that he got one day off his sentence for every day served, so long as he didn't get in trouble." He paused and tried for an ironic expression. "I mean, really, how much trouble could a man in a wheelchair get in at Stateville? Look at how much fun Richard Speck had inside. Ever see those videos he made?" Pearson shook his head. "And, for whatever reason, the parole board felt that a man in a wheelchair, now suffering from emphysema, was no longer worth keeping behind bars. In fact, it was costing the taxpayers more money to keep him inside."

Colby had had enough. "We all know he's out. Have you considered looking at him as a suspect for these copycat murders?"

Pearson frowned. He obviously didn't like being thrown off his game.

"I'll get to that," he said, the irritation creeping into his tone. "But right now I want to bring everyone up to speed on the Laird case, if you don't mind. It'll help if we're all on the same sheet of music."

"That was my case," Colby said. "I should be doing that."

"Take it easy," Bosworth said. "Maybe you can see where you messed up."

Colby felt his face flush. This was like pouring salt on a reopened wound.

Pearson must have realized he'd lost his rhythm because he licked his lips and shot a glance at O'Keefe, who turned on the rest of the lights. "Let's all take a five-minute break."

Colby stood up, glancing at Bosworth. The big man

snorted a laugh and went to the table with the donuts and coffee.

Colby took a deep breath, restraining himself from going over to give Bosworth a good gut punch. He exited the room and joined the procession heading to the men's room. But since he didn't feel like standing around with the rest of the guys, he took a detour and went to the water fountain. After taking a long drink, he straightened up, wiping his mouth with the back of his hand, and saw Leslie standing a few feet away. Her dark eyes were scrutinizing him.

"Enjoying your visit to the US?" Colby asked, not knowing what else to say.

She smiled again. Nice teeth. Real nice teeth.

"So far, so good," she said. "I'd feel a bit better if I were making some progress in my own investigation, though."

It struck Colby as strange once again that Pearson had her sitting in on what was apparently an unrelated case. "Yeah, a homicide, right?"

She nodded.

"Well, I'm sure Agent Pearson will go the extra yard to get you all the assistance you need down here."

"I hope so."

After the break, Pearson glossed over the latter facts of the Laird case, ending with Fontaine finally obtaining Laird's release on parole eight months ago, citing that "the man was no longer a threat to society."

A smaller sub-headline appeared on the screen: *Morgan Laird Granted Parole*.

"And, not so coincidentally," Pearson added, "this was about the same time that the first copycat homicide occurred."

A new image of a farmhouse projected onto the screen.

"This was a double homicide that occurred on September sixteenth." He flipped the remote and another image shot into place of a dangling man, suspended from the crossbeams of a barn. He flipped to another image, this one of the knot securing the rope to the rail. "A clove hitch. Just like,"—Pearson flashed to the next image, another knot—"this one, from the original crime Laird confessed to in Monticello, Indiana. Same MO, same setup of the bodies." He flashed through a series of images contrasting the two crime scenes. "This is nothing most of you don't already know, if you've had time to go through your case file packets."

Yeah, Colby thought, doing a slow burn again. Nothing we don't know.

"The two most recent homicides show a bit of promise, however," Pearson said, his face twisting into a wry smile. "This one,"—the image showed the partially clothed body of a young man—"is that of Benjamin Pike, a young homosexual prostitute that Laird admitted killing in an alley in Uptown." He paused. "Despite his numerous incarcerations, Laird was apparently very homophobic. I suspect this might be related to latent tendencies on his part."

Skip the psychobabble, and get on with it, Colby thought.

"And this is the copycat crime scene." A new image appeared, looking strikingly similar to the previous one. "This victim was also left in an alley in what has come to be known as Boys Town. He was homosexual, young, but apparently not a prostitute. His name was Jonathan Watts, age twenty-two." He flipped to a new image of a young woman tied to a bedpost in a grotesque position. "I have something more to tell you about the Watts crime scene, but first, this one also has something of interest. You'll notice the similarity." The image changed, but not the subject. "Laird's handiwork. Linda McKenny, circa nineteen-eight-seven." He flipped back to the previous one. "Copycat, October 12th, this year, Kelly Turner." Pearson motioned and O'Keefe switched the lights back on. The fed glanced at Colby as he reached under the lectern and withdrew a copy of *Blood Trails*.

Colby grimaced. He knew what was coming next.

"I'm sure all of you are familiar with this," Pearson said, holding the book aloft. He turned to a section bookmarked by a yellow sliver of paper and began reading. "The investigating officers found a partially smoked cigarette butt at the crime scene. It was a Pall Mall, and the lab techs managed to get a blood type off it. A-Positive, the second most common type." Pearson paused for a moment, then resumed. "However, if the DNA technology we have today, had been available back in eighty-seven, this bit of trace evidence could have identified Laird, and put him at the crime scene." Pearson looked at Colby. "Nicely written, Detective."

Colby nodded, feeling his face burning again. Bosworth's puss had a big, stupid-looking grin plastered all over it.

Pearson closed the book and said, "Now this is where it gets interesting for us. The copycat killer also left a partially smoked Pall Mall cigarette butt at this scene, too. In the exact same spot as in the original." After a significant pause, during which he looked at each person sitting around the table, Pearson answered the question burning in everyone's mind. "And, yes, we were able to recover enough trace saliva to do a DNA test."

"Any matches?" Bosworth asked.

Pearson shook his head. "Not available yet. Those tests take time, unlike the ones on *CSI*."

No shit, Sherlock, Colby thought.

"Now, that," Pearson continued, "was an obvious act

of arrogance and conceit. The killer's taunting us, saying, 'I know you'll find this, so go ahead, try to catch me.'" He held up his index finger. "This could mean he left the cigarette knowing his DNA is not on file. Or, two—" He extended a second finger. "He used a cigarette that he found, just to throw us off. Or—" He held up his ring finger. "He actually slipped up and left it there."

"In the same spot as the original?" Colby said. "I don't think so. This guy ain't stupid. Everything he's done has been orchestrated. We need to focus on figuring out his motivation."

"Ooooh, I love it when you use them big words," Bosworth said with a laugh. When no one else did, he blinked twice and shut up.

Good, Colby thought. *I knew if I waited long enough that asshole would step on his dick.*

Pearson stared at Bosworth as he picked up the book again. "Nonetheless, we can't afford to rule out any possibilities. Which is why we've got to check out every possible lead as if it were a valid one. Basic homicide investigation."

Colby couldn't help rolling his eyes at that one.

"We're passing out our latest VICAP projections," Pearson said. "Obviously, this new killer has some connection to the Laird case. We just have to establish what it is."

O'Keefe began moving around the table passing out manila folders. "Inside this you'll find your assignments for the day. You'll also find your partner assignments. Plan on being back here at three o'clock." She stopped and looked at Bosworth and Colby, and then smiled. "That's fifteen hundred for you military and police types."

At least she has a sense of humor, Colby thought, hoping he wasn't partnered up with Bosworth.

Pearson accepted the last manila folder from O'Keefe and held it toward Colby. "Before you leave, Detective, I need to speak to you in my office."

———————

When the midmorning attendants came back, Matthew bided his time, shuffling listlessly into the grooming line to get his hair cut and new clothes. He bundled his street clothes and underwear into his laundry bag and sat naked on the plastic barber's chair. The attendant acting as barber looked shocked when he saw Matthew's long hair.

"Take it all off," Matthew said, sitting in the chair. "I want to look like everybody else."

"You're…very articulate," the attendant said, his hand poised with the clippers.

"Yeah, I'm the exception," Matthew said. "Now, just do it."

Seconds later the burning tingle as the electric clippers swept over his head. He felt, more than saw, his fashionable locks falling. It was over in about twenty-five seconds. No final trimming was needed.

No tip, either, Matthew thought as he got up from the chair and moved into the shower line, receiving his bar of soap as the line edged forward.

After walking through the specially designed showers, he grabbed a towel from the stack and dried off. He was given a clean set of scrubs and elastic slippers that he fitted over his bare feet. His regular shoes had been taken from him when he'd been assigned to C ward with the rest of them. Memories about being forced to work there as a teen, taking care of his "brethren," as the old man had put it, made his blood boil. Me, like them? But actually they all were cut from the same cloth, so to speak. It's just that his cut was the only good one.

He wondered if he should try to feign repentance, throw himself on the old man's mercy. If there was such a thing. He doubted Jetters harbored any. No, it was better to continue with his plan. Morgan had gone through worse. Far worse. Matthew knew he could get through this. After all, he estimated it would only be a matter of hours now.

So he practiced looking dumb, stupid, and listless as he shuffled forward, through the line, accepting his paper plate and watching them plop a scoop-full of tan colored slop and one piece of bland, unbuttered toast onto his plate. He was given a plastic bottle of orange juice on the way to the tables. The food disgusted him, like everything about this place. He watched the Blems shoveling it in, chewing without closing their mouths. Feeding time at the zoo.

But soon, he'd be out. And revenge would be sweet. All he had to do was find someone who looked exactly like him to take his place. And that was easy.

They all did.

———

Colby felt the irritation and impatience starting to bubble up and overflow. While part of him knew that to challenge Pearson and the way this investigation was being handled was probably the kiss of death for his chances to stay on the task force, the other part of him felt compelled to take command. The vague, dithering focus was only going to lead to more people getting killed. But that was the way the feds operated: slow and slower. Their strategy was totally reactive. They needed to start shaking some trees, rattling some bushes.

Pearson held out his hand, indicating Colby should sit in front of the big desk. It set Colby's teeth on edge.

Pearson settled into the big chair opposite him. "You were a bit confrontational in the briefing. I don't appreciate someone interrupting my flow when I'm speaking."

Colby took a deep breath.

"Sorry, I didn't mean to be," he said. "I'm just concerned that we're not proceeding in the best direction on this."

Pearson raised his eyebrows. "Oh? In what way?"

Maybe he'll listen to me, Colby thought. He edged forward.

"For one thing, this offender has made a case study of Morgan Laird. And he's duplicated Laird's crime pattern to the point of precision."

Pearson brought his fingertips together and nodded.

"Well," Colby continued, "in order to figure out who he is, we have to figure out why. What's his motivation?"

Pearson sighed and dropped his hands. "If you would have taken the time to study our VICAP profile, you'd know that we've already addressed that."

Colby felt like grinding his teeth. Their profile was so generic that it was like painting an autumn landscape in black and white.

"Have you considered the possibility that Laird might be involved in these new killings?" he asked, trying to regain a measure of composure. "I mean, there's no way the new killer could know all the nuances of his activities."

Pearson shot him a patronizing smile. "Unless he studied your book."

Colby compressed his lips and let a slow breath out through his nose. "My book does detail the crimes that Laird confessed to after he was arrested, but—"

"We do consider Laird as a person of interest,"

Pearson said, interrupting, "but to suggest that he is the major perpetrator is ludicrous."

"I'm not suggesting that. Only that there has to be some kind of connection. If we can figure out what it is—"

"Which is exactly why we're going to interview Laird this morning," Pearson said, interrupting again.

"What?"

Pearson looked at his watch. "His lawyer is bringing him by later today."

"Great," Colby said. "I'm looking forward to that."

"Not possible," Pearson said. "Mr. Fontaine explicitly stipulated that you were not to be involved in the interview."

"Fontaine? Who the hell is he to set the terms?"

"He's Laird's attorney."

Colby frowned. "Listen, I know Laird. I know how he thinks. He's a natural-born sociopath. A habitual liar. A killer. I can cut through his bullshit."

Pearson's right cheek twitched slightly, and he shook his head. "I have another assignment for you today. You're to accompany Detective Labyorteaux out to backtrack on a homicide victim."

"What? Who?"

"Dr. John H. Norton," Pearson said. "He worked at a private research facility called New Genesis in Oakbrook Estates. She has the information."

"How's that related to the copycat case?"

Pearson leaned forward. "As the Special Agent in Charge, I hand out the assignments, not explain them."

Colby glared at him for a solid five seconds. "Why can't I at least watch your interview with Laird?"

"As I said," Pearson began.

"Look, I'll know if that bastard's trying to feed you a line of shit."

Pearson recoiled at the word choice.

"Laird said he would feel intimidated by your presence," he said. "I gave him my assurance that you would not be in the building."

"Oh great, coddle the son of a bitch, why don't ya?"

Pearson stared back in placid fashion. "That's your assignment. Do I need to remind you again that I am in charge?"

Colby met the stare, suppressing the urge to tell the FBI man to go to hell. This battle was already lost.

"Besides," Pearson said, his smile looking smug and self-satisfied again. "There's something of an overlap."

"An overlap?"

"When Morgan Laird was in prison, John Norton was one of his doctors."

CHAPTER 9

Knox watched as Jetters took off his glasses and sat heavily in the padded chair behind his desk. The old man's face looked pale and gaunt, with each wrinkle as deep as a groove in a marble statue. But he looked fragile, too. Not marble. More like porcelain. He looked bad, that was for sure. Perhaps the worst that Knox had ever seen him. Taking a slow, deep breath, he waited, wondering if the old man was finally going to crack right in front of him.

"You're absolutely sure?" Jetters said, using his fingers to massage the bridge of his nose.

Knox waited for Jetters to look up, but the old bastard just kept at it, his eyes tightly shut.

"Yes, I've checked it out thoroughly," Knox said, finally. "There is a student named Potts, which was the name he gave us, but the boy and Matthew don't even know each other that well. The story was a complete fabrication. That's in addition to the other details I mentioned."

Jetters recoiled slightly.

"And you're certain he's done..." Jetters hesitated, "the other crimes?"

This time Knox didn't wait. "As certain as I could be without making my interest too obvious. If I checked into it any further, it might start attracting the cops' attention."

Jetters compressed his lips, dropping his hand from his face. He replaced his glasses and sat forward.

"First that problem with Norton, and now this." He looked at Knox again. The pale blue eyes looked clear now. "How difficult is it going to be to clean this mess up?"

Knox considered the question. "That depends."

"On what?"

On how much money you're going to pay me by the end of this, he thought. The words kept ringing in Knox's mind, but he didn't speak them. Instead, he said, "Don't forget we've already run more than just a few risks taking care of Norton, and his domestic partner. We need to start thinking about overall damage control."

"I know, I know." Jetters brought his hand to his face and traced the lines on either side of his mouth. "Perhaps I gave him too much freedom, too soon. But Matthew has been my crowning achievement. The jewel in my metaphorical crown, so to speak. The embodiment, the vindication of all of our research. Without him, and the Others, we could have never perfected the..." He stopped, lifted his glasses, and began the massage again. "The program."

The Program? It was all Knox could do not to laugh. Was that what the old man called growing new organs for rich assholes and getting paid those big bucks?

Jetters heaved a sigh. "If only John hadn't been so stubborn about insisting on announcing our findings at that conference."

Knox felt a surge of glee thinking about his "insurance" policy: the hard drives from Norton's laptop and PC. He'd kept the originals and given Jetters the crushed remains of two duplicates. Money in the bank. Or, they soon would be, at any rate.

"Look, Professor, I'm concerned they're going to trace this back to New Genesis. There is a trail, for somebody skilled enough to find it." He paused to let that sink in, then added, "Like I said, damage control."

Jetters considered this, then nodded. "I must think this through."

Knox thought about asking if Matthew had one of those genetic triggers that he'd read about in Norton's files. From the sound of it, the professor was very adept at developing them. Was there a grave reserved for Matthew in the unmarked cemetery at the far, south end of the compound? But Knox kept silent. No sense in tipping his hand too soon. When the time was right, he would tell Jetters that he'd done his last clean-up job, that he was retiring on the company's dime to someplace nice and warm, where the women walked around wearing next to nothing. The more information he could gather now, the more leverage he'd have when he needed to make his closing pitch. The copies of the hard drives were his trump cards. A pair of bullets. The aces of clubs and spades. He caught Jetters staring at him, his expression going from worry to anger in an instant.

"I'm glad to see you're amused by all this," the old man said. But before he could continue with his chastisement, the phone rang. Jetters snatched it up.

"I told you I was not to be disturbed!" he yelled into the phone, but then his voice changed into little more than a croaking whisper. "What? Did they say what they wanted?" His face paled again, worse than before, and his eyes shot a glance up toward Knox. "Tell them I'll see them shortly." He replaced the receiver with an uncharacteristic gentleness.

"Is everything all right?" Knox asked.

"The police are downstairs." Jetters had turned as white as a sheet. "They want to talk to me."

———

Dix watched her slow smile as she sat across from him, sipping coffee in the small shop on Harrison Street. He would rather they were having martinis in a bar someplace, but all in good time. After all, it was early in the day, and here he was sitting at the same table with the gorgeous Carmel Washington.

"So, Mr. Dix," she said, "tell me again why it was so important that I meet you this morning."

"Please, just call me Dix. All my friends do."

Her brown eyes studied him over the rim of the cup.

He grinned. "Believe me, I live up to that name, too."

"I'm not sure how I should take that."

Dix laughed and patted his hairpiece, secretly smoothing it out over his bald spot. "Like I said, there may be snow on the roof, but there's plenty of fire in the furnace."

Carmel took another sip of her coffee. She suddenly looked distracted, and he was afraid she was going to make some girlie excuse and take off on him. He couldn't let that happen.

"Everything's moving perfectly according to my plan," he said quickly. "Colby's been assigned to the task force investigating the copycat serial killer, and I'll be working the case with him."

Her eyes widened again, ever so slightly this time. "*You're* working the case? I thought you were retired?"

He nodded. "Yeah, well, technically, I am. But Colby

always likes to run stuff by me. Back in the day, I was one of the top homicide investigators in this city."

She took another long sip and Dix watched her full lips curling over the edge of the cup. Something stirred inside him. God, she was hot.

But, all in good time.

"That's why you gotta trust me and back off a tad," he said.

"We've already made our FOIA requests. Both to the city and the feds." She set the cup down. "I don't know how much longer my editor will want to sit on this." She set her drink down and looked at him. "You're sure there's more to it than just some copycat murders?"

Dix grinned and nodded. "Believe me, you'll be astounded. It's the biggest cover-up since Nixon." Maybe he was exaggerating a little bit, but anything to impress a lady.

She rolled her eyes. "It would help if you gave me some more access to that report, then. So I could decide for myself."

"Like I said, you gotta trust me." He reached over and lightly touched the back of her hand. "Once I crack this new one, you'll have an exclusive."

He pictured himself being interviewed on her show in a tailor-made suit and a new hairpiece, pushing a book about his own life story, and how he'd come out of retirement to solve a string of gristly murders.

"Suppose I can get him to wait," she said, all business now. There was no naiveté in this babe. "How can I be sure you'll deliver?"

His mouth twisted into a lopsided grin. "Baby." He reached over and touched her hand again, this time letting his fingers linger. She didn't pull away, which he took as a good sign. "I always deliver. And you can take that to the bank."

He watched her smile back at him, still letting his fingers dance across her caramel-colored skin. It felt good, but he wished he actually was as confident as he was trying to sound. But hell, he'd solved big ones before. He was the one who'd pinched Laird, for Christ's sake. Well, him and Colby. The guy was good, no doubt about it, but that was only because he'd learned from the master.

He looked into her dark eyes again. It was crunch time, but, dammit, he could do it. Make it all come true. One way or another, he'd solve this damn thing, even if he had to go around Colby to do it.

––––––

Matthew peered out the small, eight-by-eleven-inch window in the door of his cell. Luckily, they'd left the covering shutter open, so he could see out, like from a prison cell. This reminded him of his initial discovery about Morgan Laird, and himself. The overheard conversation between the old man and Norton, the slip that led him to sneak into the records room, finding the master file on Morgan, the experiments, and...

The attendants were now long gone, having pushed the meal cart through the safety doors, and into the waiting elevator. It was set up that way. You could only get on and off this floor with one of those special keys to operate the elevator, and once it had stopped at this level, it stayed in place until the key was inserted again. They'd return again in about two hours.

Just like a prison. Predictable and simple.

Not complex. Like him.

He kneeled beside the door and wedged the remnants of the plastic spoon he'd managed to stuff up his sleeve during breakfast into the narrow space between the solid metal door and the jamb. It moved slightly. Enough for him to discern that the lazy idiots had neglected to flip the deadbolt lock.

Lazy bastards.

That would be their undoing. He'd see to it.

He wedged the plastic in some more, increasing the gap a few millimeters. Tiny, but enough, he hoped.

Removing the cloth slipper from his left foot, he quickly began to pick at the elastic band that secured it around the ankle. In about thirty seconds he was able to pull it free, giving him a strip of about five inches. Wetting one end with his spit, he rolled it into a needle-like shape, and began working it into the space he'd created between the door and the jamb. He started right above the latch.

Time and again he mashed it into the narrow gap, only to have it curl out too soon. His fingers grew raw from the continued effort, but he knew he couldn't quit. He knew, too, that Morgan had escaped from a little country jail somewhere by using the same technique. He'd seen him describe it on one of the news documentaries that had been filmed about him.

The elastic curled out again and Matthew slammed his fist against the door in frustration. The searing pain from hitting the metal brought tears to his eyes. He wanted to roll over and quit, but if he did that, he'd lose his only chance to get out, his only chance to complete his mission. Wetting the end of the elastic again, he worked in into the space. This time it went in easier, traveling all the way down past the latch, like he wanted. He pressed the spoon fragment upward, working it closer to the right-angle lip of the jamb. His breathing quickened.

The elastic was right on top. If he could just …

Almost afraid to breathe, he worked some more of the elastic into the space from the top. If he could force enough excess on the top, the wispy end might travel between the latch and the jamb and work its way downward and out, so he could grab the end of it. The spitslick pointed end began to edge outward, along the top of the white plastic, and toward him. Swallowing hard, he pushed down from the top.

The twisted end appeared through the space. He managed to grab it between his fingernails and pull.

The end came out, leaving it wrapped, in effect, around the latch. He hoped all the cardboard, chewed food, and paper he'd managed to stuff in there would have kept the latch from fully engaging into the slot. If he could pull at the right angle, it should then retract back into the door, allowing him to open it.

Wrapping each end of the elastic around his fingertips, he began a sawing motion, designed to exert pressure on the latch.

He heard something click, and the door popped open. Matthew nearly fell forward, but grabbed the inside doorknob to keep the whole door from swinging outward. There were still the cameras to contend with.

Matthew slowly got to his feet and peered out the window again.

The coast was clear, except for the oval eye of the closed-circuit camera above the door.

He knew that as long as the morning attendants hadn't secured all the deadbolts, he should be able to open the room across from him by turning the outside knob. He'd have to be careful not to shut it completely behind him, but that shouldn't be a problem.

So long as they hadn't secured the dead bolt. But why would they? They were used to dealing with a bunch of morons. Idiots with perfectly healthy bodies but scrambled brains, only looking forward to their next meal. And their next sweet treat.

He touched the candy bar in his pocket for reassurance. There were enough tranquilizers in it to incapacitate a horse. What it would do to a person was anybody's guess, but that wasn't his concern. He was only dealing with Blems, and they didn't count.

He stared at the camera again, taking a chance to push the door open just enough to work the rolled elastic completely into the latch-slot. Now he could shut the door behind him and it would never lock. But the cameras ...

Matthew remembered a television show he'd seen about Special Forces teams, and how they'd emphasized the effectiveness of cameras was over-rated.

"The best way to deal with video surveillance systems," one soldier had said, "is to pretend they're not even there."

The theory was that the people watching were so bored, that quick movements tended not to be noticed.

Time to try out the man's theory, Matthew thought, and moved out of the room. He was across the broad, tiled hallway in seven steps.

Lucky seven.

His fingers curled around the knob and it twisted open.

Perfect, so far.

Matthew stepped inside, wedging his slipper in between the door and the jamb this time to keep the latch from securing. The Blem in the room sat up with a start and stared at him with a perplexed expression.

Moving slowly, Matthew straightened up and smiled as benignly as he could.

The Blem smiled back.

Good. Trust.

Matthew reached into his pocket and removed the

Lorazepam-laced candy bar, holding it up for the Blem to see.

The brown eyes followed his every movement. Like a dog watching a treat in his master's hand.

Extending his palm, he held the candy bar out toward the Blem.

The Blem blinked and pointed to the candy bar.

His hoarse voice creaked as he made a "Me?" gesture.

Matthew nodded, still smiling. He was careful not to move when the Blem got off the bed and shuffled forward. Each movement was tinged with caution. Finally, he got close enough and reached for the candy bar, his eyes watching for any signs that Matthew was going to snatch it away.

But he didn't. He let the Blem take it. He continued to smile as the Blem peeled off the wrapper and let it flutter to the floor. Matthew picked it up. The Blem took a bite and rolled the chocolate around, not bothering to close his mouth.

The disgusting pig.

Matthew heard the crunching sound as the Blem chewed. The pills being crunched, obviously.

But something must have seemed different to the Blem. He stopped chewing and put a finger in his mouth.

Shit, if he doesn't down all of them, Matthew thought, I'll have to pry open his mouth and shove them down his throat.

Instead, Matthew made a quick motion, as if he was grabbing for the partially eaten candy bar. "Gimme back!" he yelled.

Startled, the Blem backed up a few steps, almost tripping over the stainless steel toilet and sink extending from the wall. He shoved the rest of the candy into his mouth and began chewing vigorously.

Matthew watched him continue to masticate and then

swallow. The Blem began running his tongue over his teeth.

It was down. Now it's just a matter of luring him across the hall.

Matthew smiled. "More?" he asked, waving the candy bar wrapper.

The Blem nodded.

This was almost too easy.

———

At least the weather's still nice, Colby thought, looking at the bright October sunshine filtering down over the cluster of trees visible through the huge glass window. He was still wondering exactly how to broach the subject of his dissatisfaction with Pearson to Leslie as the security guard handed them the beige visitor badges and took them to the special elevator. Special because you needed a key to operate it. The guard's shoulder patch spelled out New Genesis Corporate Security in bold black letters against a yellow background. The guy's uniform shirt was starched khaki.

The place was ultra-modern, too, and looked as elaborate as a Vegas hotel. The inside walls of the office building were a mosaic of artfully arranged rocks, tapering around to a waterfall display in the center behind the security guard's main desk. Colby glimpsed at the row of television monitors under the lip of the desk and thought, Vegas-style security, too, although the guy watching them didn't seem particularly attentive.

As the elevator doors opened, he was reminded of the task at hand and let Leslie enter first. She'd hardly spoken on the drive out, perhaps sensing his lack of enthusiasm.

The sooner I get this babysitting assignment

completed, he thought, the quicker I can jump into the meat and bones of the investigation.

He compressed his lips and wondered how the interview with Laird was going—an interview he should have been on, despite any objections from the likes of Laird or Fontaine.

The thought of Laird being out after admitting to all those murders... He shook his head. Our criminal justice system at work, he thought. What a joke.

The doors opened and they stepped into a long carpeted hallway, with rows of closed office doors on the opposite side. No windows. Whatever they did here, they valued their privacy.

"Dr. Jetters's office is down this way," the guard said. He was a short, burly type who looked like he'd probably played football in college, but was a shade too small for the pros.

Colby watched Leslie smile at the guy, and thought about how pretty she was. A Canadian knockout, that was for sure, and with just that right amount of reticence to pique his interest. This would be a good test to see if she could execute the game plan they'd discussed.

The guard knocked on a solid oak door marked with *Dr. H.A. Jetters* in gold letters against a black background.

The door was opened by a tall guy with a black goatee, a mustache, and a ponytail. He had thick wrists and a lean, wiry build that told Colby that the dude could probably take care of himself in a fight.

Ponytail stepped back and Colby saw a much older man in a white lab coat standing behind a cluttered desk. He wore gold wire-rimmed glasses and had an unruly shock of white hair. That had to be Jetters; Colby wondered who the lean guy was.

"Dr. Jetters?" Leslie asked, stepping forward and

extending her hand. "I'm Detective Labyorteaux of Toronto Police Services."

Good girl, Colby thought. Always shake their hands. If you feel sweat, you'll know how the rest of the interview will probably go.

"Toronto?" the old man said. "I assume this about John?"

"I'm afraid it is," she said.

Jetters nodded and rubbed his hand through his errant hair. "I was shocked, totally shocked to hear he'd been killed. Do you know who did it yet?"

Colby felt something stir inside him. The old guy was talking too fast. Like he was nervous, or something.

"We're working on it," she said. "Right now, though, I'm trying to find out a little more about Mr. Norton."

"*Doctor* Norton," Jetters said. "He was my partner and a world renowned geneticist."

"Yes, of course," she said. "As I'm sure you know, the more we know, the better we'll be able to investigate."

Nice recovery, Colby thought.

"May we sit down and take a few minutes of your time?" she asked.

Another plus, Colby thought. Sit down, stretch out, establish territorial imperative.

"Yes, of course." Jetters held his hand toward some chairs against the left wall. "This is Mr. Edward Knox, our head of corporate security here at New Genesis."

Watching ponytail nod and smile, Colby had the sudden urge to do the handshake test with the guy. He extended his open palm and saw Knox stir with a flash of discomfort before reciprocating. His palm felt hard and callused. No wetness there. An iceman.

"How long had Mr. Norton worked here?" Leslie asked.

"Almost thirty years," Jetters said. "Since our formation."

"You knew him well, then?"

"Yes, of course." Jetters worked his lips and then said, "We were fairly close, but...I assume you heard about Peter?"

"Peter?" Leslie repeated.

"Yes, Peter Davids," Jetters said. "John's—" A quick, lips-only smile stretched across his mouth. "His significant other. He was gay."

This guy's dodging the questions, Colby thought.

Leslie looked up from her papers. "The local police informed us Mr. Davids was deceased as well."

"Yes, yes. An accidental fall." Jetters looked like an old groundhog cautiously peering out at the sun. "Tragic case. Absolutely tragic."

This guy was uncomfortable. He was hiding something.

Colby could stand it no longer. "Anything you can tell us about their relationship?"

"Meaning what?" Jetters asked.

"Did they fight? Were they happy?" He glanced at Knox. "Know anybody who'd want to do harm to Doctor Norton?"

Pony tail sat there impassively. If the old guy was a groundhog, Knox was a cobra.

"Why are you asking me this?" Jetters was expressing something akin to a mild case of outrage. "I thought this happened up in Toronto? A street mugging, from what I was told."

"May I ask who told you that?" Leslie asked.

Colby watched Jetters blink and lower his gaze momentarily, before snapping back with, "Why, I believe it was someone from your agency."

"I doubt that," she said. "We're not usually prone to offering unsubstantiated conjectures about open cases."

She was pressing the advantage, Colby noticed. He wondered if she was picking up on the same vibes that he was.

"Perhaps it was a reporter," Knox offered from the side.

His comment gave Jetters just the break he needed to regain his composure.

"Yes, yes, I believe it was." He fixed her with a baleful looking stare "Regardless, you haven't answered my question, young lady. Was it a random street crime, or not?"

Leslie started to talk, but Colby cut her off. "We'll let you know when we solve it. Now, if you don't mind, we're not here to answer questions, just to ask them."

She shot him an almost wicked-looking glance, then turned back to Jetters.

"What did Dr. Norton do here?"

The old man pursed his lips. "John was a researcher. We do highly speculative and scientific work. Genetic engineering. We're on the cutting edge of a great many new discoveries. I'm sorry I can't be more specific."

She nodded and asked about the conference Norton was attending.

"Was he representing New Genesis?"

Jetters nodded.

"Was anyone else from your company there?"

"I don't believe so."

Knox stirred slightly. "I think we did send someone else, sir."

Jetters raised his eyebrows. "Did we?"

"Krems," Knox said.

"We do show a Vernon Krems crossing the border in a

vehicle registered to New Genesis," Leslie said. "Does he work here?"

"Krems?" Jetters looked almost theatrical as he grasped his receding chin with his right hand. "Yes, I believe he also said he was attending."

"You 'believe?'" Colby asked. He was beginning to like playing the bad cop. "You don't know for sure?"

"Listen, Detective." Jetters assumed the air of a haughty professor, giving a recalcitrant student a dressing down. "We have a large contingent of highly valued and highly skilled scientists working here, under my direction. To ride rough-shod over them, and by that I mean micro-managing their every move, would stifle their spirit, not to mention their creativity."

"Creativity?" Colby said. "I thought you were into research?"

Jetters stared back smugly. "We look for creative ways of approaching a problem. Something police would do well to consider from time to time."

"I'll keep that in mind," Colby said. "In the meantime, we need to interview this guy Krems."

"I'm afraid he's not working today." Jetters said it a little too quickly.

"Go figure," Colby said. "Who'd have thought you'd be keeping that close of an eye on him?"

"When will he be back?" Leslie asked.

"I'll have to check," Jetters said.

"How about giving us his address?" Colby asked. "We can save you the trouble."

"You'll need a subpoena for that," Knox said.

Colby turned and stared at him. "A subpoena? Why's that?"

Knox smiled. It was an attempt to look benign, but Colby had already caught a glimpse of the guy's fangs.

"Civil liabilities, and all that," Knox said. "I'm sure

you understand. We can't very well violate an employee's privacy on the whim of the police now, can we?"

"Heaven forbid," Colby said. He glanced at Leslie, who had an interesting look in her dark, brown eyes. "I guess we'll go get one."

"Good luck with that," Knox said. "Toronto's a bit far out of this jurisdiction, isn't it?"

Looking from Knox to Jetters, Colby couldn't resist taking one more shot. Plus this one was related to his own task at hand. "What was Norton's connection to Morgan Laird?"

Jetters looked like somebody'd punched him in the gut.

"Uh...Who?"

Colby took his time replying. "Morgan Laird. The serial killer. Norton was listed as one of his doctors from prison."

"Well, John was an altruist." Jetters took off his glasses and gripped the bridge of his nose. "He did a lot of charitable work for the less fortunate."

"And of course," Knox said from the side, "anything of that nature would be excluded under doctor-patient confidentiality. We wouldn't be at liberty to discuss it."

"Fine," Colby said. "We'll just have the US Attorney write up a couple of subpoenas, then."

"US Attorney?" Jetters said, his face darkening. "What would he have to do with a murder that occurred in a foreign country? You'd better be careful throwing around idle threats."

Colby smiled and took out his Chicago star. "Actually, I'm a lot closer to home than she is."

CHAPTER 10

Dix knew it would come to this as he sat slouched down in his car and watched the front of the building, trying to decide his next move. He'd used up more than just a few favors calling around to get Laird's address, a broken-down old apartment building that had seen better days a long time ago. A perfect shit hole for someone like Laird. And because there was no elevator, a guy in a wheelchair had to be in a first-floor room.

Dix tried to imagine what the asshole did all day. Not that much different from the joint, except Laird could come and go as he pleased. That's what had bothered most of the ex-cons Dix had talked to in his career. Knowing that they couldn't leave. Most of them made do with the prison food, the dangers, and the boredom. Some of them even learned to enjoy the prison pipeline of drugs and sex. But knowing that if they tried to go past a certain point, they'd be cut down, knowing some other dude was on the outside, doing what he wanted, going where he wanted, that was the roughest part.

But Laird was still severely limited, being in that

wheelchair. The parole reports said that he was on oxygen, too.

Good, thought Dix. At least the bastard's paying in some fashion for all the grief he'd caused.

But what was the next move? Dix was beginning to rethink his boastful comment to Carmel that he could solve this thing before the task force. Not that she believed him, but, hell, that was part of why he was pushing so hard. To prove that he could. But being out of the game for so long made it more difficult than he'd figured. In the old days he always knew where to look, where to go next. Now, that sixth sense eluded him. But he also wasn't restricted by any rules this time out. That was perhaps his one advantage.

Laird was involved. He had to be. The crime scenes matched too well... But what was his motive? And who was helping him? Obviously, if Laird was in as bad physical shape as he appeared to be, he couldn't be doing it alone. The asshole was supplying someone with the info, the know-how. That had to be it.

But who?

So shadowing the son of a bitch was the only option.

Dix chuckled slightly, thinking that poor Colby must be pulling his hair out being trapped on a task force run by some know-nothing fed like Special-Dick-in-Charge Pearson. Colby had opened up when they were drinking about what an anal prick the guy was.

If something materializes from this surveillance, Dix thought, it'll give me and Colby something solid to work with.

Then it'd be the two of them, working the case, just like the old days. He closed his eyes for a moment, picturing the headlines:

RETIRED COP SOLVES NEW SERIAL MURDER CASE

Maybe *Retired Detective* would be better. Certainly, he'd make sure Carmel addressed him as Detective during any TV interviews.

Carmel, he thought. What a dynamite looking broad. Exotic. He wondered what she'd look like without her clothes, what she'd be like in bed.

Suddenly he perked up and saw a guy in a wheelchair coming out of the front door, an oxygen tube tucked between his legs.

It had to be Laird, but, Christ, the guy looked old. Shrunken, too. Just a shell of his former self. The Laird that Dix remembered had been wiry and strong, even after Colby's bullet took out the guy's legs. This pathetic, shriveled asshole looked anything but formidable.

Dix leaned forward and his gut pressed against the horn, startling him.

Laird's head jerked around, looking but apparently not seeing much.

Guess both of us have lost a step or two, Dix thought.

The limo pulled up to the curb and Laird wheeled himself next to it. A chauffeur jumped out, ran around to open the back door, and helped Laird inside. The chauffeur folded the chair, stashed it in the trunk and got back behind the wheel.

Dix started his own car, watching for an opportune time to pull out into traffic. He let two cars go past before he had the chance, wheeling out of the parking space so quickly that his bumper tagged the car in front of him.

No occupant, no damage, he thought, smiling. And no witnesses, either. He'd have to make sure he repeated that scenario when he had his long-overdue interview with Laird.

The limousine was still visible farther down the block.

Dix didn't know whose limo it was, or how they tied

into this, but something told him he was well on the way to getting that leg-up that he needed.

———

Colby mulled over the interview as they drove out of the immense facility, a security vehicle following along behind them. Knox and Jetters were hiding something, but what? They were obviously not anxious to talk about the late John Norton, and this guy Krems. How it all fit together with Leslie's case, he had no idea. It piqued his interest, and any time something did that, he felt an almost irresistible urge to figure it out.

Colby's cell phone vibrated. Grabbing it off the clip on his belt, he flipped it open and saw that he had a voice message.

"This is Special Agent In Charge Pearson," the disembodied voice said. "I'm sending this out to all team members. It is imperative that you all return to the command center here at the federal building as soon as possible. I say again—"

Colby disconnected. Pearson sure loved the sound of his own voice.

Leslie hadn't said two words since they'd left, and he wondered if she was upset.

"Pearson wants me to return to base," he said, re-clipping his phone.

She turned and looked at him without speaking.

"Don't worry," he said. "I'm in no hurry. Let's proceed to talk to the coppers at Oakbrook Estates PD, and then grab something to eat."

"Are you sure you'll have time?"

"I'll make time."

"You don't care for Special Agent Pearson much, do you?"

Colby said nothing.

She canted her head. "Why were you so antagonistic with Jetters and Knox back there?"

"Antagonistic? Those two guys were hiding something. They weren't about to give up any information unless we pried it outta them."

"Still, I really wish you'd have let me handle it. I had some more questions I needed answered. After you interceded, they closed down completely."

He swallowed his snappy comeback. "Sorry. Force of habit, I guess. How about we split the difference and I'll promise to keep my big mouth shut during the interview with the police about Norton's deceased significant other?"

Her expression softened slightly. "Sorry for being snippy, but this is a very important case for me. My inspector sent me down here to cross all the T's, and dot all the I's because he doesn't think I can handle things back home."

"I know that feeling," he said. "My boss is an asshole, too."

That brought a smile to her lips. "I wouldn't really call mine an asshole. He just doesn't have a lot of faith in me. He even kind of likes to look out for me, in his own way."

"Count your blessings, then," he said. "And keep in mind that in a homicide investigation every lead has to be checked out, so they're all important. You never know what you're going to uncover that can lead you to something else."

She smiled. "Thanks. I appreciate the advice."

"Not a problem. And one thing's for sure. Those guys are hiding something." He glanced at his watch and wondered about the Laird interview. "Once you find out what, you may have a bigger piece of your puzzle than you thought."

———

"It was nothing more than a fishing expedition," Knox said, trying to keep his voice calm and low. "They have nothing to tie us to any of it."

The old man's face looked more lined than usual.

"How can you say that? They knew about you going up there. As *Krems*, at least…how are we going to explain that he doesn't really exist?" He took off his glasses and wiped at his forehead with a handkerchief. "And that business about Morgan Laird. It's only a matter of time before they connect Matthew to all this."

"You're jumping to conclusions," Knox said. He was beginning to wonder if it was time to expedite his little retirement plan. Still, he couldn't leave with all these complications hanging.

"We need to handle this," Jetters said. "Quickly, definitively, permanently."

It's just like that asshole to speak in absolutes, Knox thought. Like he was running one of his fucking experiments.

"What do you know about Laird's whereabouts?" Jetters asked.

"Not much. But I can find out."

Jetters nodded. "Find him." He looked off into space, his face suddenly sad, then replaced his glasses on his nose. "In the meantime, I've got to decide what to do about Matthew."

Knox said nothing. Jetter's "prodigal son" was a liability for both of them, but the old man would probably just keep the little psychopath locked up here for the rest of his life. "Anything I can do to help in that regard?"

Jetters shook his head.

"He's my responsibility. I'd always hoped that he'd be

a legacy of sorts, a testament to my work. One that I could be proud of."

Knox said nothing, but wondered again if Matthew had one of those "genetic triggers" he'd read about in Norton's files. A pre-programmed terminal defect that could be activated at a selected time. Handy thing to have, if you wanted absolute control over somebody.

"You want me to eliminate Laird?" Knox asked.

"That's certainly an option we have to consider. It wouldn't do to have him eventually associated with us in any way. What I need is to find out exactly what the police know, and then make my decisions." He looked up at Knox. "Can you handle that?"

"I can."

"And we'll have to figure out what to do should they come looking for this imaginary Krems person."

"Leave that to me," Knox said. "I'll see to it that he disappears. Permanently."

Along with me, at the right time, he thought.

———

Matthew had removed his undershirt, torn it in half, and woven the two pieces into a tightly knotted rope. Thin, but strong, with plenty of purchase for his hands when the time came. And it was almost here. From his vantage point inside the new room, he saw the elevator doors open and the two technicians pushed out the big cart with all the goodies. The pre-lunch meds, regular as clockwork.

Tranquilizers and candy bars. What more could a Blem ask for out of life?

They went immediately to his old room, just across the expanse of floor. He shifted his body to the side of the door-slot window, looking out with his right eye only, so as to be less noticeable.

Stealth mode.

They reached down and opened the door to his old room—his old cell, and called to what they thought was him.

"Matthew, time for your meds."

No reply. The Lorazepam had done its job. The Blem in his bed was down for the count, and then some.

"Matthew," one yelled. He moved inside the room, then rushed back saying, "Oh fuck!"

"What?" the other one said, pushing aside the goodies cart.

"He's foaming at the mouth. Turned all blue. The old man will kill us if anything happens to him."

"Shit."

"I'll start CPR. You do mouth-to-mouth."

The second technician recoiled. "Forget that."

The first one, obviously the more dedicated of the two, or maybe the most fearful, shook his head in frustration.

"Go down and get some help, then. I'll do it."

The first tech disappeared into the cell, while the second man rushed back toward the elevator. Matthew shifted again, watching as the guy placed his key in the silver hole, twisted it, and jumped inside the car as soon as the doors popped open.

When they closed, Matthew pushed open the jimmied door to his new cell and strode across the floor. The tech was leaning over the Blem, doing compressions on his chest, then bending over to blow air into the deflated lungs. Matthew stepped in behind him and looped the knotted T-shirt over the tech's head just as he rose up to begin the series of compressions again. With the long ends wrapped around his hands and the knotted section deftly catching the tech's Adam's apple, Matthew crisscrossed the lines and pulled back, twisting around so that his back slammed against the tech's as the man rose upward. Just like he'd seen demonstrated in the hand-to-hand combat tapes.

Matthew pulled down with all his strength, lifting the tech off the floor, all the while hearing that gurgling sound indicating the tech was struggling to catch his breath. Continuing to hold the position for what seemed like a small eternity, Matthew finally felt the tech go limp.

Exhausted, but exhilarated, Matthew turned and let the man's body fall to the floor. On the way down, the man's head banged into the tiles with a loud thud. Like a watermelon being dropped. A puddle of blood began to stream outward from a gash on the tech's head.

Excellent, thought Matthew. He quickly grabbed the tech's cap and placed it on his own head, then twirled the T-shirt around the cut. As he stripped off the man's clothes, taking time to do a quick feel of the pants' pockets, he grinned as he felt what appeared to be a wallet and a set of car keys along with another, larger ring of keys. Slipping on the pants and tech-shirt, he grimaced as he crammed his oversized foot into the too-small shoes.

What size did this guy wear?

But they would have to do.

He grabbed the tech under the arms and managed to flop the body onto the bed. After covering it with the blanket, he dragged the unconscious Blem out of the cell and dropped him. He then pushed the cart back over to the entranceway. Stepping on the shelves, he climbed up and managed to retain his balance long enough to grab the extended front lens of the surveillance camera. Twisting it upward, he adjusted the angle so that the only thing it would be showing now was the ceiling. Then he jumped back down. The cart tipped over, spilling its contents on the floor. Matthew stooped and crammed as many of the tranqs and chocolate bars as he could into his pockets, then grabbed another handful of the candy. Running past each room, he opened the doors to each one, waving before tossing the candy bars and yelling, "Candy! Candy!"

The Blems migrated out like a flock of hungry chickens, watching with interest as he tossed a few bars into the center of them. He mentally calculated how much longer he had, and decided he had to move fast. Scrutinizing the crowd of Blems, he picked one he thought still most resembled himself, and placed a hand on the Blem's shoulder, holding a new candy bar in front of the retard's face.

"Come," he said.

The Blem's eyes followed the candy bar, and he reached for it. Matthew drew it back, pulling the Blem along toward the room with the fallen tech. He dragged the Blem inside long enough to recover the blood-soaked T-shirt and pressed the bloody material up to the Blem's face. The creature whimpered.

Good, thought Matthew. This one's pretty docile. Good candidate for a transplant, should he ever need one.

Grinning, he let the Blem have the candy bar and pulled him toward the elevators. He fished in his pockets for the ring of keys and withdrew it. The special elevator key was long, narrow, and familiar. He knew which one it was from the days when the old man had made him work with the techs, feeding the retards to show him how fortunate he was.

The elevator doors slid open after he inserted the key, and he pushed the Blem inside.

As the elevator descended, Matthew twisted the

emergency stop switch and the descending car jerked to an abrupt halt. He had to time this just right. So the other tech, the one going after the medical response team, would be on the way up before the doors to his own elevator opened. A bell, the damn emergency stop signal, began ringing somewhere inside the shaft.

This won't work, he thought, switching the switch back to the off position. The car jerked, descended a few more feet, and stopped again. The doors opened a few seconds later. Matthew held the bloody T-shirt to the Blem's forehead, ignoring his moaning protests, and walked him out of the elevator. A security guard glanced at them.

"Better get up there," Matthew said, pulling the cap down closer to his eyebrows. "All hell's broken loose. I gotta get this one to the infirmary." He twisted the bloody head in the guard's direction.

"Shit," the guard said, lifting his radio. "We got a situation in D-Ward. Send backup."

Matthew yelled, "Good luck!" as he watched the guard jump into the elevator and punch the buttons several times. All the while, Matthew kept moving the Blem toward the doors. Pushing through into the bright sunshine, he wondered what time of the day it actually was.

Close to noon, maybe. The fresh air and sun felt odd after the protracted period of confinement he'd endured. Still, it was nothing compared to what Morgan had gone through. Matthew dragged the Blem down the sidewalk, toward the area where the employees parked their cars.

A group of security guards rushed by him, one scrutinizing the odd couple marching in the other direction.

"What happened?" one of the guards asked.

"A bunch of the Others escaped from D-Ward,"

Matthew said, pointing to the Blem. "Better hurry up. It's bad up there."

The guards quickened their pace and Matthew reached into his pocket for the tech's car keys. A GM model, from the look of them. The ring had a plastic remote attached and he punched it twice, hearing the responding beep. Repeating the movement several more times, Matthew finally saw the headlights of a Chevy Impala flash on and off, with an accompanying toot of the horn.

Perfect, he thought. He hit the trunk release button on the remote and saw the rear lid pop upward. Leading the Blem to the rear of the car, Matthew took out a candy bar and tossed it into the trunk. The Blem reached for it, but when Matthew tried to push him inside, the Blem gripped the sides in frantic resistance.

Dammit, this was not the time. Time was what he had so very little of at this juncture. He relaxed slightly, smiling and tossing another candy bar into the trunk area. The Blem still gripped the side of the car, frozen and unmoving.

Well then, Matthew thought as he reached inside the trunk and gripped the tire iron, you've brought this on yourself.

He bashed Blem's fingers first, causing him to lose his grip on the car. Then he swung the long metal rod against the retard's left temple and watched his legs sag. Matthew grabbed the Blem's fluttering legs and lifted him into the trunk. He slammed the lid shut, keeping the tire iron as he got into the car. He'd grown kind of fond of it.

The Impala started right up and he backed out of the parking spot and drove immediately toward the main gate. Even though he figured most of the security force would be heading over to quell the disturbance, he forced himself to drive with slow deliberation. There could still be a roving patrol. But he saw none as he approached the gate. Everybody was probably heading over to the disturbance in C-Ward. The guard, obviously intently listening to the gaggle on his radio, waved him through with a dismissive gesture.

Matthew lifted his hand in a wave, obscuring his face as much as he could. As he turned out onto Route 83 and accelerated to just a few miles over the speed limit, he allowed a long, slow breath to escape his lungs. He'd made it. And hopefully those idiots would be chasing shadows for a while before they even realized he was gone.

CHAPTER 11

The Oakbrook Estates detective, MacEllroy, tapped his pen on the case file on Peter Davids. "We sent a couple of guys to the house to do the death notification, as requested by you guys, but there was no response. One of the officers looked through the window and saw somebody lying on the floor." He shrugged. "They forced entry and found him. Deceased. Looked like he fell about ten, twelve feet from the upstairs balcony overlooking the living room."

"Were you able to determine how long he'd been dead?" Leslie asked.

MacEllroy shrugged again. "Couple days, maybe. There were several unlistened-to messages on the answering machine from his, un, partner Norton. We figured that Davids must've fallen while Norton was on his way up your way. We sent word back about the situation up to you guys."

"I got that," Leslie said.

Colby couldn't resist. "What are you guys calling it?"

"Accidental," MacEllroy said. "Looked pretty cut and dried. No signs of forced entry, other than what the officers did. The house is pretty elaborate. Two-story, with one of those winding staircases, marble floors, the whole nine yards. Looks like Davids slipped at the top and fell over the banister. Popped his head open on the solid floor and bled out. Broken neck, too."

"Had he been drinking?" Leslie asked.

"Open bottle of wine on the table."

"The ME do a blood-alcohol test?" Colby asked.

"Took some routine tissue samples. Results ain't back yet." MacEllroy paused and squinted. "I told yous, it was ruled an accidental. What's with all the twenty questions?"

Leslie and Colby exchanged glances, then she said, "Does it strike you as a bit strange that this man fell to his death and then his significant other was murdered shortly thereafter?"

MacEllroy considered this, then clicked his tongue and nodded. "Yeah, I suppose, but like I said, down here we had no reason to believe it was anything other than an accident. No proof, anyway. No forced entry, no signs that anything was tampered with, nothing missing. The doors had been secured with dead bolt locks, which indicated that they'd been locked from the inside."

"Perhaps they were opened with a key?" Leslie said.

MacEllroy flushed a bit. "To be on the safe side, we dusted the doors. No prints except the decedent's and Dr. Norton's."

He was going on the defensive now.

"Norton's prints were on file?" Colby asked.

"Yeah, he was listed in the FBI database. Some kind of government affiliation."

"He worked for the state prison system at some point too," Colby said, champing at the bit to take over the interview.

Leslie shot him a quick glance and he dummied up again.

"Did you know John Norton?" she asked.

"Yeah," MacEllroy said slowly. "He's been with the New Genesis Foundation for years. Before I started, even."

"Aside from what's on their website," Leslie said, "exactly what can you tell me about New Genesis?"

MacEllroy raised his eyebrows and shrugged. "They do a bunch of things. Government projects, medical research, lots of stuff. They're big donors to a lot of local charities and community functions too, including the PD. They bought all our officers new vests. Plus, they got a school and dormitory at the facility for, un, special kids." He paused. "You know, retarded. You got to admire a corporation that helps people in need like that. In fact, our former chief is now their head of security."

"His name Knox?" Colby asked.

MacEllroy's brow furrowed. "Knox? No, Hank Meister. He's in charge of the uniformed division. Knox, I think handles special corporate stuff."

"Mind if we nose around Norton's house?" Colby asked.

"Well," MacEllroy said slowly, "we officially closed the investigation, so it's no longer considered an active crime scene, but you'd have to get permission from the owner."

"And who might that be?" Leslie asked.

"New Genesis Corporation," MacEllroy said. "They own a lot of property around here, and let their important employees live in the various houses."

Colby glanced over at Leslie to gauge her reaction. She looked pensive.

"I guess we could go back and ask them," he said with a grin. "Maybe they'll give us a tour."

Knox surveyed the once pristine ward, now decorated with scattered blankets, pills, and torn candy wrappers. The rest of the techs, along with the security force, had rounded up the now sugar-buzzed Others and shoved them back into their rooms. The place was a collection of noises as the retarded idiots pounded on their doors and screamed creating an unintelligible dissonance.

Feeding time at the zoo, gone awry, he thought. No wonder Jetters kept them tranquilized all the time. Two security guards had loaded the dead tech onto a gurney along with the expired Other. His bluish color, along with the residual foam covering his mouth, told Knox all he had to know. Overdose.

At least he figured it was an Other. But then again, he'd heard that Matthew had gotten his hair buzzed, so it could be him. They were all virtually identical, in looks, anyway.

"I never dreamed he was capable of something like this," Jetters said, watching the gurneys move past him. He'd kept his voice low so only Knox could hear.

What did you expect? Knox thought. It's in his genes.

Jetters must have been thinking something similar because he leaned over and whispered again.

"We have to stop him. Before something gets traced back here."

"How sure are you *that* isn't him?" Knox asked, gesturing toward the Other on the second gurney.

The old man looked close to cracking, but he reverted to his professorial tone.

"I won't know for sure, of course, until I've scanned all their chips. But my guess is that it's not. Plus, we're missing two, and this escape showed high intelligence and planning." He took off his glasses and mopped his face. If it had been under other circumstances, Knox would have enjoyed seeing the old bastard sweat. "Still, as a man of science, I must never assume. I have to deal in facts. Empirical evidence."

Save yourself the trouble, Knox thought. He too, was sure the body on the gurney was just one of the many identical Matthew rejects. A formerly sentient mass of protoplasm that nobody really cared about. Too bad he hadn't figured out how to place a transmitter in Matthew's microchip. It would make finding him easier.

He watched as the elevator doors closed. The dead tech, on the other hand, presented a different set of problems. He had a life outside of here that had to be closed off now. All the bases had to be covered.

"I'll need the personnel file on the dead tech," Knox said.

"They're getting it now. We'll have to notify his family, of course. Say it was an unfortunate accident... offer them a substantial monetary settlement." He stroked his chin several times. "Perhaps we can say his neck got caught in the pulley system on the dumbwaiter." He pondered this, then nodded. "Yes, we'll say he was trying to loosen a snag. Tragic accident, tragic."

Knox didn't care about that. He knew his window for catching up with Matthew was rapidly closing. He'd need to trace the dead tech's credit cards in case the kid tried to use them. They'd taken all of Matthew's money and personal identification when Knox had brought him back two days ago, but he knew Matthew was smart enough to use the tech's cards to get some operating cash.

"Have Meister make the notification," Knox said. "I need to start tracing our prodigal son as soon as possible."

Jetters squinted. "Meister? Is that wise?"

Knox shrugged. "He is the official head of security.

Who better to break the news to any family members about the terrible accident? Besides, he's had plenty of experience delivering bad news."

Jetters considered this for a moment, then went to a nearby guard.

"Where's Chief Meister?" he asked.

The guard, a middle-aged flunky type, twisted his heavyset body and mumbled something unintelligible into his radio. After an equally indecipherable reply, he said, "He's on the way, Professor."

Jetters frowned and pulled out a cell phone. He flipped it open and pressed a few buttons. "Chief, are you there?"

The phone chirped, and the reply came. "I'm on the way in now, sir."

"Good. There's been a terrible accident. Report to my office as soon as you arrive."

After a few moments, the phone chirped again. "Have the police been summoned yet?"

Jetters's mouth twisted into a frown. "No. No police. This was an unfortunate accident. Nothing more."

"But, sir, we still need to—"

"We need to do nothing but notify the family that there's been an accident. A very unfortunate accident." He enunciated each of the last four words. "Is that understood?"

A moment of silence was followed by an almost inaudible, "Yes, sir."

Bought and paid for, Knox thought. Guess it helps to know who signs your checks.

They'd hired Meister on as a figurehead security chief about a year ago, luring him from his job at the police department with a lucrative offer he would have been a fool to turn down. Now he was finally going to see how much of his soul he'd traded in the process.

"I'll be reviewing that file," Knox said, as he started for the elevators.

"Wait," Jetters called after him.

Knox paused.

Jetters came up close and grabbed him by the arm. His breath was hot and stale as he said, "Take care of that Laird business. I can't have that old cretin being associated with New Genesis."

Knox nodded. He reached out and placed his key in the slot to summon the elevator.

"And then make it your next priority to find Matthew," Jetters said.

The elevator opened and Knox stepped inside. His last vision of the devastated ward was obscured by Jetters, who framed himself between the doors.

"Remember," he said. "No loose ends."

———

Dix had been slouching down in his car so long his legs were starting to cramp up. The limo was still sitting there by the curb in front of the federal building, idling.

Shit, Dix thought. The damn chauffeur probably has a wet bar in that thing.

It was going on two hours, and his only diversion was getting out periodically to feed the meter with his credit card, which the limo driver hadn't even bothered with. Of course, it had livery plates on it.

That's the kind of ride I want hauling me around once I crack this one, Dix thought, leaning back in the seat. He started to fantasize about the shape of things to come, among them, Carmel Washington.

I'll play her body like a Stradivarius, he thought. Then a pair of pedestrians, a man and a pretty woman, caught his eye.

171

It was Colby, that son of a bitch, with some nice looking broad. They were walking and talking, the girl's head tossing back, all laughter and smiles.

The guy was slick, he'd give him that. But why wasn't he working the case like he should be? Dix made a mental note to call him that night and give him the old lecture about keeping his mind on the game, not pussy.

He smiled to himself.

Just like me, thinking about Carmel, he thought. But then again, it takes one to know one.

———

As they were stepping out of the elevator, Colby saw Pearson holding the door of the main office open for some guy in a wheelchair and some other, gray-haired mope in a three-piece suit. It took a moment before Colby realized who they were, but when he did, he grinned.

"Hey, Morgan. How you doing?" He waited until the seated man's head swiveled in his direction. "Good to see you up and around."

The man in the wheelchair looked gaunt, his once dark hair, now a wispy silver, thinning at the crown. A plastic tube was hooked into his nostrils, fanning outward and looking like some grotesque image of a mustache. As soon as the recognition dawned, he smiled.

"Yeah, no thanks to you." His voice was weak as he looked. Rusty sounding, as if from disuse.

Colby snapped his fingers. "I knew I shoulda aimed higher."

The other guy in the suit held himself more erect. It didn't work. Colby still towered over him.

"Fontaine," Colby said, nodding. "Caught any ambulances lately?"

The lawyer bristled and turned back to Pearson. "This

is exactly the type of inappropriate conduct I warned you about. We are not going to stand for it."

"Well, hell," Colby said. "Just tell us what type you want, and we'll be glad to accommodate you."

"Detective—" Pearson's quavering voice started to say.

But Fontaine cut him off, thrusting his index finger toward Colby's face. "I'm giving you fair warning. Any more harassment of my client, of any kind, and your head will roll. *Your head will roll!*"

Colby watched him for a few seconds, saying nothing.

The finger wobbled again in front of Colby's nose. "Am I making myself clear?"

"Perfectly," Colby said. "Now get your finger outta my face before I break it off and shove it up your ass."

"Detective," Pearson said again, a bit more forcefully this time.

"What's your badge number?" Fontaine demanded. "I'm going to have a conversation with your commanding officer."

"Yeah?" Colby said, continuing to ignore Pearson as the dialogue between him and the lawyer escalated. He knew he should stop, back off, but something about seeing Laird again, in conjunction with everything else going on, didn't make sensible behavior an option. "Why don't you stop by the ACLU's office first and complain to them about the First Amendment? It allows me to call an asshole an asshole."

Fontaine took a deep breath, but Laird reached up and put a hand on the lawyer's forearm.

"Aww, please." His eyes looked rheumy and tired, his color like death warmed over. "I gotta get outta here. I ain't feeling so good."

"Maybe there's some justice after all," Colby said.

Laird turned his gaze back to Colby. "You think you

can get a rise outta me, after all I been through?" He shook his head and gave a short, chopping laugh. His lungs sounded like they were filling with water. "Ain't gonna happen. Come on, let's go."

Fontaine bit his lower lip but remained silent as he pushed the wheelchair toward the elevators. When they stopped, Laird turned in his chair and looked back.

"How's your book doing?" he asked.

"Great," Colby said.

Laird smirked. "Maybe I'll write one to tell how it really happened."

This seemed to give Fontaine inspiration. His head swiveled around and he raised his hand in another pointing gesture.

"Believe me, you'll be hearing from us about that book," he said. "Consider this the pre-warning of an upcoming defamation suit."

Colby nodded. He glanced at Pearson, whose mouth had twisted into a sullen frown.

The elevator doors opened and the lawyer started to push Laird inside.

"Cheer up, guys," Colby called. "I heard Hell's only half full."

———

Matthew could hear the damn Blem screaming and pounding on the trunk lid as he drove. It was only a matter of time before someone else heard it too, and called the cops. With all the damn cell phones out there, his escape could be over before it began. And he couldn't afford to let that happen. Not when he was this close to the finish line.

Considering his options, he looked for a secluded stretch of road. He wasn't ready to terminate the Blem yet. No, he needed the creature alive for the time being. But manageable. The answer came to him as he reached into his pocket and pulled out a candy bar and a handful of tranqs. He decided that three pills would probably put the Blem down, but not permanently.

He took a right at the next intersection and when the traffic around him had subsided, he pulled onto the shoulder and parked. The moaning and pounding were more noticeable now.

Did the idiot think he could actually get out?

After a quick look around, Matthew pressed the three pills into the soft chocolate and then slipped the key into the trunk lock, raising the lid.

The Blem's face twisted into a mask of terror and he raised his arms, afraid of getting beaten.

Instead, Matthew smiled and held out the candy bar, wiggling it slightly.

The Blem's eyes opened wider, and he moved his head fractionally, in a questioning gesture.

"Sure, it's for you, buddy," Matthew said. He wiggled the bar up and down again. "Take it."

Matthew held the candy steady. The Blem grabbed it and shoved it into his mouth. It would take about fifteen minutes before the tranqs kicked in, so he'd have to stick to the back roads until the whimpering stopped. Matthew pushed the Blem back into the trunk, gently at first, but then with more vigor as the creature tried to resist. Balling up his fist, Matthew cocked his arm back. The Blem recoiled in fear, and Matthew slammed the lid down, noticing at the last moment that a pair of the Blem's fingers had gotten in the way. They withdrew just as quickly, accompanied by a howl of pain.

Chuckling, Matthew re-slammed the trunk lid, this time making sure it caught.

That'll teach him, he thought.

CHAPTER 12

Pearson's scowl told Colby he was in deep shit as they walked inside the main office. The FBI man halted in the hallway and turned. His face had a flushed look as he stared first at Colby, and then at Leslie.

"Detective Labyorteaux," he said, "I received a call from your superior. You're to contact him right away."

She nodded and he directed her to a nearby desk. Then he turned back to Colby.

"My office," he said.

Colby mulled over his options. He could tell Pearson to kiss his ass, and get permanently kicked off the task force, if he wasn't already. That would go over like a lead balloon with Kropper, not to mention Mannion. Or, he could just throw himself on the FBI man's mercy, claiming that he knew he was wrong, but the sight of freed, serial killer Laird and his asshole attorney had been too much for him. Pearson liked to talk, and he liked to assert his authority. Maybe if he felt he had Colby kowtowed that would be enough.

After deciding that was the best, or more like the only, course, he tried a preemptive move.

"Look," he said once they were in Pearson's office. "I'm sorry I blew my top back there. I know it was wrong."

Pearson's eyebrows rose. "Oh? Is that so?"

Feeling like a delinquent youth in the principal's office, Colby clamped his mouth shut, silently reminding himself that this guy had no real authority over him.

"What do you think your superiors will say when I tell them how you practically ruined the case we've been building so carefully?"

Colby said nothing.

Pearson glared at him. "You practically told Mr. Fontaine to go F himself."

Colby looked down. "I was sorta hoping you'd keep it between us."

"Between us?"

Colby nodded.

Pearson's head began bobbling up and down, like one of those artificial dogs on a car's dashboard. He was obviously winding himself up.

"You have no conception of what you almost did there, do you?" he asked.

Almost did? That didn't sound too bad.

Colby shook his head, still focusing his gaze at the floor.

"We asked Laird, and his attorney, to come in today for an interview for a specific reason," Pearson said. His enunciation was exact. Like he was explaining the Pythagorean Theorem to a fourth grader. He sighed. "Did you get my message to report in immediately?"

Colby nodded.

Pearson exhaled again. "There's been a significant development. One that could break this case wide open."

The fed seemed to have expelled most of his anger.

"You going to tell me about it?" Colby asked.

"I have a meeting planned for three p.m., at which time I'm going to brief the entire team." His eyes caught Colby's. "You know, I have the greatest respect for you as an investigator, but you have to learn to exercise restraint."

Colby nodded again.

"As you may know," Pearson continued, "we have a very sophisticated forensics lab in the Chicagoland region. I was able to pull some strings. They shelved all their other lab work in favor of evaluating the evidentiary samples I've given them regarding this case."

Colby's excitement was beginning to grow. This could be the game point.

"The cigarette butt from the Kelly Turner crime scene," Pearson said. "It was a Pall Mall cigarette, the same brand as in the original crime, placed in the exact same place as in the original. And..." Pearson paused and let a smile creep over his lips. "It came back with a positive match for Morgan Laird."

Colby was in momentary shock. This was too good to be true. Almost.

"When did you find this out?"

"About an hour ago. I then sent out the message."

"I'm assuming Laird and his lawyer don't know this yet?"

Pearson nodded. "You got a look at him today. He's physically incapable of carrying out these crimes."

"But it still places him at the scene. He's got someone helping him."

"Or it could have been planted there."

"Planted?"

"It's unlikely, but we have to consider it." Pearson began lapsing into his lecture mode again. "If, in fact, he is working in concert with someone. A younger, stronger person who's following his directions, it could also explain how a confederate would have such in-depth knowledge of the crime scenes."

Colby doubted Laird would have such clear recall, but he said nothing.

Pearson flashed a self-satisfied smile. "That's one of the reasons we asked Laird to come in for the interview, with his attorney present. To make it seem routine to ask about his whereabouts. Naturally, they don't know the extent of our DNA findings."

Something gnawed at Colby.

"Laird may not be a Rhodes Scholar, but he must know about DNA. Why would he leave such an obvious piece of evidence?"

Pearson shrugged. "Perhaps he isn't as aware of our technological advances as you may think."

Bullshit, Colby thought. But what he said was, "How certain are you about the results?"

"Well, there is one more conclusive test that has to be completed. It was an exact match for the monochromic test. The nuclear DNA results should be available shortly. But as of now, we're confident that it's a high percentage probability's match for Laird." Pearson's jaw twitched slightly. "Unless he has an identical twin brother no one knows about."

"What's our plan?"

Pearson moved forward, tenting his fingers. "We've placed him under surveillance. Our interview got him locked into a statement of his recent whereabouts during some of the crimes. What we need to do now is backtrack and see how many holes we can punch in it. Once we have that done, and the final test result, we should be able to tie this one up with a nice ribbon."

It took Leslie several minutes of waiting on hold until she finally heard Graven's gruff voice come on the line. When she identified herself, his tone softened fractionally.

"How's things south of the forty-eighth, luv?"

"Not bad," she said. "They're very helpful down here."

She heard a low murmur, then he said, "Good, good. Where are you at in the investigation?"

She gave him a quick update, including her suspicions that something didn't seem quite right at New Genesis Corporation and the coincidental death of Norton's partner.

She heard him sigh and could almost picture the classic eye-rubbing gesture that usually accompanied it. That normally meant bad news was imminent. "Let's leave that investigation to the appropriate authorities, shall we? One of our informants gave us a possible lead. Local punk who was bragging about stabbing some guy with a knife."

It figured. She was down here, a thousand miles away, and the real detectives almost had the case solved back home. "Anybody I'd know?"

"I don't think so, luv. Name's Willis Campbell. Got a nice long record of arrests for everything from pissing on the sidewalk to shoplifting."

"Nothing violent?"

"No, but he might be trying to move into the big leagues." He paused, then added, "We're sweating him now."

Oh great, she thought. They didn't even wait for me to call with my update. She couldn't bring herself to say anything, so his voice filled the empty silence.

"You still there, luv?"

"Yes," she managed to say, clearing her throat. "You want me to come back?"

"Nah, stay down there and finish what you started. We'll need to show we covered all the bases on this one." She heard his deep chuckle. "See some of the sights if you have time. I've always wanted to visit Chicago myself."

"You'll let me know how the interview goes, right?"

"Of course, luv," she heard his distant voice say. "You're part of the team. Maybe the next time we speak, we'll have this one all wrapped up and ready to go."

———

Matthew waited until the whimpering and pounding in the trunk had completely subsided before he started driving around looking for places with automated teller machines. His first stop was at a jewelry store in a strip mall. Desmond Kirby, the dead tech, had about fifty dollars cash in his wallet, but he'd been stupid enough to write his PIN on the top of his ATM card. It was just a matter of hitting several of these machines and doing the maximum withdrawals each time. Matthew didn't even worry about the built-in camera systems. He had the perfect, identical twin fall guy in the trunk.

The lights of another strip mall shone up ahead in the dwindling afternoon light. There were several smaller shops and a grocery store. A fast-food joint too. He was getting hungry, and he probably should get something for his rider in the trunk, when he woke up, of course.

But first I'd better drain the Kirby account, he thought with a smile. After all, time is money, and he was running short of both. A shiver went up and down his spine, like he was on the verge of coming. This proved that he was smarter than all of them. Smarter even than Jetters, his surrogate father, whose perverse manipulation had caused all this.

But that's what he gets for trying to play God, Matthew thought.

He took a deep breath. Everything up to today, before his exquisite escape, had been more or less scripted. Sure, he'd done it all with a panache that Morgan would be proud of, but he'd still been following the set script of Morgan's old crimes. The escape today, on the other hand, had been all him, his own ingenuity...the plan, the execution, everything. It'd been more intense, too. Way more. He felt a thrill, an almost sexual pleasure as he remembered the strangulation. The adrenaline coursing through him, his heart pumping, all of it. Intense, vivid, invigorating.

After finding a parking spot near the doors, he surveyed the lot. If he was going to keep the Kirby car, he'd better get some new plates. This lot didn't look crowded enough. He'd be too conspicuous ripping off someone's plates. One thing he didn't need was to attract the attention of some cops. Better to wait. More than likely, the car wouldn't be reported stolen right away. The old man wouldn't dare go to the cops.

Matthew exited the car as gently as he could. No sense waking Sleeping Beauty. The electronic doors slid open at his approach, making him feel almost regal. And why not? He was back in the game.

The ATM was located near the front entrance, allowing people quick and private access before they went shopping. Matthew punched in the PIN, wondering how much longer before this cornucopia would dry up. He had to factor in the possibility, albeit remote, that they'd cancel the card. But that would mean reporting the guy's death, and he figured the old man would try to cover that up. They'd probably notify the widow that her husband died in some kind of freak accident.

The bills slid down into the slot in front of him. He

pocketed the money and headed back to the car, whistling as he walked.

A cover-up. That's how they operated. That's what they did best.

But soon, very soon, all that would be changing. He patted the silent trunk and smiled.

———

Knox looked up and caught a hazy reflection of himself in his car window, the settling dusk making it almost mirror-like. But it was an incomplete image, a vague suggestion instead of a crisp reflection. Much like his quest. Figuring that Matthew would be shrewd enough to use the resources he had at his disposal, Knox immediately went to the personnel records and found where Desmond Kirby's direct deposit checks went. After that, a series of quick phone calls later, he had the location of the corporate security office of the bank. Luckily, it was in an office complex in nearby. The building was only one-story with the front being composed of a wall of glass windows.

Nice for the employees, but unfortunately, it was also an easy mark for someone with an interceptor-cone scanner and a laptop. He set up about fifty feet away and put the scanner on his dashboard. In no time he'd intercepted enough internet signals from the high-speed broadcasters to tap into the bank's security records. From there, it was only a hop, skip, and a jump into monitoring the recent activity on Kirby's ATM card.

The pattern of recent withdrawals was obvious, and when the list first popped up on the screen, he realized he might be too late. Matthew had been a busy boy. Knox scanned the list of figures, quickly adding them up in his head. Ten stops so far, at three hundred bucks each. The kid had some walking-around money. The list of locations indicated he was moving toward the city. Back to his apartment?

Where else could he go? He needed operating money, and now he had that. But he also needed his IDs, a change of clothes, and another car. He had to be going home.

Knox glanced at his watch: four-twenty. With the rush hour in full effect, he had at least two hours before it began to fade. He might be able to make it over to Matthew's apartment on an intercept course. But then again, even if he didn't, he still had the GPS transmitter that he'd hidden on the Corvette. Why not let him get there, settle into his own car, and then track the little fucker down? Plus, Jetters had instructed him to get rid of Laird too.

Knox stared again at the screen. Another cash advance popped up, showing a jewelry store in Bridgeview. The direction of travel was unmistakable. Knox decided to go for the intercept and the quick ending. Should be a simple enough matter of setting the trap, then waiting.

His cell phone rang, jarring him out of his reverie. He picked it up and heard the old man's frantic voice on the other end.

"He did it. That son of a bitch did it."

"Did what?" Knox asked. "Who are you talking about?"

"Those two cops," Jetters hissed out the last syllable. "Dirkenstein just told me they faxed him a copy of a federal subpoena for Norton's records concerning Morgan Laird. And for Vernon Krems's address and personal information."

Knox let out a slow breath. This was an inconvenient

complication, nothing more, yet it was coming at a time when he least needed it.

"What are we going to do?" Jetters asked. His voice sounded brittle, on the verge of cracking.

"First, we don't panic."

"Panic? How dare you say that to me? You've made a royal mess out of this entire situation."

Knox could picture the old man's face reddening, and he was glad this conversation was over the phone so he was spared the old bastard's hot breath in his face. "Can we fight the subpoena? Get it quashed?"

"And look even more like we're hiding something?"

Knox couldn't resist. "Aren't we?"

"Don't be crass."

Knox heard the old man's rapid breathing in the receiver. At this rate he'd be ready for that new heart sooner rather than later.

"I'll take care of it."

"You'd better." Jetters emphasized each word. "What are you doing?"

"Closing in," he said, keeping things vague. "It shouldn't be long now."

"Laird?"

"I've got a meeting with his lawyer in a bit," Knox said, trying to sound reassuring. "I'm not too far from his office."

"The lawyer. No telling what he knows. Remember, I don't want any loose ends."

Knox repeated he would take care of it but suddenly found himself listening to a click and then silence.

The old bastard had hung up on him.

He replaced the phone in his pocket with slow deliberation, then dropped the Taser on the seat.

He left the laptop on the console and went to the trunk.

After pulling aside the ersatz leather lining at the right rear fender, he leaned over and pulled open a small metallic door that, for all appearances, looked like a storage compartment. The small safe had been set into the fender wall behind it, and Knox punched in his passcode. Four red lights glowed on top of the door, and it popped open.

The area inside was more spacious than it looked. Knox removed a plastic case that held something about the size of a hardbound book. Through the blue translucence, it looked to be a rather thick computer reference manual. Knox shut the door of the safe and recoded the security combination. He handled the case gingerly as he walked back to the driver's seat and shut the door. Setting the item on his lap, he glanced out the windows to make sure no one was watching him. His hands slid into his pockets, and he slipped on the thin, black leather gloves before sliding the computer book from the blue transparency. He opened the book to the cut-out pages and ran his gloved fingers over the Beretta 9mm semi-automatic pistol that reposed there. Hefting it, Knox racked the slide back and locked it in place. He reached into the book again and withdrew the long, circular silencer and screwed it onto the end of the barrel.

CHAPTER 13

As Colby stepped out of the shower, he marveled at the quick response the feds had gotten on the subpoena for New Genesis. Pearson had been obliging about that, at least.

Of course he'd probably only did it to impress Leslie.

He dried off and thought about how perfectly everything had fallen into place: Laird leaving DNA at the scene of a copycat murder, him being allowed to stay on the case despite blowing his top at Fontaine—that had been worth almost any price, Pearson agreeing to get the subpoena for Leslie...she'd seemed so deflated after she'd talked to her boss.

"It looks like they have it just about wrapped up," she'd said. "Nothing for me to do but spin my wheels down here."

"Then why not let me show you a little bit of Chicago tonight?" he said. It had been spontaneous. Her shocked look gave way to one of those demure, lips-only smiles that she did so well. "I can show you Ontario Street."

"I think," she said, "I'd like that very much."

After wrapping the towel around his waist, Colby ran

a comb through his hair, using a hair-drier to hurry the process up. With his hair sufficiently fluffed, he grabbed the deodorant and was just about to apply it when the phone rang.

Leslie calling to cancel?

He stubbed his bare toe on the molding rushing to the other room. Barely controlling his anger and pain, he glanced at the caller ID and saw it was a cellular call with a local area code. He answered with a growl.

"That any way to answer the phone?" It was Dix.

"This better be good," Colby said. "And quick. I got a date."

"Oh? With who?"

"None of your business."

"Oh, must be that good-looking babe you were walking with outside the federal building."

"How the hell did you know that?"

Dix's laugh echoed in the receiver.

"Relax, buddy-boy. I used to be a detective, remember?"

"You didn't answer my question. You been spying on me?"

Dix laughed again, with a trace of nervousness. It was covered well, but Colby noticed it. His old partner wasn't the only detective.

"I was downtown looking for you," Dix said. "I was getting ready to call you for a meet, when who do you think I spotted?"

"I give up."

More laughter. A bit more self-assured.

"Our old buddy Morgan Laird. He was in a wheel-chair getting into a limo. That shitbird Fontaine was with him."

"Yeah," Colby said, not wanting to mention the DNA discovery. "They were guests of the bureau today. Served them milk and cookies, like good little Boy Scouts, and powdered their asses before they left."

"Just remember what I always told ya," Dix said. "The only difference between the feds and the Boy Scouts is that the Scouts have adult supervision."

Colby glanced at the clock. It was almost six thirty. If he wanted to get some flowers and get down to her hotel relatively soon, he'd better get moving.

"Look, Dix, like I said, I got a date."

"Yeah, you did say. You gonna tell me about her?"

Colby sighed. What could it hurt? Maybe the old guy was getting some vicarious thrill, or something. "She's Canadian. A copper from Toronto PD."

"You know what I always told you about cops dating cops."

"I thought you were talking about male cops," Colby shot back. "Anyway, I got to scoot."

"Just give me a quick update on the case." Dix's voice had gone from salacious to imploring. When Colby didn't answer, he added, "Come on, Rog. I'm really interested in this one. We worked it together in the old days, didn't we?"

"Yeah, we did."

"Then just give me a head's up. Come on, for old times' sake."

Colby thought about it, then figured what the hell. He'd throw him a bread crumb, and it would probably satisfy him. "Can't really say too much, but it looks like looks like a cigarette butt with our old buddy's DNA might be tied into the new murders."

"No shit?" Dix's voice sounded renewed.

"He definitely knows something. He's not in it alone, that's for sure, but he's mixed up in things."

"Say, maybe I oughta go try and talk to him," Dix said. "Maybe he'd open up to me."

"Stay away from him. The feds have a surveillance team on his place. He'll fuck up, and when he does, they'll nail him."

"*They'll* nail him? What kind of an attitude is that? In the old days you'd have been chomping at the bit to take him down, even if we had to sit out there round the clock."

"It's *champing*," Colby said. "Now promise me you won't go trying to nose around Laird. The feds got all the bases covered."

"The feds," Dix said, the derision obvious in his voice.

"Dix."

"All right, all right, I promise." His voice got jovial again. "Now go on your date and don't eat too much."

Colby heard the line go dead.

Same old Dix, he thought. Always figuring he could take a few steps over the edge and not fall off.

———

Knox had done a Google search on the phone number listed for M. Laird in the lexicon of Lance Fontaine's cell phone. The address had popped up in a matter of seconds. And the GPS system he had in his BMW made finding the run-down flophouse where Laird stayed as easy as one, two, three.

God bless modern technology, he thought, smiling as he circled the block and decided on a safe parking spot on the next block down.

He smiled again as he got out of the car, remembering how smoothly things had gone with the esteemed counselor. The greedy prick had been eager to meet after Knox's phone call. All it took was a vague claim that he had information for sale regarding the police trying to set Morgan Laird up by manufacturing evidence.

"I'm all ears," Fontaine had said.

"Give me your cell number and go outside your office building. I wanna make sure you're alone, then I'll call you and tell you where we'll meet."

The greedy bastard fell for it, seeing dollar signs, no doubt. He was thinking lawsuit—official misconduct. A big-time suit against the G.

What he got instead, after Knox lured him into a multi-level parking area at the nearby shopping center, was a couple of jacketed hollow points. Fontaine was driving a Jaguar with tinted windows. Once inside the Jag, Knox took out the Beretta and began his little interrogation. The first shot hit Fontaine in the right thigh. With the sound suppressor attached, it made a subdued, plinking sound.

The lawyer's eyes widened as he cupped both his hands over the spreading stain on his gray trousers.

"I'll take these," Knox said, reaching over to grab the keys from the ignition.

Fontaine tried to open the driver's door and flee, so Knox shot him again in the upper ass.

"Where's Morgan Laird living at these days?" he asked, reaching up and pulling the lawyer's upturned face back toward him. Knox was wearing his tight leather gloves. The ones he loved to work in.

"Don't kill me," Fontaine grunted.

"Morgan Laird," Knox repeated.

Fontaine rattled off an address. "Please. I'll give you money, anything you want."

Knox glanced at the lawyer's cell phone and picked it up from the console between the seats. Pressing a few of the buttons, he came to *Call Contacts* and scrolled down until he saw *MLaird*.

"This his number?" Knox asked.

"Whose?" Fontaine's voice was a sharp grunt.

"Laird's."

"Yes."

"Good," Knox said, pocketing the lawyer's cell phone and bringing the barrel of the silencer up to Fontaine's right temple. "Then this will be all I need."

The Beretta made the plinking sound again.

Dix slipped his cell phone back into his pocket and stretched out as best he could in the cramped car. In the old days, this stuff hadn't bothered him. He could sit all day and all night watching if he had to. But then he'd had Colby with him. Four eyes instead of just his two. He sighed and watched the dumb feds sitting down the block. At least he figured them for feds. Dark suits in a standard black, four-door Ford. Could they be any more obvious?

They were so busy chatting on their phones that he was somebody could slip past them. Maybe they had another team watching the back. The flophouse obviously had more than one door in and out. But these guys were amateurs.

Dix curled his fingers around his binoculars and studied a lean, lanky guy with a ponytail, a set of chin-whiskers, and a gray trench coat going in the front of Laird's building. The guy stopped and eyed something, then trotted inside. Part of the surveillance team going for an inside look-see? Not with that ponytail. Probably one of the shitbird tenants.

The two *federales* paid no attention. They were probably focused on watching for a man in a wheelchair, so they were blissfully ignoring everyone else.

Time to take the bull by the horns, Dix thought, and stuck the binocs in the glove box. He felt his hip for the comfort of his old .38 snub nose, popped open the door, and got out, pulling his shirt tails out of his pants. Ruffling his hair lightly, to give it a disheveled look, he made sure his rug was still in place and began ambling down the block toward the flophouse.

Out of the corner of his eye, he watched the feds as he stumbled past their car. One was reading a magazine while the other chatted on a cell phone, occasionally looking in the direction of the front doors.

Hell, he thought. This is gonna be even easier than I thought.

———

Matthew had enough money to proceed with his plan, but he still needed his notes, not to mention a change of clothes. Wearing a dead man's shirt and pants didn't bother him as much as the way the garments fit. Too big in the waist, too small in the shoulders. The stupid prick had deserved exactly what he got, though. Trying to do CPR on the Blem... What a chump.

Matthew needed to get back into his apartment. Get his own car back too. Maybe put it somewhere where he'd have access to it once the plan was complete. Someplace Knox wouldn't find it.

Knox.

The name sent a momentary flash of panic through him. Perhaps they'd towed his car back to New Genesis? But that might attract unwanted attention. They'd obviously been holding him to find out what he'd been up to. As usual, the old man's primary concern was preventing bad publicity for his fiefdom.

Just wait. The old bastard would get that, and more. Way more. In spades.

He smiled at the word choice. Him, the ultimate

bastard, calling anybody else by that name. It was ludicrous, hypocritical. But soon, very soon, his surrogate father's elaborate house of cards would come crashing down and everyone would know the truth.

————

Inside the front door, Dix paused to tuck his shirt back in his pants. Looking like a bum to get past some lazy feds was one thing. Going to interview a suspect looking sloppy was another.

The guy who looks sharp, feels sharp, Dix thought. But the fatigue and frustration of the long day were starting to wear him down. Still, the tidbit that Colby had given him had been enough to plant the seed. If he could get Laird to open up, to talk to him, then maybe, just maybe, he could do an end-run around the rest of them. He imagined the feds coming to him, begging for his help.

The small hallway opened into another room that was completely deserted. A worn-out couch and a couple of equally shitty looking chairs were in the center of the floor to try to make the place look like a half-assed lobby. Beyond it, rows of cheap wooden doors lined a hallway.

Next to the door, a twin series of buttons, resembling doorbells, and a speaker graced the wall. A few of the buzzers had hand-printed slips of paper next to them with last names written in. Dix scanned the list. No Laird. Another hand-printed sign on the top button taped to it saying: *Super—Ring for Service*. Dix pressed it and heard the corresponding chimes inside the door closest to the dilapidated foyer. The floor was covered with a putrid-looking carpet, threadbare in so many places that it actually had a worn path leading to a payphone mounted on the wall. The rest of it showed the remnants of more than just a few seasons. Dix went to the windows and peered out through a grayish film. The darkening sky made it impossible to see anything. He waited a few more minutes, just to satisfy himself that no one from the surveillance team was going to do a walk-through.

Fat chance of that, he thought, mentally chastising the new breed of copper who'd rather sit in his car instead of pounding the pavement tracking down leads.

Dix smiled at his reflection in the dirty windowpane. Time to resurrect his old, confident persona. Reaching in his pocket, he fingered the badge case, hoping the super would be too drunk or too disinterested to notice the "Retired" stamped beneath the seal. He placed his index finger over it, obscuring the letters and did a few practice draws, whipping the badge case out as he walked, striving for the appearance of nonchalance.

When he got to the door, he ignored the buzzer and pounded hard on the flimsy wood. A voice inside gave a garbled yell that sounded something like, "Whaddaya want?"

Dix gave another series of heavy knocks, watching the door buckle slightly.

He heard another yell, then the sound of footsteps. The door whipped open displaying a round face, flushed red and covered with a crop of stubble. The guy was White, middle-aged, and probably looked a good ten years older than he actually was.

"What?" he said, small bunches of spittle gathering at the corners of his mouth. His big gut stretched the fabric of a soiled T-shirt and sagged down over a pair of filthy blue jeans. Behind the guy, Dix could see an open pizza box on a TV tray in front of a flat-screen television playing a porno flick.

"Police," Dix said, holding up the badge. He dropped

his hand just as the guy's eyes began to narrow. "What room's Morgan Laird in?"

"What, the right hand don't know what the left one's doing?" the guy asked. "I told the other guy, he's in number eleven."

Dix squinted at the guy. "Other guy?"

"Yeah, he was just in here a couple of minutes ago. Said he had a message from Laird's lawyer."

Shit, thought Dix. I'm a day late and a dollar short. "What did he look like?"

The super shrugged. "I dunno. Like somebody ringing my buzzer. At least he had the courtesy to use the intercom over there instead of disturbing me by pounding on my door." He pointed to the panel with the speaker beside the rows of buttons.

Dix frowned. "He still here?"

"Can't say. Been busy."

"So I see," Dix said, grinning, looking at the room beyond the guy's sagging gut. "Why don't you go call Mr. Laird and see if he's alone?"

"Why should I?"

Dix held up a ten. "Let's just say Mr. Hamilton would appreciate it."

A venal glint flashed in the super's eyes and he reached for the bill.

Dix moved it back out of the guy's reach. "First, the call."

The super frowned and walked back inside the room. Dix watched him through the open door, straining to listen as the guy picked up the phone and dialed.

"Yeah, this is the super. You alone?" The guy paused, cocked his head back, and said, "Because I got a fucking cop down here asking, that's why." After a bit more of unintelligible conversation, he slammed down the phone and came back. "Yeah, he says he is."

"That other guy leave?"

The super shrugged and held out his hand. Dix slipped him the bill and the guy said, "I assume so. Is that all now?"

Dix nodded. "Enjoy your movie."

The super frowned and slammed the door in Dix's face.

In the old days, Dix thought as he walked down the dirty hallway, I woulda kicked the guy's door in on general principles and slapped the info outta him.

He sighed. But these weren't the old days.

The wallpaper next to lucky eleven was sagging down like drooping skin. Dix glanced up and down the hall. The door of the adjacent room was half open, providing a glimpse of an old washing machine and dryer inside. Each had a hand-printed sign on top which proclaimed, Out of Order in uneven, block letters. It smelled like someone had pissed on the tile floor, which was so discolored that it was hard to tell if the odor was recent.

Dix raised his hand and knocked on the door, then tried the knob. It twisted open at his touch. The room was a hole, barely twenty feet long, with walls so close together you could almost touch each one standing in the center. A cot-like bed was on the right side, and a small television rested on a card table along with a hot plate. A closet-sized bathroom jutted out from the left. No tub or shower, just a shitter and a sink. At least the wallpaper stuck to the walls, but it looked like it hadn't been washed since Reagan was in the White House. At the far end of the room, Dix saw a figure hunched in a wheelchair, talking on a cell phone.

"Yeah, Mr. Fontaine," Morgan Laird was saying into the phone, "I'm leaving you this message at"—he paused to glance at his watch—"six fifty-three p.m., and I'm informing you that the police have come here harassing me." Laird's eyes blinked and he lowered the phone from his face. "Dix?"

"How ya doing, Morgan?"

The man in the wheelchair studied him, then a faint smile crossed the pale lips. He pressed a button on the cell phone and set it on the flimsy table.

"What happened?" Laird asked. "You got old."

Dix smiled. Same old Morgan. "Yeah, you too." He walked over and looked for a place to sit. There was one other chair, the kind you'd pick up at a cheap yard sale, but Dix decided not to trust the spindly-looking legs. As much as he hated to, he plopped down on Morgan's unmade bed, hoping no roaches would find their way into his pockets. "You know, you really oughta lock your door. Never know who could walk in on you."

Laird coughed a phlegmy laugh. "Yeah, well, after spending all them years in an eight-by-twelve cell with a lock on the door, I kinda like leaving it unlocked sometimes."

"Nice place," Dix said.

Laird blew out a puff of air. "It's a shit hole, and you know it." He wheeled himself closer to Dix. "But it beats Stateville. At least I can come and go as I please."

Dix saw an open pack of cigarettes on the card table.

"Still smoking Pall Malls I see," he said, wondering how the hell Laird could still be smoking at all, considering the oxygen tube between the footrests of the wheelchair.

Laird nodded. "Yeah, pass me one, will ya?"

Dix reached over and grabbed the pack and the plastic lighter, holding it out and flicking it after Laird put a cigarette between his lips.

"Thanks," he said, leaning forward to hold the end of the square in the flame. He inhaled, then let out a smoky breath. His eyes narrowed. "So, whatcha want, coming here?"

"Morgan, you remember me from before, right? I always treated you fair, didn't I?"

Laird drew on the cigarette again, then smirked.

"Well," Dix continued, "I been hearing things. Bad things."

"What the fuck you talking about?" Laird's brow furrowed. "Hey, you still a cop, or what? You gotta be too old now."

Dix stared at him. Maybe he could play this into an advantage. "Let's just say I'm semi-retired. But I still have connections. I can help you out of the jam you're in."

"What jam? I ain't done shit."

"That's not what I heard."

"Oh yeah? What *did* you hear?"

Dix paused to watch him. He'd broken down enough criminals in the old days to know the psychological effect of a good, solid stare. But all Laird did was stare back, puffing away at a leisurely pace. He sure didn't look nervous.

Finally, Dix asked, "You know what DNA is, Morgan?"

"Sure. Don't everybody?"

"They've got a lot of new techniques nowadays," Dix said. "For instance, you remember that half-smoked Pall Mall you left in Linda McKenny's bedroom back in the day?"

Laird let some smoke drift from between his lips.

"Well, back then, if they'd had the DNA capability that they have now," Dix said, "they'd have nailed your ass."

"From what? A cigarette?"

Dix nodded.

Laird shrugged. "I already copped to doing her. And

the rest of 'em, too. It was all covered by the immunity deal. Now I done my time, and you can't do shit to me for any of that."

Dix tried another stare. Was the guy starting to sweat? He looked more befuddled than nervous. Time to unleash a big bomb.

"That a good smoke, Morgan?"

"Exquisite."

"You know, you left some of your DNA on that butt last week."

"Huh?"

"At the copycat crime scene."

Laird rolled his eyes. "More of that shit." He took a last drag on the cigarette and stubbed it out on the edge of the card table, letting the butt fall on the floor. "Those cock sucking feds tried to run that game on me earlier today. I told 'em I didn't know what the fuck they was talking about."

"But we know better, don't we?"

"Fuck you."

Dix smiled. In the old days, he'd have plucked Laird out of that damn chair and smashed him against the wall a couple of times, just to loosen the asshole up. But, he reminded himself again, these weren't the old days.

"Give it up, Morgan. I'm probably the last chance you have to help yourself."

"Help myself do what?"

"Get out of a new murder rap," Dix said. "I know you're working with somebody on these copycat killings. Advising them, reliving your past glories, whatever."

"Bullshit."

"Tell me who's in on it with you. Tell me."

"Go fuck yourself." He suddenly coughed and a gob of yellow phlegm shot from his mouth and landed on Dix's hand.

Dix leaped to his feet in a surge of rage. His fist flew out, before he could stop himself, backhanding Laird's mouth.

Laird leaned over from the blow, which hadn't been very hard at all. His face shook with fury momentarily, then the emotion drained out of it. He wiped at his mouth, his fingers coming away red.

"Big man, hitting a cripple, huh?" he said.

Dix swallowed. In the old days, there'd be somebody watching. Colby, maybe, who would come in and pull him out of the interrogation room. Somebody to play good cop. Here, there was nobody, and this whole interview had gone south. He shuffled over to the jutting washroom wall, angry at his lack of control. Still, he couldn't show any weakness in front of Laird.

"Morgan, I ain't gonna beat you." Dix stood and took out his pen. "I don't have to. Like I said, it's just a matter of time before they come knocking down your door." Reaching across Laird, Dix grabbed the cigarette pack and scribbled his cell phone number across the top. "Think about this number the next time you have a square. It'll easy for you to find. Then call me when you wise up." He tossed the pack back down on the table. "Remember, just like before, I'm the only fucking chance you got."

He tried the stare one more time, before he turned to go.

———

Knox stood behind the door, next to the washer, and watched the images on his tablet that the fisheye lens of the camera provided from the small hole he'd drilled through the thin wall of the defunct laundry room. After he watched Dix exit and heard the sound of his footsteps going down the hallway, Knox stepped from behind the door and peeked around the jamb. The old cop was almost out the front door. Knox leaned back inside and adjusted his latex gloves. He didn't want to risk getting any gunshot residue on his fine leather ones. Those he reserved for special, non-firearm encounters.

He'd originally stepped inside the laundry room to put on the latex gloves and the special paper hospital slippers over his shoes when he'd heard the buzzer go off, and the old guy yelling at the super about being the police. Keeping out of sight behind the door in the laundry room, Knox twisted the pointed blade through the flimsy wall and inserted the camera lens. As he watched and listened to the conversation, a new plan suddenly emerged. What he needed was a subterfuge, a smoke screen to keep the cops busy while he tracked down Matthew and then escaped to greener pastures.

And now, with a little finagling, he had one.

He listened as the front entrance door closed, then with two deft steps, Knox was out of the laundry room and at number eleven. His gloved hand carefully twisted the knob. The door opened.

Morgan Laird looked up in surprise, then said, "Who the hell are you?"

"Like the man told you," Knox said, pulling out the Beretta with the extended sound suppressor, "You really should lock your door."

Laird's eyes widened when he saw the gun.

"You ain't no fucking cop," he said. Not with a piece like that."

"No, I ain't," Knox said, mimicking Laird's wispy voice. Perhaps he could do it well enough, but why not enlist the aid of the original? He picked up Laird's cell phone. The cigarette pack, with the numbers written across the top, was on the table. Knox set it up so he could read them as he punched them into Laird's phone. Before he pressed the last digit, he looked down at Laird and held the end of the silencer to the convict's forehead. "Here, call your buddy, Dix, and tell him to come back."

"What are you, nuts?"

Knox swiped the barrel across Laird's face, opening a big gash above his eyebrow.

"Call him," Knox said. He pressed the last digit of Dix's phone number, held the phone against Laird's ear, and then put the barrel back to the other man's head.

A flash of something—fear, realization, or perhaps resignation, crossed Laird's face. He licked his lips and waited. It rang twice and then he said, "Yeah, Dix, it's me. Come on back in here. I need help."

Knox heard a garbled reply. It sounded ecstatic. He moved the phone away from Laird and pressed the button terminating the call.

"Very good," Knox said. "Matthew would be proud of you."

"Who's Matthew?"

"You wouldn't believe it even if I told you," Knox said, and pulled the trigger. Twice.

CHAPTER 14

They walked along Michigan Avenue and stopped when they came to the bridge. Colby had suggested they stroll to a restaurant nearby instead of trying to search for a parking spot. As they paused and looked down at the dark water, he pointed.

"The Chicago River. Many a body's been found floating in that one."

"You said they dye it green on St. Patrick's Day?"

"Yeah. Bright, Kelly green." He turned and pointed to the brightly displayed clock on the smallish skyscraper a few blocks east. "And that is the Wrigley Building."

"Like the chewing gum?"

"Yep. And the same one Frank Sinatra sings about in 'My Kind of Town.'" He paused. "You do know who Sinatra was, don't you?"

"Of course, silly." She slapped his arm playfully. He took that as a good sign, but that still didn't change the facts. She was way too young for him.

"Is Billy Goat's Tavern around here someplace?" she asked. "That place they used to show on *Saturday Night Live*?"

"Yeah, it's over there in the lower section off Wacker. But you don't want to eat there, do you?"

"I might. But not tonight if you don't want to. I just want to see the place before I leave. I've heard so much about it."

"You got to be kidding me, right?"

She shook her head and smiled. "Isn't this where that famous reporter used to hang out?"

"Mike Royko? How the hell did you hear about him?"

"I read his book in college," she said. "You know, the one about your famous, powerful mayor."

"I remember," Colby said. "But that was a while back. Royko's long gone now. What was this class, anyway?"

"It was about historical patronage and corruption in big cities in the United States," she said.

Colby nodded thoughtfully. "Probably lots of material there. You learn anything worthwhile?"

"Just that the FBI is the most honest police organization in the States."

When he did a double-take, he saw her break into a laugh. He liked the way it sounded. Musical, sort of, and he wondered where this evening was going to lead. When they started walking again, Leslie blew out a deep breath and watched the condensation float away. Almost accidentally, their hands brushed together and he took hers in his.

"It's just down here," he said, pointing to the lighted place overlooking the water.

"Looks fabulous," she says. "We have a lot of restaurants overlooking Lake Ontario back home."

Her voice was light enough to float on air, and she smiled again.

Easy, old man, he thought, remembering again she was young enough to be his daughter.

He sighed and told himself that all he really wanted

out of this evening was a pleasant dinner with a pretty girl. Anything else, if it happened, would be gravy.

"So how's the investigation going back home?" he asked.

"My boss says they've pretty much got things wrapped up. Said to keep going through the motions down here. Like it matters."

"And it doesn't?"

Her smile faded and he realized he'd ruined the moment.

"I guess I should have expected it, my first homicide and all." She looked down at the street. "Not quite like dropping the ball, but bad enough because it means the coach was afraid to let me carry it."

Colby raised his eyebrows trying to salvage things. "A football metaphor? I had you figured for a good Canadian girl."

"Meaning what?"

He shrugged. "Oh, I don't know. I usually don't associate football with Canadians. You folks are more the cold-weather type. Hockey players."

"For your information, winter is only one season in Canada. We also have spring, summer, and autumn. And we do have football. Didn't you ever hear of the Canadian Football League?"

"They any good?"

"Of course they are."

"Is it made up of lackluster hockey players?"

"In Canada there's no such thing as a lackluster hockey player."

"I'll bet," Colby said, watching her gestures and thinking that body language was signaling him that she was loosening up. "But just remember one thing. It ain't over till it's over."

A crease formed between her eyebrows. "That seems a bit redundant."

"It's meant to be. In a homicide investigation, every lead has to be checked out. You never know what's going to make or break the case."

"So you're saying I shouldn't feel bad about being sent down here to check out a dead end?"

"Like I said, it ain't over till it's over."

———

Dix strode back toward the flophouse with a purpose this time. He was sure the federal surveillance boys had taken notice of him this time, but he didn't give a shit. Laird had invited him. Dix felt a surge of adrenaline. The asshole was ready to flip on his partner in the copycat murders.

And he's going to spill it to me, Dix thought.

He practically ripped the flimsy door off its hinges. The same old pathetic, smelly lobby greeted him. It might make a good panoramic shot when they did the movie version, though. Or maybe he could walk Carmel around it, narrating how he'd broken the case. In a few seconds, he was at Laird's door again. Lucky eleven. That had turned out to be true after all. He twisted the knob and was pleased to find it still unlocked.

Some fuckers just don't learn, he thought, as he stepped inside.

Laird sat at the far end in his chair, his cell phone on the card table, his head slumped to one side, like he'd fallen asleep.

Maybe he's praying, Dix thought. Maybe he got religion spending all those years in the joint. Or maybe he's having second thoughts.

"Okay, Morgan, here I am," Dix said, strolling past the

jutting bathroom toward the wheelchair. "Whatcha got to say to me?"

Laird didn't move. He was facing away, with his chair turned toward the window. Not that you could look out with the damn blind pulled down tight.

Something made the hairs on the back of Dix's neck stand up. Something wasn't right. He was just about to speak to Laird again when he heard the squeaking of a door behind him, and felt twin spitballs hit him between the shoulder blades. Then a powerful force gripped him and sent waves of pain shooting through him. Tingly pain. Like he'd stuck his finger in an electric socket. He couldn't move. His body wouldn't obey. It just jerked in an uneven, spasmodic rhythm as he plunged face-first toward the shabby rug.

His body landed with a flop, stealing his breath. Before he could try to move, the pain soared again, along with the involuntary jerking. Spit dribbled from his lips, as though his mouth too, was under someone else's control. He felt like a helpless puppet. The tingling increased, sending his body into even a more uncontrollable spasm, until he finally descended all the way into blackness.

———

Knox didn't ease up on the Taser until he was sure Dix was completely out cold. Still holding his finger on the trigger, he stepped over and peeled back the fallen man's eyelid. Only the whiteness of the sclera showed.

Good, he thought.

He left the trailing wires connected to Dix just in case and carefully moved over to the dead man in the wheelchair. Knox had used the special Taser cartridge that held none of the traceable confetti. Turning Laird, so his unblinking eyes now gazed down at the prostrate Dix, Knox grabbed Laird's cell phone off the table using only two fingers of his left hand. He stepped back to Dix, stooped and straightened the prone man's right arm. Knox rubbed the back of his right latex glove over Dix's, confident it would leave enough traces of barium and antimony to produce a positive result for a gunshot residue test. He stood and stepped behind Dix, standing between the man's outstretched legs. With the utmost care, Knox removed the Beretta from his pocket and unscrewed the silencer. Slipping that in his pocket, Knox dialed 9-1-1 on Laird's cell phone and readied his voice.

When the emergency operator answered, Knox screamed out in his best imitation of Laird's husky, southern-sounding voice, "Dix! No!"

He held the unsilenced Beretta straight out and shot Laird in the chest. He then tossed the phone over by the right side of the wheelchair and placed the gun in Dix's open right hand, taking special care to press the limp index and middle fingers onto one of the smooth surfaces of the gleaming black metal.

Damn, I'm going to miss that gun.

———

Matthew paid cash for two different outfits, taking extra care not to do anything to draw attention to himself. Pushing open the exit door, he stepped out into the well-lit parking lot and strolled leisurely toward the tech's car, making it look like he didn't have a care in the world.

He needed to get in and drive away, then try to make it back to his apartment. Risky, but he'd have to chance it. And tonight too. For one thing, the building superintendent, Mr. Webber, would easily buy into a story about lost keys and open the door for him. Once inside, he could pick up enough supplies, clothes, and money to see him through the rest of it. He'd decided to expedite the plan. Move things up. Jump ahead if he had to, just so he could beat them to the punch. "Them" being the old man and Knox.

The old man. *His pseudo-father.* Matthew had long since stopped thinking of Jetters in that context. He was far from it. The worst example of fatherhood there was. A phony. Dr. Frankenstein.

Matthew smiled. If the old man was Frankenstein, what did that make him? The monster? No, better described as the experiment—the first perfectly cloned human being.

Knox, on the other hand, was pure trouble. He could be in the area now, watching the apartment, ready to swoop in like some bird of prey. The old man would order it. Matthew knew he'd have to be extra careful. Park the car, leave the Blem in the trunk, and walk through an adjacent yard. Hopefully, no one would call the cops on him. But even if they did, he doubted the old man would have alerted the authorities. He couldn't afford to. Too many skeletons rattling around in his closets. Or the graveyard. Lots of them. Literally.

But soon, very soon, everything would be unearthed. He hit the remote and watched the car lights flash with an accompanying beep.

I hope that didn't wake up my sleeping brother in the trunk, he thought, smiling.

My brother?

He'd have to stop thinking of that thing in those terms.

———

Colby was feeling better than he had in a long time as they stood by the elevators. Dinner had gone very well, and afterward, they'd taken an easy stroll along Grand Avenue back to the Marriott, even though the evening had become a little brisk with the hint of the coming winter. He pointed out different sights and buildings along the lighted skyline as they walked. While they'd been eating, she'd told him a little about herself, but mostly she asked about him. She seemed particularly fascinated about his book and how he'd come to write it. Flattered, he'd told her more than he usually did. Now, as they stood next to each other he could feel the heat from her body.

She's still way too young for me, he thought.

She turned toward him as they walked. "Your first name's Roger, isn't it?"

He nodded.

"So why does everybody here call you Colby?"

He shrugged. "I guess I'm just a Colby kind of guy."

She laughed. "And what do people who like you call you?"

"Haven't met any of those yet."

"Come on."

He considered the question, then said, "People have called me Rog from time to time, but that was mostly my ex-partner."

"Rooog." She drew the word out, as if tasting the sound of it. "I like that. It has a nice ring to it."

"Which is exactly why I prefer to be called Colby," he said with a grin.

She turned and looked at him for a moment. "You averted your eyes yesterday. When Pearson showed the picture of them finding those two little girls."

That startled him. Had she been watching him?

"Did I?"

"What were their names?"

"Elsa and Anna Swanstrom," he said, letting out a breath. "I dedicated my book to them."

"Oh, that was nice of you."

The doors of the ornate elevator slid open. Colby felt a sudden awkwardness. Like a kid on his first prom date. Should he make his move, or what?

She made it for him, grabbing his hand and squeezing. He squeezed back, figuring it would end with a warm handshake, but instead, she stepped back and gently pulled on his arm.

"Want to come up for a little while, Rog? There's a wonderful view."

Colby felt the warmth of her hand holding his.

"I'd like that very much," he said.

"Good," she said as they stepped inside.

When the elevator doors closed, she leaned forward and kissed him.

CHAPTER 15

"What the hell am I doing here?" Colby asked himself as he suddenly awoke in the strange room. They'd left the drapes open and the ambient lighting filtered through the window giving everything a velvety softness. He turned his head and studied Leslie's beautiful face in the semi-darkness. Her steady, regular breathing told him she was still asleep.

And still way too young for me, he thought.

He asked himself again, *What the hell am I doing here*?

Carefully extricating himself from the bed, he shuffled to the bathroom, the lush carpet feeling soft against his bare feet. When he'd finished, he went to the window and looked out at the cityscape, his city, with the myriad of lights creating a twinkling design against a backdrop of elegant blackness.

Their lovemaking had been immediate and intense, both of them seeking the comfort and release of the unexpected passion. Her body had felt slim and taut beneath him, like an athlete's, but also soft and inviting...the smooth texture of her skin, the tangle of her hair as he ran his hands through it... he could hardly believe it had happened.

Yeah, he thought. Way too young for me.

As he was picking up his clothes in the darkness he heard her voice.

"You leaving?"

He came and sat down on the edge of the bed. "Yeah, I guess so."

Her hand came up and caressed his face.

"Don't," she said. "Stay with me tonight."

Her fingers curled around his neck, gently pulling his head toward hers, until their mouths met.

He crawled back under the covers, and they made love again. More tenderly this time.

The sunlight peeping in between the parted drapes woke him. He was alone in the bed. The digital clock on the nightstand showed seven forty.

Getting in the bathroom first for a quick shower would be essential if he wanted to get to the task force office by nine. But then he heard the water running and knew she'd beaten him to it.

He sat on the edge of the bed and considered his options. Why not take her to breakfast? Someplace nice. Besides, with Pearson virtually guaranteed to exclude him from anything important, it wasn't like he had to punch in, or anything. He'd be lucky to get an assignment to the nighttime surveillance team.

The door opened and Leslie stepped out, holding a towel around herself. Her eyes widened and she gasped.

He smiled at her sudden modesty. "Don't you think I've already seen everything there is to see?"

"No, you haven't seen one of my bad-hair days."

"I'll look forward to that," he said, stepping toward the bathroom.

After a quick shower, Colby came out, gathered up his underwear and socks, then plopped down on the bed. He leaned over to the nightstand and grabbed the remote, turning the TV on to *Chicago Today*.

Might as well see how Dix's fantasy gal is looking this morning.

The picture materialized like an electronic jigsaw puzzle, displaying a black guy dressed in a country-and-western shirt singing about the virtues of a fast-food franchise.

Colby slipped on his right sock and shook out the left one. Just as he was pulling it over his toes, the screen displayed a "Breaking News Story" emblem, and the picture morphed into his old buddies, Carmel Washington and Pierce Nolan, both trying to look like serious reporters.

"As we reported earlier, *Chicago Today* is following a story involving the Morgan Laird copycat murder investigation this morning," Nolan said, his mellifluous voice enunciating every word perfectly. "A source close to the investigation confirmed a few minutes ago that a 'person of interest' was being held in connection with two murders that occurred overnight. Carmel?"

Colby jumped up and snatched his pants, stepping into the legs as he felt the pockets of his sport coat for his cell phone.

They must have caught Laird in the act, or something, he thought.

"Yes, Pierce," Carmel said. "As you know, I've had a personal interest in this story—" He tuned her voice out as he hastily dialed the task force office line and waited, listening to the solitary ringing. Finally, Pearson's voice message came on.

"This is Special Agent Stephen Pearson. I'm not available to answer your call at the moment. I'm either on another line, or—"

Christ, thought Colby. Can't this guy ever just say something simple?

"Please leave a message," Pearson's voice continued, "after the tone, and your call will be returned as expeditiously as possible."

Colby took a deep breath and was just about to speak when a picture of a familiar face flashed on the screen next to Carmel's pretty features.

"...and it has been confirmed," she was saying, "that one of the victims was prominent defense attorney Lance Fontaine."

Colby stood there holding the phone, stunned.

Damn, he thought. This might be too good to be true.

Matthew had given the Blem another of his tranquilizer bars and stuck him in the locked storage space he'd rented. He made sure to tie him up first. The twenty-four-hour access, courtesy of a swipe-card, made it the perfect base of operations. He'd looked around as he closed the overhead door on the compartment. No one in sight. Video cameras monitored the entrance and exit, but none on the inside, as far as he could see. No prying eyes. Nobody gave a shit what kind of garbage he put in here.

He figured the Blem would be safe enough in there sleeping it off until his return. The creature stank, too. He'd obviously pissed his pants. But the storage area was deserted, so no one would notice the smell. It was also large enough to store his Corvette inside if he wanted to. With that in mind, he parked the dead tech's car in the lot of a nearby department store and called a taxi to take him to his apartment. He'd have to get rid of the tech's car soon, but it had a few more uses.

Matthew told the cabbie to circle the block a few times while he looked for Knox or his car. He had the tire iron tucked inside the left sleeve of his shirt, just in case.

"What? You ain't sure where you live?" He was a nosey asshole.

"I'm seeing somebody," Matthew said. "Got to make sure her boyfriend ain't around."

The cabbie chuckled. "In that case, you want me to stick around?"

Matthew weighed the option of killing him instead of paying, but decided it was too risky. The asshole might have called in his destination when he was chatting on his cell phone before.

"Just pull over here," Matthew said.

He got out, paid, and began walking down the sidewalk. The area where he lived was close to the college so people were coming and going at all hours of the day. His eyes kept scanning for Knox. Hopefully, Mr. Webber would be in.

Shit, if they hadn't taken my cell phone I could have called, he thought as he continued his brisk walk. Get in and out quick. Just pick up essentials and the car.

He turned on the sidewalk that led to his building, opened the door, and pressed Webber's buzzer.

"Whaddya want?" the voice asked.

"Mr. Webber, sir. It's Matthew Jetters." Keep it polite. Keep it simple. "I got robbed and they took my wallet and keys. I need you to let me in, please."

He silently marveled at the pitiful whining sound he was able to create in his voice. The safety door buzzed and Matthew pushed it open. He went to the super's first floor messy apartment and waited. Presently, the door opened and the old man shuffled out and stopped with a look of sudden surprise pulling at his sagging face.

"You got a haircut?"

Matthew rubbed his hand over his shortly cropped scalp. "Yeah, I'm joining the ROTC."

The old man smiled approvingly.

Matthew smiled back at the dimwit.

"What'd you say happened now?" Webber asked. "To your keys?"

Matthew quickly repeated the bullshit story he'd come up with, watching the wrinkles deepen on the old fart's face. He was swallowing it, hook, line, and sinker.

"I'd better have the locks changed then." The old man shook his head as he walked on stogy legs toward the stairs. "Come on, I'll open your door with the master."

Matthew put a hand on the old man's arm. "Would you come in with me, sir? I'm still a little shaken up."

Webber sighed and nodded. "I ain't heard nobody come in or out, but I'll be glad to go in with you if it'll make you feel better."

Matthew resisted the urge to take out the tire iron and beat the old son of a bitch to death. After all, he was still useful at this point. Matthew could use Webber as a shield if Knox had hidden himself in the room.

Knox felt an undercurrent of anger at the old man's insistence that he report in person to New Genesis. This was slowing his search for Matthew. Jetters had also hinted at a further development, so perhaps it was a necessary delay. Besides, it was a matter of when, not if, he found the errant fugitive from a science lab, but Knox knew if his plan were to work, he'd need to accomplish the capture sooner rather than later.

He used his special key to open the elevator and took it to the second floor. As he got out, he wondered about the condition of the dormitory, three floors above, that Matthew had left in such disarray. All was quiet in the building today.

Jetters looked up from his desk as Knox entered and closed the door behind him.

The old man looked like he'd aged ten years overnight.

"I saw the news," Jetters said, his mouth puckering as he looked downward. "Both Laird and the lawyer dead."

"As you instructed."

Jetters took in a deep breath, sighed, and nodded. "We've achieved stability on the fifth floor. However, there's another problem."

Knox assumed he meant the federal subpoena. "Give them the dummy personnel file that I came up with for Krems. It was painstakingly created."

The old man's mouth puckered again, this time with irritation.

"What the hell are you talking about?" His tone was demanding, angry. "Give who what?"

"You're referring to the subpoena, right?" Knox asked.

"No, I was *not* referring to the subpoena," Jetters said, looking away.

Knox stood there without inquiring further. The two of them locked eyes, and the old man was the first to blink. Knox was glad he'd remained standing, forcing Jetters to look up at him. It gave him a feeling of dominance.

"I shall do as you suggested with that," Jetters said. He blew out a puff of breath. "Do you think the tidying-up you did last night will be enough to forestall any further questions?"

"I laid the groundwork for a plan I think will put us

totally in the clear," he said, smiling slightly. Perhaps it was time to go on the offensive and set up his lucrative exit from New Genesis. "Look, if I'm to clean up this mess totally, I need to know the whole picture."

Jetters leaned forward, his shaggy eyebrows rising slightly. "And what exactly do you mean by that?"

Knox waited before replying. Always keep 'em on the edge of their seat, his father used to say. The man had been an amateur magician, and Knox had acted as his assistant as a boy, watching him perform.

"This whole thing's rather complex," Knox said. "I only know bits and pieces, and that's not enough."

Jetters was starting to show signs of irritation again. "You know all you need to know."

Knox paused, almost wishing he smoked so he could take out a cigarette and slowly light it before speaking again, like James Bond did in the movies. But this was real life, and the upper hand was now his. Finally, he said, "Matthew left some trace evidence at the scene of one of his little excursions. They have his DNA."

Jetters's eyes widened momentarily. "My god." Then he recovered. "You're sure?"

Knox nodded. "But, as I've said, I've taken steps."

"What steps?" The old man's face reddened. "What goddamn steps?"

"To throw the police off his trail." Knox stared down at him. "That is, if what I'm thinking is correct."

"And, what, pray tell, is that?"

Their eyes locked.

"That Matthew's DNA matches Morgan Laird's." Knox smiled again. "Matches it exactly."

The old man's upper lip twitched slightly. Knox stared back at him, waiting for a reply. When he got one, it was curt. "You seem to know everything already." His gaze was as steady as an ancient reptile's.

Still smiling, Knox continued. "The authorities believe that Laird himself, was somehow involved in this string of new murders, but due to his confinement to a wheelchair, they assumed he was involved with a confederate."

Jetters was sitting still now, his eyes unblinking.

"By dispatching Laird and his attorney," Knox said, "I've eliminated any chance the authorities would be able to prove or disprove this."

The old man's head jerked slightly in assent.

"So," Knox continued. "What we're in need of is someone whom they would think was the confederate. A fall guy. A patsy." He held Jetters's gaze momentarily. "And I've given them one."

"Who?"

Knox shook his head. "Nobody you know. An ex-cop who happened to be badgering Laird. It'll look like he and Morgan conspired to create a little havoc together and then had a falling out."

"You're sure this will work?"

It'll work long enough for me to get to an island somewhere to spend my money and live like a king, Knox thought.

He nodded his head and said, "Of course."

Jetters considered this, rubbing his hands together in front of him then tented his fingers. "And the flaws in your plan?"

"Well, it's imperative that I catch your prodigal son before he commits any more such acts."

"Don't call him that. He's not my son anymore." The old man frowned. "He's an abomination. An egregious misjudgment on my part. I treated that boy well. Made sure he had every advantage. A first-rate education, a proper upbringing, college, financial support...and now, he rewards me with this."

Knox suppressed a smile. This was quite a switch from the old man's quasi-paternal musing of yesterday.

"And as for catching him," Jetters said, "there's a new development in that, too. We've determined he's got L-Seven with him."

"L-Seven?"

"One of the Others," Jetters said. "We didn't realize he was missing until we'd restored order yesterday. Then I had the men search the grounds, but there was no sign of him. The surveillance tapes showed the two of them exiting, Matthew was in Kirby's uniform."

"Any idea why he took him?"

Jetters looked up, ready to explode. "How the hell should I know? He's already proven he has the same sociopathic tendencies as his—" He stopped short of completing the sentence, and his lower lip engulfed his upper. "But there's something we can use to our advantage here. Something that Matthew doesn't know about. All of the Others have a microchip implant, including L-Seven. It's not designed to broadcast a long-range signal, since we never envisioned they'd get off the compound. Only about a hundred yards, or so. But we're working on enhancing the scanners so they can pick it up at a greater distance."

Knox was beginning to like what he was hearing. Maybe this would turn out to be a productive morning after all. It was time for the coup de grâce. "I can't proceed unless I'm sure I can cover all the bases."

Jetters squinted. "What do you mean?"

"I need the whole story," Knox said. "The total picture."

Jetters rolled his tongue over his teeth as he looked down at his desk and then sighed. "Very well. I'll tell you. But I must have your strict assurance that it will go no further."

"Of course," Knox said, settling into the chair in front of the desk as he mentally added, *until it's time for me to pass Go and collect the cool million you're going to give me.*

———

Leslie finished getting dressed and eyed the rumpled sheets and the now-empty room. Colby had been brief, but urgent.

"I've got a situation," he'd said. "Gotta run. Call me and we'll tag up. I'll buy you lunch, okay?"

Then he was gone.

So much for her brief US romance, she thought. *He's dumping me already.*

She smiled to herself and assessed how she felt. There was the age difference, which obviously was giving him cold feet, but things like that had never mattered much to her. It was more about kindred spirits and good hearts, and she sensed he had one.

Sighing, she went to the phone and checked the time. Eight twenty. It was an hour later back home. Certainly a respectable time to be calling in.

It took her about five minutes of solid waiting to get through to Graven. She'd pretty much decided to have a leisurely breakfast in before strolling over to see Colby. To hell with his "situation." Or had he gotten what he was after last night and now wanted to ditch her? Cops—male cops—were apparently all the same, on both sides of the border.

"Inspector Graven," the voice said.

"It's Labyorteaux, sir. Checking in."

She heard him sigh. His voice sounded weary. Like he'd gone to bed late and gotten up early. Or maybe hadn't been to sleep at all.

"How's the investigation going?" she asked. "The perp crack?"

She heard him grumble.

"No. In fact, it looks like we've brought in the wrong man, luv."

"Really?" She was stunned.

"Yeah. I'm going to need you to continue backtracking down there. You got anything?"

"Not much. Some people where the vic worked are acting a bit suspicious."

Graven was silent. After a moment, his voice came back. "Stay on it then. Like I said, the perp we had in custody here kept claiming he had an alibi. It took us half the damn night to check it out, but turns out he did. So it's back to square one."

"Did those digital photos I requested from the border crossing ever come in?"

She heard his breathing again before he answered. "What photos?"

"I'd requested any digital photos and records of any Americans crossing the border two days before and after Norton's crossing," she said.

"Oh, those. Yeah, I think they did, somewhere." She heard the sound of shuffling papers and could visualize him making a mess of the desk. "I know they're here, dammit." After a few moments more of frustrated breathing, he said, "I'll have to find them and email them. Just be careful not to open any official emails on your unofficial tablet. You might get hacked."

Leslie rolled her eyes. Did he really think she would be that careless? She didn't even access her departmental account on her personal phone.

Then she saw Colby's business card lying on the desk next to her purse. She picked it up and saw that he'd written *Call Me*, with his cell number under it. He'd also drawn *xx oo* above his name. Maybe there was hope for them after all.

"I'll find a secure server I can use, sir," she said, holding the card. Through Chicago PD.

———

Colby sat waiting in Pearson's office for a good ten minutes, certain that the damn fed was letting him stew for losing it with Fontaine yesterday. But the curiosity was eating away at him, driving him nuts. A suspect, or rather "a person of interest" in custody. This whole thing was going down without him.

Who am I to blame them for not waiting? He thought, remembering, with a twinge of sadness, the Swanstrom twins. If somebody would have acted sooner, they might have survived. Maybe it was better that they hadn't waited for his sorry ass to catch up.

But who had been working with Laird on these new murders? And why?

Pearson strode in holding a manila file and went behind his desk, not bothering to look at Colby or utter a greeting. When their eyes finally met a few seconds later, the FBI man gave a nod of approval. "I see you've dressed up a bit. Turning over a new leaf?"

Colby had changed into his best dark suit for the date. And he'd worn a silk tie with a light green and blue floral design that matched his shirt. He could feel himself blush as he got to his feet.

"Of course," Pearson said, his mouth curling slightly, as if amused, "you could have shaved, too."

Colby felt his blush deepen. He automatically rubbed his hand over the stubble on his jaw, then let it drop to his side.

"You got a suspect in custody? I heard it on the news this morning."

The amused curl faded slowly from the fed's mouth. "Yes. I tried to call you. There was no answer."

Colby waited to reply. What was this asshole getting at? Did he mean last night or this morning?

"You try my cell?" he asked.

"Left a message," Pearson said. "Do you check them?"

Colby pulled the phone out and saw the little rectangular envelope feature flashed on the screen. He'd had it on vibrate and forgotten it in his coat pocket.

"Battery's low," he said, putting it back. "Why don't you bring me up to speed?"

Pearson stared at him a moment, then said, "Sure. Sit down."

Colby waited until he was sure Pearson was going to sit as well. There was no way he was going to sit in a chair and let this guy address him from a standing position. The fed tented his fingers before he spoke.

"Since I'm not sure what you do and do not know," he began, "I'll give you a thumbnail sketch. Yesterday, at exactly six forty-seven p.m., Morgan Laird dialed 9-1-1 on his cell phone in his apartment. Apparently, what sounded like a gunshot was heard in the background along with Laird's voice. A call for assistance."

He paused, as if considering just how to word the rest of it.

"We had a surveillance team on site, and they were monitoring the police calls in the district as well. When they heard the dispatch, they immediately went to investigate, and found Laird shot to death. The offender was still on scene and was taken into custody."

"Great," Colby said. "Who—?"

Pearson held up his palm and continued talking.

"Approximately an hour later, the body of attorney Lance Fontaine was discovered in his vehicle in a shopping center parking area. He had been shot to death as well."

"I heard that." Colby was getting frustrated by the other man's circuity. He tried a joke. "Look, if you're wondering about my whereabouts when Fontaine was killed, I do have an alibi."

"The thought never entered my mind." Pearson's mouth drew up at the corners again. "Besides, we're confident that the weapon recovered at the scene of Laird's murder will match that of the one used to kill Mr. Fontaine."

"Outstanding," Colby said. "Now, you gonna tell me who this guy is?"

Pearson stared at him a moment more, smiled, and then said, "Yes. I am."

CHAPTER 16

Instead of the leisurely breakfast, Leslie opted instead for a bagel with cream cheese and a medium coffee, both of which she consumed very unceremoniously in the taxi as she rode to the federal building. Between bites, she tried several times to reach Colby on her cell phone. It let her complete her dialing sequence, then flashed the ominous *LOW BATTERY* sign.

She stuck the cell phone back into her purse. The driver turned onto Dearborn and slowed to a stop in front of the Dirksen Federal Building. Leslie paid him and hurried as quickly as she could across the extended walkway. Luckily, she'd worn flats, which made the accelerated pace less cumbersome. Inside, she flashed her Canadian police ID at the security checkpoint and placed her purse and coat on the conveyor belt. After stepping through the metal detector, she grabbed her items and scanned the banks of elevators, wondering what Colby would say when she told him her investigation was going active again. Funny that she still thought of him as "Colby" after making such an effort all night to call him "Rog."

But after all, you never really know somebody until you sleep with them, she thought, allowing herself a wicked smile as the elevator doors closed.

The secretary manning the upstairs checkpoint was looking a bit addled as Leslie stopped to show her ID again and explain she was here to see someone in the taskforce.

"And who's that?" the woman asked. Her grayish-brown hair was pulled back in a severe bun, and deep lines bracketed her mouth.

"Detective Colby."

The woman's expression stiffened, and Leslie added, "Or Special Agent Pearson."

The woman picked up the phone. Although she held the receiver close to her ear, and made only murmuring whispers herself, Leslie could hear Pearson's voice booming on the other end. The woman hung up and said to go right in.

Leslie opened the door and went down the now familiar corridor toward Pearson's office. She was surprised to see him standing halfway in the hallway without his suit jacket on. The shirt sleeves had been rolled up, and he was wearing latex gloves.

"Good morning." His expression was sour as he disappeared back into his office.

Stepping to the door, she realized he hadn't gone completely inside the office, but was right there, wiping the frosted glass on the front of his door with a crumpled-up paper towel.

"What can I do for you, Detective?" he asked. He sprayed some cleaner from a plastic bottle on the glass and dabbed at it with the towel.

"I was looking for Detective Colby," she said, watching his movements with great curiosity. "Have you seen him?"

"Oh yeah," Pearson said, with a telling emphasis. "He's not here right now, though."

"Do you know when he'll be back?"

Pearson started to say something then caught himself. He lowered his arms and turned to face her. "Is there something *I* can help you with?"

Taking a deep breath to give herself a few extra seconds, she said, "He was helping me check on some things regarding my investigation."

Pearson's eyebrows twitched, like a confused rabbit. "Oh. Right."

His eyebrows twitched again, and he shrugged. "He's probably going to be indisposed the rest of the day. I sent him back—I mean, he went back to his own area. I can get you the number if you want."

"That would be great," she said. "And if I could use a phone. My cell's out."

Pearson nodded, gave the door one more scrutinizing look, and walked back into his office.

Leslie gazed at the door on her way past it, the wood still slick and smelling slightly of ammonia from the cleaner. She wondered what that was all about.

———

Colby was sitting in the small restaurant at the corner of Clark and Jackson contemplating the situation. Laird being dead was a godsend. Divine justice. And Fontaine, the devil's disciple, was no loss, either. But Dix...there was no way he could have been involved. Not the Dix he knew.

Colby tried thinking about his next move, trying to assess just how badly he'd fucked things up, when his cell phone rang. He glanced at the number and after seeing it was from the federal building, debated whether or not to answer it. What if it was Pearson wanting him back there for round two? Still, could he afford not to find out?

He answered it with a quick, "Colby."

"Hi, it's Leslie. What's going on?"

"Long story."

"Where are you?"

He wondered if he should tell her. Maybe it would be best to keep his distance. Better for him, and certainly better for her. But he needed help, and he hoped, after last night, that she was someone he could trust. He gave her directions to the restaurant and said he'd be waiting. After he pressed the END button, terminating the call, he took another swig of his coffee and found it had gone tepid. He motioned the waitress for a warm-up, and when she asked, "Regular or Decaf?" he shot her a wry grin. Maybe he should switch to decaf as he recalled the confrontation between him and Pearson.

"I want to see him," he'd demanded after hearing that Dix was in custody. "This is bullshit."

Pearson's eyebrows rose as if his sensibilities had been offended. "I don't think that would be a good idea."

"Fuck that, I want to see him."

The FBI man's eyes flickered. This guy was a pussy. "Detective, remember what I said initially about you being too emotionally involved in this case?"

"Where's he at?"

Pearson compressed his lips, then said, "At the moment, we've got him at the Metropolitan Correction Center."

Colby wrinkled his brow. "The MCC? He should be at a district lock-up. Murder's a state charge, not a federal one."

"In due time," Pearson said. "But, since the task force was on the scene and made the arrest, we're still sorting out the facts. So he's being held in federal custody right now."

Federal custody...they were stalling for time. Colby took a deep breath. This banter wasn't getting him anywhere. He decided to switch tactics.

"Look, I was Dix's partner for a lot of years. I'm sure there's some logical explanation for all this—"

"It's extremely logical," Pearson said, cutting him off. He held up his fingers as he counted off each point. "One, your ex-partner was caught at the scene. Two, we recovered a weapon that was used to shoot the victim. Three, a GSR test on your ex-partner was positive. We're running ballistics on the weapon as we speak, but believe it's the same weapon used to murder Lance Fontaine." He held up his little finger beside the other three. "And four, Laird's dying declaration named Dix as his assassin."

"Dying declaration?"

Pearson nodded. "The 9-1-1 call was recorded."

Colby felt like he'd been sucker-punched.

"Plus, there's the wound pattern on Fontaine's body," Pearson said. He held up a finger on his other hand. "Whoever shot him obviously had a grudge against him."

"How do you know that?"

"One of the first shots was to the man's behind," Pearson said, pursing his lips.

Colby frowned. Was this guy so much of a pansy he couldn't say, "ass?"

Pearson held his gaze for a moment more, dropped his hands, and assumed a thoughtful expression.

"Of course," the FBI man said. "I might consider allowing you to speak with him." He ended the sentence with a bit of an inflection and brought his fingers up to caress his chin.

Colby didn't like the sound of this.

"You and he were close?" Pearson asked.

"We were partners."

Pearson nodded. "Good. Then it should be clear to you that it would be in Dix's interest to make a clean breast of things."

"In other words, get him to confess?"

Pearson's lips twisted into a smile. "Do you think you could obtain a confession from him? It would save a lot of man hours. We'd also like to know the extent of his involvement with Laird."

"What do you mean?"

"We have to consider the possibility that Dix may have been involved in the copycat homicides." Pearson canted his head. "As I said, that's going to take a lot of man hours. You could speed things up for us."

Colby bit his tongue, suppressing the rage he felt. How could this federal idiot sit there and suggest Colby would use his friendship with Dix to stab him in the back? But before he could say anything, a voice came from behind him: "Give me a shot at Dix. I'll bust his ass and get him to come clean."

Bosworth.

Colby turned and saw the big man leaning against the doorjamb. He stood and turned around. "Yeah, I'll bet you would. You're great at stabbing people in the back and kicking them when they're down, ain't ya?"

Bosworth's mouth twisted into a scowl. "Hey, fuck you, asshole."

"You ain't fit to carry Dix's jockstrap."

"Like I said, I calls 'em as I sees 'em." Bosworth straightened up and balled his fists. "Why? You wanna do something about it, old man?"

Old man?

That was it. Colby stepped toward the big cop just as he threw a looping overhand right. Slipping the punch,

Colby moved in with an uppercut aimed for point of Bosworth's chin, but the big man ducked his head at the last second and Colby's fist smacked into the nose area instead, sending a crimson spray all over the frosted glass window of Special Agent Pearson's nicely monogrammed door.

Colby smiled at the memory of Bosworth twisting drunkenly as he sagged to the floor holding his bloody schnoz.

"Rog," Leslie asked. "What's going on?"

He looked up. She had a worried expression on her face.

He held his hand toward the chair across from him. "Sit down and I'll tell you."

———

Matthew felt like things were getting back on track. He was in a race against time, but as long as he could stay one step ahead, he'd be all right. With the Corvette now safely stashed in the storage facility, ready for a quick getaway, and the Blem tied up, sedated and sleeping blissfully in the cheap motel room he'd rented, it was time to address the next pressing issue: getting some food. He'd used the Kirby card again, renting a very nondescript van to carry out the final phases of his mission. It was something he could drive virtually everywhere, and no one would be suspicious. Plus, with the large tarps and sleeping bags he'd purchased, he could take the trussed-up, gagged Blem with him as needed. Grudgingly, he realized he should probably get some food and drink for the creature, too. Maybe a carryout from the restaurant he was pulling into.

It was a small place located in the corner of a strip mall. He went inside, sat at the U-shaped counter, and ordered a standard breakfast of eggs, bacon, and toast. The waitress, a middle-aged bimbo with the most artificial red hair that he'd ever seen, had the audacity to smile at him as she filled his coffee cup.

Matthew smiled back, thinking just how nice it would be to watch her tongue loll as he strangled the bitch. Then he noticed the moron sitting across from him staring. Matthew returned the man's stare, giving him a steely look. The guy, who looked to be in his sixties, recoiled slightly, glanced at his paper, then back to Matthew before shrugging and picking up his coffee cup.

"Any more of that good coffee, Rosie?" he asked.

Even his voice sounded intrusive. Matthew allowed himself a brief fantasy of walking over and smashing the old man's face against the counter until it was reduced to a bloody pulp.

In a perfect world, he thought. Then he caught a glimpse of the newspaper's headline and froze.

Feeling his throat dry up, he looked around, searching for a discarded paper or a vending machine.

Nothing.

"Excuse me," he said to the waitress, "do you have any newspapers?"

Rosie turned to the old coot. "You about finished with that one, Ken? You been reading it all morning."

Ken grinned, showing a perfect set of dentures. "Sure." He folded the paper and handed it to her. Rosie snatched it and strolled over to Matthew, saying, "Don't mind him, honey, he ain't got no life, except for this place."

Matthew accepted the paper with a nod and a thanks. He smoothed it out on the counter and glanced at the headline: *FREED KILLER AND LAWYER SLAIN*. Beneath it were photos of Morgan Laird and Lance Fontaine.

Matthew stared at the paper for a long six seconds. It was an old mug shot picture of Morgan.

This can't be happening, he thought.

When he looked up, the old coot from across the counter smiled and said, "That one fella kinda looks like you, don't he?"

———————

The GPS location was unmistakable. The Corvette had to be in one of the garage-like storage bins. Knox surveyed the place again. Key card entry only, a sturdy cyclone fence surrounding the facility, and a surveillance camera at the front gate. Not a bad setup. Matthew had chosen well.

At first Knox had figured that allowing the kid to get his Corvette back would simplify the search. He hadn't figured on the prick stashing it. After waiting here two hours, it was obvious Matthew had another set of wheels. And there was no telling, given his twisted psyche, just when he'd be back to collect the 'vette.

Nothing to do now but wait.

Wait, and contemplate early retirement.

Jetters had agreed to give him a healthy severance package once this last job was completed, as long as all the bases were covered.

Knox smiled at the recollection. If the old fart only knew.

He must have supposed telling me everything would keep him off the hook, Knox thought. And after all, knowing the story was one thing. Being able to prove it was quite another. Especially as fantastic as the claims would be. He'd had a hard time believing it himself. He'd always known that Jetters had some heavy-duty connections, but now that he knew the entire scope of the operation reached all the way to Washington, from the former president's new heart, to the senator from Massachusetts' new liver. Secretly cloning organs for the rich and powerful. It was dynamite, and the elite would never want it to come out. To think it all started with some cloning experiments with a serial killer's DNA...Knox was glad that he'd had the foresight to keep Norton's original hard drives. Not only would they be worth a bundle, they were the best life insurance policy he could have.

It was all about thinking one or two moves ahead. Keep them watching your right hand while you were setting up the next trick with your left. Sleight-of-hand, and he was going to be a very rich man, once this final matter was run to ground.

Knox checked the GPS monitoring position for any movement. Nothing. But that was okay. Sooner or later the kid would come back for that damn car.

And when he does, Knox thought, it'll all be over.

———

Colby stood on the sidewalk at Van Buren and Clark, just outside the Metropolitan Correction Center waiting for his cell phone to ring. Inside, he knew Dix was being held in a detention cell and wondered if he was somewhere looking out one of those slit-like windows. Colby hoped that his little fracas at the office had slowed Bosworth and whomever they were sending over for the interrogation. The phone rang in his pocket. He took it out and pressed the button.

"Yeah," he said.

"I'm in position," Leslie said.

"What's your extension?"

He heard her giggle. "It's four-five-two-six. None other than his office itself."

Colby couldn't help but smile. "How'd you manage that?"

"I told him I had to make a sensitive call to Toronto and my cell was still out. He offered his office without hesitation."

"I think he's sweet on you," Colby said, suddenly wishing he hadn't. "Anyway, after we get this little matter taken care of, you'd better really call your boss in case he checks the phone records later."

"Go for it," she said as the connection went silent.

Colby slipped the phone inside his pocket and stepped through the doors, flashing his badge at the guards manning the doors. He had to get this done fast... in the next few minutes.

"I'm part of a federal task force," he said. "Here to see a prisoner."

The guard asked for the pertinent information and punched Dix's name into a computer terminal. Colby felt the sweat trickle from his armpits. His internal clock kept ticking away. If only Pearson stays away from his office long enough.

The guard looked up and shook his head. "Sorry, Detective, but there's a flag on this prisoner. Gotta have special permission from the SAIC to see him."

Colby tried to affix a perplexed look on his face. "Special Agent Pearson put it on there?"

The guard checked the screen and nodded. "He did."

Colby chuckled. "You don't know Pearson, do you?"

The guard shook his head.

"He's a she," Colby said. "*Marion* Pearson. A real pistol, too, if you know what I mean." He gave the guard a knowing, guy-smile. "Carries her penis in her holster, and wants everybody to know it."

The guard smirked. Colby took this as a good sign.

"She's the one that sent me over here." He handed the

guard one of Pearson's cards. "Here, call her and confirm if you want."

The guard looked at the card for a few moments, then back to the screen, before picking up the phone and punching in the numbers. Colby felt more sweat trickle down as he watched the man navigate through the answering service menu. Finally, he sat up a little straighter, and said, "Is this Special Agent Pearson?" He paused, then recoiled slightly. "Sorry, ma'am. I meant to say that."

He paused again and Colby suppressed a grin. Leslie was apparently laying it on pretty thick. He hoped the timing would hold out.

"There's a Detective Colby here, CPD, ma'am, I mean special agent—in charge. He wants to see a prisoner you —" he stopped and recoiled slightly again. "Okay, I will. Thank you." He hung up and shook his head. "Shit, I see what you mean."

Colby plucked Pearson's card from the man's hand.

"*Special Agent In Charge* Pearson," the guard said, giving a haughty lilt to his voice, "that's what she told me to call her, said to tell you go on up, and that there's two more agents from the task force on the way over."

Colby suddenly felt the urgency in his gut. The clock was ticking. He pulled his jacket back and removed his Sig Sauer. "Where can I check this?"

The guard pointed to the left and picked up his phone. "I'll have him brought to the interview room on the fifth floor for you."

After securing his pistol in the lockbox, Colby literally ran to the elevators. The slow ascent seemed to take forever. Finally, the doors opened and he was escorted down a narrow hallway to the door of the interview room. Hopefully, he'd be able to get in and out before the stooges arrived. "On the way over," Leslie had told the guard. Her message to make it quick. He felt a pang of regret involving her in the subterfuge, but he had to get in to see Dix, and she was his one shot. Besides, she didn't work for Pearson. She wasn't even a citizen of this country. When it came right down to it, the fed couldn't do squat to her. Maybe he could nix giving her any more assistance, but from what she'd said last night, her investigation down here seemed to have run its course. That was something else, too. Her investigation ending meant she'd be leaving soon. How did he feel about that?

His mental rumination was cut short by two guards escorting Dix, who was still clad in his civvies, but without belt and shoelaces, into the room. Dix had a brocade of white stubble on his cheeks and they'd taken his toupee. He looked shrunken and old.

"I shouldn't be too long," Colby said to the guards. They nodded and left.

Dix sat across from Colby, who kept glancing over his shoulder at the door.

"I only got a few minutes. The feds are sending the goon squad over."

"Figured as much. Man, it's good to see you."

"What the hell happened?"

"I fucked up."

"Tell me something I don't know. What the hell were you doing at Laird's?"

Dix frowned and twisted his head away, looking at the wall as he spoke. "I was shadowing the guy, figuring maybe I'd catch him in the act. Or at least get a lead on who's been working with him."

Colby stared at his ex-partner. "How do you know so much about the case?" As soon as he said it, the answer came to him. Their night of drinking, Dix sleeping on the couch, the misplaced file…Dix must have realized it, too, because he bit his lip and looked away.

"Sorry, Rog. I just wanted to be a part of it again."

Colby blew out a slow breath and glanced at his watch.

"Apologize later. What do you remember?"

Dix leaned forward. "After I talked to you on the phone, I got the bright idea that I might be able to reason with Laird. Convince him to talk to me." He paused. "Lame, I know, but if you remember, I was the one he opened up to before."

Colby nodded.

"Well," Dix said, "I got nothing, so I left him my cell number, giving the old spiel, if you want to talk, call me. I leave, and then he calls me back before I even got back to my car. I figured he was coming around." He frowned. "No fool like an old fool, I guess."

"So you went back?"

Dix nodded and scrunched up his mouth. "I walked in there, and the next thing I know, something hit me like a ton of bricks. I was on the floor, couldn't move, then I musta blacked out." He shook his head. "When I come to, I was kinda groggy. I start to get up, and all of a sudden, a bunch of feds are drawing down on me. Laird's dead. Shot. And there's this damn gun on the floor next to me." He looked Colby straight in the eyes. "I swear to you, I ain't never seen that gun before in my life. It was a Beretta nine mil, for Christ's sakes. You know I never messed with anything other than a Smith or a Colt."

"What did Laird say to you when he called?"

"I dunno. Something simple like, 'Dix, come back.'"

"He called you by name?"

Dix thought for a moment, then nodded.

"Describe for me going in the room again," Colby said. "Did it feel like somebody cold-cocked you?"

Dix's mouth twitched. "Un-un. I ain't never felt

anything like it. It was like I was paralyzed. My muscles wouldn't work."

"Could it have been a Taser or a stun gun?"

"Didn't have those when I was on the job."

Colby thought for a minute, then glanced at his watch again. Time was getting short and he couldn't afford to bump into somebody from the task force coming to interview Dix. That'd land him in the Internal Affairs office in a hurry. He stood up and motioned for Dix to do the same.

"Take off your shirt."

"What for?"

"Just do it and turn around," Colby said. "You, bashful?"

Dix frowned and stripped off his shirt. Colby scrutinized his back and saw two small bumps in the center. He ran his fingers over them.

Dix jerked at the touch. "Shit, what's that?"

"Taser marks. We've got to get a photograph of them." He took out his cell phone and snapped a picture.

Dix began tucking in his shirt.

"You know any good lawyers?" Colby asked.

Dix shrugged. "Not too many anymore."

"Okay, I'll find one. Tell him to get proof of those marks before they fade. In the meantime, don't give any statements to anybody."

"Like you need to tell me that."

"I mean it, Dix. They'll probably be sending some guys to double-team you."

"Feds? Shit, what they gonna do? Slap my pee-pee?"

"Bosworth's working the task force. They might send him, thinking he'd be able to butter you up."

Dix snorted. "The day I can't handle a scrotum like him, is the day they'll be pissing on my grave."

Colby looked at his watch again.

"I gotta get going. Can't do us any good if I get suspended."

"Stay outta trouble, partner," Dix said. "One of us in the shitter is bad enough."

"Is there anything else you can think of that happened while you were there? Anything or anybody out of the ordinary?"

Dix thought for a long time, then shook his head. "To tell you the truth, it's all kind of fuzzy."

Colby grabbed one of his cards from his inside pocket, scribbled his cell phone number on the back, and handed it to Dix.

"Well keep going over it," he said. "And call me if you think of anything."

Dix nodded, then compressed his lips. Colby thought he saw his ex-partner's eyes mist over.

"It looks bad, don't it?"

Colby took a deep breath, then patted Dix on the shoulder. "Hang tough."

CHAPTER 17

While Colby waited back at the restaurant for Leslie to extricate herself from Pearson's clutches, he scribbled notes on his pad. His cell phone kept vibrating, but each time he checked the incoming call, he saw it was the LT's number at the district. He couldn't afford to answer it. Once he was ordered to report, to explain Bosworth's broken nose, no doubt, they'd hang him out to dry. And he had things he had to do. Number one was to figure out a way to clear Dix before the feds crammed a frame around him that was so tight he'd need a jar of Vaseline to get out of it. Still, if Dix was being straight with him, then his innocence should become clear sooner or later.

Yeah, he thought. In a perfect world.

He thought it over again. Caught at the scene, a positive GSR test, the murder weapon, probably with his prints on it, nearby, and a revenge motive that Pearson could serve up for dessert. This probably meant they wouldn't be able to clear the copycat cases, but they could try to blame that on Dix: *He killed Laird, thereby eliminating the chance to figure out the identity of his accomplice in the copycat murders.* Pearson had insinuated he liked Dix for those, too, but that case would take time, and would probably be unprovable. But Dix was certainly on the hook for Laird and Fontaine, and Pearson was going to keep turning the screws. Federally, they could hold him for seventy-two hours before bringing charges, rather than the forty-eight the CPD was bound by, which gave Pearson that extra edge. He had dreams of breaking Dix down and getting a confession.

Colby smiled. That was going to prove more difficult than they thought. Bosworth couldn't rough Dix up, either. The interviews would be videotaped. Colby suddenly wondered if he'd been recorded earlier? That was another reason not to answer the LT's calls.

The waitress came by and refilled his cup. He'd already drunk a pot full, and his bladder was feeling the call. He got up and went to the washroom, and when he came back, he saw Leslie sitting at his table.

"How'd you know where I was at?" he asked.

"I'm a detective, remember?" she said. "This is the same table we sat at earlier. I've known you long enough to establish that you're a creature of habit."

He allowed himself a quick smile. "Any problems with our buddy Pearson?"

"None. I didn't even see him at all while I was in there. And I made a point of calling Toronto just in case he checks."

Colby nodded. She was sharp. He felt a twinge of regret again at involving her in his conspiracy. After all, it wasn't her battle.

"So, what did your friend say?" she asked.

Colby gave her a quick rundown of his short session with Dix.

She appeared to hang on each word. "And what's our next move?"

He reached over and touched her hand. "Look, this

isn't your fight. I've involved you enough in this. I don't want you to get in trouble."

She frowned and shook her head. "You can't do it alone. Isn't that obvious?"

He thought for a moment and nodded. "But—"

"No buts," she said. "I'm with you on this. However, I do have to do a few things on my own case while I'm down here, one of which is that email I mentioned before."

"Okay," he said, reaching into his pocket for his cell phone. "I'll need to make a few calls first." It rang as he held it in his hand, and he glanced at the number, wondering if it was Kropper again.

But it wasn't. It was the office, all right, but it was his own desk. Thinking of someone rifling through his stuff when he wasn't there, he pressed the button and said, "Yeah?"

The voice on the other end spoke in a hushed, but hurried whisper.

"Rog, it's Ray Brewer. You'd better get in here ASAP."

───────

Knox was growing bored as he sat in his car across from the high cyclone fence with the barbed wire strands running across the top. He reread the signs, for the thousandth time: *RENTAL STORAGE FACILITY*, with *24 Hour Access/Video Surveillance* printed in smaller letters beneath it. The Corvette was in there someplace. The GPS had told him so hours ago, but it wasn't quite accurate enough to show him exactly which shed Matthew had stashed it in.

Knox took a deep breath and considered his options. He could continue waiting it out, certain that the punk would show up sooner or later. But what if it was later?

Could he really afford to let him stay on the loose that long?

The credit card transaction that he'd monitored earlier this morning on the dead tech's American Express told him that Matthew had rented other wheels. But finding out exactly what kind was too risky. No matter what cover story he came up with to get the information, if the car rental clerk sensed too many red flags, he'd call the cops. It wouldn't do to have Matthew stopped and possibly arrested before Knox caught him. Then the game would be over, and he'd have to pass *Go* and not collect his million dollars from Jetters.

Not that the old man had any idea he was going to pay that much. But once Matthew was delivered, and Knox was relaxing on a beach somewhere in the Cayman Islands, he'd call Jetters and explain how his retirement parachute needed more fluff. What choice would the old fart have? Especially after he found out that Norton's hard drive and laptop had survived their owner, after all. That was the beauty of it. Jetters would have to pay up, or be exposed for what he was: a man who'd tried to play God, and ended up making a deal with the devil instead.

Knox smiled. It was almost Faustian.

No, he thought, more like Frankenstein.

Matthew searched his deepest recesses trying to muster up a sense of loss about Morgan, but felt the same after he'd killed the first victims: nothing. He was a bit disappointed, but only that they would never meet face-to-face now. After all, he did have the man's genes, his DNA, but it wasn't like they were family.

Someone cut him off and he slammed on the van's brakes, holding down the horn and giving the other driver the finger. He turned and saw an older woman riding in the car next to him staring. He gave her the finger, too, then managed to compose himself.

It wouldn't do to fall apart now. What was that line from Yeats? Things fall apart, the center will not hold? Something equally useless like that.

Uselessness. He wondered how much longer he had. If his "father" had implanted one of those damn genetic triggers he'd found out about when he'd managed to crack the old bastard's hidden research files. When he'd found out who he really was, or should he say, *what he was*? That was when he'd found out his relationship to the Others, the Blems, and how each of them had a predetermined life span determined by the preset genetic trigger. His own file contained no mention of one, but this last time, they'd had him sedated, who knew what the old bastard had done to him?

He slowed down, letting traffic fill in between him and the cars he'd honked at. No sense taking the chance that they might call the cops or get his license plate, since the private mailbox place was just up ahead. The end of his plan so close. Sure, he'd had to accelerate it a bit, cut off his original plan to duplicate the rest of Morgan's series of murders. He wondered what Morgan had thought when he'd seen the news show about the copycat killings. Had he been pleased? Or maybe, envious. Envious that he was no longer capable of pursuing the ultimate thrill?

Matthew's mind shot ahead, thinking of the last moves of the game. Completing the final chapter, and then taking off for someplace safe, where he could leisurely watch as the old man's empire came crashing down.

The midmorning sun was high in the sky, but it was still chilly and miserable. Typical mid-October.

He'd have to settle someplace warm, where no one would come looking for him. Maybe the Bahamas or Mexico. One of those American conclaves surrounded by abject poverty. Where the cops were fat, lazy, and corrupt. Where he could continue his hobbies.

He smiled, remembering a news show about a place called Juarez, where they'd found the bodies of over a hundred women. Now that would be an interesting record to break.

———

Leslie held her breath as Colby swung the unmarked police car through the crowded streets with a wild abandonment as he kept talking on his cell phone. He was, she decided, a man possessed. Maybe that's why his cell worked down here and hers didn't.

If only she could tap into his energy and drive to solve her own case, which was growing more problematic with each passing minute. She found herself feeling stressed. Graven was expecting results, and she hadn't a clue about how to proceed. Maybe she could ask Colby for advice. He'd been more than willing to give some a few days ago, when they'd first gone out to interview Norton's colleagues. But now he was totally focused on his friend's arrest. She listened to his half of the conversation.

"Yeah, Carmel, I know," Colby said into his phone. He twisted the wheel, driving with one hand and bobbling his head back and forth like a ball on a pivot. "But I'm telling you, there's a whole helluva lot more to this." He drew his lips together as he was obviously listening.

"No, I didn't try to blow you off." He frowned. "It was more of a misunderstanding, believe me."

Leslie tilted toward him as the car made a very quick

right turn. Colby slammed on the brakes and honked at another vehicle that had begun to pull out in front of him.

Maybe he wants me to take the wheel, Leslie thought to herself, smiling at his antics. He was a colorful one, that was for sure.

"Look," he continued, "you're sitting on the biggest story of your career. All you got to do is trust me. Give me what you got so far, bring me up to speed, and I promise you an exclusive when I get to the bottom of this."

He listened, then scrunched up his lips.

"Yeah, Dix might have said that, too, but when I say it, I can deliver. You know that."

Luckily they'd turned onto a less populated street and nobody was getting in their way. Leslie wondered if her sudden stress-sweat was a result of Graven's ominous comments or Colby's driving habits. Everyone down here seemed belligerent and in a hurry.

"Okay, sounds good," Colby said. "Right, I see." After several long pauses, during which time his expression twitched slightly, he grunted a few encouraging monosyllables. Finally, he said, "All right, thanks. I'll get back to you, I promise. Just keep sitting on it till you hear from me."

The person on the other end must have said something disconcerting because his lips twisted into a scowl, and he muttered a reluctant sounding, "Okay, if that's the way it's gotta be." When he terminated the call, he held his cell phone up like he was going to throw it at something. "Bitch."

"Bad news?" Leslie asked, hoping to mitigate the tension.

"Yeah, this reporter I know is telling me she's going to run with the story of Dix's arrest tonight at five. There's no way I can convince her to wait."

"Sounds bad."

He set the cell phone on the seat between them. "I tried to tell her they got the wrong guy. Maybe she'll think about it and be too worried about a lawsuit."

"Maybe."

He slowed for a red light. "And I didn't forget about your homicide case, either. I just need to work this Laird murder until I get my buddy out of the frying pan."

That sounded a little more promising.

"I appreciate that," she said, but still heard that loud, sucking sound in her mind's ear of the chances of her solving her first homicide going down the drain. Still, that was no excuse not to give it her best down here. "Is there a secure server around here anywhere? I need to check my departmental emails."

"I know just the place," Colby said.

CHAPTER 18

Despite Colby's quick-driving tactics, when he got back to his own area office it was apparent that he'd lost the race by a landslide. In fact, the landslide looked like it was sitting there waiting to fall on him. A landslide of shit. He saw a scowl on Kropper's face as the lieutenant caught sight of him and Leslie entering the office area and waved a summoning hand. It was a big scowl, but that wasn't the worst of it. There was a corresponding expression on Deputy Superintendent Mannion's face as well. Colby swallowed hard, turned to Leslie, introduced her to Detective Ray Brewer at the desk across from his, and told her to wait there. The timing didn't seem right to get her on the department's computer system.

"Good luck, Rog," Brewer whispered. "They been waiting on you."

"Heard you wanted to see me, boss," he said as he walked into Kropper's office.

"Shut the door," Kropper said.

Oh-oh, Colby thought, knowing that was always a bad sign.

Kropper pointed to the chair in front of his desk. The

"hot seat." The lieutenant's face was a shade redder than usual, his waspy frame angling in his overstuffed chair, like he was lining up a shot on a billiard table, and it looked like he was planning on using a lot of English.

Colby sat, stealing a glance at Mannion, whose lips had drawn into a tight line.

"What the hell happened over there this morning?" Kropper asked.

Colby started to take a deep breath, but before he could answer Kropper asked another question, his voice rising an octave or two. "And where the hell you been?"

Colby cleared his throat, but the thin man cut him off again, thrusting an index finger at him from behind the desk.

"This better be good," he said, "or you're gonna be spending some time in the shit-house, dammit."

Colby licked his lips. They obviously knew about his little fracas with Bosworth. Did they know about his unauthorized visit to the MCC as well?

"Lieu," Colby finally managed to say, trying for a look somewhere between apologetic and oppressed, "if you're talking about that little misunderstanding between Bosworth and me—"

"Misunderstanding!" Kropper's hand thumped the top of his neatly arranged desk, causing the stacks of paper to jump. "You break a fellow officer's nose in a brawl in a fucking FBI office, no less, and you call it a little fucking misunderstanding?"

Colby ducked his chin and shrugged. "Hey, he took a swing at me first."

"That ain't what Special Agent Pearson said." Kropper's gaze looked like it could pierce wood. "You broke Bosworth's fucking nose."

Colby scratched his cheek. It would have been better if he would've let Bosworth's washer-woman punch connect. At least that way he would have had a bruise to show that Bosworth swung first.

"Detective," Deputy Superintendent Mannion broke in, "didn't I tell you that I was very concerned that the department not be embarrassed by this copycat thing?"

"Yes, sir," Colby said. From the DC's expression, Colby's hope that old "Take-it-to 'em Mannion" would see things in a different light didn't look too promising.

"And how do you think it looks for your section leader to get a phone call from the damn feds about two of our officers being involved in a brawl in his office?" Mannion had taken on the tone of a disappointed father. But he hated the FBI. That much Colby knew. Maybe this would be salvageable.

"I know it probably looks bad, sir," Colby said, "but Bosworth took a swing at me first. I used to box. It was instinctive."

Mannion frowned. "That might be a good excuse for clobbering some shithead on the street, but in the federal building, in front of a room full of witnesses?"

Colby thought about saying that Pearson wasn't an objective witness, but didn't. A tiny glimmer of hope emerged. Maybe Bosworth had gone to the ER instead of the MCC. Maybe the feds didn't know about Colby breaching the no-visitation edict yet. Once they did, it would be like throwing gasoline on a bonfire. But, hell, they'd find out sooner or later. He decided to take a chance.

"Sir," Colby said, bypassing the still-fuming Kropper and looking directly at the deputy superintendent, "you remember Detective Fred Dix, don't you?"

Mannion nodded, his eyes narrowing. "Yeah, we used to work together in eighteen."

"The feds are trying to work up a case against him for killing Laird and Fontaine, but he didn't do it."

Mannion's brow furrowed. He looked over to Kropper, whose cheeks still held two silver dollar-sized red spots.

"You didn't tell me that." Mannion's voice sounded like it was coming from the pit of his stomach.

"This is the first I heard about it." Kropper suddenly looked scared.

It was as he expected. Mannion hated the feds as much as he did. Colby sat up, figuring this was his best shot, and gave them a quick rundown of the events, ending with, "And it looks like the feds are trying to railroad him."

Mannion frowned. "Shit, this is even worse than I figured. Not only do I have two dicks assigned to a federal task force acting like they're in a bar brawl, but now I have a retired copper about to be announced as the prime suspect in the murder of a shitbird and his fucking attorney. Can it get any worse?"

Colby stole a glance at Kropper, who sat there, just glaring at him.

Mannion was on his feet, pacing. He parted the horizontal venetian blinds that flanked the window to the detectives' office. "Who's the broad?"

"She's from Toronto PD," Colby said. "She was working with the task force down here."

"Toronto? Canada?"

Colby nodded.

"Oh shit," Mannion said, flipping the blinds closed with his fingertips. "Not only are you acting the fool in front of the feds, but you're doing it in front of some foreign copper?" His cheeks flushed, and he held out his hand. "Give me your badge and ID. You're stripped until further notice."

"Stripped?" Colby said. "For how long?"

"Until further notice," Mannion repeated. "I got to figure out how to do damage control on this shitstorm."

"But—" Colby started to say.

"No fucking buts," Mannion said, snapping his finger. "Your badge and ID."

Colby reached in his pocket and handed over his badge case.

"Give us your weapon, too," the deputy superintendent said.

"Aw, come on, boss." Colby's voice was plaintive.

"Un-un. You give up your gun, so I know you ain't gonna be working this fucking thing on your own and causing me more heartburn." Manion glanced at Kropper. "Unofficially, you take his piece and have him sign a letter saying he voluntarily surrendered it to you."

Kropper nodded and picked up the phone.

"Boss," Colby said, "if I can just work on a few things around here—"

"No way. You're stripped, plain and simple, pending further disciplinary action. You're not to be engaged in any police investigations," Mannion said. "That's an order. Got it?"

"But I've been helping Detective Labyorteaux with her investigation."

"Who?"

Colby gestured at Leslie who was now standing next to Brewer as they both watched the office.

"Have Brewer help her." Mannion brought his big index finger up and poked Colby in the chest. "You go home."

Colby glanced down at Kropper, who was smiling ear-to-ear, and realized he had few options.

But a smart general picks his battlefields, he thought.

———

The afternoon sunlight filtered in through the dirty glass of the wig shop, shifting so that the block letters were represented as shadows on the tile floor in front of him. Matthew watched as the Asian woman combed and clipped the long hairs around his neck into something resembling a Mick Jagger cut. He felt like sticking his tongue out, but decided that it would look a bit too gauche. Actually, the reflection staring back at him from the mirror didn't look half-bad. Noticeably flashy, but that was what he wanted. Let whoever saw him remember the hair, so it'll be easier to doff the wig and slip away.

"A bit shorter here and here," he said, suddenly thinking the style was way too feminine. But maybe that wasn't such a bad idea, either. "No, on second thought," he said, raising his hands. "It's fine the way it is."

"You wait one minute," the old slant-eyed bitch said. "I fixie."

He pushed her hand away and jumped out of the chair, wondering what it would be like to kill an Asian. He wondered if Morgan ever had. He would have probably called the bitch a chink or a zip. Taking a deep breath, he forced the rage burning in his chest to dissipate.

Not the time, or the place right now, he told himself. Save it for later. Plus, he had his "brother" sleeping off another tranq-laced candy bar. It wouldn't do to get delayed giving this slant-eyed cretin a well-deserved beating, and have the Blem wake up and go wandering around the parking lot. Plus, he needed to maintain a low profile. And he had to get to his safe deposit box to pick up his emergency stash, now that he had the key back. The wig would help throw off anybody staking out the bank, just in case Knox had found out about that, too.

The chink looked nervous. She flashed a set of crooked teeth, reinforced by gold inlays.

He smiled. One of those would make a good trophy.

She smiled back. "You sure you like? You no like, I fixie."

"No, really, this is fine." He adjusted the smile to what he hoped was a boyish look and allowed a trace of femininity into his posturing. Let her think he was a fag. Less threatening and less likely to arouse suspicions prematurely.

The old woman's eyes looked perplexed under the epicanthic folds.

"You want box?"

"No," he said, and smiled, thinking all the while of the rush he'd get if he could only reach out and grab that scrawny-looking neck. "I'll wear it."

———

Knox had given up the surveillance, for the time being, but kept his GPS tracker on as he drove back to New Genesis. If the Corvette started to move, the tracker would let him know and he could begin an immediate intercept course. Without anything more, he realized, he was reduced to a sad little game of wait and see. The Kirby card had shown no new transactions after the rental thing, and although it would be nice to know what kind of vehicle the little punk had chosen, nosing around there could be counter productive. He lamented not leaving Matthew's cell phone in his apartment as a lure before. He could have tracked the signal, and used that to triangulate the little punk's location, as well. But it was like waiting for a city bus in the rain—no telling when it would show up. Plus, time wasn't on his side. Not only did he have to find Matthew, but he had to make sure that the cops didn't. Not that they'd be looking for him at this juncture. Not yet, anyway.

The subterfuge of using that stupid, old cop had been a Godsend, a gift. The guy had waltzed in at just the right moment.

Knox was on a roll, and if he played his cards right, he could ride it all the way to Easy Street.

His cell phone rang, jarring him out of his concentrated reverie. The number was New Genesis. "Where the hell are you?"

"Coming back to the center, as you instructed, sir." He figured tossing in the last bit of respectful salutation would butter the old coot up. It was like adding a new ball to a juggling routine. This one required a bit of extra attention. "Have you perfected that feature you told me about?"

"I believe we have," Jetters said. "It should be useful to you."

"Fine," Knox said. "I'll be there shortly." He was about to terminate the call when he heard the old man's anxious voice again.

"You're sure everything's...ameliorable?"

This was working out better than he had hoped. Just wait till he sprung the blackmail scheme on the old bastard. But to do that, he had to get Matthew. Soon.

"Everything," he said, "will be just fine."

———

Colby was operating in stealth mode now. He'd made a show of introducing Leslie to Ray Brewer, as he whispered to both of them to sit and wait for his call. As soon as he'd cleared the building, he dialed Brewer's desk, praying that Kropper or Mannion wouldn't be near the heavyset detective when he answered.

"Can you talk?" Colby asked.

"Yeah, your girl, Les, has been explaining the game of hockey to me."

"Great. Where are Kropper and Mannion?"

Brewer grunted, and Colby figured he was checking out the LT's office.

"They're still shooting the shit."

Colby waited a few seconds, wondering how much Leslie had told Brewer about what was really going on. "She told you about Dix, right?"

"Yeah. What you need me to do?"

Colby thought. "Find out where the Laird murder happened, and who caught the case."

"That's easy," Brewer said. "It happened down in Two. I'll call over there and see what I can find out. They're probably mad as hell that the feds came in and stole it."

"Tell 'em I'll need copies of the police reports, too. I'll go by there and pick 'em up."

"Anything else, my prince?"

"Yeah. Give me Rich Lapell's phone number."

"Who?"

"He works for the state. An ET. I'm thinking they called them to process the Fontaine murder since it was in the suburbs."

"Hey, ain't you stripped? You're just John Q. Citizen right now, till this thing is cleared up."

Colby sighed. Brewer was right. Not having his credentials was going to make things harder. Much harder.

"You still got that duplicate badge you had made a few years back?"

"Yeah." Brewer's voice sounded leery.

"Slip it to Leslie for me. And toss in your backup gun too."

"Not only do you want me to put my own career on the line for helping a *rogue cop*." Brewer's voice had an exaggerated whining lilt. "But you want my extra piece, too?"

"I'll make it up to you," Colby said. "Tell Leslie to meet me by the car as soon as she has that stuff."

He terminated the call and settled in to wait. Carmel had given him the location of Fontaine's murder, but also a five o'clock deadline for plastering Dix's face all over the evening news. He'd be tried and convicted in the court of public opinion before he was even indicted. And that was coming too, if Pearson wasn't dissuaded. Colby needed to come up with something fast.

CHAPTER 19

The four of them, Knox, Jetters, a gangly pipsqueak from technical services, and security chief Hank Meister, stood in the shade of one of the many huge trees that flanked this section of New Genesis property. Across the open expanse of field, perhaps a hundred yards away, they watched one of the Others move, tethered like an upright dog, while one of the security guards gently walked him along. The directional finder Knox held was about the size of a hardbound book. The regular series of beeps that had previously corresponded with the relative positioning of the Other's inserted microchip became obscured with intermittent static. Knox estimated they were about one hundred yards away. The signal was growing fainter.

Jetters glanced at the geeky technical guy and said, "Dammit. It's already losing the signal. I thought you guaranteed it would work up to two hundred yards?"

The old man's expression was severe.

The geek punched his glasses back up on the bridge of his nose and compressed his lips. He glanced apologetically at Knox and reached for the directional finder.

"Perhaps there's too many radio waves around here." The geek raised and lowered the finder while keeping his eyes plastered on the lights in the circular scope.

Hank Meister raised his hand to the portable radio mike clipped on his shoulder lapel. "Want me to call them back?"

Jetters ignored him, concentrating his piercing gaze on the tech.

"Sir?" Meister asked again.

"What?" Jetters shook his head, like he'd just noticed a troublesome insect.

Meister's face tightened. "You want me to call them back?"

Jetters pursed his lips, then shook his head. He immediately went back to berating the technician.

Knox gave the security chief a sideways glance. He hadn't liked it when Jetters had given Meister the chief of security position. He was ex-law enforcement, and therefore a liability to any of Knox's unauthorized assignments, even though he appeared to be a classic case of a retired desk jockey, turned useless watchman. Knox remembered the relish with which Jetters had justified his decision.

"The man's merely a figurehead," Jetters had said. "Someone to lend an aura of respectability to our enclave. Nothing more. He expects to sit behind a desk and collect a large paycheck for essentially doing nothing."

Jetters had smiled in his typical, condescending fashion after the words came out, so great was his self-satisfaction. Just like everything else the old fart did, He thought everything he planned was just another stroke of his genius. But Knox wasn't totally convinced about Meister. It had taken more than a bit of guile to persuade the ex-cop about the "tragic accident" concerning Kirby's death. The chief had finally acquiesced, but Knox detected something in the other man's gaze. A rising wariness, maybe?

It was something Knox would have to monitor and take care of if the situation merited it.

———

Matthew decided to wear the wig when he checked the UPS Store that he'd set up in the months before he'd begun formulating the plan. Since he had the wig, he felt he might as well use it. Plus, developing a comfort with something new was important, too. Get used to wearing it, so he looked natural. He could dump it if he had to change his appearance quickly. He looked at himself in the rearview mirror, brushing a few errant strands to the side, and then jamming a baseball cap on top to look less conspicuous.

He still looked like a transvestite's worst nightmare, even with the cap obscuring the unnaturally thick center part. After making a mental note to grab a rubber band inside and pull the excess hair back into a ponytail, he remembered the Blem. They had to look like twins from here on out.

Twins, he thought. More like the master and his identical patsy.

Smiling, he got out of the parked van and strolled leisurely toward the UPS Store.

The wig gave him a measure of confidence. Hopefully, even if Knox were watching, he wouldn't recognize the long-haired patron Matthew had now become. Instant transformation.

But there was no way that Knox could even know about this place. Matthew had taken every measure to make sure this part of the plan remained a total secret, using cash to pay the deposit and fees. There was no way he could be traced here. Still, the thought of Knox being on his trail tied small knots in Matthew's stomach.

He did a quick look around before he went inside but saw no one.

"Hi," he said to the chubby girl with reddish hair and pale skin sitting behind the counter playing on her iPad. As she looked up, Matthew was conscious of her eyes roaming over him, stopping abruptly at the long curling tendrils that framed his face. As a slight smirk tugged at her lips, Matthew felt his anger and rage starting.

Who the fuck is *she* to be laughing at me?

It was all he could do to control the urge to grab her.

"Can I help you?" she asked.

"Yeah," he said, brushing back some of the hair. "My name is Owen Rand. I'm in box number twenty-three-eight. I lost my key."

The girl put the tablet down and rested her arms on the countertop. She moved like a sloth.

"I'll need to see your ID," she said.

Her skin looked pasty now, her cupie-doll lips drawing back into a semi-smile.

"Sure," he said, reaching for his wallet. Luckily, he'd been able to get a few personal items from his visit to the apartment, including his laptop. Making another false identification card, and getting it laminated had been simple, but everything was when you were just a little bit smarter than everyone else. "School ID okay?"

"Sure," she said.

He laid the glossy card on the counter with a snap, watching her greenish-blue eyes move downward. She looked back to his face, then once again at the photo ID. "Wow, you look kinda different now."

"I've been sick," Matthew said, figuring her infantile mind was having trouble sorting out that it really was him in the old picture. Then suddenly it came to him. He reached up and lifted the hat and the thick wig beneath it, holding it up just enough to give the girl a glimpse of his shaved head. "I've been in the hospital. For chemo."

The cupid lips immediately formed an O-shape, and she looked away.

So easy, he thought. Confront them with something unpleasant to think about, and they forget all about rules and regulations.

"Oh, gosh," she said, lifting her corpulent butt out of the chair. "I'll go check it for you right away, sir." She flashed him a quick smile as she disappeared into the stockroom.

In that instant, Matthew fantasized about sneaking back there, grabbing a handful of those strawberry-blond tresses, pulling her head back, and slitting her throat. Of course, that would complicate the task at hand.

Still, he thought, I can dream, can't he?

———

After driving to Area Two and using Brewer's extra badge to substantiate his nonchalant identifying hello, Colby and Leslie were granted access to the big investigations' office. Brewer had been able to find out that a dick named Dave Powers had caught the Laird case initially but had passed the ball to the feds, upon an order from Deputy Superintendent Mannion. Luckily, Colby and Powers went way back, having worked together back in the Second District on a few homicides. Powers, always impeccably dressed, stood and shook Colby's hand.

"Hey, Rog, how's the book tour going?"

"Could be better. You got one you want me to sign?"

Powers grinned. "Yeah, but I left it in the shitter."

"Un-huh." Colby grinned back, then introduced

Leslie. "She's down here working a homicide case, and I'm sorta, kinda helping her out."

Powers raised his eyebrows. "Some guys get all the luck."

"You got a spare computer where I could check my email? Plus, I gotta talk to you about something."

Powers looked around the office. It was close to three and virtually every desk was occupied. He pointed to one on the far edge of the room that was vacant.

"You can use that one."

"I may need to print out some stuff, too," Colby said. "Is it hooked up to a decent printer?"

Powers raised his hand and waggled it up and down, frowning and then flashing a smile. "As good as you're going to get around here. It ain't Kinko's."

Colby nodded, anxious to get what they needed and leave. Word of him being stripped would spread fast, and the last thing he wanted was Mannion catching wind of him being there.

"I gotta warn you, too," Powers said, sitting back down in his chair. "It takes forever to download files. I hope you ain't got no pictures."

"I'll let you know," Colby said, taking two steps forward, then stopping. "Say, I heard you caught a case near and dear to my heart."

Powers cocked his head inquisitively.

"The Laird homicide," Colby said.

"Shit." Powers smirked. "I shoulda played the fucking lottery yesterday. I was over there supervising the ETs and setting up a canvass, when word comes down, from the deputy superintendent of operational services, no less, to let the feds take over." He sat back and clasped his hands behind his head. "No way I wanted any part of that cluster fuck anyway." His smile vanished, and he straightened up and sighed. "You know who they pinched at the scene, right?"

Colby nodded. "I'd like to see what you got on it."

Powers opened his desk drawer. "I was keeping a file on it, anyway, figuring the feds will eventually turn it back to us for state prosecution. Once they fucked it up beyond all recognition." He took out a manila folder with a sheaf of papers in it. A flash of suspicion flickered across his eyes and he extended the file toward Colby. "Here you go. You just curious, or what?"

"I'm working with the feds on a related case. Task force."

Powers grunted. "Better you than me."

If you only knew the half of it, Colby thought.

He and Leslie went across the expansive room and sat at the vacant desk. The computer was on the floor next to it, hooked up to an ancient-looking monitor on one side, and an equally decrepit printer on the other.

Colby turned it on and put in his CPD password to enter the departmental open the system and stood up.

"It's all yours," he said.

Leslie moved in closer and smiled. She smelled of delicate perfume, and he admired her flawless profile as she was crowded in next to him.

She accessed her departmental email account and clicked on the message. It popped up with the heading of *PHOTOS BORDER CROSSING*, with no additional text, only an attachment.

"Can we download these pictures?" she asked. "I'd really like to see what this Krems guy looks like."

Colby nodded and she started the download. The box opened up on the screen and gave an estimated time of seventeen minutes.

"That's CPD code for twenty-five," he said, pointing at the screen.

"I guess we wait on pins and needles, then."

He took out the paper with the number Brewer had given him for Rich Lapell and dialed it on his cell.

"Crime lab," Lapell's deep voice said over the phone.

"Hey, buddy, it's Colby. How the hell are ya?"

"Fine." Lapell's tone quickly became guarded as he added, "Now whaddya you want?"

"Such cynicism from a fellow public servant?"

"Come on, I'm up to my armpits in work and ain't got time to play."

Colby hesitated, then decided to put all his cards on the table. "I need a big favor."

"Don't you always?"

Colby gave Lapell a quick rundown of his needs, without mentioning Dix or being stripped.

"I already faxed over a copy of my preliminary findings to Special Agent Pearson." Lapell sounded perplexed. "He said the feds were taking the lead on it. Had a suspect they figured to tie in to both homicides."

"Yeah," Colby said, "and I'm working with the task force. Trouble is, I'm over at Area Two running down a lead and I need those copies bad."

"Didn't Pearson disseminate them?"

"He thinks dissemination has something to do with birth control," Colby said, hoping Lapell's natural cop animosity toward the feds would override his skepticism. He heard the other man sigh and took it as a good sign.

"All right, what's your fax number?" Lapell asked. "But the next time we get a body dumped on the Ryan, I'm gonna expect tit for tat."

Colby opened the desk drawers and found an area detective's card. The fax number was on the bottom, and he read it to Lapell.

"Okay," the state cop said right before he hung up, "but you're gonna owe me."

Favors and markers were the life's blood of investigations, and Colby said he was fully prepared to honor the marker whenever Lapell called it in.

If I'm still around to do it, he thought as he went to the fax machine and waited.

He hoped his little info-gathering trip would come off just as smoothly. He flipped open the file Powers had given him and began perusing it. It was chock-full of scribbled notes and crime scene sketches. A full report from the ETs, as well as the report from the medical examiner, would be forthcoming, but right now he had the basics. He looked around, scanning the office for any sign of "inquisitive brassholes." The lieutenant's office was empty, so he felt a bit safer. Leslie walked over to him and asked if she could use the phone.

Colby took out his cell phone and gave it to her. "Use this instead. I don't want any trace of our visit to be left here right now."

She nodded.

"In fact, I need to go use the copy machine," he said. "And I'm waiting for a lengthy fax. Stay here and make sure nobody else grabs it, would you?"

"For you, dear, anything. But..." She took out her own cell and shook her head. "Let me see if I can get a signal on mine from here." She punched a few digits, waited, then made a circle with her thumb touching her index finger. "This is Detective Labyorteaux. Is Inspector Graven there?"

Colby left her and strolled toward the copy machine. Powers was on the phone and not even looking his way. Resisting the urge for another quick glance around, Colby took the sheaf of papers out of the manila file and flipped through them, checking for staples. He found several and plucked them out before setting the papers in the copying tray. His cell phone rang, startling him.

"Yeah," he said into the phone, hoping it wasn't Lapell telling him the fax was off.

But an automated voice began speaking, informing him that he was receiving a collect call from the Metropolitan Correction Center, and asking if he'd accept the charges.

He waited for the message to run its course, then pressed the accept button. He pressed the button to begin the copying, too. The papers began their trek through the machine, the greenish light seeping from under the closed lid.

"Hey, buddy," Dix said. "How ya been?"

"They finally let you make a call?"

"Yeah. Bosworth and some tight-assed fed were here trying to get me to give it up." His tone had an exhausted edge to it, despite the forced merriment.

"You talked to them? I told you not to."

"Relax, I eventually told them to go pound sand. I just wanted to feel 'em out. See what they had."

Colby felt a surge of frustration and anger. Why hadn't Dix done what he'd told him to do and just requested a lawyer? Every scumbag who'd been through the system knew enough not to talk. But then again, it was just like a cop to think he could play the system to his advantage. The only problem was, it was like playing a game of tag with a Bengal tiger.

Colby heard Dix laugh. "Man, you really did a job on Bosworth's schnozz too. Looks busted for sure. I asked him if some Thirty-Fifth Street hooker closed her legs too fast."

Colby chuckled. He could picture Dix's flawless delivery. The papers had circulated through the copying machine and he collected them as he stuck the originals back in the manila file.

"What did he say to that?"

271

Dix laughed again. "Nothing. He just turned as red as a ripe tomato."

"I still haven't found you a lawyer," Colby said. "So don't talk to them again if they come calling."

"I won't." Colby detected a hesitancy in Dix's tone. "You finding anything out?"

Colby decided not to mention his current suspension status. Dix had enough to worry about.

"Working on it." He began to walk back toward Leslie at the far side of the room, casting a quick look at Powers, who was still busy on the phone himself.

"Say, Rog..."

Colby's stomach tightened. "What?"

"They musta done a search warrant on my place. They found the copy of that file I made."

Great, thought Colby. How am I gonna explain that?

"But I stoned up on 'em," Dix said, talking fast. "Acted like I never seen it before."

"F. Lee Bailey would be proud."

"Shit, to think that I might need some punk like him defending me is enough to make me consider confessing."

Colby took a deep breath. "Like I said, don't talk to them again until I get you a mouthpiece."

"Don't worry, I won't. But remember you asking me about anything out of the ordinary last night?"

Colby looked toward the fax machine and saw Leslie standing there holding several sheets, with another one slowly emanating from the slot. He glanced at the desk and saw the picture on the computer monitor was almost completely downloaded. It was too large or the screen and showed only a man's jacketed arm.

"What'd you remember?" Colby asked Dix.

"Well, when I was walking up to the place, I seen a car with a couple of feds sitting in it. I mean, they were about

as obvious as a couple of cockroaches sunning themselves in the bathtub."

Colby chuckled. Leslie looked at him and smiled,
holding up the collected sheets. He nodded.

"But when I was going in," Dix continued, "I seen
some pretty boy in a suit. From a distance, I figured for a
copper walking in ahead of me. At least I assumed he
mighta been a cop, from the way he moved and looked."

"Okay." Colby got back to the desk, grabbed the
mouse, and moved it to reduce the size of the displayed
picture.

"But the guy had real long hair," Dix said. "And a
goatee. So I figured, what kind of copper is that? I mean,
the fucker's hair was so long he had it pulled back into a
ponytail, for Christ's sake."

"A ponytail?"

Colby watched as a smaller version of the picture
popped up. The texture was a bit grainy showing the
upper portion of a man visible through an open car
window, but it was still unmistakable: Edward Knox, of
New Genesis, long hair, goatee, and ponytail.

CHAPTER 20

Matthew stared at the Taser in the clerk's hand. It hardly looked formidable, the way a gun did, but he couldn't risk trying to get a real piece. Not with a three-day waiting period and background check. Plus, he had no Firearm Owner's Identification Card, and that left him high and dry in Illinois, unless he bought one on the street. But that meant exposing himself to more risks. A Taser was something else. That only required him to be eighteen. It was smaller than he'd imagined, and shaped almost like a flashlight.

"It's laser-sighted?" he asked. He'd left the wig in the car, figuring his buzz-cut would be more welcome and less noticeable in the gun shop.

"Yes, sir," the clerk said. He removed the square cartridge on the end. "With the Taser in this mode, you can use it as a stun gun. Just hold it against your adversary, and pull the trigger." He pressed the button, causing an arc of crackling electricity between the two nodes. "And this," he held up a block-like cartridge, "can stop a Brahma bull up to fifteen feet." The clerk snapped the cartridge back into place. "And that ain't no BS, neither."

Matthew remembered the feeling of getting hit by those prongs and nodded. "Okay, I'll take it. Batteries, too."

"Great. You won't regret it. Anything else you're looking for?"

"Handcuffs." Matthew peered through the top of the glass display. "And let me see those?"

"The leg-irons?" The clerk opened the back of the case, reached in, set two boxes on the countertop, and removed the lids. "These titanium cuffs are real light. Feel 'em."

Matthew picked them up. "But are they just as strong?"

"Sure are. Plus, both open with a standard handcuff key."

Matthew held the lightweight shackles a moment longer, liking the way the light danced over the hard, polished surface.

"Okay, I'll take them," he said.

"The leg-irons, too?"

"Yes," Matthew said, then thought about recent events and being prepared. "In fact, give me three of each. And a second cartridge for the Taser."

The clerk's eyebrows arched upward.

Matthew took out his billfold, which was thick with currency. "Can you toss in some of those plastic restraint ties, too?"

"Wow, that's a pretty big order. You going to work in a jail somewhere, or something?"

"I'm going on a special operation. How was it they used to say it?" Matthew grinned, raising his index finger as if he remembered. "If I tell you about it, I'll have to kill you."

The clerk grinned back, showing a set of crooked teeth as he eagerly slipped the stuff into a bag.

"You know," he said. "I ain't heard that one in a while."

Matthew smiled again.

You don't know the half of it, Matthew thought, keeping the smile on his face. *You sad sack of shit.*

———

Leslie ordered them room service and sat at the small coffee table across from Colby. He was furiously scribbling notes on several sheets of hotel stationery. She watched him working the pen over the paper, drawing diagrams, and arrows, circling some items and scratching out others.

"So are you figuring how this whole thing fits together or doing a calculus assignment?"

"Actually, that's a pretty good analogy. I always used to tell Dix that solving a complex case was a lot like working through an algebraic equation."

"It looks a lot more complex than algebra."

"It is, but in a lot of ways, it's plain and simple logic. You just put down the facts, and see how they interrelate." He tapped the pen on the first box at the top of the page. "Our buddy Knox was in Toronto at the same time as your victim, Norton. But he lied to us about it. Gave us a song and a dance about some guy named..." His pen trailed across the paper, but she said it before he could.

"Vernon Krems."

"Right," he said. "And more importantly, Knox's boss went along with it when we were at that New Genesis place."

She nodded.

"Knox and the old guy, Jetters, are covering something up," Colby said, tapping the paper again. "You can bet it had to do with Norton's murder up by you." He sat back. "Here's where it gets interesting. Apparently, Norton knew Laird. Was his doctor while he was in prison. And Dix says he saw a dude with a ponytail," he reached over and grabbed the grainy copy of Knox's border crossing photo, "which means that our buddy Knox most likely was at the scene of Laird's murder, too."

"It's all tied together, isn't it?"

He nodded again, then frowned. "But how? It's a no-brainer to figure that Knox killed Norton and Laird. Probably Fontaine, too, if these preliminary reports are right. Two guys shot with a nine-millimeter within hours of each other, who happen to be attorney and client. Then Dix showed up at the wrong time and Knox framed him."

"Even Pearson can't deny all this stuff. Shouldn't we go to him?"

Colby's frown deepened. "We'll need something more concrete. Once an asshole has his mind made up, you need the pope to call and tell him he's full of shit. And even then he wouldn't believe it."

She giggled. "You do have a way with words."

"Plus, we still don't know how Norton's, Laird's, and Fontaine's murders are all tied to the copycats." He compressed his lips. "Still, Laird must have been involved in those. DNA doesn't lie, and they found his at one of the crime scenes."

"Do you think Knox could have been in on them with Laird?"

"That makes the most sense, but until we know all the whys of it, we're still shooting in the dark. That's what we'll have to find out tonight, if we can."

"I assume that means we're going someplace after dinner?" she asked, straightening up.

He nodded.

"All right then." She unbuttoned her blouse and skirt,

then laid them on the bed. "I'm going to freshen up a bit."

Standing there in her bra and panties, she was amused as she watched his eyes sweep over her.

The knock on the door made him glance up warily, until the muffled voice on the other side said, "Room service."

Colby started to get up, but Leslie put a hand on his shoulder and told him she'd get it. On the way, she grabbed one of the hotel robes hanging on the bathroom door. As she slipped into it, she heard Colby's cell phone ring for about the umpteenth time that afternoon.

"You going to answer it this time?" she asked.

"Nah, it's probably just my asshole boss calling me up to gloat," he said.

She smiled at his colorful language until she opened the door, and then she saw Pearson standing there with Special Agent O'Keefe, Lieutenant Kropper, and Deputy Superintendent Mannion in his dark blue uniform blouse.

Oh, Christ, Colby thought. Looks like the gang's all here now.

CHAPTER 21

Matthew watched the Blem eating his Happy Meals in the rear of the van, burping and farting, happy as a pig in a poke. Matthew drank some more of his own soft drink and picked up the group of envelopes he'd gotten at the mailbox place. God, he would have loved to have strangled that red-haired bitch. He longed to feel the rush again.

But on to the business at hand. It was clear that it was indeed time to enter the final phase of the plan. With Knox on his trail, he had to move fast. Set things in motion, make the call to the old man, and collect his hush money. He set the drink on the console and began shuffling through the material.

Blacks would probably be easier, he thought as he shuffled through the photos and applications from his bogus mailbox address. But Matthew realized he'd also stand out a lot more in a Black neighborhood, and it wouldn't do for a White guy to get stopped with two little nigglets in his rented van. He wondered how Morgan regarded Blacks. He would have called them niggers. Morgan had spent enough time incarcerated that he'd probably been victimized by them, especially being in a wheelchair.

I'll have to make amends for that, he thought. Maybe a trip down to Jamaica or Haiti and kill a few to even the score. But those future fun and games would have to wait.

He read through more of the pictures and applications he'd received. It was amazing how much personal information people were willing to give out in search of a quick buck or a shot at their fifteen minutes of fame. The ad he'd placed on the internet, stating he was an independent filmmaker looking for pre-adolescent twins to be in a commercial, had netted him a ton of resumes. Most of them from greedy parents seeking a chance at big bucks.

He came to a photograph of two very pretty little White girls, dressed identically, and both with nice blond hair. They could have almost passed for the Swanstrom twins. He knew in an instant he had to have them. Scanning the accompanying resume, he felt a suddenly, sexual arousal. He looked over the accompanying resume: single parent home, and they lived in a trailer park. He found the contact phone number and grabbed his newly purchased burner phone.

The woman answered on the first ring. Matthew could hear the blare of a late afternoon talk show in the background. Trailer park trash.

"Ms. Turner? This is Owen Rand, calling for New Star Associates. It's in regard to your response to our ad."

"Oh, yes."

He could detect the interest in her voice. She was already hooked.

"Do you still live at the same address?" Matthew read it off the resume.

"Yes, we do."

"Good. Could you have the girls ready for a quick

audition in say, an hour?" He worked at keeping his voice professional sounding and non-threatening. "I'd like to stop by and take some pictures. It won't take very long."

"Yeah, sure, we can do that," the woman said. He heard her cover the mouthpiece on her end and say, "Go get your sister now."

"Fine. Coincidentally we're setting up now in a strip mall not too far from you. I'll take a taxi over to your house." His voice was Mr. Happy with the golden prize. This was going to be almost too easy.

———

"I can see why you haven't been answering our calls," Mannion said, stepping forward as he eyed the red-faced Leslie in the robe. His face had an amused smirk, and Colby knew that they were in deep shit. That they'd tracked him here, to Leslie's hotel, shocked him at first, but hell, he should've figured on it. He wasn't at home, and they'd just been in a north side district station. Even though he hadn't been answering his cell, it was on and still sending a ping to the closest towers. It would have been a simple matter of triangulation and a few phone calls. Leslie's downtown hotel was no doubt the first place that popped up. He should have seen this coming.

"Calls?" he asked. "I must have a low battery."

Mannion frowned.

Kropper's lower lip jutted out and he shot a mean glance at Leslie, then at Colby. "You brought an unauthorized person into a district station. Let her use departmental equipment. You're gonna be brought up on charges if I have anything to say about it. Plus, you been working this case specifically when we told you not to."

Colby shrugged. There were so many of them it was

diffusing their efforts. Best to let them bluster and see where they were going.

"I was showing an officer from another country our facilities," he said. "And her superiors emailed some documents to her regarding an ongoing case. We downloaded them."

The bags under Kropper's eyes danced with fury. He looked about to respond when Pearson broke in.

"And how do you explain that little visit to the MCC this morning that I supposedly authorized?" He glanced at Leslie and said, "I had a hard time convincing them that Marion can also be a man's name."

Colby saw Leslie blush. Why had he gotten her involved in all this?

"Me seeing Dix is immaterial," Colby shot back. "You're building a case against the wrong man."

"Listen, asshole." Kropper poked a finger into Colby's chest. "I told you I ain't putting up with no more of your shit."

Colby stared back at him, then said, "Deputy Superintendent, I believe you just witnessed a battery to a police officer."

Mannion frowned.

"You ain't no police officer," Kropper said, but he drew his finger back.

"Cool your jets, both of you," Mannion said. Then, to Colby, "You're in shit up to your knees. You know that, right?"

"Look, boss." He held up his index finger and thumb, with about a millimeter separating the two. "I'm this close to being able to prove that Dix didn't kill Laird. I just need a little more time, is all."

"May I remind you," Pearson said, "that we're handling that case."

Colby stared at him. "Yeah, and you've got the wrong guy."

Pearson shook his head. "It's a moot question, since you're no longer involved. And you may as well be told that the case against your friend, Dix, is getting stronger all the time. The reason we're here is to ask you to go back downtown with us."

"For what?"

Pearson sighed heavily. It was almost theatrical. "To determine if *you* were involved."

"You can't be serious."

"I'm afraid we're serious as a frigging heart attack." The fed smirked.

Colby wondered how long he'd been waiting to use his sanitized version of that old cliché in a conversation. But the asshole still wasn't man enough to go all the way with something— "Frigging?"

"We'd like you to take a polygraph examination," Pearson said.

"For what?"

Pearson's face was placid. Like a man who thought he was holding the winning hand, and didn't care who knew it. "We served a search warrant on Dix's residence today. Any guesses as to what we found?"

It had to be the copy of the file Dix mentioned.

Colby shook his head.

"A photocopy of the copycat case file," Pearson said it like he was announcing checkmate.

"Yeah, well let me know if you find my fingerprints on it," Colby said. "I can honestly say I've never seen it."

"Which means what?" Kropper asked. "That you just handed over your file for Dix to copy?"

Colby was getting tired of this intrusion. Another knock sounded at the door, once again announcing "Room service."

"I think that's our food," Colby said to Leslie. "Now, if you gentlemen, and lady, will excuse us, Ms. Labyorteaux and I were just about to have dinner."

He was taking a chance, but the fact that they'd only asked him to accompany them meant that they didn't have anything solid. He hoped he had just enough time to get them out of there, then run Knox to ground. It was the only chance he, and Dix, had left.

The trio of men glanced at each other.

"He's your employee," Pearson said to Mannion. "But I can tell you that the bureau wouldn't tolerate insubordination of this magnitude."

Mannion's face grew redder.

Special Agent O'Keefe looked on the verge of finally opening her mouth when Mannion's gruff voice said, "Let's go." He turned to Colby. "Plan on reporting to Lt. Kropper's office at nine sharp tomorrow morning. And bring your union lawyer."

One by one, the three men moved toward the door, Mannion opening it first and stepping around the room service. Kropper slipped out behind him, followed by Pearson. O'Keefe paused and stepped back into the room. She leaned close to Colby, handing him a card, and spoke in a quick whisper.

"I'm not so sure they're on the right track, either," she said. "If you get anything solid, and need to talk, my cell's on the back."

What was she, the federal "good" cop? Colby nodded and took the card. The food smelled nice, but he knew he wasn't going to have time to enjoy it.

———

Knox was getting into his BMW just as his cell phone sounded. Jetters's nervous voice greeted him.

"Matthew called me. He says he's planning something big. Something that's going to expose everything."

"Calm down," Knox said. "Did you record the number he used?"

"Yes, yes, yes." Jetters's voice grew impatient. "Dammit, man, didn't you hear me? He said—"

"I heard you," Knox interrupted. He was getting tired of coddling this old idiot every time a new "catastrophe" popped up involving the prodigal experiment. "Now, give me the number."

Jetters read the numerals off, one at a time to Knox, between rapid breaths.

"It's a cell phone," Knox said, studying it. This was good. Real good.

"I already know that. It's unregistered."

A burner phone, no doubt. Knox knew he had to take control or he'd be wasting more time listening to the old man's babblings. "What did Matthew say? And how long ago did he call?" He was already opening his laptop and turning it on.

"About ten minutes ago," Jetters said. "He called and demanded an enormous amount of money, or he'd go to the press about what we've been doing at New Genesis."

"And implicate himself in murder?" Knox said. "He's bluffing."

"I told him the same thing, but he just laughed. Said he had it all worked out so he'd get off scot-free. Dammit, I can't afford—*we* can't afford to have a scandal touch us."

"It won't," Knox said. His Geo-linking software was already searching for tower usages involving Matthew's new cell phone number. "I'm tracking the number now. Looks like he's out southwest somewhere."

"Are you sure you can get him this time?"

MICHAEL A. BLACK

"I'm sure," Knox said. "Once I zero in on his signal, I can triangulate his exact position."

"Then do it. Do it now." Jetters made a huffing sound. "I don't care how, but you have to bring him back here. I want this finished. Tonight."

"By any means necessary?"

After a moment of silence, he heard Jetters's voice say, "Yes."

The pleasure will be all mine, thought Knox. As he was about to terminate the call, Knox heard Jetters cry out, "One more thing."

"Yes?"

"Try not to harm his brain," Jetters said. "It's the key to why he was the only successful cloned specimen. He was special. I'll need to examine it."

"Understood, sir." Knox felt the trace of a smile tug at his mouth as he turned away.

The pleasure is still mine, he thought.

286

CHAPTER 22

Colby shoveled in a mouthful of broiled chicken and rice as he watched Leslie getting dressed. After chewing it as much as he could without risking swallowing it whole, he shifted the food to his cheek and asked her, "You still got that guy's card from Oakbrook Estates PD?"

She tucked the tails of her white blouse into her dark jeans. "MacEllroy? I believe so. Why?"

Colby managed to swallow without choking and paused with another spoonful poised at his mouth.

"I need it when you have time," he said.

She nodded, grabbed a piece of the broiled chicken, and went to her stack of files on the desk. "You know, you should slow down when you eat."

"And you know, you really should wear something other than white," he said. "It's too reflective."

She glanced at him over her shoulder and frowned. "I plan on wearing a jacket, too." Straightening up, she flashed a grin and held up the card, but stopped as she approached him and pointed at the TV.

The volume was very low, but Colby saw Carmel Washington talking with Pierce Nolan. In the background, over the heads of the two reporters, a large photo of Colby's face loomed. He reached for the remote, but Leslie already had it. The volume shot up suddenly, like an intruding cold breeze.

"So tell me, Carmel," Nolan was saying with his practiced delivery, "when did you first learn of this new development?"

She smiled as the camera zoomed in for a close-up. "Actually, it began when a confidential source informed me of the investigation a few days ago. And at that time, we began a special investigation."

"Which was that a series of copycat murders has been sweeping this Midwestern area, strangely mimicking Morgan Laird's original crime spree," Nolan's perfectly modulated voice said.

God, I hate that guy, Colby thought. He suddenly felt his stomach tighten again, stifling any further hunger. "Here comes my fifteen minutes of fame."

"Fifteen minutes?" Leslie asked.

He smiled. "It's a long story. Ever hear of Andy Warhol?"

"Who?"

"Never mind," he said, and leaned closer to catch the next part of the news show.

"The authorities were certain that Laird was involved in this string of new murders," Carmel said. "In fact, they even had evidence tying him to one of the crime scenes."

Christ, was there anything Dix didn't tell her?

"But with the murder of both Morgan Laird and his attorney, Mr. Lance Fontaine," Carmel continued, "the case broke wide open."

"In what way?" Nolan asked. It came off sounding staged and theatrical, as if they'd discussed every word beforehand.

Colby's mouth drew into a tight line.

"For one thing," she said, "that confidential source I mentioned before…" Carmel let a lips-only smile hide the tease, "seemed *very* interested in getting some publicity for himself." Her face got serious. "So, naturally, I was a little suspicious."

Damn, Colby thought, she's leading right to Dix. Pearson's gonna love this.

The camera shot in for a close-up showing her high cheekbones and flawless skin. "And while reporters don't normally reveal their confidential sources…"

You wouldn't know a real reporter if one bit you on the ass, thought Colby. She was just a model with a script.

"…in this case I'm forced to, because it's become part of the story."

"And quite a bizarre story it is," Nolan said.

Colby tried to remember that old quote about not suffering fools gladly. He wanted to knock that jerk on his ass the next time they met.

"Right, Pierce," Carmel said. Another clip rolled on the oversize screen behind them. It was the one showing Dix and Colby talking together on the show. "My very own source, none other than retired officer Fred Dix, was named as a 'person of interest' by the Copycat Killings Taskforce. A source close to the investigation told me that Mr. Dix is being held at the Metropolitan Correction Center at this time."

"So they're saying he killed Morgan Laird and Lance Fontaine?" Nolan's silky tones hit just the right pitch to sound sincere. The guy was probably reading it all from teleprompter.

Carmel's face took on a serious look as the levity of the recorded scene, showing Dix and Colby laughing, played on.

"Authorities aren't saying a whole lot at this time,"

she said, "but, they did say that an indictment is expected shortly."

"What possible motive could a retired cop have to go bad?" Nolan said.

Scratch those cue cards, thought Colby. Make them idiot cards.

Colby stood up and started dialing a number on his cell phone.

"Don't you want to watch the rest?" Leslie asked.

"Nah, I've already had a belly full." He heard the voice on the other end answer with a crisp, professional tone.

"Hey, Detective MacEllroy, this is Rog Colby, CPD. I need a big favor."

———

Knox was opening the special safe he kept in his office at New Genesis when he heard the soft creak of the outer door. He removed the last of his untraceable weapons, a Heckler & Koch 9 mm semi-auto with sound suppressor, and placed it into his open briefcase. The fingers of his gloved hand hovered above the weapon as much out of habit as caution. Jetters called out to him.

"Are you here?"

"Yes." He closed the lid of the briefcase and snapped the locks.

Jetters came into the office, frowning at the darkened interior, and flipped on the lights. "What the hell are you doing poking around here in the dark?"

"I like the darkness. Sharpens the senses."

The old man's mouth puckered. "And why aren't you out there tracking down Matthew? Isn't that what I told you to do?"

The old man's breath was redolent with booze. Knox

held back mentioning that the purpose of his visit was to collect the Heckler & Koch, and then raise the stakes a tad. After all, timing was everything.

"He must have turned off the phone," Knox said. "I lost the signal and had to come by here for some additional equipment."

"I thought I told you I wanted this thing terminated tonight."

Knox let a slight smile caress his lips. "You did. And it will be." He paused to watch the other man's reaction. "But I'm glad we ran into each other."

Jetters ignored the opening. "Where was he when you last tracked him?"

Knox, in turn, ignored the question. "I mentioned before that handling this case has been very risky for me. After I bring Matthew back here, I want to be pensioned off."

"And I told you, you will be," Jetters said, his head shaking with an obvious, growing rage. "Now, what are you doing to find Matthew?"

Knox laid a pair of gloved fingers on his open laptop. "Like I told you before, as soon as he uses the phone, or turns it on, I'll be able to vector in on what towers the signal is being relayed from. From there it's a simple matter of triangulation."

"What about the telemetry we gave you the other day? You can use that, too, can't you?"

The old boy must be drunker than he looks, Knox thought. Either that, or he's really losing it.

"In case you forgot, that signal has a pretty short range." He paused a moment, then changed the subject. "Back to my retirement…"

"What about it?"

Knox reached into his pocket, removed a slip of paper, and handed it to Jetters. "I opened this account today in the Cayman Islands. I want seven million dollars transferred there immediately."

"What?" Jetters stared up at him. "Are you insane?"

Knox resisted the urge to slap the old fart. He was getting tired of the condescension, and wondered what the reaction would be if he told him he had Norton's laptop and flies.

"Hardly," Knox said. "I've taken a lot of chances handling all this for you. It's essentially placed me in a position where I'll be at risk to remain here. I need a cushion."

"A seven-million-dollar cushion? That's obscene."

"Obscene is what you've been doing here, professor. Obscene is the madman out there you created who's emulating a serial killer." Knox saw the old man recoil like he'd been slapped in the face.

"My intentions were pure," he managed to say. "My honor's intact."

Knox let the smile creep upward. "That's right, as long as you have people like me to do the dirty work for you."

The old man's mouth opened, his lips trembled, but no sound came out. Finally, he looked away, then said, "Where do you expect me to come up with that kind money on such short notice?"

"That's your problem." Knox felt he had the dominant position now. It was time to lay the groundwork for his departure, and his future. Still, it would be better to hold something back. Not put all of his aces down on the table just yet. "Call one of your politician friends in Washington. There's plenty of money there, especially when you've been growing new organs for half of them."

Jetters looked like he was on the verge of tears, his voice a whisper when he spoke. "You have no idea what it was like. No idea."

Knox used the opportunity to revel in the moment. He'd won. He was certain of it. He let the old fool ramble on.

"Before we realized how much more expedient it was just to grow the specific organs, when John Norton and I first withdrew that deoxyribonucleic acid out of that cell twenty-six years ago…" His eyes appeared distant, unfocused. "When we were able to put that nucleonic bundle into that first, unfertilized egg…to see life being created in a test tube."

Knox began to worry that the old coot was loping toward a complete breakdown.

"Professor—"

Jetters raised his hand in a sharp, cutting gesture, and continued to talk, as if he were giving a homily from a pulpit.

"And seeing the first fetus evolve through the process. Seeing the being that we'd created, right here, right in this very building, ourselves, playing God, creating life…"

He really was losing it, Knox thought. And if the old bastard cracks, I'll never see my money.

"The first ones were fragile," Jetters continued. "Their cell structure like tissue paper. Couldn't sustain itself. So many failures." His hands covered his face, muffling the words that came next. "And the slew of the Others, physically strong, capable of thinking, yet limited in cognitive development ability. So many close misses, and then finally, after so many, many attempts, Matthew. The one shining success in a sea of failures."

Knox heard his laptop alarm chime. He glanced at the screen and saw the number of Matthew's new cell phone flashing on the screen inside a little pop-up box that said, *Now in Use.*

"He's using his phone again," Knox said, eager to snap the professor out of his melancholy ramblings.

Jetters perked up, his eyes clear now, flashing toward the open laptop. Suddenly his own cell phone jangled in his pocket. His eyes focused darkly on Knox, then he held the phone to his ear.

"Yes?"

Knox knew immediately, from the expression on Jetters's face, who it was. He pressed more keys on the laptop, vectoring in on various maps, larger grids at first, then smaller each time.

"Matthew, where are you?"

Knox looked back to Jetters, gauging how long the conversation would last. The longer, the better, but as long as the little creep left the phone on after the call, Knox could resend the tracking signal and it would still pick it up. He waited, intentionally wanting to see how this little drama would play out. Jetters cringed, like he was actually in physical pain.

"Come back, son. I want to help you, before it's too late."

Knox could hear Matthew's raucous laughter over the phone, then, after a few more seconds, he saw Jetters slowly put the cell phone back in his pocket.

"He says he's going to bring down New Genesis. Unless I pay him even more than you're asking for."

Asking? Knox thought, I'm demanding what I deserve.

"Find him," Jetters said. "Bring him back here. Tonight." His face took on a look of complete and total determination. "I can't have him ruining a lifetime of work. Too much is at stake."

"Consider it done." Knox picked up his briefcase in one hand and his laptop in the other. "As long as you make that wire transfer for me."

"Yes, yes, you'll have it in the morning, dammit."

"And then you shall have Matthew," Knox said, but Jetters had that far-away expression again. He turned and walked out of the office, muttering to himself. Knox listened to the professor's parting words.

"I've got to find out why. Why I succeeded with him, and not the others. Must analyze his brain cells. See exactly where I succeeded. And where I failed."

I'll have to remember not to shoot the kid in the head, Knox thought as he watched the laptop continuing the vectoring process of the tracking signal.

———

Matthew smirked as he terminated the call. It was risky, he knew, playing his hand before he was done. But he needed to do it. He wanted to set the wheels in motion so that Jetters would know this was no bluff.

I'm capable of anything, he thought. And he knows it.

He glanced back at the Turner twins sleeping blissfully in the back of the rental van. The Blem sat beside them, his mouth taped shut with duct tape, his hands and feet secured with the new handcuffs.

"It won't be long now," he said to them, knowing that they wouldn't have the slightest idea what he meant even if they could hear him. It was difficult, though, to perform without an audience. Perhaps it was the most difficult part. No one could really appreciate the depth of his genius. Working it all out, flaunting it in the face of the authorities, and having a plan so perfect that after the final act was complete, he could just walk away.

Sprinkling some of the tranquilizers on the ice cream cones had been brilliant. He smiled as he'd watched the two little girls licking them down, the undiluted tranqs exploding into their systems as he talked with their pig of a mother.

He regretted not being able to kill her. The sight of her disgusting body writhing on the ground in the rear of the parking lot after he'd Tasered her made him smile again. She'd bought it hook, line, and sinker when he said they'd have to go around the back to go in the studio. It would have been more expedient to slice open her throat and leave her to bleed to death on the asphalt. But he needed her to wake up and call the cops. He needed the notoriety of the girls being taken. An Amber Alert, no doubt. So he'd just kept his finger on the trigger, giving her shock after shock until he grew tired and just walked over and kicked her in the head. He was confident that he'd knocked out some of her rotten teeth, the blood spilling from her lips. But her pulse was strong, so she wasn't dead. Just unconscious.

He'd left his last, autographed copy of Colby's book by her prostrate body, with the page marking the chapter about the Swanstrom Twins folded down so the cops would get the connection. No one knew to look for the rented van, which he'd parked behind the strip mall. Ms. Turner had been only too happy to drive them all back to the "studio shoot" at the strip mall. He had only to carry the slumbering twins from the mother's car to the van, and drive away.

It was all he could do to steer around the pig's body on the ground, too. But Morgan hadn't killed Mrs. Swanstrom, so this one had to live, too.

Symmetry, he thought. Perfect symmetry.

———

"Detective MacEllroy gave us your number, Chief," Colby said, standing on the man's front porch. It was cold now that the sun had gone down, and he could see his breath. Hank Meister stared back through the screen door. He was a big man and Colby reflected that they weren't that far apart in age. He hoped that he didn't look as bad as Meister did. The man's gut hung over his pants like a sagging bladder.

"I'll be outside for a bit," Meister called to someone inside the house. He disappeared for several moments, then came out slipping on a jacket as he stepped outside. He looked at Colby, then at Leslie, and said, "He called me. Said you gave him some life-and-death story about New Genesis?"

Colby debated how much to tell Meister. The guy had all the earmarks of an ineffectual police chief from a bedroom community, who was loafing through retirement with some glorified, do-nothing, security position. Still, he had little choice. He had to get something to take to Pearson. Something that would get Dix off the hook before they indicted him.

"It's looking more and more like that," Colby said. "What can you tell us about New Genesis?"

Meister strolled away from his front porch, over a grassy lawn and toward the yellowish glow of a streetlight by the curb. His big face puckered. "Look, I signed a confidentiality agreement when I took the position there. If I go talking about the company, I'd be opening myself up to civil litigation."

"Civil's civil, Chief," Colby said, hoping the respectful use of the man's former title would establish some cop-to-cop line of communication. "We're talking criminal here. Big time."

Meister's pucker deepened, sending wrinkles lacing down his cheeks, his gaze shifting to the ground.

He's almost there, Colby thought. But does he need a push to go over the wall?

"Chief, I'm asking you, one cop to another, trust your gut."

It was all the push Meister needed. "Okay. What do you want to know? I'll try to see if I can answer it."

"New Genesis. What is it they do there?"

"It's mostly a research center," Meister said. His voice swelled with something akin to pride. "Medical research. Cutting edge, too. They get a lot of important people there for stuff ranging from cancer treatments to transplant operations. But they do lots of other stuff there as well."

"You know this guy?" Colby asked, holding up the picture of "Vernon Krems" crossing the border into Canada.

"Sure." Meister nodded. "That's Mr. Knox. He works there."

"What's his job?"

"He's kind of a jack-of-all-trades." Meister raised his eyebrows. "He mixed up in something?"

Colby shook his head. He'd been here before, knowing that he had to take control of the interview and not let Meister ask the questions, but still soft-soap the man enough so that he didn't clam up.

"Chief, I can't say right now. What I need from you is just your unbiased answers. I'll tell you everything once I get the facts I need."

A slight smile grazed Meister's lips. "Yeah, I guess I'd do the same. Once a cop, always a cop, I guess."

That's what I'm counting on, Colby thought.

"Knox is sort of in charge of internal security matters," Meister said. "I'm really just a glorified groundskeeper, if the truth be told. I oversee the uniformed division, but our function is mostly just security. Checking doors, patrolling the grounds for people wandering in and resident escapees."

"Escapees?"

"Yeah, the professor runs a school there. For retarded kids."

Colby wrinkled his brow. "Where did they come from?"

"From the program he runs with the prisons. Women's prisons. Takes a select few each year, the ones that are pregnant, and keeps them incarcerated, giving them good nutrition and schooling until their babies are born." Meister shrugged. "Most of them are probably little crack babies anyway. Nobody wants them."

"So the kids stay there?" Colby asked. He was trying to get a semblance of the big picture, but too many pieces were missing.

Meister nodded again. "Like I said, crack babies. Most of them turn up mentally challenged, or so I'm told. I really don't have much to do with them. But I hear that the professor is real particular that they're treated well."

"I'll bet he is." Colby glanced at Leslie, who was standing there with rapt attention. "What's Knox's background?"

Meister shook his head. "Don't have access to his personnel file, but I heard through the grapevine that he used to work for the government before he came here."

"That professor sounds like he's too good to be true," Colby said. "What's his story?"

"He's probably," Meister said, raising his eyebrows again, "the smartest fella I ever met. Like he's on a different plane from the rest of us."

Colby looked at Leslie and nodded.

"Did you know Professor John Norton?" she asked.

Meister's brow flicked and wrinkled some more. "Yeah. Heard he was killed in a mugging up in Canada."

"Were he and Jetters close?"

"Used to be," Meister said. "But lately, I got the feeling they'd had a falling out."

"How so?"

"Well, I heard them arguing a lot. Norton was upset over something that was happening in Europe." He paused and shifted his eyes upward. "Italy, or someplace. Something about a cloned horse, and how they were passing us by."

"A cloned horse?" Colby asked.

Meister nodded. "I was in the outer office waiting to see Professor Jetters when I heard it. He laughed and said, 'Just like those gooks with their dog? Let the accolades fall where they may.' I thought it was a funny way of putting things, so that's why I remembered it."

"And then what happened?"

Meister shrugged. "The professor saw me standing there, gave me a glare, and walked over and slammed the door shut. I got the message and left. But I remembered what he said."

"When was this?" Leslie asked.

Meister's lower lip engulfed his upper. "About a month or so ago, I'd say."

"Right before the Toronto convention," she said. "An international geneticist's convention."

"Know anybody named Vernon Krems?" Colby asked.

Meister shook his head. "Why?"

This was spiraling out of control again. But he needed to keep Meister with him.

"Chief, can you get us into New Genesis tonight?"

"Tonight?"

Colby nodded. "I need to get a handle on this guy Knox. Can you let us see his personnel file?"

Meister's head shook in little movements. "I dunno."

"Look, Chief," Colby said. "Like I told you, we're talking some major crimes here. Homicides."

Meister looked at him, his mouth now a tiny, gaping hole.

"Homicides? Who?"

"John Norton, for one. And a couple more, we think." Colby watched the expression on Meister's face go through several transformations, then turn resolute.

"Let me get my coat," he said, all serious business now. "And my keys."

CHAPTER 23

Meister led them along the winding, tree-lined streets toward New Genesis. It was Friday night, and close to seven. Colby hoped to get something to take to Pearson. Hopefully, it would be a way out of the downward spiral he was caught in. But hoping wouldn't cut it. Still, he had to try.

Leslie had been silent beside him, but he knew she shared the same doubts. This feeling was reaffirmed a moment later when she looked over at him and asked, "Have you figured out how all this ties together?"

He sighed. "Not totally. It must have to do with Laird's original connection to Norton, and hence, this place."

The brake lights of Meister's Cadillac flashed. Colby hit his brakes as the big El Dorado slowed to a stop in front of them.

"Are we there?" Leslie asked.

Colby shook his head. "Close." His cell rang.

"Detective?" Meister asked. "You see that BMW that just passed us?"

Colby vaguely remembered it. Meister's brake lights

still shone brightly. His car edged to the side of the road. "I'm pretty sure that was Knox."

Colby glanced in the rearview mirror. Twin taillights were receding into the darkness.

"You want to go after him?" Meister's voice asked. "I can call some of my ex-boys on the PD to pull him down on traffic or something."

Colby considered this. He was still officially stripped, as Kropper had so vividly reminded him. That meant his police powers were nonexistent. Plus, he needed more of an edge.

"Let's try and tag him, Chief. He know your car?"

"Probably," Meister said. "He's pretty sharp."

"Okay," Colby said, glancing in the rearview mirror again as he shifted to reverse, backed up a tad, and made a sweeping U-turn. "We'll stay in the lead. You keep about a hundred feet behind, in case he makes us. We'll do it in tandem."

"Ten-four," Meister said and ended the call.

Colby figured this was probably about as close to police work as Meister had gotten in years, but his presence was a plus. He was pretty sure Knox was armed. They had one gun and two cell phones between him and Leslie. Colby had forgotten to ask Meister if he was packing. If it got hot and heavy, backup would be a 9-1-1 call away. He found himself longing for his fifteen-shot Beretta instead of Brewer's old five-shot, snub-nosed revolver. Hopefully, the ammunition hadn't turned green.

The distinctive row of the BMW's taillights appeared ahead of them, and Colby eased off the accelerator a bit. He didn't want his headlights to become noticeable in Knox's mirrors.

He turned to Leslie. "Maybe he'll lead us to another one of the copycat conspiracy boys. Laird had to have help."

"That's what I was thinking," she said.

"I thought I smelled rubber burning."

She gave him a playful slap, which he also considered a positive sign. It was going to be hard when it came time for her to go back to the Great White North. He thought about that for a moment. Maybe he could ask her to stay. But there was about as much chance of that as baseball replacing hockey as Canada's national pastime. Besides, his immediate priority was nailing Knox and getting Dix off the hook.

His cell rang again, and Colby fumbled to answer it, wishing he had his Bluetooth.

"You on him?" Meister asked.

This guy had ants in his pants. "Yeah. We're still heading west, I think."

"How about I pass you and take over? I know this area a lot better than you."

"Sounds good," Colby said, hoping Meister wouldn't lose their quarry. But traffic was pretty sparse. Maybe it would be better if Knox noticed a new set of headlights in his rearview mirror.

Colby watched as Meister's Caddie went around them.

"Okay, I'm on him," Meister said. His voice imbued with excitement. Colby knew every copper dreamed of the big case that would evolve into an adventure. Looks like the ex-chief had finally gotten his.

"I think we're heading for the Tri-State," Meister said. "He's moving at just under the speed limit."

"Great, Chief. Stay on him."

Colby thought about it. Knox was driving at an average rate to avoid getting stopped. That must have meant he was en route somewhere where he couldn't afford any delays or distractions. Things might be looking up after all.

"Yeah, we're definitely getting on two-ninety-four," Meister said. "I'm on him."

They got on the Tollway and began heading south. It became an easy tail, with the enclosed distances allowing them to back off slightly and still keep the BMW in sight.

"Colby?" It was Meister. "I think he might've made me. His head's moving around like crazy."

It was pretty dark. Meister might just be experiencing the phantom jitters. Common enough for somebody inexperienced in the art of tailing.

"Go ahead and drop back," Colby said, figuring he'd feel better being in control anyway. "We'll pick up the slack for a while."

"All right, I'll switch to the right lane and come up on your six."

Our six? Colby grinned. Old boy must have been a former Marine.

"Don't you want to know what I was thinking about?" Leslie asked.

"Yeah."

"Remember Chief Meister saying they specialize in organ research and transplants at New Genesis?"

He nodded, focusing on looking inconspicuous as he shot past Meister's vehicle.

"Well," she continued, "there was something I remembered about Norton's autopsy. He'd had numerous organ transplant operations." She patted the file on her lap. "I was reading the autopsy report on Norton's significant other. He appeared to be an organ transplant recipient, too."

"What are you suggesting?" Colby slowed down, keeping a watch on the BMW's taillights.

"The tox-screen didn't show the presence of any anti-rejection drugs," she said. "Usually people who have had organ transplants have to take them continually to keep the body's own defensive antibodies from attacking the foreign organ."

"Yeah, I've heard that."

"Plus," Leslie continued. "The coroner said Norton's organs were in remarkable shape for a man his age. Almost like brand new."

Colby considered this as he watched the BMW's taillights. This case was getting weirder and weirder. He wondered if they'd find any answers when they got where they were going.

————

It hit Matthew like a gut punch as soon as he crested the bridge. The refinery, or rather, what had once been the refinery, was now in a state of shambles. Instead of the massive, block-like rows of isomerization units, production towers, blowdown drums, and cement distillation columns, the entire area looked like it had been hit by a bombing raid. Only a few scattered columns remained, and most of those had long plastic coverings draped over them. Piles of rubble, brick, fractured cement blocks, and tangles of rebar filled the area in between. Matthew braked and turned left at the intersection. Across the street the rows of huge storage tanks reposed in a rusting tranquility. The barrel storage area was gone as well. That was where Morgan had stashed the Swanstrom twins.

They're tearing it down, he thought. All of it. They can't do this. It'll ruin the last act.

Furious, he rolled by the main entrance. The twelve-foot cyclone fence was rusted and sagging, running up to the gate where he could see a lighted guard shack. A huge sign on the front gates said it all:

NO TRESPASSING

DEMOLITION IN PROGRESS

He was sure that this was the same place where Morgan had made his last stand, where the cop shot him in the back. But now, it was all different.

Matthew licked his lips and let the changes in the scenario run through his mind. The few houses across from the refinery looked dark and unoccupied.

Probably abandoned. Good. No witnesses.

He glanced back over his shoulder at his passengers. The twins still appeared to be sleeping. They'd feel less pain that way, and that would cheat him out of the thrill of watching their terror. Still, he needed to concentrate on setting this up as best he could. A few minor changes wouldn't hurt. And it would even allow him to put his own personal stamp on things. Plus, this was more about setting up the finale than mirroring Morgan's last battle with the police.

Matthew came to the end of the fence line. The refinery's property gave way to a grassy slope and a set of metallic stairs descending from the railroad tracks running above them. He got to the corner and turned left, going under the cement columns of the viaduct. The stop light was red about forty feet ahead, and across the street was the truck-storage facility that Morgan had driven the stolen cop car into when he was being chased. Right before they shot him down like a dog, ruining what had been a very active and productive life.

That place looked abandoned now, too. A row of high weeds had crept up through the patches of green alongside the front. Everything had changed. Nothing was the same as it had been for Morgan.

But Matthew knew he could still make it work. He'd just have to be a little more creative.

He turned right driving parallel to the railroad tracks

on an elevated embankment. He'd go by the Franklin Hotel. See where Morgan had stayed in his last night of freedom, before outwitting the cops and shooting two of them. Three, if you counted that fat asshole, Dix. But Matthew had already made up his mind to avenge Morgan, in his own special way. He slowed down and pulled out the cell phone. There were two more calls he had to make before stashing the burner phone on the Blem.

Knox had the laptop on the seat next to him and glanced at it intermittently. The vector arrow had slowed almost to a stop, and from the map he figured he was a good ten or twelve miles away. As he got closer, the mapping would enlarge, but from the general area depicted, he knew that Matthew had last used a tower in the South Suburbs. The Blue Island area from the looks of it.

Knox tried to think what the little prick would be doing there. It was typically blue collar, and a bit rough for a twerp like him. Still, he had overpowered and strangled the health technician in the escape. Of course, Desmond Kirby wasn't exactly a formidable opponent and was probably figuring on nothing more challenging in his afternoon than feeding the Others.

Nevertheless, Knox had been surprised at Matthew's resourcefulness. The punk was not only smart, he was dangerous, too.

Knox veered over and went into the I-Pass lanes as another toll area approached. In his rearview mirror, he noticed another set of headlights do the same. Nothing unusual about that, except this pair of headlights looked familiar. The car had been behind him for quite a while.

A tail? But who?

Knox saw the vectoring arrow flutter slightly, showing Matthew was on the move again. But it didn't move far. The arrow stopped again. If Matthew was driving, he must be going in circles. Looking for something, perhaps?

Knox accelerated and smiled.

He'd find out soon enough.

CHAPTER 24

"Looks like we're getting off at Cicero," Meister's voice said over the cell phone. He'd taken over the tail again.

"Which direction you heading?"

"Gotta drop back a little." Meister's voice sounded strained.

If Knox spotted Meister, the whole game could be blown. "Stay on him, chief."

"I will," Meister grunted. "He's going left, toward... Cicero Avenue. You know this area at all?"

"A little," Colby said. He pressed the accelerator, shooting around sets of slower-moving vehicles, and then cutting right to make the exit. The ramp curved out of sight under a bridge.

"I'm still a few cars back," Meister said. "Don't think he spotted me. Looks like he's jumpy, though. His head keeps bobbling."

Colby took that to mean that Knox must have seen Meister's Caddie at some point, and was, at the very least, alerted.

"He's turning left now," Meister said. "Coming up to

—" His voice faltered. "Dammit. No street signs I can see. It's the first light after you go over the bridge."

"Ten-four," Colby said. He could see the superstructure just up ahead. "I'm coming up behind you." He swore as traffic ahead of him slowed to a stop for a red light.

"Is it always this nerve-racking?" Leslie asked.

"No," he said with a grin. "It's usually a lot worse."

She laughed.

"A good partner can mean the difference between success and failure," he said. "They have to be tuned into each other."

She was silent for a moment. "Like your friend Dix?"

Colby smiled at the thought. The truth of the matter was that Dix had shown him the ropes when they'd first partnered up, even saved his bacon more than a few times. But at the end, Colby hadn't been totally sad when Dix pulled the pin. When it was time to go, it was better to go while you still had game.

"He was a good partner," Colby said.

Leslie seemed to consider this, then asked, "Is it hard, tracking down someone like Morgan Laird? Trying to stay one step ahead of him?"

"At the time, we didn't even know what we had." Visions of that last chase flashed through his mind as he silently willed the light to change to green. "It was more of a lucky break. Being at the right place at the right time."

"We're heading northeast now," Meister said. "On an angle street. Viaduct ahead, houses on either side."

"Okay, Chief," Colby said into the phone. "We're bogged down in traffic, but we'll catch up to you."

"Do you have any idea where he's going?" Leslie asked.

He shook his head, but in the back of his mind, some-thing had occurred to him. Something from a long time ago.

No, he thought. No chance. It would be too coinciden-tal. Like déjà vu all over again.

———

The Franklin Hotel didn't look anything like it did in the old pictures. They'd completely re-sided it, and instead of a dilapidated sign advertising low SRO rates, the sign now said, *Island Condominiums*. Things had really changed.

Matthew's mouth drew into a tight line as he sped past it, taking the same route that Morgan had taken twenty-eight years before. Over the railroad tracks, past the bank building and stores, back toward the oil refinery. Or what was left of it. Nothing was working out the way he wanted.

He slammed his fist onto the seat next to him. It had been his plan, his artistic desire to re-create Morgan's work with painstaking accuracy, in some hope that he could someday contact him and explain the perfection with which he'd been able to execute things. But it was too late for that now. Everything had changed. Still, he needed to tie this up with an appropriate Gordian Knot. Something that would say case closed, but still leave a sliver of doubt to keep them guessing.

He and the Blem were dressed exactly alike, and they had identical DNA. Morgan's DNA. When they found the Blem's body, everything would point to him. Matthew would be in the clear to make a new start with the money he'd saved. Once established, he could begin to extort more from New Genesis. With all the old man's connections, he was bound to prolong prosecution. But hopefully, he'd still be discredited, ruined. Exposure of his hideous experiments would be the ultimate revenge. It would be his time to sit in the Petri dish waiting for the next development.

Matthew fingered the length of rope he'd purchased and fashioned into a noose. A quick suicide note, identifying himself as Laird's son, would be sufficient for the stupid cops, who'd be looking for the path of least resistance. Probably wouldn't question anything, and if they did, how would they prove it? The Blem was practically untraceable, and they'd probably just write case closed on what they'd say was a genetic anomaly. Then, later, when he'd settled in Mexico and amassed a fortune from Jetters, perhaps he'd start dropping clues that all wasn't settled so neatly in what they thought was the final act.

He fingered his cell phone, ready to make his last call. After selecting the number, he pressed the send-key and waited. The mechanized voice answered.

"You have reached the news offices of WWDF Television in Chicago. If you have a news tip for *Chicago Today*, please press one. If you have a news tip for—"

Matthew pressed one, and listened to another automated voice give instructions to leave a message after the beep. "And be sure to leave your contact information along with it," the cheerful voice added.

Yeah, right, thought Matthew. He needed to word this carefully, and he was almost at the abandoned truck rental facility. As he stopped for the light, he said into the phone, "Listen, I've got those twins wanted in that Amber Alert, and I'm going to kill them in revenge for that fucking cop killing Morgan Laird. I'm leaving a note that will explain everything."

He disconnected as he passed the metallic staircase,

and the silhouettes of the few remaining towers of the old Penicolt Oil Refinery came into view.

———

Knox turned and looked at the vehicles parked by the Island Condominiums, hoping to see one of Matthew's cars there. He had to be driving a rental truck, since Knox was sure the Corvette was still tucked away in the storage facility, but there was also a chance he would try and use Kirby's vehicle for a getaway car. Knox saw the vectoring arrow make still yet another turn. He waited for the damn screen to update its mapping image. But he was close now. Very close. In the meantime, he glanced in the rearview mirror again. That Cadillac was still behind him. The same one from the tollway. It had to be a tail, but who?

Time to find out. Knox slowed his BMW slightly, forcing the car behind him to pass. That left no one between him and the Caddie. It slowed down as well, maintaining a long space interval. Knox hit the brakes abruptly as he went under a streetlight, watching the Caddie almost rear-end him. He studied the image of the other driver in the mirror. A face jerked into view, then disappeared as the driver leaned back. It was just a flash, but it was enough: Meister.

What's that incompetent idiot doing way out here? Knox thought. And why is he following me?

Up ahead, he saw the red lights activate on the black-and-white arm of a railroad crossing barrier. It started to descend and Knox glanced at the vectoring arrow. He had to make it though, and hit the gas pedal hard, shooting around the lowering arm.

Let's see if this loses fat-boy, he thought. If not, more drastic measures might be called for.

"He's going west on a street called Vermont," Meister said on the phone. "Hold on. He's cutting around some railroad gates. Gonna follow him."

Colby shot through the traffic and unfamiliar streets, trying to catch Meister.

"Got through," Meister said. Colby could hear the ringing of the warning bells over the phone. "Barely. Don't think you will."

Colby hit the gas, shooting around a car in front of him.

"This damn place has more train tracks than Union Station," he said. "And most of them are slow-moving freights."

"You've been here before?" she asked.

He nodded. "Long time ago."

Colby twisted the wheel and turned left onto Vermont, seeing the blinking red lights on the now fully descended gates. He floored it, edging over into the oncoming lane of traffic. Several cars were heading toward them and honking. Colby cut back to his own lane, then veered out again, just as the deep resonance of the approaching diesel blared out.

"You're going around the gates?" Leslie said, her eyes wide with fear. "We'll never make it."

Colby glanced over at the approaching freight train, perhaps two hundred feet away and speeding toward the crossing. It was moving pretty fast. The powerful whistle blasted another warning.

Colby did a quick computation of his chances of making it across without getting creamed, glancing to his left at the two hundred tons of steel barreling forward, horn blaring and headlight cutting through the evening darkness, and decided the chances beating it were slim and none.

And slim had left town.

"Shit," he said, and hit the brakes, twisting the wheel, to send the Chevy into a side-wrenching skid, but stopping just short of the lowered, black-and-white arm with the flashing red lights.

"Oh my god," Leslie said, her voice little more than a gasp.

The huge engine rumbled by, looking like a specter from the Grim Reaper. Colby pounded his fist on the wheel. The cell phone had gone flying and he bent down to feel for it on the floor. When he finally found it, he immediately held it to his head and said, "Chief, we caught the damn train. Where you at?"

Meister's voice sounded even more flustered.

"We're turning onto a street called…Francisco. Now we're turning right onto one hundred thirty-first," he said. "Hey, wait a minute, he's pulling over. I think he's made me."

"Shit," Colby said again. This wasn't working out the way he'd hoped at all. "Drive on by him. We'll find a way around this train."

"Aaaah." Meister grunted. "He's waving me down. Like he wants to talk, or something. I'll make a cover story."

He hung up before Colby could tell him not to. Staring at the dead phone, he swore again.

Leslie tapped him on the shoulder and pointed.

"There are a bunch of cars turning around," she said. "Do you think that means they know another route?"

Colby watched the endless stream of passing freight cars, which were going noticeably slower now. He glanced to his left and saw the turning cars.

What the hell, he thought, cranking the wheel. It sure beats sitting here and waiting.

———

Knox waved again as he stepped out onto the roadway, tucking his fingers into the tight leather driving gloves. Nothing around but abandoned houses and an old oil refinery, he thought. Not a bad place for a little interrogation. But he knew it would have to be quick. Matthew was close, just on the other side of the cyclone fence.

He saw Meister slowing to a stop, a false grin plastered over his face.

"Chief Meister," Knox said, stepping around to the driver's side as Meister lowered the window. "Am I glad to see you."

"Yeah," Meister said. "Funny meeting you out here. I thought that was your car, so I wanted to say hi."

"It's good that you showed up when you did," Knox said, spotting the cell phone in Meister's lap. "I'm on company business and I can use some help. Anybody with you?"

Meister shook his head and pointed to the phone. "Just talking to the missus, is all."

Knox could tell he was lying. "What are you doing out this way?"

"Visiting a friend," Meister said, a little too quickly.

Knox smiled.

Probably shadowing me since I left the compound, he thought, shifting his stance slightly, away from Meister's line of vision.

"Our quarry's right over there," Knox said, his lips pulling back into a smile. His right hand flipped up the flap of his jacket, and his fingers fitted themselves around the thick grip of the Heckler & Koch.

"Huh?" Meister said.

Knox brought the long-barreled pistol up with a smooth motion. He stopped when the sound suppressor was an inch away from Meister's left temple.

The plinking sound was barely audible.

Knox watched Meister stiffen, his jaw going slack at the same time, like he'd been slapped when he was just getting the punch line of a dirty joke. The ex-chief slumped over on his right side, and Knox stuck his arm in through the window space and pulled the trigger three more times, each bullet making a neat, round hole as it entered the side of Meister's head. He pushed the smoking extended barrel against Meister's open left eye.

Not a flinch.

Smiling, Knox opened the door and plucked the three brass casings from the space between the seat and Meister's back. Then he picked up the final casing from the street and placed them all in his pocket.

That was the only thing about using a semi-auto, he thought. Plenty of rounds, but you always have to police your damn brass.

———

Matthew pulled into the gravel driveway and stopped just short of the wire gate. He laid on the horn until a heavyset security guard came shuffling out of the gate shack. The guy wore some sort of half-assed uniform, with a big revolver swinging in a holster on his belt. Probably interrupted his evening snooze.

"Hey, what's the big idea with the damn horn?" the guard asked. His glasses were perched regally on his nose, and despite the flaccid look of his jowls, he'd managed a pretty fair imitation of a tough guy.

"I'm sorry, sir," Matthew said. He'd slipped on the

wig again, but had the hair pulled back into a ponytail. It would be easier to fit onto the Blem that way. "But the other guard told me to come down here."

The guard's face wrinkled between the eyes.

"What other guard?"

Matthew brought the Taser up with his right hand and pulled the trigger after seeing the red dot on the security guard's blue shirt, just above the silver badge. The man dropped like a decapitated marionette, and Matthew let him taste the full ninety-second burst. He opened the door and pulled the trigger again, sending more juice down the wires as he got out of the truck. The guard's body jerked and twisted like a fish on the pier. Matthew reached down with his left hand and unsnapped the revolver from its holster. It came out quite easily, and he liked the way it felt.

He eased up on the trigger and watched the security guard's chest heave up and down with frantic breathing motions.

"There, there," Matthew said, setting the Taser down and switching the revolver to his right hand. "It won't hurt a bit anymore. I promise."

He placed the barrel directly over the man's forehead and cocked back the hammer.

Feel the rush, he thought, and squeezed the trigger.

———

The sound of the shot from somewhere in the confines of the crumbling oil refinery grounds was unmistakable to Knox as he dropped Meister's Cadillac into gear and let it do a slow roll into the overgrown bushes and shrubs at the rear of the fence line. The big El Dorado was still visible. He debated taking the time to fashion some more efficient concealment but decided against it. This looked to be a pretty deserted area, and the Meister would probably sit for hours before being discovered. It would have to do. Time was the antagonist now. He had to catch Matthew, incapacitate him, and bring him and the Other back to New Genesis before anyone discovered them here. From the sound of things, the little bastard was up to his old tricks again. And from the sound of it, possibly armed. This added a new wrinkle. The chances that he could bring him in without physical harm now were dubious.

I've come too far to get shot by some spoiled little psychopath, Knox thought as he slipped the compact scanner out of his pocket. He switched it on and watched the circular directional finder send a series of flashing dots in a northwesterly direction. Knox looked up.

The Other has got to be in that old refinery, he thought. But the overriding question was whether Matthew was still with him.

———

After dragging the guard out of sight behind the gate shack, Matthew pushed the long metal gate open just far enough to allow space for the van to pass. Then he ran back to it, put it in drive, and drove through, stopping to close, but not lock, the gate after him. The Blem was a whimpering idiot, constantly trying to pull his hands out of the handcuffs.

"Stop that," Matthew said as gruffly as he could. Suspicious lacerations on the Blem's wrists might make the scenario less believable. He steered around several piles of smashed bricks and twisted rebar and headed toward one of the four remaining isomerization units. The huge, chimney-like shape of tan bricks stretched upward against the velvet sky. Except for strategically placed lights, the yard was dark and deserted. It looked like a bombed-out city.

When the demolition crew came into work tomorrow, they would be in for a surprise. Four bodies. Of course, he'd have to do a rushed job killing the twins due to the time constraint. He'd just strangle them both and spit on their bodies. That would leave a traceable source of DNA, which the cops would match to the Blem, who'd be left hanging, literally, nearby.

A tragic suicide, replete with a note and a copy of Colby's book.

Colby. Matthew regretted he hadn't been able to come face-to-face with the man who was responsible for paralyzing Morgan and putting him in prison. But the asshole cop would have to live the rest of his life knowing that he couldn't stop the second coming of Morgan Laird. Maybe someday there would be a third.

He stopped the van between two big piles of debris and hopped out, leaving the lights on and the motor running. He needed to see what he was doing.

The first thing he did was pull both of the girls from the back and lay them out on the ground in front of the van. The stark glare of the headlights washed over their slumbering bodies. One shifted slightly, perhaps having a dream.

I hope it's a good one, princess, Matthew thought. Because it's your last.

———

"There's Francisco," Leslie said, pointing at the oversized street sign. Colby turned left. He'd managed to follow two other cars that'd turned around at the sight of the slow-moving freight, and they'd led him on a circuitous, but train-free route back to Vermont. The area was taking on that eerie look of something familiar, yet different. The old truck rental building, the strong cement arches under the viaduct were a dilapidated version of the scene that had haunted his dreams for the past twenty-eight years.

"A hundred thirty-first," Leslie said, pointing again.

Colby turned and they rolled past the metallic stairway. It looked more rusted than he remembered. And instead of the well-lighted refinery with an endless maze of twisting pipes, he saw the bleak silhouettes of the few remaining stacks and towers, illuminated only by a sprinkling of perimeter lights.

"Keep your eye out for Meister's car," he said, glancing back and forth.

"Over there." She pointed to the right.

The rear end of a vehicle was visible in the high grass, wedged into an array of bushes.

Colby leaned in front of her and shone his mini-mag flashlight through the open passenger side window.

The beam swept over the trunk, taillights, and chrome bumper.

"Damn," Colby said, and stopped.

———————

Matthew bent to place his hands over the girl's slim neck when he heard a scream, accompanied by a banging. The damn Blem. Angry, Matthew stood and walked over to the van. He'd taken the guard's flashlight and now shined it into the Blem's startled face.

The creature grunted.

Pathetic, thought Matthew.

"Come," he said, motioning with the beam. "Come here."

The Blem looked at him a few seconds before moving,

then scurried across the ribbed floor toward the open rear doors.

Matthew fished the handcuff key out of his pocket and roughly twisted the Blem around. The retard kept squirming until Matthew slapped him on the top of the head. It still took several tries to hold the cuffs steady enough to fit the small key into the round hole. After removing the cuffs, he tossed them onto the floor of the van.

He won't go far with those leg-irons on, Matthew thought.

Something else suddenly occurred to him.

The van. He'd have to leave it here and get out of here on foot. How else could the presence of the three bodies be explained? Otherwise, the cops would realize there was another person involved.

———

They both got out cautiously and approached the Cadillac from opposite sides. Colby had Brewer's snub nose thirty-eight out and in the ready position in front of him. Edging closer, he shone the beam inside the vehicle, sweeping over the inert form slumped over in the front seat. He opened the door and felt Meister's neck for a pulse.

"Is he dead?" Leslie asked.

Colby nodded and felt a searing rage seize his gut. This was his fault. If he hadn't let Meister take the lead in the tail …

"What do we do now?" Leslie asked.

Colby motioned for her to back away from the Cadillac and go to the street.

He knew she had no weapon, and he didn't have one to spare.

"Here." He handed her his cell phone. "Stay here and dial nine-one-one. Tell whoever answers your location and that there's been a homicide. When the cops get here, tell them the story. All of it."

"Wouldn't it be better for you to do that?"

"Knox is nearby," he said. "This is the last chance to catch him red-handed."

"But how will you find him? Looks like he already fled."

Colby glanced around, taking in the old, but new, sights, sounds, and smells. He shook his head. "He came here for some reason. Besides, I got an idea where he's at."

Leslie looked confused. "How?"

"Like I said, I've been here before."

She looked more confused. "Be careful. He's armed."

"If I can't handle some asshole with a ponytail," Colby said, getting back into his car, "it'll be time to hang 'em up anyway."

———

Matthew had originally planned to string up the Blem from one of the still-standing towers but realized that it would be just as easy to tie the rope off on the van's rear bumper and loop it over the open door. He could use the dead guard's car for his getaway, but that would tip them to another person being there. He'd have to hoof it for a few blocks until he found someplace to call a taxi, or something. Everything else would fall into place beautifully. The bitch from the rental place would identify the dead Blem as the van's renter, especially with the wig in place. And it would tie things up in a neat little bow.

He smiled at his own cleverness.

Improvisation. Easy when you're just a little bit

smarter than the stupid cops and the rest of the dumb populace.

Matthew took the wig off and grabbed the Blem's collar. The frightened eyes stared back at him, his face like a dark reflection in a twisted mirror at a carnival funhouse.

"It's okay," Matthew said in a soothing a voice. "I just want to see how it looks."

"I'd say it looks like you've been acting up again," a voice said from behind him.

Matthew stiffened. Knox.

It wasn't possible. How could that bastard have traced them here? Matthew's throat suddenly felt very dry, and he edged his hand down toward his belt where he'd stuck the security guard's gun.

"How'd you find me?" Matthew asked, trying his best to sound cordial as his fingers gripped the pistol. In one smooth motion, he pulled it up from his pants and pulled the trigger. The blast from the barrel shooting out half a foot.

As Colby drove past the gate area of the old refinery, a gunshot ripped through the night. Slowing down, he glanced right and saw the heaps of twisted detritus lining what had once been several square blocks of massive pipes, structures, and three-story chimneys. He pulled his car over to the right, next to a group of heavy bushes. A translucent tarp had been wired to the inside of the fence, probably to reduce the demolition dust blowing across the road. Hopefully, it would keep the car out of the line of sight of anyone inside. He slipped out, gently pushing the door closed with his hip. Moving to the fence line, he paused. It was cyclone fencing at least twelve feet tall with a roll of twisted concertina wire on top. No way to scale it, but about twenty feet to his left he saw a small gateway. It had been secured with a rusting lock and chain. Colby moved over to it and pulled on the gate. It eased open about half a foot. Small enough to prevent anyone from taking anything sizable out, but large enough to allow him to squeeze through. A five-foot berm ran along the inside of the fence, and he flattened out to peer over it, staring out into what looked like a big, dark field with a line of large halogen lights on twenty-foot poles planted around the perimeter. Beyond the fence were heaps of crushed bricks, tangled metal, and several large cranes. A section of cement sprouted flower-like petals of twisted metallic pipes that stuck up about three feet.

He didn't want to turn on his flashlight as he moved to the closest brick pile.

Make me too much of target, he thought.

Seconds later, he tripped and went sprawling, the hard ground and loose debris biting into his shoulder and cheek. But he managed to hold on to both his flash-light and gun. He got to his hands and knees and listened.

An uneven yell floated through the darkness.

Colby rose and peered cautiously around the junk pile.

Ahead, about thirty yards away, a pair of red taillights glowed in the semi-darkness. A van. The headlights were on and shining against a partially demolished tower or chimney of some sort. Two men were by the vehicle. Glancing around, he picked his next cover-point and took off in a low, cautious run.

———

Knox watched Matthew squirm, holding his gut as the blood drained out of the wound in his side. It looked like a through-and-through. Probably lacerated his bowel, but he'd live. Until he got back to New Genesis, anyway. The little prick's shot had gone wild, and Knox pulling the trigger on the Heckler & Koch had been almost instinctual.

Almost.

Forget going easy on this little son of a bitch. It looked like more of a mess than he'd figured. Not only did he have Matthew and his mentally challenged clone to deal with, but two unconscious, young girls lay a few feet away.

"Who the hell are they?" Knox asked, pointing to them.

"Fuck you." Matthew gritted his teeth. "You shot me. Get me to the hospital. Now."

Knox smirked. It was good to know that the little bastard had reverted to type, spitting out demands and orders just like his creator-father, Jetters.

"I asked you a question," Knox said. "Who are those girls?" He held up the Ruger .357 he'd taken from Matthew and looked at it. "And where'd you get this?"

"I told you to get me some help." Matthew's voice raised an octave or two.

Knox sighed and pointed the extended barrel of the Heckler & Koch at Matthew's left foot. To emphasize his point, he squeezed another round off, making sure that it grazed the sick bastard's shoe.

Matthew screamed like a frightened little girl.

Knox smiled again. "The next one will go through your toes. Now who are those two girls?"

"A pair of twins I picked up," Matthew said. "I wanted to replicate Morgan's final act." He began to sob, and when he spoke again, his voice was a plaintive whine. "Now, please, please, get me some medical attention."

"Believe me," Knox said, "in a little while, you'll have more of that than you bargained for."

———

Sweet Jesus, thought Colby. This was unbelievable. It'd gone from tailing a suspect to watching a couple of psychos exchange insults at a hostage situation. And who was this new guy? Knox must have been involved with Laird, helping to commit the copycats, but another helper was something Colby hadn't even considered. This wasn't just a serial killer, it was a murder committee. He knew had had to get those little girls out of this alive and unharmed. If Knox left with them, they were both as good as dead. He'd never allow some missing kids to be tied back to him. The guy was too good at covering his tracks.

The long-barreled gun glistened under the glare of the red taillights.

Silencer. High-capacity magazine, too.

Colby looked down at the truncated detective special. Five-rounds. Knox probably had twice as many. Plus, Brewer's gun had a two-inch barrel. A belly gun. Not good for a long-range shot. Colby doubted he could take Knox out at this distance.

Another figure suddenly danced around in the headlights, moving his feet with very small steps, and making some kind of keening moan.

Where the hell did he come from? Colby watched him. And who was he?

The man began moving toward a big, half-moon shaped metal tube that looked like it had once been a massive storage unit.

Knox moved forward and grabbed the dancing man, shoving him back toward the van, pushing him around the side of the vehicle and out of sight.

Was he going to kill him?

Colby's gut tightened. No backup was on the way anytime soon, and there was no time to wait. He ran to the next rubble-pile, his shoes making scuffing sounds on the broken bricks and discarded boards. If he could get close enough to squeeze off a decent shot maybe he could end this.

A snapping sound whispered between the gasps of his own labored breathing, and a round tore through the meaty part of his left calf, feeling like someone had thrust a red-hot spike through it. Colby tumbled forward, feeling something strike his left side, just above his belt. Glancing to the left, he saw Knox standing by the right rear area of the van, holding that elongated gun with both hands in a classic stance.

Can't let him get target acquisition, Colby thought, feeling a searing pain tearing through him with each little movement. He brought the revolver up, pointed it in Knox's direction, and pulled the trigger.

The gun flared like a blunderbuss, its flame lighting up the darkness, and causing a ringing distortion in his ears. Colby kept moving, he didn't know how and managed to dive behind the next pile of rubble. Rolling on his side, he peered out quickly from behind a jutting, broken cement block. He couldn't see Knox, but hoped the round would keep the bastard from advancing to finish the job.

But still, Knox had time on his side.

Taking a deep breath and feeling the pincer-like pain rack his chest, Colby tried to get his breathing under control. He felt a numbness rising from his legs and hoped it wasn't the onset of shock.

He concentrated on checking the wounds with his fingers and taking quick, shallow breaths. He heard Knox call out, "You're going to have to shoot a lot better than that, pal."

Colby debated remaining silent, trying to lure Knox toward him, then shooting him when he got close enough. But the guy had been sharper than he'd originally thought. "Government trained," Meister had said. That could mean anything, but suddenly it made Colby very nervous.

"You make more noise moving than a herd of elephants," Knox called again.

Colby gritted his teeth, wondering if Knox was trying to initiate conversation as a ruse, trying to gauge their relative positioning.

Shit, he probably knows where I'm at anyway, Colby thought. Plus, I don't intend on staying here. Might as well try to rattle him.

"Knox, give it up," he yelled. "This area is full of police personnel. You're surrounded."

Silence, then Colby heard a low burst of laughter.

"Somehow, I doubt that," Knox said. "Otherwise, why would you have an idiot like Meister backing you up? But anyway, Detective Colby, it's nice to talk with you again."

Fragments of the brick exploded in front of Colby's face as he felt another bullet whizz past. Instinctively, he held the revolver out and fired back, regretting it moments later. He was down to three shots now, and Knox knew his exact position.

Rolling to his hands and knees, Colby tried to move as quickly as he could toward a long stack of metal pipes, leaking blood with each movement. If he could hunker down there, maybe he could hold out until reinforcements arrived. If Leslie had gotten hold of some, and if he could stay conscious. Both his shirt and pant leg felt sodden, and he knew he was leaving a pretty obvious blood trail.

Leslie. What if she'd heard the shots? He hoped she wouldn't try to do anything stupid, like come after him. She didn't even have a weapon, and Knox wasn't the type to let the fairer sex sway his aim.

A sudden burst of intense pain gripped him, holding on for several seconds before fading back into the dull, constant ache.

Colby worked on controlling his breathing. He'd partially circled the area where the van was and had inadvertently gotten closer than he intended.

One shot, he thought. That's all I need. Just one fucking decent shot.

"Let the gun fall from your fingers," Knox's voice said from behind him. He felt an accompanying nudge of something hard and metallic on the back of his head. "Right now, or I'll blow your brains out."

Colby felt paralyzed. The man was unbeatable. He'd been flanking while Colby thought he was moving to a new cover spot. But why hadn't he pulled the trigger?

Must want information, Colby thought, which can buy me some time. Maybe time enough for backup to arrive and save those two little girls.

"Listen, there's a sniper with a night scope trained on your head right now, Knox," Colby said. "Pull that trigger and you're a dead man."

The extended barrel smacked against Colby's temple. Stunned by the blow, and before he could react, Knox's left hand shot forward and snatched the revolver from Colby's loose fingers.

"Now," Knox said, pushing the end of the long barrel up against the underside of Colby's chin. "You and I are going to have a talk, and for each wrong answer, I'm going to put a bullet into you. Get it?"

Colby felt the warmth engulfing him. Maybe, if there was any mercy in this world, the shock would overtake him now, lulling him into a state of non-feeling, whatever hell his body would have to go through. He hoped it would be the same for the twins, too. A peaceful voyage into tranquility. Colby managed to collect some saliva and spat at Knox's face.

Knox recoiled, wiping at his cheek, as he thrust the pistol toward Colby's head. He stopped and adjusted his aim so it was now pointing at groin level.

Colby took a shallow breath and thought, Oh fuck.

But suddenly Knox's face twisted into a grimace, and his body went spastic, leaning backward like he was doing some sort of bizarre limbo dance.

Colby blinked twice and saw a young Morgan Laird standing behind Knox, holding what looked to be a Taser.

"How does it feel, motherfucker?" the young Laird said. His face was a maniacal mask.

Colby wondered if he was hallucinating. Then another wave of pain brought things into focus again. The young Laird's shirt was bloody. He'd been shot, too. And he was continuing to keep the juice going from the Taser as he walked up on them. As he got to Knox, young Laird snatched the silenced semi-auto from the ground and then kicked away the revolver. He let up on the trigger of the Taser long enough to switch hands, and then depressed it again, sending Knox into a new series of spasms. The mad eyes looked down at Colby.

"You know who I am?" young Laird asked.

Colby tried to answer, but no words would come.

"I want you to know before you die," young Laird said. "I want you to know all of it."

Colby tried to speak, but his tongue wouldn't work.

So this is how it ends, he thought. A lousy place to die.

And he'd failed to save the twins.

Again.

"I'm your worst fucking nightmare, Colby," young Laird said.

He knows me, Colby thought. So why don't I know him? Unless he's Morgan Laird, come back to haunt me.

Young Laird pointed the big-barreled weapon toward Knox when Colby heard a shot. Young Laird dropped everything, the semi-auto, the Taser, and clutched at his chest, looking down at a spreading flower of crimson on the breast of his light-blue shirt. Two staggering steps and he curled up into a ball and fell over. Colby tried to reach for one of the weapons to put a bullet into Knox. He wanted to kill that bastard before he it was too late, if it was the last thing he ever got to do.

He reached out again, each movement causing more agony to radiate through his body. His fingertips brushed against the butt of the pistol, but Knox began to stir, raising himself up and shaking his head. Their eyes met and in a second, Colby knew he'd be too late as he watched Knox grin as his fingers curled around the butt of the pistol.

A second shot split the night and Colby's eyes focused on a circular hole that appeared on Knox's forehead.

Right between the eyes.

Colby saw Leslie's figure, silhouetted by one of the perimeter halogen lights, running toward him. She was out of breath, but still totally professional slowing down and moving in to kick the gun out of Knox's slack hand. The man's glazed eyes had that vacant look of death.

Leslie then checked Matthew and seemed satisfied that he was expired also. She moved back to Colby and kneeled beside him.

"You're a sight for sore eyes," he managed to say, nodding at the forty caliber Glock in her hand. "Where'd you get that?"

"Meister," she said. "Took his gun."

Colby nodded, a wave of pain and nausea sweeping over him. Thank God for retired coppers and concealed carry, he thought. And for guardian angels who could shoot.

He managed to look up at her one more time.

An angel, he thought, as the world suddenly went totally black.

CHAPTER 25

Colby remembered waking up twice during the ambulance ride, and once more in the ER, before the black void overwhelmed him again. When he finally managed to open his eyes again, he was in a room with tan walls and a long white curtain to his right. It was either heaven, or hell, or perhaps a hospital room. It was too cool for the second, and too dingy for the first, so he assumed it was the third. He rotated his head and saw a profusion of brown hair leaning over by the foot of his bed. The hair turned, and he saw an angelic face. Maybe this was heaven after all.

"Where—" he tried to ask.

Leslie leaned forward and her soft fingers caressed his face. "Shh," she said. "You're in the hospital. You're going to be just fine."

"Water," he managed to say.

She stepped next to him and held a plastic glass with a straw to his lips.

He sucked some fluid through it, swallowed, and felt slightly better.

"How long?" His voice sounded distant and raspy, his throat dry.

"Two days," she said. She reached up and pressed the button for the nurse.

Two days? It seemed impossible. The last thing he remembered was being on the ground at the old refinery. "Really?"

She nodded.

"How did I go to the bathroom?" he asked, trying his best to smile back at her.

She laughed softly. "You'll find that out soon enough."

"Oh, Christ," Colby said, suddenly cognizant of an intrusive penetration in his penis. He tried to move, but felt weak and somewhat shaky. But things were starting to come back to him, like pieces of a large puzzle becoming visible. He felt a sudden surge of panic.

"Those two little girls. The twins?" he asked.

"They're fine. Safe and sound."

He felt as though a huge weight had been lifted off his chest.

"You did good," she said. "You saved them."

"You mean *you* did. Keep spouting bullshit like that about what a hero I am, and my next book's gonna have to be a novel." The drip of the morphine-tainted saline suspended from the hook over his bed slid lazily down the long clear plastic tube connected to the IV on his left hand. The sheets felt smooth and clean, and his pillows fluffy and soft. "Otherwise, nobody'll believe you made a head shot like that. Way too unbelievable."

Leslie smiled.

At least now I know what an angel in heaven must look like, he thought, as she leaned over him and whispered, in that supremely sexy voice of hers, "Special Agent Pearson, your Deputy Superintendent, and Lieutenant Kropper are waiting outside in the hall wanting to know if you feel good enough to talk to them now."

Colby considered this. "So they're all lining up to kiss my ass, huh?"

"Actually, they're waiting on permission from your doctor, and he told me to ask you if you felt up to it."

"Fuck 'em," Colby said. "Let them wait. They bring in Dr. Frankenstein from New Genesis yet?"

She shook her head. "Special Agent Pearson—"

"Hey," he said, interrupting her, "that's Special *Asshole* Pearson."

Leslie giggled. "Okay. Special Asshole Pearson and company hit the place yesterday, after getting the subpoenas and search warrants despite some, and I quote, 'Some unexpected, heavy-duty government clout.'" She paused, then said, "They found Professor Jetters in his laboratory. He'd hanged himself. Destroyed all his records, too."

"Figures," Colby said. "Taking the coward's way out."

"But during the raid they found a whole section of strange, mentally challenged young men. One of them was in the refinery that night, too." The area between her eyebrows furrowed. "They all look very similar to the one I shot. And we both know whom he resembles."

Colby nodded his head. The visions of the young Morgan Laird holding the pistol flashed through his memory. His worst nightmare. The bastard had spoken the truth. "Find out who he was yet?"

"His name's Matthew Jetters, but he's not related to the professor. Not biologically, at least."

"What?"

Leslie shifted. "There have been whispers that New Genesis created him. That he was Morgan Laird's clone."

"Clone?" Colby shook his head. "No way. That's not possible. Is it?"

"They're already cloning animals." Her eyebrows rose. "And, like I said, there's a whole slew of twenty-something males at New Genesis who look just like our dearly departed Matthew. And your friend, Morgan Laird, in his younger days."

Colby shook his head. "But that means they would've had to have done it way back when…no, I can't buy it." But he suddenly remembered the shock of recognition when he saw the little pervert's face as he was standing there with the gun. *I want you to know before you die*, the nightmare had said.

Leslie shrugged. "I know it sounds pretty farfetched, but they say cloning's in our future. That it's only a matter of time."

"Time," Colby said, holding up his wrist. He realized he wasn't wearing a watch. "What time is it, anyway?"

"Quarter after nine, and…" She turned quickly and held the remote toward the television, "Oh, my god."

"We missing a rerun of *The Lone Ranger*?"

"No, something better. Your partner, Dix called and told me to make sure we watched *Chicago Today* at nine, if you were up."

Leslie carefully settled down next to him on the bed as she flipped through a few channels. Dix came into view, sitting across from Carmel Washington. Both were laughing and smiling.

"That old, randy son of a bitch," Colby said. "Turn it up, a little."

"So it was all part of our master plan for me to get arrested," Dix was saying.

Carmel's pretty face had a Mona Lisa smile.

"I mean, sometimes, in police work, you have to go undercover." He leered at her legs. "Deep under."

She smiled with her teeth this time.

"And my partner, Roger Colby and I, knew we'd have

to make everybody *think* I was responsible for killing Laird and Fontaine, in order for him to flush out the real killers."

"Is there anything more you can tell us about who these real killers were?" Carmel asked.

Dix waggled his eyebrows and grinned. He looked like an obese Groucho Marx.

"Well, Carmel," he said, "there's a lot I could tell you, believe me, but I'm bound by my oath to truth, justice, and the American way right now." He paused and looked directly into the camera. "Besides, my buddy Rog will probably want to write another one of them books of his about it."

Carmel asked another typically standard question, but it was drowned out by Colby's groan.

"That sly bastard," he said. "Maybe I should remind him that my next book's definitely gonna be a novel. A science fiction novel."

"Is it now?"

He looked up at her, the potent mix of painkillers making her face look more angelic than usual. "Have I thanked you yet for saving my life?"

"Why don't we wait till you've recovered and you can give me a special thank you?" she said, leaning forward to kiss him lightly on the lips. "Now, two things. Do you feel able to talk to your boss?"

Colby pushed his head against the softness of the pillow. "Sure, why not?"

She nodded and began to straighten up.

"What's the second thing?" he asked.

She paused, placed a hand on his forearm, and squeezed. "I have to be back in Toronto tomorrow."

Colby felt like he'd been struck by another bullet. This time in the heart. He tried to swallow, but his throat felt too dry. "Oh."

Her fingers stroked his forehead lightly.

"Guess I knew it was coming," he said.

"Toronto's not that far," she said.

"Neither is Chicago."

"You could come up for a visit sometime. When you're feeling better, of course. We could go on a trip to Niagara Falls. One of the Seven Wonders of the World."

"We could." Hell, he always knew he was too old for her anyway.

"Or, better yet, you could retire and move up there." Her fingers traced over his features. "Think how much your big American paycheck would be worth in Canadian dollars."

Now it was his turn for a lips-only smile. Live outside the United States? But like she said, Toronto wasn't really that far…he looked up at her.

Man, is she gorgeous, he thought. If I was smart, I'd make sure we turned out to be more than just two ships passing in the night.

"What's the conversion rate for Canadian dollars into real money?" he asked.

Her face took on a dreamy look as she leaned over and kissed his lips again.

"Real money?" she said. "I'll have to think on that one for a while."

ACKNOWLEDGMENTS

There are a lot of people to thank for this one. My buddy, first reader, ace writer, and top cop, retired CPD Lieutenant and now Bridgeview PD Commander, Dave Case, who helped me through the rough first draft and with a lot of the Chicago Police Department things. Retired Vancouver PD Detective, John Eldridge, was an immense help with the Canadian aspects of the story. I'd also like to thank Shauna Washington, who gave me sage advice on the female characters, Paul Bishop, for more things than I can count, Rachel Del Grosso, for her expert advice, and all the others, too numerous to mention, whom I called upon as I wrote this novel. Any mistakes I made are totally my own.

A LOOK AT: DEVIL'S DANCE
TRACKDOWN BOOK ONE

Framed. Forgotten. Fighting for Redemption...

After a botched raid in Baghdad leaves civilians dead, Army Ranger Sergeant Steve Wolf is branded a war criminal and left to rot in prison. But when he's finally released four years later, the real battle begins.

Recruited by his former mentor, ex-Green Beret Jim McNamara, Wolf reluctantly joins the high-stakes world of bounty hunting. Their latest mission takes them deep into Mexico in pursuit of a dangerous fugitive—but they aren't the only ones on his trail. Wolf's former brothers-in-arms, the ruthless private military contractors known as the Vipers, have their own deadly agenda. Their target? A priceless stolen artifact tied to a powerful and merciless man who will stop at nothing to retrieve it.

With enemies closing in, the hunt leads to the abandoned Mayan ruins of El Meco, where Wolf must fight for his life against a small army of trained killers. Outgunned and outnumbered, his only option is to embrace the warrior within —because in the world of mercenaries and betrayals, survival is the only victory.

AVAILABLE NOW

ABOUT THE AUTHOR

Michael A. Black was a US Army Military Policeman and a police officer in a south suburb of Chicago. He worked in various capacities in police work including patrol supervisor, SWAT team leader, plain clothes tactical sergeant, and investigations. He was awarded the Cook County Medal of Merit in 2010 and retired from police work in 2011. In 2022, he was inducted into the Illinois Boxing and Martial Arts Hall of Fame. Black is the author of fifty books and over one hundred short stories and articles. He has a BA in English from Northern Illinois University and an MFA in Fiction Writing from Columbia College Chicago. He wrote two novels with the late Richard Belzer of *Law & Order SVU*. Black also writes novels as Don Pendleton in the Executioner series and westerns (the *Gunslinger* series and *Concho: Border Blood* for Rough Edges Press) under the name A.W. Hart.

www.MichaelABlack.com